# CORNUBIA TO TUNDRA

Coastal Research

# Cornubia to Tundra

## Michael J. Fennessy

**Sequel novel to Exmoor Beneath the Landscape**

**Coastal Research**

Published by Coastal Research,
Tamarisks, Waresfoot Drive, Crediton, Devon, EX17 2DG

www.coastalresearch.co.uk

First published by Coastal Research in 2025

A CIP catalogue record for this book is available from the British Library.

ISBN 978 0 953 0656 5 3

Printed and bound by Short Run Press, Exeter

*This book is dedicated to all those people who have strived to create, preserve and maintain access to the countryside.*

# 1

Mark Scott had made no comment to his wife, Emma, about the extraordinary meeting he'd had with Vanessa Wyndham earlier that afternoon. At home he realised he needed to direct all his attention to Emma and not burden her with work matters. At 13 weeks confinement all she was concerned about was getting to the end of the school term and moving into their bungalow at East Quantock, near Taunton.

Weston-Super-Mare had been a convenient rented house for several years, but it was never intended to be their permanent domicile. Their marriage a few weeks ago was the real start to their future lives. They had just a few weeks treading water until they got the keys to their new home on 2nd August 2019.

The meeting with Vanessa Wyndham had probably been contrived. Mark had gone down to Exford at the request of the Exmoor Heritage Park Authority. It was a courteous addendum to the winding up meeting for the extraordinary Russian attempt to drive a tunnel up to a large country house. Exmoor Heritage Park seemed to have a high regard for the assistance Mark had given them through the summer. Why Vanessa Wyndham had tacked herself onto the Park meeting had become clear. She wanted Mark to be a discreet observer for national intelligence during his trip to China in September. Her role in the security services made Mark feel she was credible. Under her previous name of Naomi Dawson, she had successfully co-ordinated British resources to recover him and his fieldwork boss back to England the previous summer. That made Mark feel he had a duty to consider her request genuine.

Tomorrow would be Saturday, domestic tasks day. Sunday was Mark's planned visit to the mines near North Molton where Clive Mangan had agreed to take him into an old adit to look for ore samples. Almost certainly Iron, and there was the faint possibility of other metals. It was a visit Mark needed to make to convince himself, and his supervisors, that he had checked out all the significant mining areas in and around Exmoor.

Mark was nearing the end of his first year of a PhD programme in geology. He was based at Avon University, near Bristol. Prior to the PhD he had worked for several years as a Copper exploration geologist. Chalco, the company who employed him, was based in Guernsey and operated all around the world.

Saturday, Emma had a few hours of school work to prepare. She only had one more week of term. Mark was given a long list of jobs, including cleaning Emma's car inside and out. He also had to check out washing machines and fridge freezers. Their bungalow at East Quantock had a fitted oven and hotplate, but the vendors were taking the free standing white goods.

Mark still wasn't sure if Emma wanted to join him on the trip to North Molton. The arrangement was that she could sit outside with Dorothy Mangan, Clive's wife. Dorothy had always accompanied her husband on his visits to the mine, principally as a caution, so that she could sound the alarm if Clive and his fellow mine rescuers didn't emerge on time. Clive was the organiser of the local mine rescue group, and had been for 24 years. He was familiar with this particular adit, their training adit, and had also taken many geologists into the mine over the years.

Saturday went well. Car cleaned and Mark had worked out which models of fridge and washing machine they needed. Emma was happy with her school preparations and they decided to have a gentle walk along the sea front, before dinner. Emma disclosed that she was becoming more conscious of her tummy. She was starting her second trimester. On Saturday night Mark said he was aiming to leave at nine o'clock in the morning for the drive to North Molton. If she wanted to join him she was most welcome and could decide in the morning.

Sunday 14th July 2019. Emma was still keeping her alarm set for 06:30. She looked out the bedroom window. It was dry and sunny, as the forecast had said, but she decided to have a day at home. She wanted to be well rested for the final week of term. Mark set off in the truck down the M5 and then along the North Devon Link Road. He had the grid reference for Hensdown Farm.

He was on time. Clive and Dorothy Mangan were talking with Roy Farrow, the farmer who held the key to the locked gate of the adit. After introductions they walked down across the fields to a small wood surrounding the entrance to the adit. Although it was mid-July the adit entrance appeared more like a spring. A trickle was leaving the adit. It was contained in a small ditch through the wood and then meandered across the flat field towards a larger stream.

Adits are horizontal tunnels into rock that are cut by miners searching for metal ores. Most of them have a slight gradient to allow water to drain from the mine.

Dorothy was a short stocky woman in her late fifties. She was an English teacher in a comprehensive school, although she had to call it an academy now. Mark realised that there would have been a common topic of conversation had Emma joined him.

Clive had a camping chair in a nylon bag slung over his shoulder. At the wood Dorothy set up the chair in the sunshine at the edge of the

3

wood, about thirty metres from the adit entrance. It was a pleasant warm day.

Mark and Clive went across to the adit entrance and the heavy iron gate. Clive unlocked the padlock and took it across to Dorothy for safe keeping. She put it in her small rucksack. Clive said: 'Probably about one hour, dear.'

Back at the entrance Clive briefed Mark on some safety matters: 'As with all adit entrances, particularly if the ground isn't steep, the roof of the first part of the tunnel is fractured rock. Further in it's much more solid. We occasionally get roof falls of shillet in the first ten metres. There's a shovel hanging on the wall at about fifteen metres. That's just a precaution in case we have to dig our way out a bit. It doesn't happen often, but you need to be aware of it. So try not to hit your helmet on the roof in the first few metres. Further on you can bang your head on the roof as much as you like.'

Clive was dressed in a full wet suit covered by a boiler suit without arms. He had work boots on his feet. Mark was in just a boiler suit, and his boots. The floor of the tunnel was more like a stream bed. Mark remembered the first e-mail he'd had from Clive Mangan. The adit had been cut purely to drain water from the main shaft.

It wasn't long before Mark was rather damp, certainly up to his knees. The tilted oval shaped cross section of the adit required continual leaning to the side wall, and he had to crouch. After a while it was quite a tiring struggle. The sides of the tunnel were well scratched. Clive pointed them out: 'That's where the stretchers scrape along when we're doing our rescue practices.'

They reached the main shaft, three hundred metres in. Clive explained the mine's structure: 'The top of the shaft is capped, although we're not sure how well. You probably visited it when you were taken on your brisk tour by Mr Glendinning, the land agent. If we climb that short ladder over there, up to the lowest level, I can show you where the lode is a bit further in. The ladder's ok. We replace it every few years.'

The level was only about three metres above the adit. They climbed up. On advantage was that the level was dry under foot, although the headroom was low. At the mineral lode Mark unpacked his gear from the waterproof container he had strapped to his back. The Portable Infra-Red Spectrometer, affectionately referred to as PIRSy by Mark, was clearly showing the presence of Iron. There was also a slight signal for Copper, but no other elements. The lode was damp so Mark wasn't placing too much reliance on the initial readings. He used his hammer and chisel to remove some small samples and bag them. He was quite excited. This was a much better set of samples than he could have obtained, back in March, from the vegetation covered piles of shillet near the top of the mine shaft. He also took some photos and said to Clive: 'This is a brilliant opportunity for me. I can't thank you enough. I've been wondering how I was going to get realistic samples from the North Molton area.'

Clive: 'Shall we head back then?'

'Yes, all done, thanks.'

They crawled back to the ladder and carefully descended to the adit level. Standing in the bottom of the shaft was the only opportunity to stand fully upright. They were just about to adjust to the crouch position again when a huge flash emanated from the adit. 'Quick, stand here, blast wave.'

A second later a horrific pulse of air reached the main shaft. They were deafened. Their lungs felt the blast. The blast had also forced its way up the shaft, about 40 metres, to the capping. Clive shouted: 'Into the adit,'

Mark couldn't hear a thing, his ear drums were probably damaged. Clive grabbed his arm and dragged him into the adit tunnel. There was dust everywhere. Then rock and soil started falling down the main shaft. Clive took a hanky out of his pocket and covered his mouth and nose. Mark didn't have a hanky in his boiler suit pocket. He had a small towel in his back pack. He took it out and covered his face. Clive was shouting, but Mark couldn't hear. The gestures were clear. They needed to wait for the dust level to settle. It wasn't obvious how long that would take. Clive sat down on a small shelf just inside the adit tunnel. He pointed to his watch. He held up one finger. Mark assumed that was one hour. It wasn't wise to move. They needed to effectively cover their faces. Protecting their lungs from the dust was essential. They sat together on the shelf. A significant smell was in the air. Clive was shouting: 'Bomb, bomb.'

Mark couldn't hear the shouts, but guessed what he was saying. It was evident that both of them had badly damaged hearing; Clive's was not as severe as Mark's. They switched off their headlamps and sat still, covering their faces. There was definitely a smell of explosive. What had happened?

# 2

Earlier outside, two men had approached Dorothy Mangan. The taller one announceed: 'Hello, I'm Pedro Fugro from Avon University. I work with Mark Scott. Is he inside the mine?'

'Yes, they went in about thirty minutes ago.'

He strided into the wood and up to the adit entrance. He seemed to take something from his rucksack and threw it into the adit. Five seconds later, as he was running away, an enormous explosion. A blast of rock and debris blew out of the adit and through the wood, fortunately missing where Dorothy was sitting. She was shocked.

The other man was now standing next to her. As Pedro Fugro walked back to them he said: 'You're coming with us.'

The other man had removed a hand gun from his trousers, and forcefully gestured that she walk back up across the field to the farm. Dorothy was agitated and kept shouting questions at Fugro. He didn't answer. The other man, an unkempt rough diamond, kept prodding Dorothy with his gun, uttering in a strong Bristol accent: 'Move, be quiet.'

Dorothy found the brisk walk uphill a struggle: 'Wait, I need to rest.'

Fugro shouted: 'Keep walking.'

At the farmyard the other man opened the rear doors of a dirty white van.

Inside was the farmer, Roy Farrow. He was gagged and had his hands tied behind his back, and a heavy duty cable-tie binding his ankles.

Dorothy was angry: 'What are you doing? You're nothing to do with Avon University.'

There was no answer from the two men.

The other man prodded Dorothy with his gun again. Fugro had been to the passenger door and came to the back of the van with a gag and several black cable ties.

Roy Farrow was trying to make noises, but his gag was a hindrance. There was no seating or carpeting of any sort in the back of the van. There was a full height steel bulkhead behind the driver's cab. The inside of the van was empty, but dirty. Fugro tied a gag onto Dorothy, then tied her wrists behind her back. Dorothy started kicking Fugro, but he just became rougher. He lifted her into the back of the van and used his feet to slide her further in. The other man then strapped her ankles together. They closed the doors and drove off.

Dorothy and Roy Farrow could see each other but couldn't communicate. There were no windows in the rear of the van, but a chink of light was coming through the badly bent rear doors. They tried to manoeuvre themselves to sit upright. The farm lane was bumpy and the van was moving rapidly. It was unbearable sitting on the ribbed metal floor. They realised that sitting with their backs to the steel bulkhead offered the least uncomfortable position. The van reached the tarmacked lane, it was less bumpy. Whoever was driving was throwing the van around corners. They were in a hurry. After about ten minutes the road was straight and smoother, but the van was screaming along. Dorothy assumed that they had reached the North Devon Link Road. Her mind was still making rational judgements but she was petrified.

There was a lot of high speed swerving. Dorothy knew the road had no dual carriageways, occasionally there were three lanes. The speed limit was sixty, but they were probably exceeding that most of the time. The road had a bad history of accidents.

After about five or six minutes Dorothy heard a siren. Was it a police car? The siren got louder and louder. It seemed to be alongside. The van sped up and there was much swerving.

The siren was still going but it seemed to have moved back behind the van. Had they given up? Dorothy still couldn't be sure it was a police car, but she deduced that it might be some sort of strategy. Most police vehicles could easily outpace an old white van. Had the police radioed for assistance? Was it likely that a road block would be set up over towards Tiverton, if that's where they were heading. Both of them were pondering their predicament but they couldn't communicate with the tight gags. Dorothy assumed that anyone who ran a farm was quite good at resolving difficulties in a pragmatic way. Without language, or the ability to move, or use their hands, solutions were severely limited. Dorothy was on the driver's side, Roy Farrow was on the passenger's side.

Another ten minutes elapsed, the van slowed, then fierce braking. It was a good job they had their backs to the bulkhead. There were several sirens blaring. Suddenly the van sped up. A horrible bump, and a ripping sound. The van accelerated but the tyres must have been damaged. The wheels began to grind on the tarmac. The ride in the back was erratic. Then a swerve. Had they left the road? Two seconds later their heads and backs were forced into the bulkhead. The pain was excruciating. The van had stopped, partly on its side. Dorothy fell onto Roy Farrow.

# 3

'Armed police, you are surrounded.'

Several police slid down the steep embankment. The driver, it was the rough diamond man, opened his door, and pointed his hand gun at the police. He was obviously panicking and shocked, but the airbag had saved him from hitting the windscreen. A police marksman higher up the embankment shot the gun from his hand. That probably disoriented him further, and his hand was bleeding. He waded across the stream and ran through a field, in a Northerly direction.

Three policeman managed to wrench open the back doors and climb in. They could see two persons gagged and tied up at the front end of the interior. They were in a pile on the left hand side. The weight of three additional adults in the back of the van, which was already tilted onto its left hand side, caused it to slide further into the stream and fall completely on its side. With the doors open stream water rushed in. The van was now blocking the stream. The policemen struggled to reach the captives, and more of a struggle to get them out onto dry land. Roy Farrow was unconscious and there was a lot of blood. Dorothy Mangan was aware of the rescue attempt. She was trying to scream, behind her gag. The weight of water was forcing the van further downstream.

The police were equipped to tackle the radioed incident; stop the vehicle and arrest the culprit. However, the stream presented difficulties for which they weren't prepared. They could only assume that the two in the back, both gagged, were hostages. The situation was near chaos. After a muscular struggle Dorothy and Roy Farrow had been dragged from the van and laid down on the embankment.

One policeman had a special handtool that cut nylon cable ties. Another untied the gags. The hostages were lying head up on the steep embankment. 'I'm Dorothy Mangan my husband has been trapped in a mine at North Molton by these men.'

The policeman who seemed to be co-ordinating the scene was radioing for support: 'Two ambulances, and the Force helicopter, needed fast.'

Roy Farrow was not responding to any prompting.

Another policeman shouted down to the three soaked officers: 'Quick, get them up here on the flat.'

Now that her cable ties were off Dorothy Mangan crawled up the steep embankment on her own. Her head was bleeding. She counted eight officers in total but co-ordination was lacking. She shouted: 'There's another man in the passenger side, he's the ring leader.'

At that the senior officer delegated two of the traffic officers to look in the cab.

Roy Farrow was now laid out on the grass by the road. It was level. Two more officers were directed to clear his airway and resuscitate him. Attempts to revive him failed. He was considered dead. A minute later the first ambulance arrived. They had oxygen and airways and spent several minutes on Roy Farrow.

A second ambulance arrived and checked Dorothy Mangan.

The two officers sent to inspect the cab shouted up to the co-ordinator: 'There's a man, partly under water, and he can't release his seat belt. We need a knife.'

The man, Pedro Fugro, was leaning so hard to the right, to keep his mouth above water, that the seatbelt release socket wasn't reachable. One of the ambulance crew grabbed a seat belt cutter, ran down the embankment and dived into the cab. She managed to cut away the seat belt and the passenger was free. The van was now wedged across the stream and static. The young woman ambulance attendant, and the already soaked policeman, dragged Fugro out and other officers cuffed him. They dragged him up the embankment under the gaze of an officer with a gun. Dorothy Mangan came over and said this man was the ring leader: 'He told us his name was Pedro Fugro. He was the one who threw the bomb into the mine.'

The police frisked him for weapons and searched his pockets. He had a nasty wound on his forehead, possibly where he hit the dashboard. His soaked passport had the name Carlos Sanchez, not Pedro Fugro. The police arrested him and put him in one of their cars.

Dorothy Mangan had spent the last ten minutes trying to get the co-ordinating officer to phone the mine rescue group based in Barnstaple. Her own phone wasn't working; it had been submerged. She was not in a good way herself but was the only one who was aware of the whole situation.

'Madam, I'll have to take you to the station to make a full statement.'

'No. You're taking me back to Henswood Farm. My husband and Mark Scott are trapped in the mine that was blown up. When I've got them out, that's when I'll go to the hospital. When they've patched me up, that's when I'll give you a statement. Give me your phone I need to speak to my husband's friends. Only they have the ability to get my husband out. And I want two ambulances sent to Henswood Farm. And make sure a top level police officer is sent to the farm as well to co-ordinate. You've been present at just one part of this horrific incident. When the full story hits the media you'll realise what you've become involved in. It's four-thirty, we're running out of time. Get me back to Henswood Farm now.'

'What's the grid reference?'

Dorothy Mangan was losing her patience: 'Get me back to Henswood. I'll get someone to radio you the bloody grid reference while I'm being driven. It's North East of North Molton. Don't waste any more time.'

Only one person was in cognisant control of the whole situation. It was Dorothy Mangan. She'd accompanied her husband on his mine rescue activities for 24 years. Her attendance had never been tested until now. She knew what needed to be done, and she wasn't going to let her husband die.

The police helicopter came over the horizon. The ambulance teams were dealing with the body of Roy Farrow. The local traffic situation was in chaos, and the helicopter landed on the road. One of the other officers liaised with the helicopter team: 'He's English, about thirty, dark haired, stubble beard, about five foot eight, greenish t-shirt, grubby blue jeans, site boots. He headed North over there about 15 minutes ago. He's got an injury to his right hand from when an officer shot a gun out of his hand. We have that gun now, so he may not be armed any more, but he's still dangerous. One man is dead.'

The helicopter controller said: 'Climb in, you're the witness.'

The helicopter took off to search.

At last Dorothy Mangan was in a police car, siren blaring, weaving between hundreds of cars trying to continue their journeys. The rescue from the van had been near Tiverton. It was probably 30 minutes to get back to the Farm, and that was if the police car driver could negotiate the massive traffic build up.

# 4

In the mine Clive Mangan and Mark Scott had sat quietly for a full hour to let the dust settle. Mark couldn't communicate easily with Clive but he was sure in his own mind that both of them were thinking about what had happened to Clive's wife and the farmer. Whoever had detonated the bomb was obviously some sort of criminal character. Was this some revenge activity from his Ecuador experience last year, or some retribution from the Russians at Highveer Point?

Clive shouted: 'We need to see if we can dig out now.' He gestured to Mark who struggled to his feet.

Mark was not well. His hearing had been seriously damaged. His lungs felt painful and his breathing was noisy and difficult.

When they were standing they stepped back into the main shaft. That's when they noticed a tiny streak of light coming down through the cap at the top. They couldn't see a definite hole, but the cap must have been fractured by the blast. There was probably about half a tonne of new rubble on the floor. They quickly crept back into the adit tunnel in case any more rubble fell down.

The air in the tunnel was still dense with fine dust, and it smelt of something similar to fireworks. Explosives and bomb materials had never been part of Mark's scientific repertoire. He tried to keep the towel over his mouth and nose. Mark was slower than Clive in their endeavour to get back to the adit entrance.

They pressed on, but the stream water around their feet was getting deeper. They'd only struggled about 150 metres from the main shaft. Clive looked worried. Whatever rock collapse had occurred, must have prevented the water draining. Clive's foot trod on something that wasn't rubble. He reached down and pulled up the emergency shovel. The wooden handle had been broken. There was now only about twenty centimetres of wood shaft left, and the broken end was awkwardly splintered. The blast had shot the shovel well over 100 metres into the adit. Clive pressed on. Most of the adit had a height of about 1.7 metres. Clive was shorter than Mark and was finding the crouching easier. Mark was about 1.8 metres tall, plus the extra height of his safety helmet.

Clive reached a set of marks on the tunnel wall that he recognised. The rescue group knew that was a 50 metres to the gate symbol. Underfoot the rubble build up was making the tunnel even smaller. The water level was up to their chests. Clive realised that if they forged on towards the adit entrance they would have no air above the water level. And the water level would continue to rise. They were in an impossible situation.

Mark was in a bad way. His breathing was getting noisier and more difficult. He was also cold and wet. Unlike Clive, he wasn't wearing a wetsuit. In fact he'd never owned one.

Clive thought he had better take Mark back to the main shaft. There he could either stand upright or sit on the rock bench. He would also be out of the water. It was a struggle for Mark to return to the shaft. When he got there he stretched and stood upright for a few minutes then decided to sit on the rock bench. He knew he wasn't coping.

# 5

The police car with Dorothy Mangan in it reached the Farm at about 17:10. There was a civilian car in the farm yard that she recognised. It was Kevin Hammett, a local vet. He had just arrived. He was a similar age to Clive and had been in the rescue group for over ten years. His interest had been started when the group had recovered a calf who had fallen into a disused shaft.

Two empty police cars were also in the farmyard. Their occupants were nowhere to be seen. Dorothy briefed Kevin. He said he would go down to the adit and she could remain to co-ordinate further arrivals. Kevin assured her that they would get her husband out: 'In the last hour phones had been ringing and nine of the group are now heading to the Farm, one of them is bringing the group's Land Rover with all the heavy equipment.'

Dorothy asked one of the two policeman who had driven her to the farm to stay with her for communications. She asked the other to go down across the fields to the adit entrance with Kevin Hammett. The police officers obliged as they realised that Dorothy was making sense.

More cars were arriving with rescue group members. Several were already in their full gear. Wet suits, overalls, boots, helmets, headlamps. Dorothy briefed them. She was running on adrenalin, but they knew she was not exaggerating. Another group member's car arrived, this was an off duty nurse. He realised Dorothy needed attending to. Her back of head injury had just about congealed, and there was dried blood all round her neck. He was surprised she was still functioning. He cleaned her up and inspected the injury. It was a fairly deep puncture wound, but he was more concerned about concussion and its consequences.

Kevin Hammett reached the adit entrance. The policeman radioed back to his colleague at the farmyard: 'Quite a large fall of rock and soil. The stream bed is dry. Send two JCBs, urgently.'

The policeman was just relaying Kevin's message. The rescue group at the farmyard were now working on the problem. Dorothy's description of the bomb incident was clear and unambiguous. They all knew she was a reliable and clear thinker. For years she'd supplied them with sandwiches and mugs of tea at their various practice events, but now they realised her organisational abilities.

The group's Land Rover arrived and communications were now live with Kevin Hammett. They knew a nearby farm had a JCB with a two foot bucket on the back end. Two of the group were already on their way to get it, hopefully the owner was at home. They needed a second one in case the excavation was more complex than expected. Perhaps, the owner of the first one might know the quickest way to obtain a second machine.

A police major incident van trundled into the farmyard, followed by a large Volvo police car with a Superintendent from Barnstaple. The police incident van and the rescue group's Land Rover were marshalled side by side. Another officer ordered the removal of many vehicles out of the farmyard and directed them to a field. They needed a clear route for heavier vehicles to get through to the yard, and into the field that led down to the adit.

Kevin Hammett arrived back up from the adit. The team agreed that Kevin should take on the role of team co-ordinator, normally Clive Mangan's role. Hammett wanted the group's Land Rover, full of rescue gear, down at the adit entrance.

Finally, Dorothy could see that things were in place to effect a possible rescue. The nurse was concerned that she needed to go to hospital. Dorothy was sitting in a car and had briefed the Superintendent. The nurse quietly explained to the Superintendent that an ambulance was needed fast.

Down at the adit entrance, shovels were removed from the Land Rover. Six of the rescue group started shifting the mud and shillett. It was the best they could do until a JCB arrived. Their major concern was the almost dry stream leaving the adit. They had to work fast to release the trapped water. Four shovelling at ground level, and Kevin had directed two to work on the top of the ground that had slumped into the adit. Possibly they could gain access into the adit.

In all, they had to remove about twenty tonnes of loose soil and shillett. They knew that shovelling would take many hours, probably even a day. They needed a JCB, and fast.

The rescue group had no knowledge of where Clive and Mark were located in the mine when the explosion had taken place.

# 6

At the police incident van in the farmyard the four officers who were first on the scene arrived back in the farmyard. The information that had been radioed to them was that there were two people stuck in a mine. They'd seen "Shaft" printed on the map near Henswood Farm so that's where they'd headed. They found a shaft top and noticed that the ground had slumped recently. They reported this to the Superintendent.

Most rescue group members were now at the adit entrance. The woman in the incident van was the Superintendent. She had a link down to Kevin Hammett. He said they had a loud speaker system with a long cable in the Land Rover. He detailed one of the rescue group to get the policemen to take him back to where they'd found the fractured capping, and take the loud speaker system.

The first ambulance arrived. The rescue group nurse waved the paramedics over to his car where Dorothy Mangan was sitting. She was getting delirious now. There was no debate, she had to go to hospital, complex concussion. The paramedics got her into the ambulance and set off for North Devon Hospital at Barnstaple. The ambulance driver knew the traffic was busy on the Link Road. Barnstaple was almost certainly a quicker bet than Exeter. The ambulance was returning back along the farm track only to be met by a mud covered yellow JCB speeding towards them. Inside the JCB cab was one of the rescue group. The other had driven over to another large farm where they hoped a second digger would be available.

Seeing the ambulance with its blue light flashing, the JCB driver swerved off the farm lane into a field, smashing down a wire fence, so that the ambulance could reach the road.

Fortunately, the farmyard tidy up had cleared enough space. The JCB sped through the yard, down across the field and on to the small wood surrounding the adit entrance. The rescue group shovellers were greatly relieved.

There was a small problem. A tree was in the way, before the JCB could get close to the collapsed adit. One of the rescue group raced across to the Land Rover and grabbed a chain saw. Felling the tree took another three minutes. Kevin Hammett talked to the JCB driver. Apparently there was only a quarter of a tank of diesel. That would give him about two and a half hours working unless some more could be brought in. That request was radioed back to the police incident van.

In the van the Police Superintendent, Melanie Kingston, was wearing her summer clothes. She had been on the beach at Saunton Sands with her family when she had the call from her Barnstaple Control Room. Before Dorothy Mangan was slipping into delirium Kingston had talked with her. The names of the two people in the mine were Clive Mangan, Dorothy's husband, and Mark Scott, a geologist. She'd asked Dorothy if Mark Scott was associated with Avon University. The answer was "yes". That was enough for Melanie Kingston to set up a call to GCHQ to alert Vanessa Wyndham. Twenty minutes later a call came through: 'Superintendent Kingston?'

'Yes.'

'Vanessa Wyndham here, Thank you for alerting me. I should be with you in about two hours. Can you avoid any media intrusion for the time being. If there have been any leaks so far, keep it to an unfortunate mine accident. Try to leave the international context to one side, and not mention a bomb.'

At the adit entrance the JCB had manoeuvred into a workable position and was dragging out the loose shillet and soil. It was a tight site for the operator and he soon realised that a second digger was needed to drag the loosened material away from the first digger.

The rescue group members with the shovels were now working on the top of the slump. They were throwing loose material towards the digger which was making much greater progress than they were.

# 7

Back at the main shaft, Clive Mangan realised that exit from the mine via the adit wouldn't work. The water depth meant that digging out wasn't possible. Water level had now reached the main shaft and was around their ankles. He had no knowledge of whether a rescue was under way. Clive had some flapjacks in his overall pockets which he and Mark started eating. They were both thirsty, but the water in the adit was now muddy.

Clive knew he had one other possibility. Ten years ago they had discovered a narrow air-shaft leading up from the lowest mine level. The level where Mark had obtained his ore samples. The air-shaft was 400 metres further on from the main shaft.

With no communication to the outside world he couldn't assume that anyone would know of his and Mark's predicament. He didn't even want to think of what may have happened to his wife, and probably Roy Farrow.

Could he persuade Mark to walk and crawl the 400 metres along the lowest mine level? At least there would be no deep water. The first hurdle was to get himself and Mark up the aluminium ladder to the level. He gestured his plan to Mark who just assumed it was to get him above the rising water level.

Mark was energised a little from eating the flapjack. He was cold, but not shivering. Physically he was functioning except that his breathing was compromised from the dust. They were both feeling thirsty. The short ladder climb was successful. The mine level varied in height, sometimes getting as low as a metre. Crawling on broken rock was painful on Mark's knees. It took them 35 minutes to reach the air-shaft. They both knew that their headlamp batteries would be nearly exhausted. Mark still had his small torch in his rucksack.

At the air-shaft Clive pointed out the concrete tube that he and his colleagues had installed ten years ago. Mark's hearing was nil, so Clive's verbal explanations were ineffective. He just showed Mark with short uses of his torch. Mark could see that the concrete tube had an internal diameter of about 60 centimetres. It had metal steps all the way up to a closed top. When the torch was switched off four tiny slits of light could be seen entering the tube at the top. The main shaft was about 40 metres high, but this shaft was 50 metres, it obviously exited higher up on the hill. Clive held up five fingers of his right hand and illustrated a zero with his thumb and forefinger. Mark responded: '50 metres high.'

Clive nodded.

The concrete tubes had been provided by a mine rescue group member who owned a concrete manufacturing business near Braunton. The group had known of the air-shaft for many years but it was quite narrow. It took the group eighteen months to widen it so that the pipes could be lowered in. The pipes were 1.6 metres long and they interlocked. The shaft wasn't completely straight, or perfectly vertical. Eventually, the first pipe had been lowered down and firmly rooted in the floor of the mine level. They'd used an angle grinder to cut away about a third of the circumference so that access could be gained into the tube. Unfortunately the oval shape of the access was only about a metre high, so it was a squeeze. A large person would struggle to get inside the tube.

Clive indicated he would go up first with Mark close behind. Their small rucksacks had to be worn on their fronts so that they could position their backs firmly against the inside of the pipes. Progress was slow.

Their success wasn't guaranteed. They only had one headlamp switched on at a time. In case this attempt didn't succeed they needed to be ruthlessly mean with their light sources. Mark thought the attempt looked hopeful, but Clive was concerned that the galvanised lid at the top may not release. He had made it ten years ago but the locking mechanism was complex for safety reasons. The group couldn't risk any passer-by in the woods removing it. The group had a special key to open it from the outside, but release from the inside was by a wheel on the underside of the lid. Rather like the hatches on a submarine. Was the mechanism corroded? This was making Clive particularly anxious.

Climbing up the tube was slow progress. The protruding metal steps were about 40 centimetres apart. Placing each foot was tricky with rucksacks on their fronts obscuring the view of their feet. It was a case of feeling their way up. Resting wasn't a problem as their backs were firmly jammed against the inside of the pipe. Mark was a little taller than Clive and had longer legs. Each change of footstep for him was awkward. Mark's breathing was seriously impacted but he knew this was their best hope of getting out. Frequent rests were necessary but falling was unlikely as long as feet were carefully placed.

As they reached the top they were aware that the light, coming in through the narrow slits below the lid, was dimming. Clive reached the lid and started working on the wheel to release the four catches that secured the hatch. It was solid, no movement at all. Mark was almost directly below him now: 'What's the problem?'

Clive answered but Mark couldn't hear.

Mark said: 'Can you hang from the wheel as you try to turn it.'

That was a big ask, but Clive knew he had to try everything within his power. Clive kept one foot touching a step and applied his 80 plus kilogrammes. It worked. Clive carefully rotated the wheel to its full extent so that the catches were clear of all the lugs. The lid was free. One last effort and Clive was able to throw the lid to one side and it fell to the ground. Twilight flooded in. It was a shock to their eyes, even though it was late evening. Clive climbed out, then held Mark firmly as he finally reached the top and struggled over the concrete lip.

They were out. They were now in the woodland, not owned by Roy Farrow. That's was another story from four years ago when the woodland was sold to a new owner. They removed their rucksacks and put them back on their backs. Mark was just hoping he hadn't damaged PIRSy, his Portable Infra-Red Spectrometer. He knew his Iron ore samples would be ok, inside two poly sample bags.

Clive led them down the wooded slope towards the top of the main shaft. There they were greeted by four members of the rescue group who were erecting a large steel tripod in preparation for attempting a rescue down through the main shaft. Clive said: 'I can barely hear what you're saying. We've both had our ears damaged by the blast, Mark can't hear a thing, and his breathing is bad also.'

One rescue group member said: 'There are ambulances over at the Farm. We've cut a gap in the barbed wire. I'll show you where.'

Clive thought he heard the word ambulance, but little else. Mark was struggling. The surge of adrenalin that had got him up through the tube and out into the fresh air had ceased. The ground in the woods was rough and full of brambles. It was slightly downhill but Mark's energy was failing. Even though it was a warm evening, he was now shivering. He stumbled. The rescue group members got him up and supported him for the last 300 metres to the farm.

The four of them working at the tripod decided to leave it in place for now as the shaft capping would need replacing. That was a problem for another day, but the new landowners might be awkward. They seemed to be mainly interested in keeping the woods for pheasant shooting parties. A thousand pounds a gun from corporate away-day amateurs was an attractive income stream for the owners.

All six of them reached the farm yard. They had radioed their imminent arrival and the ambulance crews were preparing to receive the two survivors. Kevin Hammett, the local vet, had come up from the adit entrance. The diagnosis for Mark was confirmed; severe hearing loss, probably perforated eardrums or worse, dust inhalation, and several cuts to his knees from crawling through parts of the mine level. Clive was put in the other ambulance. He had similar injuries, but less severe, and the wetsuit had saved his knees from cuts and bruises.

# 8

The heaters in Mark's ambulance had been powered up and all his wet clothing removed. Warm tea was brought over from the farm kitchen. He was able to sip it and munch on an energy bar.

Melanie Kingston interviewed Clive Mangan in the other ambulance. With the marginal hearing in his right ear the Superintendent was able to get confirmation of the events in the mine. Definitely an explosive device.

Mark's speech was rough and raspy, but intelligible. He needed to call his wife, Emma. The paramedic found the phone in his small wet rucksack, fortunately it was enclosed in a waterproof case. Everything else was sodden. Mark was regaining his faculties. He had probably been quite near hypothermia earlier but now fully aware of his situation. The phone was working, it hadn't been affected by the blast. He told the paramedic that he needed to speak to his wife, but may need help. The phone already had six failed attempts by Emma to reach him. It was now 21:45. Mark called her: 'Hi, darling. I'm ok, but my hearing's been damaged. I can't hear anything you say. I'm out of the mine and being looked after.' He passed the phone to the paramedic.

'Mrs Scott, I'm Gordon, the paramedic attending to your husband. He's not badly hurt but we're taking him to hospital.'

Emma was in a mixture of panic and elation. She tried to compose herself: 'Which hospital?'

'Probably Barnstaple or Exeter, but we're waiting for confirmation as he needs a specialist to sort out his hearing. It may be only a temporary loss, but they'll need to do a range of tests.'

Emma: 'Can I listen to him again?'

The paramedic gave the phone back to Mark.

'Darling, I'm feeling stronger now, and they've warmed me up. I expect the paramedic will phone you when we know which hospital. Love you. There's no need to come down tonight, we both need to sleep.'

Mark ended the call.

He asked the paramedic to find his car keys in a zip pocket in his sodden boiler suit: 'Can one of you find the large rucksack in my red truck, it has my spare clothes.'

In the other ambulance Clive was being updated on his wife, Dorothy, and farmer Roy Farrow. His wife had been the one to activate the rescue attempt. She was now at Barnstaple having a blot clot removed from her brain. The outlook was good for her, but Roy Farrow's death was a tragedy. Clive had known him for nearly thirty years. Melanie Kingston came into the ambulance to hold another conversation with Clive. He told her that Roy's brother, Brian, lived in the next farm, Hawkland. If he was alerted he would know what to do. There were no milkers at Hensdown, just beef cattle and sheep, and the chickens. Brian Farrow would deal with the animals.

# 9

In the incident van, the Superintendent's civilian communications assistant had been taking instructions from Vanessa Wyndham. Her ETA was now 22:20. The instruction for the two ambulances was to go to Exeter. An hour's drive but the two casualties injuries were not life threatening. The security services would have a team arriving tomorrow morning to build an account of what had happened. It would be easier if all parties were in one locality. As for Pedro Fugro, alias Carlos Sanchez, he was already at Exeter, under armed guard at a military installation. The gun wielding driver, name not certain yet, had been arrested after a protracted search by the police helicopter, and four armed police car teams, up through the Exe Valley. He was on his way to hospital at Exeter, under heavy security. His hand injury was quite severe, and he had lost quite a lot of blood. It was the latter that caused his downfall. He had taken hostages in an isolated farm but his attempt failed when he lost consciousness and collapsed. That was fortunate for the police as somehow he had acquired a shotgun with a magazine.

The ambulances were held on stand-by until Vanessa Wyndham arrived. It was a moonlit night as a black helicopter landed in the field adjacent the farmyard. The same field as where the excess cars had been untidily parked earlier.

Vanessa Wyndham jumped out, accompanied by a young man heavily armed. Being high summer, he didn't have the benefit of a large overcoat to conceal his equipment. It was clear that the security services were treating the whole incident as high level. Wyndham asked to be taken to Mark Scott's ambulance: 'Hello Mark, this was what we were concerned about last summer.'

Mark recognised her immediately, but put his hands to his ears and then waved his hands to signify a negative. Vanessa Wyndham took a felt tip pen from her pocket. She wrote on the inside wall of the ambulance:

> I'm putting in female agents again with your wife; also a
> nurse.

She asked Gordon, the paramedic, for Mark's phone, and got him to open it. She asked him to send a message to Emma. Mark typed a message somewhat similar to Vanessa's. He showed it to her. She indicated a thumbs up.

Vanessa scribbled a second sentence on the wall:

> Instituting similar arrangements to last summer until we
> know more about the two terrorists.

Mark 'Thanks.'

At that, she waved good bye, with a smile, and went across to talk with Superintendent Melanie Kingston. The ambulances were despatched to Exeter.

Mark was finding his situation of one-way conversation frustrating. At least he'd got through to Emma, and was now feeling comfortable and warm on the ambulance trolley. It would be useful to talk to Clive again. Perhaps that would be possible at the hospital. It was apparent from the appearance of Vanessa Wyndham that the security services were intent on treating the explosion seriously.

In the incident van the two women settled down for an exchange of information. Melanie Kingston sent her communications assistant off to the kitchen for two cups of coffee.

Wyndham: 'I expect you've heard a little bit about Mark Scott's experiences in Ecuador last year. I'd like to bring you up to date with the security services position. We haven't dropped the incident from our files. We kept protection on his family, and that of another casualty, last summer until we were sure that the Ecuador terrorists didn't have an international element. With this latest event we will need to reinstate our operations. Our first priority is to interrogate the two characters and reactivate our link with the CIA; they have much more experience of South American terrorism than we do. I'm pleased how your team here in North Devon has responded to this local incident. My main aim for your team is to keep a lid on it as much as possible.'

Superintendent Kingston intervened: 'That might present challenges as we have a probable manslaughter case with the death of Roy Farrow near Tiverton. Newspapers are usually quick to pick up on road traffic accidents. This one caused huge traffic jams for several hours.'

Wyndham: 'What if the two incidents were not connected. Possibly treat the crash of the van as a plain traffic accident, and separate from the mine collapse.'

Superintendent Kingston: 'We can try, but many vehicle occupants probably saw a police marksman shoot the gun out of the hand of the driver of the van. We also used a tyre ripper to stop the van. The public saw that as well. The helicopter search up the Exe Valley will have been noticed. This whole incident is going to be difficult to smooth over, but we'll do our best.'

Wyndham: 'Thanks, but keep in touch. I assume you'll sort out action to get this farm supervised.'

Superintendent Kingston: 'We will, I've already despatched two officers to the neighbouring farm.'

Wyndham: 'I'll go down to Exeter now, get some sleep, and meet the Chief Constable first thing tomorrow. Hopefully, interviews with the two terrorists might help us determine the extent of their organisation.'

Vanessa Wyndham and her armed support agent left.

Down at the adit entrance the rescue group were tidying up. The digger had pulled away the collapsed roof of the adit, and the second digger had moved the loose rock to the edge of the small wood. There was a moment of excitement as the last few tonnes were flushed out by the pressure of water built up in the mine. Quite a mess, and it was by then fairly dark. The JCB was nearly swept away by the muddy wave but it was heavy enough for driver to stay in control.

Kevin Hammett, the local vet, and now the *de facto* leader of the group, decided they could do little more that evening. It was 23:00. He had just returned from seeing Clive Mangan to assess his injuries. Hammett asked the group if they could return tomorrow evening to work out how they were going to secure the modified entrance to the adit. As it was a crime scene, the police would maintain a watch overnight. Daylight would allow their forensic people to gather samples of the explosive from the walls of the adit.

At the incident van Melanie Kinston was detailing some officers to maintain a watch and secure the farmhouse. Mark Scott and Clive Mangan had given up their keys in the hope that their vehicles would be driven to Exeter. Clive Mangan had been more concerned about his wife than himself. He wasn't intending to stay long in Exeter. His chat with Kevin Hammett had confirmed his ideas that Mark was in a worse state than him. Clive could just about hear and he certainly hadn't suffered as much blast and dust as Mark.

Just as Superintendent Melanie Kingston was about to leave, a truck came into the farmyard. Its occupant was Brian Farrow, brother of Roy. He'd been informed of his brother's death and had come over to get some more information from whoever was in charge. This was a difficult meeting at the end of a long day. She needed to calm him down as well as stress what the police needed over the next few days. Caring for the livestock would be the least of the problems for Brian Farrow.

# 10

At the hospital in Exeter Clive and Mark were given cursory examinations, cleaned up, fed and placed in a ward overnight. Clive was made aware that the captured van driver was in the same ward, in a side room. Two armed officers were guarding him. Other patients were probably unaware of the significant patient, and some were already asleep. The van driver's hand had been cleaned and bandaged and he was scheduled for surgery in the morning.

Mark Scott's breathing overnight was noisy and uncomfortable. He didn't sleep well. After breakfast the next morning, two consultants arrived. They assessed both patients but spent a lot more time on Mark. The thoracic surgeon wanted Mark in theatre straight away for a more detailed examination. Both had perforated ear drums, but the outlook was considered good. Clive's right ear was still giving him moderate hearing.

Mark was scheduled in theatre for 10:20. Fortunately, Emma arrived at 09:30, accompanied by two minders, one man, one woman The gentleman was obviously armed. Emma gave Mark an enormous hug. Their conversation was one sided but aided with a notepad and pencil that Emma had brought with her. At least Emma could see that Mark was not as injured as she had been informed. She remarked that there were two armed police at the ward entrance and it took several minutes to get clearance to enter. Mark was sitting up in a chair in a hospital gown. At 10:15 a policeman and an orderly arrived with a wheelchair to take Mark to theatre. Emma was told that she could wait if she wished. Mark would be about forty minutes.

The thoracic surgeon was waiting with one nurse. Mark was given some sort of relaxant then interviewed in depth for ten minutes. As the surgeon spoke his questions appeared in text on a screen so Mark could read them. When Mark had answered the question about distance from the blast, he'd said about 300 metres, the surgeon was quite relieved.

'Although you were in a confined environment the pressure wave would have reduced considerably. I suspect you have experienced little physical damage to your lungs, but the dust may be what gave you the breathing difficulties. As a geologist do you know what rock type was in the mine?'

Mark answered: 'A fine sandstone and mudstone.'

'At 300 metres you were probably breathing in the mudstone particles which would have been mostly clay rather than sharp quartz. Hence silicosis is unlikely. I'll just check your upper airways with the endoscope.'

The relaxant was obviously working now as Mark didn't find the tube uncomfortable. He could see the images on another video screen.

Surgeon: 'I'm quite happy with that, no indications of serious damage to the lungs. I'll get some steam therapy and controlled coughing set up for you. That can be done in a ward side room. I'll review you again in 48 hours.'

Mark was wheeled back to the ward, under heavy guard, to see Emma again.

Mark, still with a gravelly voice: 'It seems no long term damage, but I'll be here for a few more days.'

Emma scribbled on her notepad: 'Well that's a relief, what about your hearing?'

'I'm seeing the hearing consultant after she's finished with Clive.'

The lady doctor came over to Mark's bed and introduced herself in a strong Irish accent: 'I'm Catherine Ryan, hearing consultant.'

Emma heard, but Ryan had to show Mark her i-pad with the transcription.

Emma sat to one side while Mark was examined. Dr Ryan spent some time with the otoscope in the left ear, then a quicker examination of the right ear. Mark was given an i-pad by one of the nurses. As with the thoracic surgeon, the specialist's words appeared on the i-pad screen. Her diagnosis was: 'Your right ear has a minor perforation, that should heal itself within a week. Your left ear has a much larger perforation, but there is no other physical damage, and no sign of any bleeding from either ear. A specialist nurse will give you some medications and clean your ears carefully. I'll be back to see you on Wednesday.'

Emma heard all that.

The ward nurse came over to see them both, but spoke directly to Emma. 'As far as I know your husband will be here for between four and six days. The knee injuries are minor and we will continue to change the dressings on those here in the ward. Apparently, some officials will be here at 11:30 to see your husband and Mr Mangan.'

The nurse turned towards Mark and the hospital i-pad: 'Mr Scott, you'll keep that i-pad for the duration of your stay. Let us know when it needs charging. Before you're discharged we'll bring over one of the techies to put an app on your phone. That'll do the same as the i-pad.'

It was Monday 15th July 2019. Mark and Emma had only two and half weeks until they moved house. Emma didn't raise the subject but she hoped that Mark would be agile and back to his usual physical competence. Her Mum and Dad would be helping, and probably Mark's parents, but she didn't want them doing any heavy lifting.

The couple chatted together until the arrival of Vanessa Wyndham. Emma gave Mark a big kiss and said she would be down again Tuesday evening.

Vanessa Wyndham had walked in with Dominic Wright, who Mark remembered from the helicopter day at Heddon's Mouth. Vanessa talked with the ward sister first and a side room was provided for the four of them; Wyndham, Wright, Scott and Mangan. Mark's impression was that Dominic Wright may have been Vanessa's boss.

Vanessa conducted the meeting: 'Gentleman, we've had a meeting with the Chief Constable this morning. We have a rough idea of the events yesterday but need to get a recording of your perspectives, from the time you arrived at Hensdown Farm and met Roy Farrow. Let me know if your i-pads are not picking up any of my sentences and I'll slow down.'

Mark and Clive Mangan recounted their recollections. Vanessa and Dominic interjected from time to time, to get precision, particularly up to the time of the explosion.

Vanessa: 'Thank you for that. We have to have these details on file for legal purposes because it's almost certain that the van driver will be charged with the manslaughter of Roy Farrow, as well as various firearms offences. The van driver's name is Colin Jones, well known to Bristol police. It's likely he was just a hired gun and van. Mr Mangan, the last we've been given about your wife is that she had the blood clot removed and is well on her way to a full recovery. I understand that the hospital in North Devon has been keeping you up to date. In a few days, when her doctors allow, we need to get her account of the arrival of the terrorists. Mr Mangan, please can you leave us now, we'll probably talk to you again after we've interviewed your wife.'

Mangan: 'Ok, thanks for bringing me up to date on Dorothy. I've had a couple of calls from North Devon but the voice to text i-pad doesn't work so well with phone calls.'

Vanessa Wyndham to Mark: 'We're not sure how the South American visitor will be handled. He will be treated as a terrorist and it will be up to higher authorities than me and Dominic to make decisions on him. His Brazilian passport showed his name as Carlos Sanchez, but one of his credit cards had the name of Pedro Fugro. If the passport is correct, then it appears he's the son of one of the late terrorists in the attack helicopter that injured you last summer in Ecuador. There is the possibility that he's also the one that the Ecuador authorities want for the missile attack on our evacuation aircraft. When we're back in London we'll be knitting all this together with our CIA contacts. The Brazilian connection is interesting to them. It may be why the Ecuador authorities haven't been able to find him. National borders are rather fluid for terrorists in the Northern Andes of South America.'

Mark: 'Do you think Carlos Sanchez has any associates in this country?'

Vanessa: 'We're not sure yet, that's why we've instituted a high security level again. The fact that he appears to have hired a local gun man in Bristol might indicate he's a lone operator, but we can't be sure. We'll keep you in the loop. I'll be back after we've been able to interview Dorothy Mangan. Please don't give any details of what we know about Sanchez to Clive Mangan until we've spoken with Dorothy Mangan. Hopefully, she can give us the best, in fact the only, account of the terrorist arrival and up to the van crash.'

Mark: 'Thanks for trying to resolve all this.'

Vanessa Wyndham and Dominic Wright left Mark. They went across to another side room where Colin Jones was under guard. They spoke with him for half and hour. They were only interested in how he was involved with Sanchez. They were trying to assess his intellectual level. They made no attempt to tell him how he would be charged. His hand injury had been attended to and he was to be transferred to police for them to pursue traffic, firearms and manslaughter charges.

Wyndham and Wright were certain in their own mind that he was nothing more than a jobbing criminal. Their focus needed to be directed to Carlos Sanchez. They left the hospital for their meeting with the South American who was under guard at a military base nearby.

At the base, even though they had all their security passes, the process of getting in to see Sanchez was complex. The security services, the military, and the police are all highly structured organisations. All sectors were accountable to government, but they were all hesitant and bureaucratic when personnel from another sector wanted to intrude or require assistance.

After feeding and cleaning up Sanchez had been left overnight, and through the morning, with minimal contact and no verbal interaction from the military police.

Dominic Wright and Vanessa Wyndham were processed slowly by the military officials and given a strict briefing on how they could conduct their enquiries. They realised that would mean they would be watched and almost certainly recorded.

Sanchez was not forthcoming. A great deal of shrugging, and denials. He said hardly anything, although his standard of English was more than competent. He refused an offer of diplomatic assistance. He didn't admit to being an Ecuador citizen. Wright and Wyndham made no comment on how he would be charged, or by whom. They were just trying to build a picture of what had happened yesterday. They also knew that this initial meeting was a preliminary. Until they had gleaned an account from Dorothy Mangan, they realised the legal situation was unclear. This wasn't going to be straightforward data gathering, and there was only one eye witness. Had Roy Farrow not been killed, he, as a second witness, could have provided corroboration.

Wright and Wyndham decided to end the preliminary meeting with Sanchez. Perhaps a few days in isolation might make him more communicative. They had a short discussion with the base commanding officer before they left.

Their helicopter arrived to take them to Chivenor airfield. There they would wait until they could talk with Dorothy Mangan at Barnstaple hospital.

# 11

Following the various visits to the ward at Exeter Hospital, the nurses were able to perform the treatments for Mark. That occupied Monday afternoon. It was a little uncomfortable but it was quite effective at getting a mucky mess out of his lungs.

Tuesday morning Mark was feeling much more comfortable. His chest was less irritating. His speech was less gravelly, according to Clive Mangan. Hearing for both of them was still much the same.

Mark had another steam therapy session in the morning. He was looking forward to Emma's visit later in the day. From feeling totally desperate for his life in the mine on Sunday he could now see that the house move on 2nd August was realistic. He felt he had been lucky.

Mark slept on Tuesday afternoon, then Emma arrived early evening, accompanied by her minder. Conversation was more relaxed, and use of the i-pad speech to text device was becoming easier.

While Mark was asleep Clive Mangan had been discharged. He was taken to Barnstaple hospital to see his wife.

At Barnstaple hospital Wright and Wyndham had been allowed to see Dorothy Mangan. In fact the interview was conducted by a senior police detective. The security services were just in attendance. It was crucial that the interview was legally sound as a manslaughter charge was involved. Vanessa Wyndham felt that Dorothy Mangan's statement was cogent and it gave her and Dominic Wright a clear understanding of the actions of the terrorists. The statement was also sufficient for any government actions dealing with Carlos Sanchez. Wright and Wyndham had all they needed to go back for a second interview with Sanchez.

Vanessa Wyndham wanted to ensure that Mark and his family would not receive any further intimidation. She did not wish to see Sanchez being deported to anywhere in South America. She felt it safer if Sanchez could be imprisoned in Britain for terrorist activity. Unfortunately, those sort of decisions would be out of her control. She was conscious that some countries had an unfortunate history of releasing prisoners for political reasons when new leaders were elected, or took power. Hence keeping Sanchez on British soil seemed safer in the long run.

Vanessa Wyndham felt her inquiries were complete. Others would work through the legal and political consequences. That was well above her pay grade, and that of Dominic Wright.

Wednesday at Exeter hospital Mark received another visit from Dr Ryan, the hearing consultant. The right eardrum was healing over well, but the left was a mess. Surgical assistance was needed. Mark's knees had a few scabs but they weren't affecting his mobility. His breathing was now much easier, and less noisy.

Later that evening, when Emma arrived, they discussed their impending house move. Emma suggested asking Pete to help out on 2nd August. Mark thought that was worth pursuing. Emma had been wearing loose dresses since Monday. That was quite appropriate in the warm weather. She was conscious that her bump was now visible if she wore tight clothes. Mark's strongly suggested that she should take a directorial role during the house move; others could do the lifting and carrying.

Mark asked Emma to phone Richard Ericson, his supervisor at Avon University, and explain what had happened near North Molton on Sunday. Richard Ericson would need to inform Redruth Institute of the reason for Mark's cancellation of the visit. Until he got a speech to text app on his phone communication was awkward. Emma had a number of tasks to complete this week, as well as going into school for the last two days of term.

Thursday Mark was seen by the thoracic surgeon who indicated that lungs were now clear of dust particles and there was no permanent damage. He could be discharged. However, the prognosis from Dr Ryan, the hearing consultant, was less encouraging. The right eardrum would probably heal by itself completely within a few days, but the left one definitely needed surgery.

When Mark said he was moving house in about two weeks and wanted to be able to be involved, the dialogue moved to discussing possibilities. Dr Ryan said she would need to study her lists and contact him. Mark would need to be in hospital for one or two days after surgery, then no swimming or air travel for several weeks.

After the consultation Dr Ryan agreed that Mark could be discharged for the time being. Emma came down after school to collect him.

# 12

Friday evening Emma had finished term, faitly confident that no one had suspected her pregnancy. Mark was preparing himself for working from home. That meant both of them would be in their rented house with a security services minder. Mark decided to press on with his preparations for China, and start packing for the house move. In two weeks' time they would be in their own bungalow.

On Saturday Mark typed a carefully worded letter letter to John Shackleton at Redruth Institute of Mining. He'd missed the visit to the Institute and the tin mine. He didn't wish to lose the connection with the Institute. Cornwall could be a significant fieldwork area over the next twelve months. The letter was a mixture of apology, limited explanation, and a courtesy letter to someone he valued highly. He didn't disclose the terrorist element of the mine incident.

Emma wanted a supermarket visit. The three of them climbed into the truck and set off. Today's minder was aware that his long winter coat was conspicuous. He tried hard to follow the couple without giving any indication of being associated with them. He had his own trolley and had already briefed Mark and Emma to go through the checkout first, then hover nearby as he took his turn. The minder was much more sensitive to his role than some of the others they'd had recently.

Domestic routines were a little strained through the weekend, but they managed a short country walk on Sunday afternoon.

Monday, Mark had two messages, one from the hospital in Exeter and one from Vanessa Wyndham about a visit. The hospital were offering Mark an operation on his left ear on Thursday 8th August, six days after the house move. Mark accepted the surgery offer.

The Vanessa Wyndham visit was at 11:00 that day. It was mainly an update. The two characters involved in the mine explosion were going to be handled differently. Jones would be processed by the police and put through the criminal justice system. Carlos Sanchez was going to be kept out of the standard criminal justice system, and treated as a terrorist. The mine explosion would be treated as attempted murder but security services didn't want to route him through open courts. For the time being, he would be kept incognito at various establishments in Britain, and not passed back to either Brazil or Ecuador. As far as enquiries had ascertained, Sanchez was not closely connected with known South American groups, narcotics or kidnapping. No one had come forward to represent him, and Ecuador no longer wished to pursue any charges for the missile attacks at their military base. Wyndham was content that the government could keep him out of circulation. The mine incident was going to be allowed to drift into being a non-event as far as the public was concerned.

The security services minders, would cease at 18:00 today. Vanessa Wyndham left, her investigation of the mine explosion incident was over.

Domestic life for the newly married Mark and Emma would return to normal.

Emma, with her usual organisational flair, was now writing lists of where everything was being packed, labelling all the cardboard boxes, and where they would go in their new home. Every so often Mark was called upstairs to carry another box down for stacking in the front room.

Mark wasn't getting a great deal of geology work done.

It was now 26th July, the China trip departed on 14th September, seven weeks away. From the comments of Dr Ryan, and the A4 sheet of instructions issued to tympanoplasty patients, Mark felt confident he would be perfectly fit for the journey.

Phone calls that evening were quite satisfying. With no other sound in the house Mark could hear moderately well with the phone pressed up against his right ear. A catch up call from Richard Ericson was encouraging. Richard told him to relax and focus all his efforts on removal day, next Friday. His Mum and Dad confirmed they would be coming down for the move. Pete, Mark's long term friend, announced he was bringing a van to transport the cardboard boxes. He would do all the lifting and carrying. Mark had already insisted to Emma that she would have nothing more than a directorial role on move day.

Friday 2$^{nd}$ August finally arrived. The family turned up. Pete arrived with a van. Everyone followed Emma's carefully planned schedule. She should have followed a career as a film director. No hiccups, everything went smoothly.

Mark, Emma, and her bump, spent their first night in their new home, and in the new bed. The next morning was sunny with a light breeze. Many jobs to turn cardboard box city into a real home. Saturday lunch was brought over by Emma's Mum and Dad. On Sunday they invited Mark and Emma to theirs for lunch. It was only a four kilometre drive. Emma could envisage the near future when local familial support would make such a difference to her work and family life, particularly child care.

Mark made one trip to Avon to gather up some details he needed.

Thursday morning 8$^{th}$ August, Emma drove Mark down to the hospital at Exeter. He had the tympanoplasty surgery on his left ear, that afternoon. Dr Ryan saw him after he had come round. She said she was more than happy with the operation and he could be discharged on Friday afternoon.

Emma came down to bring him home. Mark was still a little dizzy, but quite cheerful. Over the last few days he was also regaining more hearing in his right ear. Dr Ryan had told him that it may be several weeks before the left ear, on which she'd operated, would be returning to normal.

That weekend Mark relaxed, unusual for him, but probably caused to some extent by the residual anaesthetic. Their new home was functioning perfectly well. Mark had developed a few ideas of what he'd like to do with the property, but they weren't urgent, certainly not until the baby arrived. Sunday, Richard Ericson turned up with his family. A social call, but his gentle message to Mark was not to race to catch up on the lost weeks. Compared to many PhD students Mark was firmly in control of his research and not struggling. He should spend some time with Emma, gather his strength and fitness and focus on the China trip. The visits to the Tamar Valley and Redruth could wait until they returned.

The woman were busy chatting. Richard and Angela's well behaved twin eight year-olds were exploring the garden.

Richard turned the conversation to academic benefits of the China trip. They both knew that the programme of visits would probably only be made available to them each day. Their role would be to just absorb whatever information that came their way. They were a high powered team. Two highly qualified academics in geology, and one experienced field worker in Copper detection. As for Jeremy Chudleigh, the fourth member of the party, there was unspoken puzzlement. Mark had detected earlier that Gordon MacPherson, head of geology, was not happy with the attachment to the China visit of a barely known administrator.

Richard said that mutterings in the departmental lounge hadn't shown much confidence with the Vice Chancellor. He'd only been in post for two years and the signs were becoming evident that the University management was moving towards money, particularly the building of residential student accommodation funded by private equity investors. The VC was an economist, no higher degrees, but had written a text book for under-graduates. He was a rapid riser from one of the business focused colleges in the Midlands. As for the VC's appointment of Jeremy Chudleigh, no information seemed to be available about him other than the fact that he had spent three years in the USA before joining Avon a year ago.

Anyway the puzzlement would continue, the geologists would just have to focus on their aims and objectives, even though they knew they would be guests in a different country to the European nations with which they were familiar.

The afternoon was encouraging and low stress for Mark and Emma. They both waved the Ericson family off after the congenial get together. Their twins, as usual, had been incredibly well behaved.

Now that Emma was on school holidays, and in her new home, she was thoroughly relaxed. The previous few months had been hectic for her, but happily things had fallen into place. Mark spent the following week gently tackling garden tasks, mostly the August weed growth. The bungalow itself was in exceptionally good order. They were extremely fortunate. One afternoon Emma, completely out of the blue, said to Mark: 'Can we have our honeymoon now? What about a week on Alderney?'

Mark was taken aback: 'Well yes, but why Alderney?'

'I just want a quiet week in a quiet hotel. Jersey would be busy and crowded, and we've done Guernsey.'

'Ok. When?'

'Next week, perhaps. I could make the arrangements, so you can concentrate on some reading.'

That was settled. Emma decided to book the ferry from Poole, conscious that Mark had been advised to avoid air travel for several weeks.

Saturday 17th August they were off. The crossings to Guernsey then onto Alderney were relatively calm. The hotel sent a minibus to the quay to collect them. This was a dream location for Emma, a beautiful room with a view and an indoor heated pool. Mark was happy, he had no expectations other than to support Emma in her choice. Emma's bump was still small but she paraded herself confidently, gently and smoothly, no longer feeling the need to disguise her pregnancy.

The holiday, their honeymoon, was actually quite active. They set off for a walk each morning. Over five days they covered much of the island, one day was drizzly so that deteriorated into perusing the local gift shops. Afternoons were by the pool or sunbathing on the hotel balcony. Mark fitted in quite a bit of reading and internet searching. For Emma it was her romantic week away, one that she hadn't been sure she would get a few weeks ago.

They returned home on the following Saturday. Emma's holiday planning skills had clocked up another success.

# 13

The bungalow was their rural idyll, the garden was tidy, Emma was really relaxed, so Mark decided to go back to Avon. The Geology Department was quiet, the Library almost empty, no undergraduates. Then Mark realised it was Bank Holiday Monday. He drafted a couple of letters to Tamar Valley mine and Redruth Institute. He explained the reason why he wasn't able to keep the arrangements for late July. They were more courtesy letters as Richard Ericson had informed the two venues in the week after the explosion. Richard hadn't disclosed the terrorist involvement and it seemed that the lid on the media had been respected. It had been one of those events that Whitehall wanted to keep at a low profile.

Mark spent the week on his China preparations. He got translations from the Library of several Chinese articles on rare earth mineral mines, although they had no location detail. He also found an article on physical processing and the hazards of chemical processing. This was quite a find because it laboured the "care of environment" mantra. It was an interesting paper.

Friday afternoon Mark decided to leave early. He was quite pleased with what he had gleaned that week. He made sure he had enough material, particularly maps of China, to do a bit of work at home next week.

He walked across to his truck, unlocked it, stowed the rolled up maps of China carefully behind the driver's seat. Then a voice behind him asked: 'How was Alderney?'

Mark recognised the voice straight away.

Vanessa Wyndham announced: 'I have a few things you need to know to bring you up to date. Can we walk across to the trees over there?'

They walked across the grass to a wooden seat, in the shade, about a hundred metres from the cars.

Vanessa started: 'First the explosion incident at the Hensdown Farm adit. We don't see the gun episode with Colin Jones as having any consequences for you and your family. Jones has never been a gang member in Bristol. He's just a gun for hire. He'll probably get about six years.

Mark: 'Will he be prosecuted through open court?'

'Yes.'

'What about Carlos Sanchez?'

'He's still being held by our people. Security forces in Ecuador are rather busy. We get the feeling that Ecuador don't really want to deal with him, and Brazil are not interested at all because his Brazilian passport is a fake. Both countries will be happy if we can keep him out of circulation in Britain. He'll be put in an ultra-secure establishment for many years.'

Mark: 'So you don't see any further repercussions from the Ecuador incident?'

'No we don't. But, I want to give you these. They are alarms. They work through the police telephone system. The leaflet explains how to keep it charged. The one for Emma is marked "E". Keep them with you at all times. If you press the red button, the national alert desk will know who you are, and they'll have your location at the time of pressing.

They'll continue to monitor your location and alert the appropriate action team. It's the same alarm system that we give to High Court judges, certain Members of Parliament, and other people we need to protect.'

Mark: 'If you don't see Sanchez as a continuing problem, why do we need them?

'It's not about Ecuador, it's about the Russian involvement at Highveer Point. We don't believe it was promoted by the Kremlin. It appears to be an oligarch project that put money in to set up a secret base that they could "sell" to the Kremlin when it was complete. That sort of gesture would have won Brownie Points for the project masterminds. Unfortunately for them, they could now be several hundred million pounds out of pocket following the destruction of their tunnel, the big house, and the lifting barge. They could be rather aggrieved. For months they were waving cash around in Whitehall to buy various smoothing influences. The matter is all about money. We know that oligarchs are buying their way into favours from all sorts of influential people, including Members of Parliament. London is a hot bed of corruption. If you're an oligarch with a billion pounds, or even more, then you can do a great deal of persuading.'

Mark: 'Are we in imminent danger?'

'We don't know. Most oligarchs don't like eliminating people, they need people to assist them in their endeavours. They know that money is their main method of influence, and it works. That leaves oligarchs free to build a generous, well meaning, reputation within British society.'

Mark: 'So you imagine it's a slim risk?'

'Yes, but we're keeping you on the list.'

Vanessa lifts the tone of here voice: 'I'll leave it like that for now. but the second reason for talking to you today is to tell you that Canada and the U.S, want Professor Zhou out of China, if they can see an opportunity. Zhou's son has been eased out of the Beijing inner circle and

Zhou can see it's now the time to go. Don't mention this to anyone. What you need to know is that if a local Chinese man, or woman, approaches you with a phrase including "geraniums and "terracing" then you can follow their suggestions. It may not arise. Just pursue your academic interests as planned, but we are there, in the background, to support unexpected events.'

Mark: 'It sounds like a spy novel.'

'I know, but everything could go quite smoothly, with no unexpected events. We'll catch up again when you get back.'

Vanessa walked back to her insignificant car and drove slowly out of the car park. There was hardly anyone around on the Campus. If anyone had been watching from a window they may have assumed it was lover's meeting. Mark didn't even want to consider that. He remained on the wooden seat for a few minutes cogitating the latest briefing. He then walked to his truck and drove home.

Emma had enjoyed her week, she'd had the bungalow to herself during daytime and immersed herself in her new home, the family home.

After dinner Mark quietly explained the alarm, in a matter of fact way. He just hoped Emma would see it as a minor matter.

# 14

Monday 2nd September, less than two weeks to the departure for China. Mark decided to work at home for a few days and await the call from Richard Ericson. He studied the maps intently and gradually built up a mental image of the whole of China. The mining areas were not easily evident, but from his reading of numerous articles his understanding was increasing.

Tuesday was Emma's 20 week scan at the local hospital. They both went along. The sonographer firmly announced that all was well and gave them a print out of the scan. It was definitely a girl. Studying the print out Mark had a feeling of welling up, almost a tear of joy in his eye. The visit was a great assurance to Emma who would be starting back at school on Thursday, following a staff meeting on Wednesday.

Mid-week, an e-mail from Richard Ericson detailed the proposed meeting scheduled for Monday 9th September. A long agenda. The e-mail was addressed to Gordon MacPherson, Mark and Jeremy Chudleigh, so all four of them would probably be at the meeting.

Mark's hearing was improving. Not as good as it was before the explosion but he was confident he would be able to follow everything on the visit. He'd checked the various aviation web sites and was happy to find that the aircraft to Beijing would be a large modern jet with a higher cabin pressure. He couldn't find anything about the domestic aircraft down to Fudong.

That weekend Mark and Emma went to the supermarket together on Saturday. Emma was feeling well and confident. She was keen for a walk on Sunday. They walked for nearly two hours in the sunshine across local farmland. Their move to East Quantock had given them new areas to explore. Emma's two days at school wearing her floppy jumper had given no indication to anyone that she was pregnant. She'd decided, on the advice of her Union, to draft a handwritten note which she would present to the Headmistress next week.

Monday, Mark headed up to Avon. The new commuting route only added about ten minutes to his journey. The meeting started at 11:00 in Gordon MacPherson's office. All four were there. Jeremy Chudleigh introduced himself. Only Gordon MacPherson had met him up to now.

Jeremy Chudleigh: 'I'll chair the meeting as I've got the tickets.'

Gordon MacPherson arrested his statement straight away: 'I'll chair it Mr Chudleigh, this is largely an academic meeting. As the Head of Department, I'll be leading this delegation. Academic rigour of this proposed tie up is central to our mission. I've had clear instructions from the Vice Chancellor on how we are going to make this arrangement work. The last item on the agenda is administration, we'll deal with tickets then.'

Mark could see a weak grin developing on Richard Ericson's face.

Gordon MacPherson launched: 'Professor Ericson can you explain how we will be promoting our aims for the proposed exchange programmes.'

Richard Ericson: 'Thank you Professor, I'll start with the Doctoral arrangements . . .'

The two of them had obviously planned this strategy. They spent nearly forty minutes going through their "academic" agenda. It seemed to Mark that they were determined to keep Chudleigh in his place. He was the administrator, not a person who would be involved in any of the teaching, support or keeping the researchers focused. MacPherson wasn't sure of the relationship between the Vice Chancellor and Chudleigh but he was determined to keep to his principles. Higher Education was about bringing on the next generation of scientists and technocrats, not extracting large amounts of cash for privatised accommodation projects.

The meeting concluded with a short item on administration. MacPherson stated: 'Mr Chudleigh I understand you wish to say something about tickets.'

Chudleigh: 'Yes chairman, I have the airline tickets, we need to be at Terminal 5 Heathrow by 04:00 for the Beijing flight.'

MacPherson: 'Give us the tickets then, and the ones down to Fudong.'

Chudleigh stuttered a bit but eventually passed the individual tickets to the three academics. Richard Ericson was pleased that MacPherson had demonstrated beyond doubt that he would be leading the China visit. Throughout the meeting Mark Scott had listened attentively to every word but made no comment. It was clear that he was being left to focus solely on his research objectives. That suited him.

Jeremy Chudleigh left the meeting with a simple 'See you on Saturday gentlemen'.

At that Gordon MacPherson quietly said to Richard and Mark that he would book a hotel at Heathrow and arrange for one of the University's minibuses to take the three of them up on Friday afternoon.

The next three days Mark spent at home studying his maps and reading up as much as possible on mineral processing. He cooked dinner for Emma each evening. Friday morning was an early start as Emma drove him to Avon before school.

Her parting words to Mark were: 'I love you very much for getting me through this summer, take care.'

The three of them piled into the minibus at 15:30 and set off for the Heathrow hotel. Dinner, paid for on Gordon MacPherson's faculty credit card, then an early night. At airport departures there was no sign of Jeremy Chudleigh until they noticed him at the boarding gate in the business section. The three others shuffled through the economy queue.

At Beijing there was a two hour wait before the three hour flight down to Fudong. Actually, to an airport about 40 km distant. It was on this flight that Chudleigh joined them. It was so unfortunate for him that the domestic flight was all one class.

On landing they were met by a man in a dark suit and impeccable English: 'Professor MacPherson, welcome to southern China, I trust you and your colleagues have had a comfortable journey.'

They were ushered to a waiting minibus, labelled in Chinese, but with FUDONG UNIVERSITY clearly marked below.

By the time they reached the University Campus it was nearly daybreak. They were offered a light buffet breakfast and told by their guide that there would be a meal at 14:00 local time and then a start to proceedings with Professor Zhou at 15:00. They were shown to their rooms: simple, clean, single bed, desk, kitchenette, shower and lavatory. Mark said he needed a short walk and some fresh air, and then a sleep. They all agreed to meet in the refectory at at 13:55. Mark sent a short message to Emma. Within 20 seconds the phone showed it had been received. He planned to send a message when he got up at about 06:00 each morning, Fudong time. That would mean Emma would receive it at 22:00 BST.

After the meal, Professor Zhou met them and showed them to a conference room for introductions. Jasmin Wang, secretary to Zhou, and Ling Hahn the gentleman who met them at the airport were there, together with University staff in uniforms who were introduced as drivers. All spoke reasonable English. Zhou indicated that Hahn would be advising them on all diary and travel times. From Zhou's expressions and gestures it seemed that Hahn was the party official. He may have been a sort of tourist guide, but he was meticulous and making frequent notes. It was difficult to assess his purpose. Without any conferring the group could sense that they needed to treat him with caution.

Zhou outlined the week ahead. Monday to a Samarium mine, about a 90 minute drive. Tuesday to a Neodymium mine, about a 2 hour drive. Wednesday a local processing plant, on campus. Thursday lectures and seminars. Friday organisational matters of the proposed exchange system.

That evening was taken up with a tour of the traditional geology laboratories and engineering workshops. It seemed that Fudong was a University devoted solely to geology and mining and processing. No other subject disciplines.

The evening tour was quite formal and highly structured. No opportunity for the sort of chatter that was common at conferences. Hahn accompanied them for the entire evening. Each lab and workshop had a team of lecturers and technicians. They were briefly introduced by Zhou, then each specialist embarked on a monologue of what they did. All in well rehearsed English. Brief opportunities for questions at each lab, but the answers were given by Zhou. An A4 sheet of the monologue was given out as they were ushered towards the next lab. The handout was identical to the monologue but with numerous diagrams included.

The tour finished at 21:00, Zhou departed quietly. Hahn said breakfast at 07:00, assemble at the entrance at 08:00 for the minibus journey to the mine. Mark Scott, MacPherson, Ericson and Chudleigh, the group, were led back to their accommodation by Hahn. MacPherson mouthed: 'My room.' to his colleagues, except Chudleigh, and held up three fingers.

Hahn had disappeared. The three of them assembled in MacPherson's room. Richard Ericson switched on some recorded music on his phone and said in a soft whisper: 'I've been on many orchestrated tours at conferences but this evening's march was particularly strange.'

MacPherson: 'It's been a dense introduction to the set up here, actually quite informative, but I'm concerned that it's all rather robotic.'

Ericson: 'Zhou is behaving differently to how he was in Innsbruck. He was much more relaxed there and reflected a typical academic conversation. What did you think Mark?'

Mark: 'Yes, he's certainly different. I was talking with him for nearly two hours on the mountain walk and in the coach. He was quite relaxed then. At times I could sense his Canadian accent. His minder was not all that bright and it was easy for Zhou to conduct conversations in English.'

MacPherson: 'Well, it's still a valuable visit. I've picked up quite a bit this evening, but we'll have to see if we can get Zhou on his own tomorrow. I'll look for opportunities to distract Hahn and you two can try and resurrect the rapport you had at Innsbruck. Anyway, we'll get some sleep now, and have another short get together here tomorrow night. Thanks for switching on the music Richard. We can't be sure our rooms aren't being bugged.'

# 15

Monday morning they all turned up for breakfast at 07:00. Chudleigh said: 'I'm coming on the minibus today.'

After breakfast they got into the minibus. Hahn sat next to the driver. Zhou sat with the group. Chudleigh isolated himself at the back of the minibus. Everyone commented on the weather, it was already warm. Zhou quietly took a small electronic bug with its short wire from his anorak pocket and showed it to MacPherson, Ericson and Mark. They gently nodded in acknowledgement. After a few minutes, when the minibus had reached the main road, Zhou started his prepared statement: 'Today we are travelling to a Samarium mine. As you will know Samarium is valued for its ability to sustain high temperatures in magnets, but also for development work in X-ray lasers. The latter requires highly purified forms of the element. There are other Lanthanides in the mine but in quite small quantities. On the world market Samarium's value is fairly low, but its uses are still being investigated within the advanced electronics world. The mine has no radiation problems but dust is present. You'll be given active filtration headwear. The background geology is fine grained granite about 50 milion years old, the ore veins are about 40 million years old.'

The academics of the group were listening intently. Zhou paused his delivery and didn't wish to take questions yet. He gestured a zip across his mouth. The journey itself was interesting. A great deal of market gardening in the surrounding countryside, with a few cows and goats.

About an hour into the journey the road started to climb. Zhou resumed his delivery: 'We keep this mine in our field visit list because of the way that the waste is managed. The mine has been going for over 30 years and has had forty-five workable veins. As those have become exhausted waste material has been moved back into the disused levels. Much of the waste is gravel down to dust. The fine processing unit is about two kilometres away. The waste from their processing is also brought back for packing into the disused levels. The fine processing unit itself is never open to visitors or graduate students. We'll get to see some coarse processing in the red building during the afternoon.'

The minibus drew up in a large car park. Some lorries, a large number of small motor bikes, more like mopeds. At this point, Hahn took over: 'Please walk across to the blue building. You will be equipped with overalls, boots and a ventilator helmet. You may leave any items in an individual locker. You are welcome to take your camera or phone into this mine and take photographs at will.'

After they had donned the safety clothing, Hahn introduced Mr Wu, the mine manager. He took the group into the mine. Mr Wu's English was limited, but the group could identify many of the mine's features and equipment by his gestures. There was no clear opportunity to separate Hahn from Zhou. There was also the electronic bug in Zhou's pocket.

Mark was taking many photos in the mine. The vein that was being shown to them was about 40 centimetres thick. They were then taken further into the mine to where waste material was being firmly packed into a disused working level. They were using small amounts of water in the packing process, and also a hosepipe that was spraying a cement slurry. Hahn was standing next to the machine that was mixing the cement. One of the workers accidentally knocked a leaver on the machine and the engine raced. The hosepipe uncoupled itself at the outlet valve and Hahn was badly sprayed with cement slurry. It covered his helmet and appeared to have squirted some into the side of his visor which affected his right eye. He was in agony.

Someone must have activated an emergency bell. Within a minute a stretcher team ran into the level where they were all standing. Hahn was loaded onto the stretcher and carried briskly out of the mine. At this point Mr Wu escorted the group back to the blue building. There was no sign of where Hahn had been taken, The group removed their protective clothing and were directed into a washing area. After ablutions they were shown into a canteen and invited to sit down. There were six miners on another table and a loudspeaker was blaring out nationalistic music. Richard Ericson was sitting next to Zhou. Zhou removed the bug and gave it to MacPherson who put it into his own pocket and walked across to the window to admire the view. Mr Wu was at the other end of the canteen negotiating with the canteen staff for some lunch. The group's arrival was probably earlier than planned. Richard said quietly to Zhou: 'Are we able to talk now?'

Professor Zhou: 'Possibly, Hahn is the problem. He was sent down from Beijing two weeks ago. That was a few days after my son was removed from his government position and sent to the rice fields. I had planned an opportunity to talk openly with you tomorrow when we are at the Neodymium mine. If Hahn returns from the medical unit you must return the bug to my pocket and revert to our structured programme. I don't know Mr Wu particularly well. Only enter into technical discussions in his presence.'

Richard Ericson: 'Understood.'

Mr Wu returned and spoke to Zhou. Zhou explained to the group: 'Lunch will be served in a few minutes. It will be chopsticks.'

Professor MacPherson returned to the table and discretely passed the bug back to Richard Ericson, who put it in Zhou's pocket.

Lunch arrived. Rice, egg and vegetables. It was an amusing slow progress. It was the first time the group had seen a smile creeping over Zhou's face. Mr Wu finished his lunch quickly and got up from the table. He bowed graciously to Zhou and muttered something.

Zhou announced clearly: 'Mr Wu has gone to the medical unit to check on Hahn. He will be back shortly to conduct the afternoon's programme.'

Jeremy Chudleigh had tagged along so far. He wasn't familiar with such a visit. In the mine he was decidedly nervous. It was the least of MacPherson's concerns. Only Richard Ericson and Mark Scott had met Professor Zhou at the Innsbruck conference in May. Professor MacPherson hadn't. On seniority he was the notional leader of the Avon exchange visit and so far he was unimpressed by the fact that Professor Zhou wasn't free to conduct his own conversations.

Mr Wu returned to the lunch table and had a tense conversation with Professor Zhou. Apparently, Hahn had been sent to hospital. His eye had been cleaned in the medical unit, but the pupil had been physically damaged by the pressure of the jet of cement slurry. Mr Wu would be taking the group on a tour of the workshops and equipment stores.

After the culturally traditional lunch, typical of rural China, the group were guided to the equipment stores. This was the yellow building. Hard hats required in these buildings. Professor Zhou was able to do the explanations. Photography was encouraged, except one piece of electronic sensing equipment. It wasn't a spectrometer, but some form of laser device, evidenced by the symbol on the side of the box. Mr Wu was quite protective about this item. The stores had numerous types of electrical equipment such as diamond saws and hammer drills. A considerable number of hand tools of various sizes, typical of mines throughout the world.

The next building, green, was a workshop. Several operatives sharpening cold chisels and changing diamond blades. Another bench was cleaning dust accumulations from electrical tools.

The third building on the tour, the red building, was adjacent the mine entrance. Paper face masks were issued, but inside was quite clean. The building housed what appeared to be sophisticated shaking tables. Twenty first century versions of what was still in use in West Cornwall Tin mines until quite recently.

The ore material from the mine was being tipped into a hopper outside the building. Conveyor belts moved the material into the building and through three separate shaking tables. Professor Zhou explained the process. It was a coarse handling unit. A rotary mill reduced the material to fine sand sized particles. The output was loaded onto shaking tables to cause separation of the quartz and other granite particles. That waste went onto another conveyor belt which went to dumper trucks for return to the mine's disused levels.

The remaining shaking table contents were scraped off manually by four workers who continually monitored the table. The scrapings went on to another conveyor that delivered the material to a tall tank full of water. As it settled, particle size and density gave another form of sorting. The tank was complex with many columns near the base. Pumps moved the water, with the settling particles, slowly across the tops of the columns. As the particles were collected in the different columns small bucket conveyor belts moved from the base up to bins at the top of the tank. In this way the less dense quartz, feldspar and mica particles were removed from the valuable Samarium ore. The waste was sent to another dumper truck.

All this was visible since the side of the water tank was made of armoured glass so that the separation could be observed. The Samarium ore went into a tanker parked outside the red building. The coarse processing operated 24 hours a day. The tanker was changed at 16:00 each day. It was driven down the hill to the fine processing building 2 kilometres away.

The coarse processing unit was returning ninety percent of the mine's output back into the mine for packing into the disused levels.

Outside the red building, by the tanker, Zhou gave a summary and then began answering questions: 'You can see why I've brought you to this mine. In the last five years we've reduced mining waste by over a half. This policy change has also made the fine processing plant more efficient. This mine is maintained by Beijing more as a research establishment than a full scale production facility.'

The three academics in the group were impressed but noted the number of people in the coarse processing unit was quite high. Technical questions continued. It was clear that Zhou was much more relaxed and conversational in the absence of Hahn.

Richard Ericson asked: 'It was mentioned earlier that the fine processing unit isn't available to visit. Is there a reason for that?'

Zhou: 'There are similar physical process to what you've just seen, but it also uses chemical techniques.'

Throughout the afternoon Jeremy Chudleigh was passive. He showed little interest.

They got back in the minibus. Without Hahn the driver was in control of the journey. He pointed out the fine processing building as they turned off the hill road and rejoined the main road. The building was about 30 metres wide by 80 metres in length. There was a tall chimney at one end. Probably indicative of the presence of volatile chemicals. Technical conversations between Zhou and the group continued for much of the journey back to Fudong.

The evening meal was at 19:00 followed by a lecture from one of Zhou's colleagues. That dealt with the theory behind physical processing they had seen during the afternoon. Topics included density of the ore, settling rates, frequency variation for the shaking table. Many equations. Mark made notes but a handout was also issued at the end.

Jeremy Chudleigh didn't attend the lecture. The group of three gave their thanks to Zhou and the young lecturer. They went up to their rooms and for their group meeting three minutes later.

MacPherson welcomed the other two into his room: 'This is a weird set up. I went to a conference in Shanghai about seven years ago. It was much more open than what we've experienced today.'

Ericson: 'I agree, Zhou has been most cautious. His persona is quite different to Innsbruck. Perhaps it's all due to his son's demise. He must be quite worried.'

MacPherson: 'What do you think Mark?'

Mark: 'Yes, he's quite nervous most of the time. I don't think this exchange proposal is going to fly. For my part I'm just going to soak up everything we're being shown this week. It's still valuable to me, even if the exchanges don't come to anything.'

Mark didn't mention the recent alert he'd been given by Vanessa Wyndham. He needed to be careful. He wasn't sure how and when he was going to convey a "Tin, Copper, Cornwall" phrase to Zhou as he'd been briefed by Vanessa Wyndham two months ago.

The meeting of the group of three went on for half an hour. There was value in soaking up all that had been prepared for them, but also a realisation that Zhou was in a particularly delicate situation. They would have to wait for tomorrow's trip to the Neodymium mine to see if Hahn was back in control.

# 16

At breakfast on Tuesday Zhou approached the group with a weak smile: 'Gentlemen I have to announce that Mr Hahn has been kept in hospital, so Jasmin Wang, my secretary, will accompany us today. Our conversations will be technical, as yesterday. See you at the minibus at 08:00.'

There was 25 minutes spare. MacPherson said, looking at the other two: 'I'm going up to my room to clean my teeth.'

Ericson: 'Good idea.'

They avoided Jeremy Chudleigh and all piled into MacPherson's room. He announced: 'The unknown today is the secretary, Jasmin Wang. We need to follow Zhou's lead, he did say we should have an opportunity to talk informally. Caution is the watch word.'

Down at the minibus they were introduced to Miss Wang, an attractive, dark haired, 30 year old, quite petit, in a figure hugging, high necked traditional dress.

It was a long drive, conversation was more relaxed, but only technical matters. Miss Wang was joining in, obviously trying to practice her English.

At the Neodymium mine there were fewer buildings than yesterday's site. Zhou introduced the group to the mine captain who could not speak English. Zhou explained: 'This mine is all about volume. No attempt to limit waste or backfill old levels. The coarse ore goes to a large processing plant West of Shanghai. Then the Neodymium metal itself goes to a factory that makes magnets for the automotive industry. This mine has been run commercially since the metal was proved seventeen years ago. Bedrock again is granitic, and the ore veins were introduced only a few million years after the granite cooled. There are other Lanthanides in the mine, but they aren't recovered in a big way. Neodymium is the main prize.'

Jeremy Chudleigh's ears had pricked up when he heard the word "commercially".

The group were kitted out with protective clothing again, then taken into the mine. Many veins, 10 to 30 centimetres thick. The pace of the mine was much greater than yesterday. Yesterday's Samarium mine was about precision and not missing anything.

At today's mine coarse material was being taken out in large dumper trucks. The majority to a spoil tip, but the actual Neodymium ore was tipped into waiting lorries. The group were led into the mine about twelve hundred metres and they still hadn't reached the end. On the return walk Richard Ericson counted 38 veins that were being worked.

Zhou explained that the mine was highly valued by the government's economists, but the damage to the environment was severe. Finer sediments were being washed into the river from the spoil tip and that resulted in contamination and siltation downstream.

They were led out of the mine after about two hours. Miss Wang had a meeting in the mine office to arrange some dates for student visits. The mine captain gave each of the group a small polybag with fragments of Neodymium ore. Jeremy Chudleigh declined his. Mark grabbed it instead. The mine captain showed them to the canteen. A special table had been laid for them. Five of them sat down for lunch. Knife, fork and spoon this time. Zhou pointed to the large wall display of the production targets and achievements over the seventeen years. Jeremy Chudleigh went across to study it.

Zhou started: 'Hahn wasn't coming on this trip anyway. I don't know if he'll return tomorrow. Today, I've left my electronic bug in the minibus. With my recent change in status, I'm now on a watch list by Beijing, it's highly unlikely that I'll be running Fudong next semester. It's also unlikely that a new regime will maintain the momentum for the exchange scheme. For your part, please use this week to gather as much information as you are able, but be nice to Mr Hahn when he returns. I'll do my best to keep you informed.'

Mark decided this was his moment: 'Professor Zhou, I'm finding this visit incredibly useful. I'm just starting to investigate Tin and Copper mining regions in Cornwall. Thank you so much for this visit.'

In this slightly more informal setting Mark had fulfilled the request of Vanessa Wyndham.

Zhou made a slight nod. MacPherson and Ericson thought that was an odd remark, particularly Mark's emphasis on the words Tin, Copper and Cornwall. At that point Jeremy Chudleigh returned from studying the large wall display. MacPherson asked him if he'd found it useful. That evoked a positive sounding "Uhm", nothing else.

The three academics were clear on their objectives, but they weren't sure how to handle Jeremy Chudleigh. Another unknown was Jasmin Wang. Was she a party official, or just a young woman trying to earn a salary, and not rock the boat? Gordon MacPherson wanted to ask Zhou about her loyalties, but he'd lost the opportunity when Jeremy Chudleigh returned.

After they'd finished their late lunch Zhou said he wanted to show them the size of the spoil tip. They walked across to where the dumper trucks were discharging their loads. The mine captain accompanied them. A bulldozer was moving the waste particulates, some large, irregular shaped boulders, but mostly gravel and sand sized grains. As the bulldozer pushed the material to the edge, gravity took over and the material slipped down into the valley. The three academics took photographs. Miss Wang walked back towards the minibus with the mine captain. Gordon MacPherson quietly asked Zhou if he was able to trust Miss Wang. Zhou replied: 'Mostly, but she is often under scrutiny from some of her family. She's been exceptionally supportive to me for the last six years, but her cousin, also in Fudong, is a party official. He makes her life difficult. Since my wife died four years ago she's been most helpful. She doesn't like Hahn.'

MacPherson thought that was an unusually frank answer, but Zhou was still unable to give up everything. Conversations with Zhou would be so much easier if he wasn't in such a delicate position. Zhou was older than MacPherson but a mutual respect was growing between them.

Mark and Richard Ericson were also chatting on their walk back to the minibus. Mark said: 'This visit is not what I expected. I suppose it's still an incredible experience towards my programme of study but I'm so sorry it's not going to Zhou's original plan.'

Ericson responded: 'Well, it certainly isn't your fault. It's world politics. We're just the technocrats.'

They thanked the mine captain and all got back into the minibus. The drive down the hill gave them a clear view of the spoil tip, it was huge. At the local town, they joined the main road and passed over a bridge with the river below. Considerable suspended sediment coloured the turbulent water. This was late summer, probably much greater discolouration occurred during winter rains.

Discussion on the return journey was a little more open. MacPherson was leading it, mostly technical topics, but also trying to gauge the remarks of Jasmin Wang. Her desire to practice her English meant she was engaging quite a bit, and her geological knowledge was a credit to her. MacPherson pushed it with a direct question to her: 'Where did you study geology?'

She was slightly taken aback. She paused, glanced at Zhou and then said: 'I did the undergraduate course at Fudong, before Professor Zhou joined the University.'

MacPherson wasn't sure if he was pushing her too far, so he brought the conversation back into the whole group.

They arrived back at the University just in time for the evening meal. After eating they met in the lecture theatre. Jasmin Wang gave out synopses of the two mines they'd visited, then Zhou embarked on a description of the processing equipment laboratories that they would visit tomorrow.

The group of three had another meeting in MacPherson's room. They all agreed that Miss Wang was not a continual threat to their informal discussions with Zhou. She wasn't shadowing Zhou in the same way that Hahn did. They still had to be cautious with their comments, and just follow the programme, with interest and enthusiasm.

After breakfast on Wednesday morning Jeremy Chudleigh used the first opportunity to talk to Professor Zhou to ask him how he could have a meeting with the bursar, or financial controller. Zhou retorted that all the administration matters would be dealt with on Friday. Zhou was aware that there was little engagement between the administrator and the three academics. He had other things on his mind than finance at the moment. Zhou turned to the three academics and said: 'Mr Hahn will be joining us for today's visit down to the processing equipment labs. We'll walk down in five minutes. Zhou was tense.

As they left the refectory, Mr Hahn arrived with an eye patch over his right eye. He made no remark about his injury, but took command of the morning programme: 'Today we visit the processing equipment laboratories down near the river. These labs are principally for research. The undergraduates use the labs in the main building, which I showed you on Sunday evening.'

Jeremy Chudleigh was nowhere to be seen. At the laboratories, it was just one huge industrial type building, the group were issued with safety goggles. Different equipment areas separated by lines of yellow paint on the concrete floor. An uneasy double act between Hahn and Zhou ensued as they explained the unit.

Fudong Geology and Mining University had been built 35 years ago. The architecture was similar to that found at several new British universities established in the post war years. The research processing equipment laboratories were new. They were conceived by Professor Zhou when he took over at Fudong six years ago. They were completed three years ago. The whole unit is Zhou's baby. The building is situated close to the river as several processes involve water. The river water is taken into a leat about a kilometre upstream. Then held in a 75,000 litre covered holding tank. There are several filtration systems before the water arrives at the laboratory building, and many more stages of filtration before the water is released back into the river. Because the laboratories are only processing small amounts of material the accumulation of solid waste is quite small, less than one small skip a week.

This was an opportunity for the Avon group to see the sort of research work that the different sections could provide. Each piece of equipment was in the hands of one researcher, some were PhD students, some postdocs.

The researchers had been briefed by Zhou to relate their equipment in English. Some were perfecting the equipment and making adjustments and alterations, then collecting data on performance of the system. The engineering section with six technicians at the far end of the building made any new components that were required.

The group spent about fifteen minutes with each researcher. There were no limits on questions or photography. Each researcher issued an A4 sheet with their project and that included diagrams.

As they moved from one section to another they could see the complexity of the whole unit. Some techniques were completely new to all three of them. There were shaking tables – three types, sieving systems, settling tanks similar to the one at the Samarium mine, centrifuge systems – batch and continuous, crushers, magnetic separation. There was also a large section dealing with electrolysis.

There were no chemical systems. From the way that Zhou introduced each of his researchers, it was clear that this was the culmination of his long career trying to develop less environmental damaging mineral process systems. He made no comment about Beijing's attitude to his crusade. From yesterday's visit to the Neodymium mine it was evident that efficient extracting of metals was the national objective.

Half way through the tour of the unit the group was taken back to the refectory for lunch. For some reason Zhou was absent for this, but Hahn sat down with them. That was a bit of a conversation stopper.

Mark was quite excited while talking to Richard Ericson. The equipment shown to them through the morning had captured Mark's imagination, and he was asking more questions than the other two. His collection of handouts were all stuffed in his jacket pockets. He'd taken many photos on his phone.

The afternoon toured the second half of the unit. Hahn was introducing each researcher and their project, but embarrassingly he demonstrated his weak understanding of geology and mining in general.

After an hour Zhou rejoined the tour. He was as white as a sheet. For a man over sixty he was looking ill. He gave no reason for his absence, but just tried to continue his task.

The group had reached the last two sections when Jasmin Wang rejoined them. She whispered into Hahn's ear. He left rapidly. She smiled politely at everyone. Zhou continued, still looking nervous. They completed the tour of the equipment and were then introduced to the engineering technicians, none of whom spoke English. Zhou explained the various lathes, cutting and drilling devices. Every bench was spotless. Many waste bins for off cuts and swarf. The waste was mostly metals and acrylic sheet.

Zhou completed the guided tour and said: 'After the evening meal we'll meet in the seminar room we used yesterday evening.'

As they walked back up to the main building Zhou departed and left them with Jasmin Wang. When he was out of sight she turned to the Avon group and explained that: 'Your colleague, Mr Chudleigh, has been arrested by security officers for stealing computer equipment and files from our administration building. Professor Zhou has been summoned by Mr Hahn. She said nothing more as they walked back up the path. Near the main building she stopped, waved her arm and said: 'Do you like the way we have arranged the "terracing" for our display of "geraniums".'

Even though her English speaking skills were limited she clearly annunciated the two key words. She'd obviously been briefed by Zhou.

Ericson and MacPherson looked at each other in puzzlement. Mark was working out how he should explain what he'd just heard.

Miss Wang left them. Mark said to the other two: 'Before the evening meal can we have a brief meeting upstairs?'

In MacPherson's room Richard Ericson switched on the music again. Mark started: 'I think I need to explain that I was given two code words by the security services, "terracing" and "geraniums". You heard Miss Wang deliberately use those words just now. We don't know what's happened with Jeremy Chudleigh but it sounds like we're going to get help in some form, British or American, but they'll be local people. We need to be ready. Keep any valuables on your person. We should go down to the refectory now, then to the seminar room.'

MacPherson asked for more information. Mark said: 'Just trust me.'

They sat through the meal in the refectory. Everything the same, except the absence of Jeremy Chudleigh. Table service as before, they were still the honoured guests of the University. The three of them were there on their own. No sign of Zhou, Hahn or Miss Wang.

The Avon group finished eating, and were just drinking a cup of tea, when the head waiter announced in perfect English: 'You may go to the seminar room now.'

# 17

The three of them walked along the corridor towards the seminar room. Hahn stepped out of a side room and directed them in. Zhou and Miss Wang were waiting. Zhou said: 'Gentlemen, we hope you've enjoyed today's tour. We've had to amend our evening programme.'

At that point a door opened behind where Hahn was standing. Two Chinese masked men came in, grabbed Hahn, and put a cloth over his face. Within three seconds he fell to the floor. One of the men gave Hahn an injection into his neck. The other spoke clearly to the Avon three in an American accent: 'Terracing, geraniums. Follow us please.'

Mark looked firmly at Ericson and MacPherson: 'It's genuine.'

The Avon three, plus Zhou and Miss Wang, walked swiftly through the door where the two masked men had entered. One of the masked man was leading. The other dragged Hahn's limp body through the door and locked it. Hahn was left at the top of the concrete stairs. This was a service staircase that led down to a garage area where a laundry van was waiting. The group of five were ushered into the back of the van. They were asked to put their phones in a special case so their location wouldn't transmit. The garage door opened. The van drove off. There was a small window between the inside of the van and the driver's cab so the five of them could see the road ahead. No one said anything. An intercom clicked on, a woman with an American accent announced: 'We'll be stopping in about about ten minutes when we're out of Fudong town. It'll be quite dark by then. Hang on to something for now.'

The inside of the van was like a mobile biology laboratory. There wasn't much traffic on the road. The driver was probably keeping to local speed limits. After a few minutes the van left the main road and pulled into something like a roadside warehouse building. The two drivers got out and opened the door at the back of the van. They invited the five to climb out for a short break, and pointed to lavatories at the far end of the building. They pulled a few bolts and moved the left hand side bench and cupboard unit out to reveal a long seat, with seat backs on the left side panel of the van. The rear of the bench and cupboards was hollow. The group of five were put in behind the false bench and the unit was slid back into place.

Richard Ericson said to Gordon MacPherson: 'Did you see the sides of the van? The signwriting has changed. It now has a picture of a lobster and the bottom line reads "National Lobster Hatchery".'

As the van moved off and back onto the main road the intercom clicked: 'We now have a three hour drive. You can switch on the video screen in front of you. The split screen shows the front and the back view. If we get stopped, keep quiet. We'll show the traffic police that the back of the van is empty. If there is a thorough search then you may get arrested. We have another van, one kilometre behind, who will immobilise the traffic police if necessary. We won't tell you any more yet in case we're stopped and you're detained. You can then say you've been kidnapped against your will. If anyone needs a restroom break give us ten minutes warning. You can press the green button by your video screens to wake up the intercom.'

The seating arrangements were a little cramped but there was just about enough room to stretch legs. Under each screen was a shelf with snacks and bottled drinks. The three Avon members of the evacuation group said little. Without any information on their destination they had little to talk about.

It was nearly midnight when the van stopped. They could see they were by the sea. The rear screen showed the second van pull up behind them. The two women drivers opened the rear of their van, moved the sliding false bench and helped the slightly stiff passengers climb out.

The large sign on the side of a concrete building had the same signage as the van "National Lobster Hatchery". There were no lights on anywhere. The waning Moon gave enough light to see what they were doing. Gordon MacPherson noticed that two men from the second van were carrying the Avon group's suitcases. They were the Chinese men who had immobilised Hahn. No one said anything.

The five of them were directed towards a waiting speedboat tied up to a pontoon by the quay. The group climbed onto the rear portion of the speedboat and then shown to seats down inside the lower cabin. No words were spoken by the van drivers or the speedboat crew. The boat left the pontoon and was soon travelling at over twenty knots. Repeater displays in the lower cabin showed speed, depth, compass heading and Latitude and Longitude.

The boat was unusually quiet. They could hear and feel the boat slamming into small waves but no engine noise. Mark muttered to Richard Ericson that it must be electric drive.

After five minutes the skipper, a Caucasian American, announced that they were heading for a large cargo vessel coming out of Hong Kong harbour. He advised them: 'More information later.'

Zhou and Miss Wang said nothing to the other three. Mark and Richard were occasionally exchanging thoughts. Gordon said nothing.

It was now Thursday 19th September at 00:45. The skipper announced firmly: 'Coastguard vessels trying to intercept. Preparing to submerge. No problem. Stay seated.'

The vessel slowed. Looking to the stern of the boat they could see a large panel move slowly down to enclose the cabin space. The skipper said: 'You'll see large orange bags emerge into the lower cabin and on the rear deck. They and others are filling with water and we'll submerge. They won't leak. You'll be kept quite dry.'

The noise of the pumps was getting louder. If the skipper had said any more they didn't hear it. The boat slowed and started to submerge. There were no leaks. At a depth of one metre, another display had appeared on the repeater screen, and the boat speed increased to eight knots. They were now in a submarine. This futuristic situation continued for nearly an hour. Hence they would have travelled about seven or eight nautical miles, about 12 or 13 kilometres.

The skipper announced: 'Coastguard vessels have lost us. We're going to surface. Prepare for pump noise.'

The orange bags began to collapse and fold back into their lockers. The boat rose up and the skipper engaged full power again. Fortunately, the sea was almost flat. After a few minutes the large panel covering the rear deck opened up again. It was was nearly 02:00, the skipper announced that they would soon be craned up onto a cargo ship.

It all happened without a hitch. The boat was lowered onto a substantial cradle. The group of five disembarked. At that a large shutter door opened up in the ship's superstructure and the cradled boat was railed into a substantial workshop area.

It was a warm night. A uniformed man greeted: 'Welcome aboard SS Sunflower, registered in Honolulu. I'm Captain Greg Burton. We're heading for Luzon in the Philippines where I'll be handing you over to U.S. and British officials. We'll give you your phones back when we're on land. They're still in a protective case so no one can track you. Follow me, I'll show you to your cabins. We'll give you a call at 08:00 China time and Philippines time. We'll collect you for breakfast at 09:00. Weather is predicted calm. You'll get a longer briefing after breakfast. You're quite safe now.'

Gordon MacPherson said to the other two: 'I'm not sure what's happening but we need to get some sleep, and listen to what we're told at tomorrow's briefing.'

Mark was concerned that he wouldn't be able to send his usual message to Emma at 06:00. He was uneasy. He just hoped this was all going to work in their favour.

# 18

Everyone was collected for breakfast and taken to a tidy galley area. Not as flamboyant as cruise ship dining areas but the service, Filipino, and quality of food was excellent.

The Avon three were light on sleep but hadn't missed a meal. The extraordinary evacuation from Fudong had gone smoothly. What would have happened if the van or boat had been intercepted didn't bear thinking about.

Captain Burton arrived at 09:50: 'Good morning everyone, hope you slept well. Please come along to the Officers' Mess for a briefing.'

All five sat down in the mess. Captain Burton started: 'I can't comment on the diplomatic issues that arise from this evacuation, but I can bring you up to date on the timetable. We'll dock in Manila Bay, Philippines, at 13:00 tomorrow, Friday 20th September. We'll be met by a team from the U.S. Embassy and another team from the U.K. Embassy. Professor Zhou and Miss Wang will go to the U.S. Embassy as agreed last week. Professor MacPherson, Professor Ericson and Mr Mark Scott will go to the U.K. Embassy. Basic administration details will be dealt with at both. The two groups will be able to meet again on Saturday afternoon. Your phones will be waiting for you at the embassies. Families of the U.K. group have already been informed by London that you are safe and that your return travel plans have been delayed a little. Today you can relax and discuss your shared academic interests. Any questions?'

There were several from the Avon group, but they were all batted away by Burton who advised them to talk to their embassies. He finalised his briefing with: 'Your meals will be served in the galley, where you had breakfast. You can ask the steward here in the mess for anything you need. There are three small conference rooms over there that you're free to use. World news on the TV here in the mess. We're not a regular cruise ship, as you've probably realised, no swimming pool I'm afraid. Just make yourselves as comfortable as possible.'

Gordon MacPherson approached Zhou and asked if he could have a discreet chat in one of the conference rooms. Zhou accepted the request. McPherson wanted an explanation of Burton's statement "as agreed last week". Zhou replied that the plan for the Avon visit was thrown into chaos about ten days ago when his son was removed from his position in Beijing. That was also the day that Hahn was sent to take over from Zhou at Fudong. The U.S. wanted him out as quickly as possible and a plan was cooked up to evacuate. The Avon group visit had to be woven into the plan. Trying to give as much experience and information as practical to Avon, but use the visit as a vehicle to control Hahn.

MacPherson asked: 'Was the cement slurry incident at the Samarium mine part of the plan?'

Zhou: 'Yes. Hahn had an enforcer, you didn't meet him, but we had to get him away from Fudong. The enforcer raced to the hospital when Hahn was taken there. Mr Wu made sure that Hahn went to a specialist eye hospital 300 kilometres away. Wu's first aid team even made sure that a sharp piece of quartz was pushed into his eye. That gave us about 24 hours when neither Hahn or his enforcer were at Fudong. That was enough for the U.S. security people to prepare the Wednesday episode. I do hope that we were able to still give you and your colleagues a clear picture of what I've been doing at Fudong.'

MacPherson: 'Well you certainly did that. You packed a lot into three days. We're most grateful.' Pause. 'How were you able to set up the cement slurry incident?'

Zhou: 'The Samarium mine has been part of Fudong for many years. They are a sort of research establishment. They work closely with us. Hahn and his enforcer went up there last week to assess what his new administration empire involved. The miners didn't take too kindly to him. They were the ones who devised the cement slurry incident. They told me to leave it to them.'

MacPherson: 'I'm beginning to see the plan now. How do you feel about leaving your son in China?'

Zhou: 'He's already in Manila. The U.S. got him out on Monday. He and Jasmin Wang are a couple.'

MacPherson realised that he and the Avon group had only experienced one half of this evacuation plan: 'Do you know how your future is going to take shape?'

Zhou: 'Not fully. I'll know a little more when I get to the American Embassy.'

MacPherson: 'What is the U.S. hoping to get from you?'

Zhou: 'I know a great deal on the whereabouts of rare metals in Africa that have been proved but not yet exploited. Twenty three sites in total. China has had prospecting groups all over Africa for at least twenty years. They've had mining operations in many countries by persuading the governments and providing infrastructure and health provision in return. By Western standards these health centres might appear modest but they've been well received in many impoverished rural communities. The metals recovered far exceed the cost of China's sweeteners. Unfortunately, some communities have been left with bad pollution and environmental damage. China's actions have been similar to European colonial occupation a hundred years ago. Morally, those metals should be exploited by the African countries, many of which have weak economies. With education those countries should be able to do the mining themselves and with much less pollution. The Americans want to see if they can move in and make the process work. I realise there is a risk that some American mining corporations will be involved, but the United Nations might be able to keep an eye on that risk.'

MacPherson: 'Have the U.S. offered you an academic position?'

Zhou: 'They've indicated such, although no specific institution. I'm 63 now so I'm unlikely to take up a new role. If I can just continue my interests. that I had developed at Fudong. I'll be content. If it was an emeritus role that would be ideal.'

MacPherson: 'What will happen to your son and Jasmin Wang.?'

Zhou: 'That's to be decided. Chen is 31 and highly qualified in fluid dynamics. That's what he's been working on in Beijing, but using his abilities to clean up some of China's industries has gone out of favour.'

In the officers' mess Miss Wang had left and gone back to her cabin. Richard Ericson and Mark Scott were alone musing and recollecting how fortunate they were to have been removed from a delicate situation. Richard asked Mark how he seemed to be aware that something was going on: 'Are you part of secret services?'

Mark: 'No, although they're keeping an eye on me and my family. This came about first, following Ecuador, and second after the Highveer Point illegitimate mining operation. The day before we left Avon I was given the two key words: "terracing" and "geraniums". In retrospect, I think that Whitehall where aware of some plan but the U.S. hadn't given them any detail.'

Zhou and MacPherson left the conference room and rejoined Mark and Richard. They all wanted some fresh air so rang for the steward. As it was a cargo vessel it wasn't safe to wander around most decks but the steward showed them the way up to the stern deck which was a crew recreation area. The four men sat on the seats chatting and enjoying the Sun which was high in the sky.

After lunch and dinner they decided to have an early night after the long day on Wednesday. Gordon MacPherson knocked on the cabin doors of Richard and Mark and suggested a quick catch up in his cabin. He summarised the discussions he'd had with with Zhou.

After breakfast on Friday, all five were on the rear deck watching the coastline of Luzon as they steamed towards Manila.

Gordon MacPherson started another conversation with Zhou, attempting to clarify some of the things he was told yesterday. He raised the question of an emeritus professorship at Avon, something he was sure was in his gift as Head of Department. It would have to be confirmed by Academic Board but he was sure that such a prize would be approved. He could probably get a salary sponsorship from a British geology or mining company. Zhou's response was one of gratitude but he wouldn't decide until after the Embassy meeting. In any event he was more concerned about getting his son and future daughter-in-law settled. He wanted to be in close proximity to them if possible.

Manila Bay opened up. The steward came out onto the rear deck and announced that everyone would be able to go ashore in a little over an hour. Would they like to go down to the galley for an early lunch and prepare to disembark.

Transport was waiting at the foot of the gang plank. One large American vehicle, and one minibus. The five evacuees were put in the respective vehicles.

At the British Embassy the Avon group were welcomed by the Ambassador and introduced to Ms Julia Pentland. She took them off to some accommodation rooms and said she would return to collect them in twenty minutes. They would need their passports.

They were first processed by a young man with a passport reader, similar to the ones at airports. He also photographed them and took fingerprints. Then they had individual interviews with Ms Pentland.

No difficulties were encountered but it was all civil service procedural matters. They were each given their mobile phones at the end of their session. Gordon MacPherson asked Ms Pentland if she could enquire about the formalities for accepting Professor Zhou as someone seeking asylum. 'That's above my pay grade, but I'll pass your enquiry to the correct officials.' Wait outside with the others was her reply, accompanied by a gentle smile.

The three were sitting in a row, checking their phones which were fully charged. Several messages on all three. Mark had a message from Emma:

Where are you?

It was 15:00 Philippines local time. That meant it would be 07:00 for Emma. He sent a message:

I'm ok, slight hiccup with phone. Now in the Philippines due to travel changes. Should be home in a day or two, when flight details confirmed. Will let you know times. Avon minibus will collect us from Heathrow. I may need collecting from Avon. Missing you xxx

Mark couldn't explain the full story in a text message. It would take a whole evening. The main priority now was to keep everything sounding completely normal.

Ms Pentland came out of her office and said everything was in order. She said that the various departments in London had been updated.

As she said various departments she stared momentarily at Mark. They were free to enjoy the garden, if they wished, but not leave the Embassy grounds. Tomorrow, Saturday, they would be taken to the U.S. Embassy after lunch. They would give them the flight details to London from Manila Ninoy Aquino airport but it would route via Denver Colorado in the U.S. The last thing Ms Pentland said is that they were invited to have dinner this evening with the Ambassador and his wife at 19:00.

Much polite conversation at dinner. Both the Ambassador and his wife quizzed the three of them on matters surrounding rare earth minerals.

The following day they were taken by minibus to the U.S. Embassy for lunch. There they were surprised to meet Jeremy Chudleigh who, together with Chen Zhou, were evacuated by a route they declined to discuss.

Yesterday Zhou had been interviewed by nameless people. He assumed they were appointees of the National Security Agency (N.S.A.). This was Zhou's part of the deal. He was asked to disclose the locations of the 23 sites where rare earth minerals had been proved. The U.S. wanted to move in and set up the infrastructure so that the minerals could be mined and sent to the U.S. Zhou was concerned that the contracts would go to U.S. owned multi-national mining corporations. He didn't want the African countries trampled on. Many were severely underdeveloped. He thought that he still had one trump card up his sleeve. During his career in China he was responsible for keeping the database of future exploitations. That morning he had given the Agency interviewers the country and approximate locations, but not the precise Latitude and Longitude. He knew enough to know that keeping some information back was advantageous, so he still had room for negotiation.

It was becoming apparent to Gordon MacPherson and Richard Ericson that their Fudong adventure was just a small part of a well conceived U.S. plan to acquire knowledge of African rare earths in Central Africa. Mark Scott had no concept of the master plan. He was only aware of security services interest from the two sets of words: Tin, Copper, Cornwall and geraniums, terracing.

It was also becoming clear that Jeremy Chudleigh's time in the U.S. had involved connections with the N.S.A. He was a different man in the U.S. Embassy to what the three had come to know from the pre-visit meeting at Avon. Possibly his disinterested role at the two mine visits earlier in the week was a ploy to separate him from the three academics.

Apart from the black Range Rovers, and occasional helicopter use, British security services operated on significantly slender budgets than their U.S. counterparts.

Scott, Ericson and MacPherson were muttering to each other, but the puzzlement was beginning to grate. Had they been woven into a complex plan by the U.S. agencies.

The U.S. now had Professor Zhou. Quite a prize for a nation that had to improve its knowledge and control of rare earth resources. The Avon three had certainly boosted their own knowledge but it seemed they had been used. How would Jeremy Chudleigh report back to the Vice Chancellor. The rumours swirling around the Heads of Department were that the VC and Chudleigh were rather chummy.

'Gentlemen and Ladies can we meet in the conference hall.' was called by a man in a suit with one of those curly wires coming out of his ear.

The Ambassador was introduced, and he announced: 'Welcome all to Manila. I think we can say that the operation has been successful. We understand from our local operatives in Hunan Province that Mr Hahn has fully recovered from his assisted sleep, so we have left China with a clean slate, no casualties. We have arranged a direct flight, Business Class I might add, to Denver this evening. The flight will be by one of our respected airlines. Our reasons for routing the UK contingent that way back to London is to avoid any possible interference from Chinese controlled air operators. We are sure Professor Zhou and his family will wish to take up a position at the local mining university, and we've arranged accommodation for our UK friends to have a good look around our world class academic and engineering facilities. A second flight will take the UK party back to London on Monday evening. We hope you've enjoyed your time here in Manila, and on behalf of the President may I thank you all for your assistance with this operation.'

Gordon MacPherson whispered to the other two: 'Well that confirms our suspicions, we have been used.'

MacPherson approached Jeremy Chudleigh after the speech was over. He asked him to join the English contingent out in the rear garden to share perceptions of the past week. Chudleigh looked a little uneasy but agreed. He knew the four of them would be on the plane together for the flight to London but he was a little reticent.

While they were in a group of four, MacPherson decided to the take an informal line: 'How are we going to relate this experience to our colleagues when we're back at Avon.'

Richard responded first: 'I think we can say it's been a bit of adventure but we haven't achieved our intended aim. The original proposal to set up research exchange programmes has evaporated.'

Mark thought he would stay out of the discussion, but surprisingly Jeremy Chudleigh contributed: 'It's quite clear that global control of rare metal resources has become more open and the inappropriate Chinese domination will be reduced.'

MacPherson: 'Has it been the sort of operation that academics should be caught up in?'

Chudleigh: 'It's only in the last two weeks that the U.S. involvement has become necessary.'

Ericson: 'Are you happy to publicly disclose the role you've had for the Americans?'

Chudleigh: 'All this only came about when the Zhou family situation became unsustainable.'

MacPherson: 'Are you on a retainer from the Americans?'

Chudleigh: 'Not exactly. Only expenses.'

Chudleigh was visibly uncomfortable. MacPherson didn't see any benefit pursuing the discussion. Chudleigh walked back into the Embassy building.

Mark had been following all the questions and statements carefully. He'd decided to keep out of the politics. He felt a little guilty about having been groomed by the British security services, but it had been for his own safety.

MacPherson noticed that Mark had not taken part in the discussion. In the presence of Richard Ericson he said clearly to Mark: 'I'm not putting you in the same category as Chudleigh. Your involvement with the British security services only came about prior to our current episode. Chudleigh appears to have played an active part of the American plan.'

Mark wasn't sure how this would affect his position at Avon. Richard Ericson could see he was unsettled. He whispered: 'The way this week has changed from its original schedule is not down to you. If there is any muck sticking it'll be on Chudleigh. Anyway, one of your objectives was to boost your understanding of rare earth mining and processing in a country with limited information transfer. You've achieved that, so have I.'

MacPherson stepped in: 'No Mark, none of the second half of the week has been your doing. We've all gained from this adventure in many ways, but we've still got to decide how we're going to present this in the departmental staff-room.'

At that, the man with the curly wire coming out of his ear approached them in the garden: 'Gentlemen, there will be some refreshments, I guess you English call it afternoon tea, in the dining room at 16:00. A security convoy will take all seven of you to the airport at 16:30, for your flight to Denver. There will be several air marshals on the flight.'

At the airport all seven were ushered through checks and into a secure departure area. They were marched down the boarding tunnel and into business class along with more men, and one woman, all with curly wires in their ears. The U.S. operation had gone successfully for them. It seemed the authorities weren't going to let anything go wrong at this stage.

With the big reclining seats and pillows and blankets, all seven were able to get a comfortable sleep on the long flight across the Pacific.

It was late afternoon, Mountain Standard Time, as they approached Denver. There was some early Autumn snow on the highest peaks. A welcome party greeted them at Arrivals. This was headed by the President of the University, and a Dean. The group of seven were put into two large minibuses; one for the English party and the other for the China party. That was the last that the Avon group saw of Professor Zhou until the Monday evening farewells. There appeared to be another minibus with security people.

At the School of Mines the Avon group were shown to accommodation. Not typical student rooms, but mini apartments. Dinner would be at 19:00 and an escort would be waiting in the corridor at 18:55 to take them down.

Mark Scott was glad to take a shower after the long flight. He guessed the other three would as well. Gordon MacPherson thought it was prudent, and politic, to treat Jeremy Chudleigh as a full member of the Avon group for the various proceedings over the next 24 hours. They went down to dinner in a large restaurant full of students. They were put on a top table with elaborate service. Afterwards, the escort took them to a seminar room where they were given a schedule for tomorrow.

Monday morning 23$^{rd}$ September started well. They were certainly being treated as honoured guests. MacPherson wondered if this was a consolation prize. The U.S. had got Zhou, and Britain was getting a glossy tour of a well funded academic institution.

What would be happening to Zhou wasn't known. He had some negotiating power, but his main aim was to get his son Chen into some solid position. He realised his own position would be some sort of emeritus role, but he still had to give the U.S. the exact locations of the 23 sites in Africa. Whether he would be able to see the African countries develop mines, or whether large American multi-nationals would do the exploitation remained to be seen. If it was the latter then Zhou had only swapped one form of colonial control for another.

The Avon group, now numbering four again to maintain harmony, were taken on a guided tour of the laboratories and workshops at the School of Mines. For Mark this was useful experience but he couldn't help making comparisons with British geology and mining departments. There were a couple of areas with mineral processing equipment and they were given examples of how such equipment operated. Whether Zhou would be given the opportunity to continue his ideas of physical processing of rare earth minerals was something that might need time to assess.

Monday evening there was a five minute meeting with Zhou, his son Chen and Jasmin Wang, as the Avon group were assembled for their departure. Handshakes and best wishes, but no opportunity for real discussion.

A minibus took the British group back to the airport for the flight to Heathrow. Mark sent Emma a message of the timings. They were booked into business class again so opportunities to sleep were quite good. They arrived early morning. Gordon MacPherson had put in a request to Avon for a minibus to collect the four of them. They were back at Avon by midday. As they got out of the bus with their luggage Gordon MacPherson quietly whispered to Mark and Richard: 'My office first.'

MacPherson had been pondering his public account all the way back from Denver. There was to be no mention of an undercover operation by the Americans. He was quite sure that China wouldn't be making accusations of having one of their top geologists captured. The Avon Geology Department line would be that Zhou had agreed to move to Denver as part of a Sino-U.S. agreement on world standards for eco-mining protocols. They were routed back via Denver to share in the arrangements. No mention of an evacuation, no mention of the speed boat submarine. It was to be a low key agreement with difficult but long term objectives to move towards low energy, minimal pollution, mining standards. As for the exchange programme that was to be a secondary objective and would be formalised with China, or the U.S., at some point in the future. All in all a successful ten days.

Richard Ericson was in complete agreement, particularly the emphasis on low key. Mark nodded, and said his priority was to stay out of departmental and global politics. He would take the line that he had been a passive attendee with the sole intention of learning as much as possible about rare earth minerals. and the mining and processing techniques being used in China.

Gordon MacPherson concluded that he would be making a similar statement during any other business at the next Departmental Meeting.

Mark went to his office. Xavier had already left for his new contract in Sweden and Brian Potter's desktop hadn't altered so Mark assumed he was still on fieldwork in Wales. Fortunately, all the handouts from the Wednesday tour of the processing laboratories were still stuffed into the pockets of his crumpled up jacket. In total eighteen handouts, many quite detailed with diagrams. He decided that reading through the handouts would be his sole task for the next two hours before Emma arrived. Many of the sheets of paper would need ironing, but he had a treasure trove of ideas.

Emma arrived with big hugs: 'You must have had an incredible journey.'

Mark agreed: 'But it's great to be home.'

The Department consensus would have to be smoothed a little more for Emma's ears. Mark couldn't help thinking he was lucky to be home, and not locked away in some Chinese institution.

# 19

Back home Emma asked how his hearing had been. Mark replied: 'Almost back to normal. Haven't had any problems. All the flights were in large modern aircraft with well controlled cabin pressure.'

Mark had to be careful. Too much information might invite more questioning from Emma. He didn't want to manufacture false narratives about the journey from Fudong to Manila. Emma would detect if there were fibs.

It was relaxing to be back in the family bed, and with Emma. Mark slept well. He'd already told Richard Ericson that he was having a day off on Wednesday. Fortunately, he had all his luggage, including the Neodymium ore samples. Emma went off to school, she'd felt well all the time Mark was away. She told the headmistress of her pregnancy, and the predicted birth date. The response was: 'That's wonderful news, congratulations, I wondered if you might be at the end of last term.'

Mark did his washing, ironed the crumpled handouts and checked the truck over. He wrote up an addendum to his diary with the details of the exact journey. He would put that in his China folder tomorrow. It was more a case of anonymised lists. He just needed a structure of the unusual days, so he could recreate it if it became necessary. To anyone else it would appear unremarkable. He cooked dinner that evening, to which Emma remarked: 'I've missed my personal chef.'

That evening he phoned Bernard Hosegood to bring him up to date. Mark was effusive on how helpful the visit had been and then created the story that the Zhou connection had been modified. He was now going to be based in Denver, but will be pursuing his ideas to persuade the mining and processing industry towards cleaner working. Bernard's response was: 'That's admirably altruistic but I can't see it working with many of the multi-nationals. I won't ask how the Americans managed to persuade him to work for them.'

Mark didn't respond to that point. He wondered if Bernard believed his sanitised account.

Thursday and Friday Mark went up to Avon. Brian Potter was back in the office and probed Mark on how the China visit had gone. Again, Mark gave a positive account of its success.

Mark thought he should have a quick chat with Richard Ericson to make sure he was up to date on the sanitised account. Unsurprisingly, several staff yesterday had commented to MacPherson and Ericson that the project had been unlikely to be achieved.

Digging metals out of the ground was expensive at the best of times. If there was to be a new code of environmental conservation, then mining accountants would not be super keen.

Two members of staff who had backed the intention to set up research exchange programmes were a little taken aback at the lack of progress. Richard wasn't sure if the "official" account agreed on Tuesday afternoon was credible. That, however, was Gordon MacPherson's problem.

Mark's ears were better, the surgery on his left ear seemed to have been successful. He could now resume his PhD programme and the fieldwork objectives. He made contact with both Tamar Valley old Copper mine and Redruth Institute of Mining. Both had been alerted in July, by Richard Ericson, of Mark's hearing loss from the explosion. They were quite amenable to setting up days to complete the original objectives. This time, Mark would do two visits and not suggest too strongly to Emma that she could join him. He knew that Emma wanted to focus on putting in a good performance as Head of History at her school. She would finish at the end of term, just before Christmas, and start her maternity leave.

The Tamar Valley visit he could do in one day. They'd offered him a window of 09:00 to 11:00 on 1st October, and the drive down was only about two hours. Emma had got used to early morning starts and decided to stick with them. That meant Mark might be able to do the visit and be back home to cook dinner for her.

John Shackleton at Redruth Institute of Mining had written Mark a warm letter after the explosion incident, encouraging him to resume his programme when he was fully recovered. Several e-mail exchanges resulted in revised dates of Tuesday 15th to Thursday 17th October. Mark could join one of the undergraduate trips down into the Tin mine, so that would reduce the cost.

Mark's diary was filling up. He needed to do some lab work on his samples from China as well as a few others. He thought he could manage everything when an e-mail arrived from Guernsey. Andrew Norris wanted him over Sunday 6th to Saturday 12th October. Apologises for such short notice but this coincided with four prospecting teams being at Head Office in between field deployments. Mark would have to give a seminar to some experienced staff, as well as others whom Andrew Norris wanted updated on rare earths.

October was going to be a busy month, but he'd had a fairly light summer, so he'd just have to piece it all together. The seminar was all in his head. It was only a matter of selecting what he wanted to include, orchestrating it, and writing himself a paper. He would almost certainly be required to create a handout.

On Saturday Mark followed Emma's agenda. They went to the supermarket together in the morning. After lunch Mark cleaned both vehicles, mowed the lawn and made dinner. Sunday they had a day over at Porlock Weir. Emma could have a walk on the flat footpaths behind the shingle ridge. Emma had endured two weekends on her own and Mark thought he needed to give her his full attention. She was keeping well, was enjoying teaching, and planning how she wanted History to be taught to the girls in her school.

Monday Mark was up at Avon, preparing for his visit to the Tamar Valley. The early start on Tuesday worked well. At the old Copper mine he was greeted by a particularly knowledgeable guide and taken in way past the small gauge railway line. The mine level was angled about twelve degrees to one side. It was nearly eight metres from floor to the top. There was a collection of ladders and ropes at the end of the level. Mark wasn't sure how secure they were. This part of the mine was never open to the public but it had been inspected and worked upon by a large number of mining archaeologists and geologists. Mark could see a lot of green colouring in the roof of the level, normally an indication of Copper minerals. The guide said the ladders were quite safe so Mark clambered up. He didn't take the spectrometer; the green Copper ore staining was highly visible. He just chipped away with his hammer at the brightest specimens. He had a collecting bag around his neck so just kept putting loosened fragments into it. The fact that the walls of the level were sloping actually made his position at the top of the ladder fairly secure, but it was still a risky situation. He gently negotiated his way down the two ladders and thanked the local guide. He had about a dozen samples which he could assess when he was back at Avon.

The rest of the week at Avon Mark used his three pieces of equipment to work through the North Molton, the China and the Tamar samples. The pattern was repeating. First PIRSy, his field infra-red spectrometer, then the Bench X-ray spectrometer and lastly the mass spectrometer over in the Chemistry department. They were used in that order to measure the elemental content of each sample. Generally a greater number of elements were found with the higher precision instruments. Mark was still hoping to identify any rare earths metals that might be mixed in with the Copper ores. The North Molton samples were the last of the Exmoor mines. An area of predominantly sedimentary rocks, but with crystalline intrusions. China, and now the Tamar valley were intrusive igneous rocks, but with subsequent hydrothermal intrusions that contained metallic ores.

Towards the end of the week Mark pieced together his talk for Guernsey. The visit to the Head Office of Chalco was a significant stage in his 42 month sponsored PhD. He was required to spend one week a year at Head Office as part of his sponsorship contract. He was conscious that his efforts so far, mostly on Exmoor, hadn't found any appreciable quantities of rare earth metals. They were certainly present but not in quantities that would repay any investment to recover them. That was why he was switching some of his interest to processing methods. Going to Guernsey and speaking to fellow Copper prospecting teams might not be providing much assurance to a Company that earned its money from advising where metal ores were located.

He decided to use the seminar as an opportunity to float his ideas, mainly Zhou's ideas, to a geology audience. The feedback would be useful.

Mark spent Friday afternoon selecting images from his fieldwork, including Austria and China. Perhaps he could sell the idea that Chalco could become consultants on eco-mining and eco-processing.

Saturday at home was supporting Emma with domestic tasks, getting the shopping, and packing for his flight to Guernsey on Sunday.

Emma drove him to Bristol Airport for the afternoon flight to the island. He checked into the usual hotel and noticed that a large number of rooms were blocked out to Chalco. Probably for the four teams that were currently at Head Office. The Company had a standard pattern of prospecting. Send a team of about four geologists, surveyors and engineers to a commissioned location. They work on site for about two months to find the Copper ore and prove it's viability. In other words assess how much ore could be found. Back to Guernsey to finish writing up the report, then sending the report to the mining company or government that had commissioned the prospect. The team get typically seven or eight weeks leave. When the next prospect is activated the senior geologist comes to Head Office for about two weeks to work with the remote sensing department. In the second week the rest of the team joins to carry out the pre-fieldwork preparations. So Mark was expecting that there could be over a dozen field staff in attendance during his visit.

The seminar, or mini-lecture, was scheduled for Wednesday morning at 11:00. Mark would have meetings with Andrew Norris and Bernard Hosegood on Monday. He guessed he would have to run through his proposed talk with both.

Mark's meeting with Andrew Norris was mildly encouraging although he did conclude that integrating site processing with mining might not go down well with many of their commercial clients.

The meeting with Bernard focused more on the PhD programme. Was he moving away from his original thesis where he was intending to find rare earth minerals in the spoil of historic mining operations? Or, was he addressing the central problem that wherever rare earth minerals were found they would need significantly more processing than traditional metals like Copper or Tin?

Bernard was not trying to put Mark off but suggesting that the whole world of mining was going to need to tidy up its act could be controversial. Mark appreciated that, but there had been over a century of wealthy countries exploiting metals in poorer countries, particularly in Africa and South America, many of those had caused environmental damage. With world attention being placed on energy reduction and limiting pollution, mining needed to demonstrate a more planet friendly *modus operandi.*

The in-house coaching was helpful. All the images he had prepared were still relevant but he placed a little more emphasis on processing. On Wednesday he gave the talk. Twenty six people in attendance, including the remote sensing specialists and the lawyers. Also David Gresham, Mark's senior geologist for his first two years of field work. David had flown over specially for the talk. He was now walking almost unaided and looking his normal self.

Mark started hesitantly and then noticed that he had the full attention of his audience. He became more confident and summed up with: 'As we move into the future we have to show leadership in advocating on-site low energy processing, particularly if we can develop expertise at finding rare earth minerals.'

Mark received a warm reception. There were many questions, but the most useful benefit over the next two and a half days were the discussions that were prompted by the talk. It was also the first opportunity that Mark had to meet with other teams.

Several useful comments arose. Probably the most helpful was that some environments weren't suitable for water assisted on-site processing, particularly deserts and high mountains.

Mark also acquired a deeper understanding of how the Company operated and how different geologists tackled their projects.

Back on the plane on Saturday, Mark was quite satisfied with his performance. Emma met him, then home for the shortened weekend. With a smile she asked: 'Were you in our bridal suite this time?'

Mark gave her a kiss and responded: 'No, a bog standard business class room this time. Anyway, without you it wouldn't have been the same.'

Emma drove them home via the supermarket. On Sunday Mark took Emma up onto Exmoor for a pub lunch. They'd found one with a vegetarian menu during the Summer. After lunch a walk down along the River Barle. The seasons were changing, a few leaves on the woodland floor and it wasn't a particularly warm day. Emma was on good form. Her notified and recognised pregnancy was giving her mild benefits at school. Other staff weren't dumping jobs on her and the girls were unusually courteous and agreeable.

Monday Mark went off to Avon to catch up with his post and grab the stuff he needed for Redruth. Richard asked how the seminar had been received. Mark replied: 'Ok, I think. I put some emphasis on eco-mining and eco-processing. I wasn't shot down and it prompted some sound questions, and several follow-up meetings with some of the senior geologists that I hadn't met before.'

Richard: 'That's good. I watched your seminar on Zoom. As did Professor Zhou.'

Mark was shocked: 'I didn't know that. There was a camera at the back of the room, but I thought that was because Andrew Norris wanted a recording.'

Richard: 'You're now in a world of international broadcasting!'

Mark was back home by 15:30 and started cooking dinner.

# 20

Tuesday Mark set off early for Redruth. He aimed to arrive by 11:00 for the first meeting with Professor John Shackleton.

Shackleton was intrigued by Mark's progress with rare earths and was particularly interested in his trip to China. The meeting lasted a full hour and focused quite a lot on the eco-processing concepts. Shackleton conceded that on-site partial processing was relevant for rare earth minerals. This was because the small quantities involved with most intruded veins of Monazite required a great deal of sorting to obtain the intended metal. Thus on-site processing was an economic essential. If that could involve effective methods of reducing energy and pollution then there were benefits all round.

Shackleton concluded by saying that he'd like Mark to meet Graham Stanley, a new postdoc at Redruth who was studying all the Granite Plutons in Cornwall to identify undiscovered sources of Cassiterite, the principal ore of Tin. 'We'll go and collect him and take him down for lunch.'

Graham Stanley was a year younger than Mark. A short, thickset man with a strong Yorkshire accent. Following his graduation from Edinburgh in geology he took a job with a multi-national working in the Caucasus, on the Georgian side. His experiences were quite horrific. People were just a disposable resource for the company. He had to be his own health and safety adviser.

The three of them recounted their varied careers and how experiences had steered the choices. Shackleton's reason for introducing them was to see if they could interact with fieldwork. Graham was looking for Cassiterite, Mark for Monazite crystals which are the source ore of the rare earth elements. Graham had only started at Redruth two weeks ago and his programme for the rest of Autumn was to get to know the Cornish granite plutons and the known occurrences of Tin. John Shackleton thought that working with Mark until winter weather closed in could be a benefit to both of them. Mark had no objection to that. It would enable him to pick up samples from a variety of sites. Graham was also on the list for the Tin mine visit tomorrow. Shackleton left the two of them to talk.

After lunch Graham suggested they go to the Map room to peruse the modern and Victorian large scale plans. Mark was impressed by Graham's understanding of the Cornish landscape. That was a consequence of him spending many summer holidays with his Aunt in St Ives. As a geography teacher she took him on scores of visits to places of interest. Mark could see some advantages of joint fieldwork. Having a near local showing him around was useful in his strategy to look for mineral samples in the igneous regions of Cornwall.

On Wednesday Mark and Graham had to be at the Tin mine gates. The mine was currently inactive but there was considerable ore still unexploited. If and when the world price of Tin recovered then the tinners hoped their mine would re-open. Equipment and pumps were all being kept operational, partly for safety, partly to prevent flooding. The money for that came from the European Union.

The tinner who took them down explained the safety protocols for the mine shaft cage. They descended about 150 feet, 25 fathoms. After exiting the cage they walked about three hundred metres along a level with reasonable headroom. There were four undergraduates in the group, plus Mark and Graham. The Cassiterite lode was on one wall and the ceiling. The level was about six feet high, Mark had to stoop with his helmet on. Graham's short stocky figure was similar to many indigenous Cornish so he didn't need to stoop.

At the lode face the tinner gave the undergraduates a hammer and some chisels. They could chip away and collect about a matchbox size of the ore. Mark and Graham had brought their own tools.

Mark also had his spectrometer, PIRSy. They spent twenty minutes at the face while the tinner gave them the history of the Tin mine tradition in Cornwall. Mark collected slightly more than a matchbox quantity of the ore, mainly Cassiterite, mostly black crystals, but he also collected some samples at the edge of the Cassiterite veins. Using PIRSy he was getting strong signals for Tin and Silicon, and slight signals for Neodymium and Praseodymium. Graham was familiar with portable spectrometers. He was required to use X-ray types in Georgia. John Shackleton had ordered an Infra-Red one for him. There were also several new Bench X-ray instruments, often called Bench XRF (X-Ray Fluorescence), in the Redruth labs.

The group of six, and the tinner, returned to the mine shaft cage and rang the bell to request the lift. Back on the surface Mark and Graham thanked the tinner and walked back to the Institute for lunch. Mark was pleased with his collected ores. He and Graham returned to the Map Room to work out how they were going to plan their survey of granite plutons. What that meant was visit anywhere where there was known evidence of recent or ancient mining. They would start at West Penwith, the area to the west of Penzance and North of Land's End.

Back at Mark's B&B he sent a long message to Emma. He floated the idea of spending part of half term week at Penzance. Whether that would be acceptable he would have to wait until he returned home.

Thursday morning Mark had another meeting with John Shackleton. Mark's interest in on-site processing had registered with Shackleton who offered Mark the use of the labs and engineering workshops at Redruth: 'We have some processing equipment including a working example of a shaking table that was in use at Geevor Tine mine until thirty years ago. As for on-site eco-processing techniques we're not there yet, but we fully realise that's a direction in which we might need to invest.'

Mark showed him some photos on his phone of what he'd seen in Fudong. Shackleton was quietly impressed.

Mark headed for home after lunch. The nearly three hour drive would make trips to Cornwall, to work with Graham, rather long days. He would need to plan some three or four day stays at hotels or B&Bs. He was sure that he could square that with Bernard Hosegood.

Back home Emma welcomed him. Mark's offer of a few days at Penzance sounded perfect for her: 'How about Sunday evening to Wednesday evening next week, which is half-term. That would give you three days for fieldwork with your new friend Graham. I can have a relaxing few days strolling around Penzance and shopping.'

Mark was happy with that and pleased that Emma was giving herself a break. He sent an e-mail to Graham. That received a positive response within five minutes. Mark booked a modest guest house near the sea front.

A quick trip to Avon on Friday to assess his Tin mine samples on the Bench XRF. He entered the results in his spreadsheet. Strong Tin signal in all pieces he collected. Some of the vein edge samples had a signal for Silicon which was also expected. The signals for Neodymium and Praseodymium were varied. No signal on some pieces and slight signal on others. Separating out the rare earths on-site would be a challenge.

On Saturday Mark and Emma went shopping. Not the usual tour of the supermarket as Mark needed some snack food and Emma didn't want to overstock the fridge when they would be away next week. Mark cleaned both cars and did a quick tidy of the garden. Sunday they had a short walk around the local lanes, then an early lunch.

The road down to Penzance was quiet. The guest house was comfortable, but showed signs of being at the end of season. The evening meal was excellent. Emma's remark was that the accommodation was simple but quite adequate for her three day perambulation of the town, the libraries and the museum. Early starts were still in favour so they opted for a 7 o'clock breakfast.

Graham turned up at 08:00 as planned. He was dressed in his full motorcycle kit. Mark suggested he put the bike in the guest house car park and they travel together in the truck. The West Penwith pluton of granite had numerous attempts at metal mining over many centuries. Some archaeologists advocate a history going back over two thousand years. Graham suggested a brief visit to Geevor Tin mine first. The mine was functioning until 1990. It was now a Museum and tourist attraction with some of the old tin miners acting as guides.

It was useful to see the exhibits in the Museum and the old equipment in the Mill. They spent an hour there then set off to look for disused mines and spoil tips. West Cornwall's mining industry flourished from the work of Thomas Newcomen, of Dartmouth, who invented the low pressure steam beam engine in 1712. The engines were used to pump water from mines and greatly benefited Copper and Tin exploitation in South West England.

The Cornubian batholith is a large intrusion of granite, about 290 million years old, running from West of the Isles of Scilly to East of South Devon. The granite outcrops, the big plutons, of the Scillies, Penwith, Carnmenellis, St Austell, Bodmin and Dartmoor are the exposed sections. The older sedimentary rocks that once covered them have now been eroded. Mineral veins have been intruded, or created in metamorphic contact zones. This is why there is so much metal ore in the South West Peninsula.

Much spoil, the waste rock after Copper and Tin ores were separated from the granite, cover the land around the West Cornwall cliff tops. Soil development on a granite landscape is slow so recent waste broken rock is often readily identified.

Hundreds of thousands of tonnes of metal ores have been extracted from mines in Cornwall over the last few hundred years. Tin mining was active back to the Bronze Age but steam engines, from the Eighteenth Century onwards, greatly increased the efficacy of mining. Some mine shafts reach depths of over 1,000 metres. Steam powered winding gear enabled men to be lowered to the deeper levels, as well as lifting the recovered ore. Before the advent of steam power men used ladders, and buckets of ore were lifted up by donkeys powering winches at the top of the shafts. Many shafts have now been capped, some with old timber railways sleepers, which have rotted and become a hazard. Modern capping methods are much more solid, comprising steel and concrete. The Ordnance Survey large scale plans have recorded a huge number of shafts, but not all. They appear of maps and plans as "Mine", or "Shaft". A great proportion of those are also marked on walkers maps. Other estimates put the total length of all the horizontal mine levels, or tunnels, as several hundred kilometres. Mine captains would ensure that sketch plans of their mines were made and updated daily. Large numbers of these original plans are still extant and held by mining enthusiasts, academic institutions, libraries, company archives, mine rescue groups.

The task for Mark and Graham was to search spoil tips for evidence of metal ores. Scores of amateur geologists, gemstone hunters, and academics have been doing this for decades, but with limited success.

Miners who worked with simple tools were not prone to wasting even small quantities of ore. Hopefully, modern electronic technologies might be able to detect evidence of such residues.

Visually searching for Cassiterite among spoil was relatively easy as the blackish crystals, some small, were the key indicator. Unfortunately, crystals of tourmaline, common in granite, can also be black. Spectrometers are able to distinguish between the two. Mark's PIRSy, the Infra-Red Spectrometer, was quite useful in that respect.

Both Mark and Graham were quite fit and visited nearly fourteen mine shaft areas on the coast between St Just and St Ives. Mark would need to buy another batch of sample bags. They got back to the Penzance guest house just after 18:00. Mark was able to introduce Graham to Emma who told him about her visit to a museum where she had seen many pictures of by-gone miners. Graham got on his bike and set off for home, in Truro. Emma had spent most of the day in Libraries and Museums, with a little bit of window shopping in between.

Mark and Graham had been talking most of the day. Graham's wife was Dr Jean Green, a junior doctor at Treliske Hospital. They both had two year contracts which would take them up to September 2021. Graham wasn't sure what they would do after that, but it might be overseas, so Jean could get some experience working in a third world country. Graham hoped he could find something in the same country, hopefully not for a high risk mining outfit.

Tuesday, the weather was cloudy but dry and not too cold. They did another tour of old mine sites. Graham was particularly interested in one mine. The amount of Cassiterite fragments lying around was considerable, many large crystals. Most Cornish mines had spoil with lots of quartz but little metal ores.

On Wednesday, the weather was still usable and they were able to complete their survey of the principal mining areas of West Penwith.

Mark had accumulated forty six sample bags. Back at the guest house Emma had laid out the various items of baby clothes she'd purchased: 'This has been a relaxing few days for me. Thanks for bringing me down with you.'

They got home late Wednesday evening and had to drive through heavy rain and strong winds. Mark went into Avon on Thursday. He had a quick catch up with Richard Ericson then established himself in the lab with the Bench XRF. He had 46 samples to crush and then put through the instrument. He was there until 19:00. A lot of data, many elements recorded.

He was exhausted when he got home. What he'd achieved in the last four days was similar in quantity to his entire Exmoor sample collection. It wasn't really about quantity, but more to do with what he'd found and where. On Friday he entered all the data into his spreadsheet. A total of nine rare earths as well as significant results for Tin, some Copper and Arsenic. Mark could see a possible article coming from the West Penwith survey. He had a chat with Richard over lunch and floated the idea of submitting a paper to a journal. Graham would be a contributor, he'd also been the source of the background knowledge of the area. He'd also navigated the two of them to the various sites. Richard agreed that it was a good idea. Mark would send Graham a copy of the spreadsheet and a draft article. That would take him next Monday and possibly Tuesday.

The weekend was as normal. Supermarket on Saturday. Mark cleaned the truck in the afternoon. Then Sunday a gentle walk with Emma over at Minehead. The weather was benign and the holiday crowds had disappeared. Unfortunately, the clocks had gone back and it was getting dark by 17:00. Emma had done some school work on Thursday and Friday and was now all set for her last 7 weeks of teaching before the baby arrived in January. The trip to Penzance had been quite inspiring for Emma. Her time in the museums and libraries had prompted the idea of a module on Cornwall's mining and industrial heritage. That would give her something to focus upon during maternity leave.

Mark rattled off a draft article on Monday and e-mailed it down to Graham. The reply was supportive, and he would work through it that week. As for further field surveys he suggested they watch the weather. At the moment it wasn't looking hopeful, a lot of rain.

Their next campaign would be the Carnmenellis pluton, and the several satellite plutons: St Agnes, Tregonning and St Michael's Mount. That might have to wait as a memo from Gordon MacPherson appeared in his pigeonhole on Tuesday. The Vice Chancellor wanted to mount an inquiry into the China episode. Mark went to see Richard Ericson. His understanding was that the VC had become rather irritated over the difference in accounts from Gordon MacPherson and Jeremy Chudleigh. Apparently, Chudleigh was blaming Mark for the sequence of events involving the evacuation to Manila.

The VC had been hoping for a prestigious exchange arrangement but the whole thing had just dissolved. Richard had been summoned to the VC's office on Thursday, and Mark on Friday.

Richard said to Mark: 'You've got to keep this completely under your hat. There have been rumours floating around the various departments for several months that the relationship between the VC and Chudleigh is more complex than just university administration.'

Mark was left wondering how he would account for his instructions from Vanessa Wyndham. He went home that afternoon considering his position. He talked to Emma about it. She recommended that he should talk to Bernard Hosegood. That evening Mark phoned Bernard and unloaded the whole problem. Bernard's main point was that as Mark had no tenure at Avon, the VC didn't have any right to treat him like staff. Being a sponsored student the University had certain obligations to him for unhindered study. Bernard said he would fly over and accompany him to the inquiry meeting, and would act as advocate.

All that didn't make Mark feel any easier. Wednesday and Thursday he took some of his West Penwith samples to the mass spectrometer in Chemistry. He found Phillip Warren, the technician, and explained that he had put 46 samples through the Bench XRF but wanted to get quantification on the seven most significant. These were the seven with the higher quantities of rare earths. That took Mark all of Wednesday and most of Thursday morning. He got the results, quite a bit of Neodymium in five of the seven samples. Back in his office he entered the data into his master spreadsheet and also looked at the locations on the map. All the high Neodymium was in a mine cluster only 1200 metres across.

Mark had been unsettled doing the analyses; the first time his heart wasn't in his work.

Friday, at Avon, Bernard Hosegood turned up at 09:30. That gave him time to get Mark's account. Bernard's advice was to hold to the agreement he had with Vanessa Wyndham, don't give her name, just refer to "them" as "Whitehall". He would step in if the VC was becoming too intrusive or assertive.

Mark was called in at 11:05, Bernard followed him in and boldly announced himself as Professor Bernard Hosegood, Mark Scott's sponsor and professional advocate. They both sat down, Bernard had to pull a chair across to sit next to Mark. The VC introduced the panel: himself, then Humphrey Wilson, local manufacturer, and Jeremy Chudleigh, financial adviser.

The VC asked the questions. Mark gave his answers. After about seven minutes Bernard stopped Mark and gave his summing up: 'Mr Scott has conducted himself for the last 13 months at Avon with the full confidence of myself as Chairman of Chalco Prospecting Limited. His relationship with Whitehall has continued since they extricated our staff from a dangerous situation in Ecuador. He was awarded the Queen's Gallantry Medal for actions in saving his colleague. He and his family receive continuing security support from the British Government. Further than that I cannot comment. As your Inquiry progresses I anticipate you will analyse how Mr Chudleigh's involvement with the U.S. authorities impacted on events in China.'

That caused visible signs of embarrassment from Jeremy Chudleigh, and an element of confusion from the VC. Bernard stood up, indicated to Mark to do likewise, and they both walked out.

Outside, Bernard commented to Mark: 'How on earth a sociologist got a Vice Chancellor position at a science and technology university I find astonishing. I expect you'll hear of a resignation shortly.'

Mark didn't want to get involved and just said: 'Thanks for supporting me.'

Bernard: 'I had a long chat with Gordon MacPherson yesterday afternoon. You've done nothing inappropriate. Next time you see Naomi Dawson, or Vanessa Wyndham, if that's her current name, bring her up to date on this complete waste of bureaucratic time.'

Bernard went off to talk with Gordon MacPherson again. Mark decided to go home. He was relieved to have had the support of Bernard, but just wanted to separate from the stress.

That weekend Mark focused solely on Emma and the new home. Sunday it was raining heavily, but Emma's Mum and Dad had invited them to lunch. That was relaxing, the first time for several weeks.

A message from Graham Stanley came in on Sunday evening. The wet and windy weather was settling down later in the week. Would Mark like to come down for another fieldwork campaign Wednesday to Friday? Mark didn't take long to consider that. He replied yes. He found a B&B at Porthtowan and booked to arrive Tuesday evening. Monday he called in to the big farmers' store near Taunton to buy 200 sample bags. He needed the ones with good seals and made of sturdy polythene. Supermarket food bags were too flimsy for sharp stone fragments.

At Avon later on Monday Mark went to the staff lounge. He detected that there was an unusual amount of quiet whispering. Richard Ericson was there. Mark asked what was going on.

'Chudleigh resigned this morning. The whole campus is elated. It seems he's been exerting his pressure on all departments. So now he's going, all the stories are coming out.'

Mark: 'That's interesting.'

Richard: 'Yes. Amongst the mutterings are that Bernard Hosegood was the one who stirred the pile of manure.'

Mark thought he would quietly go back to his office and stay out of the campus politics. He put PIRSy on overnight charge and decided to go home to pack.

Tuesday he enlarged maps of the Carnmenellis area on the photocopier and made a few other preparations. He updated Richard Ericson and set off for Porthtowan after lunch.

Wednesday morning Graham turned up on his bike. The weather was dry and cool but not windy. Graham's assessment of the area was that although Camborne and Redruth had the highest concentration of mine shafts, they were unlikely to provide undisturbed spoil tips because of all the urban development and redevelopment over the last three hundred years. Rural sites might offer better chances of finding less disturbed spoil tips.

They set off for the Tregonning-Godolphin satellite pluton, over near the South coast. They went to the Wheal Roots mine, operating as the Poldark Mining Heritage tourist attraction. It was closed for the winter but they managed to talk their way in and got a private tour of the actively used levels. The mine was known for its Tin production. There wasn't much ore material extant in the public levels but they took some samples. That took two hours out of their day but at least they were *in situ* samples.

They spent the rest of the day around the area but were slowed down by the mud. The recent rain had brought the water table up to winter levels of saturation. Mark had brought the small pick axe from the truck which was useful for getting through to the actual mine spoil. Several of the sites they visited were on farmland. At one site they were waved away by a farmer. They found a couple of real spoil tips, probably untouched for a hundred years. At two sites they could visually detect black Cassiterite, and PIRSy indicated the same. No rare earths detected. Those pieces were bagged; perhaps the Bench XRF would give more elements.

Graham's objective was to build up a picture of the 19$^{th}$ century activity and then use field evidence and mineral records from the archives to assess which mines would be most suitable for re-activation if world Tin prices became favourable. There had always been a strong feeling amongst the indigenous Cornish that Tin mining would resurge. It would need a higher world price, newer detection and mining techniques, and more efficient processing. It may be a pipe dream but in the Information Age local knowledge might still prove valuable. The Redruth Institute of Mining was unusual as an academic institution. It had a massive knowledge base that wasn't recorded anywhere else. They were even careful not to digitise old paper records as internet trawling and interrogating connected computers was rife. The massive databases held by U.S. and China were attempting to become the all knowing repositories of total world knowledge.

On the way back to Porthtowan Graham asked Mark if he would like to come to dinner tomorrow evening. Jean had a day off and would like to meet Mark. That invitation was accepted. Mark said he could pick Graham up from home tomorrow. They planned to have a day in the middle of the Carnmenellis pluton, just South of the two towns where land was less developed and hopefully less disturbed.

Thursday morning Mark drove down to Threemilestone, near Truro, where Graham and Jean had rented a house for two years. It was only about two kilometres from Treliske Hospital where Jean was based. Graham wanted her to be closest to work as she often had night shifts.

Graham suggested they start on the high ground of Carn Brea, just South of Redruth. It was undeveloped and he had some other information on the geological formation. There was less of a wet soil problem than yesterday and they were getting some useful responses from PIRSy. They then moved South to the Carnmenellis high point near Stithians Reservoir. They got many samples from there. Other sites on farmland were a bit muddy again. There was one site which appeared to have a large spoil tip. Graham though it wise to ask the farmer's permission as the site was particularly exposed to public view. It was worth asking as the PIRSy readings gave strong signals for four rare earths as well as Tin. They were quite pleased with their findings. It was 17:00 and the clouds were getting lower and darker. Graham suggested they call it a day and head off to his house.

Fortunately Mark had a clean pair of shoes in his truck. The ones he used at the B&B. He tidied himself up and walked into Graham's home. Jean was particularly welcoming. She admitted she didn't get much time for proper cooking so she'd had an unusually interesting afternoon. Jean was a similar height to Graham but quite slender. She intended to specialise in paediatric medicine eventually, but was just building up her general medical experience. The evening was quite convivial as they exchanged accounts of their careers and families.

Mark drove back to the B&B at Porthtowan for his last night. The owners had put an envelope on his pillow. Mark opened it:

Mark, can we meet in my car, blue Mondeo, at 08:00
Friday morning. I'll be parked across the road from your
B&B. Allow 10 minutes.
Vanessa

Graham would arrive about 09:00 so Mark asked the owners if he
could have breakfast at 08:30. Two days of fresh air and a healthy
walking pace had made Mark quite sleepy, but as he climbed into bed he
wondered what Vanessa Wyndham would have to say about China, or did
she just want to debrief him.

Mark got up and showered and went down and across the road to
Vanessa's blue Mondeo. 'Morning Mark, apologies for interrupting your
fieldwork.'

Mark: 'Good morning, I guess this is about China.'

Vanessa: 'Yes, it didn't go exactly as we had thought. I gave you the
"geraniums and terracing passwords" after we were told, at short notice,
by our U.S. contacts that they were intending to extract Zhou. As usual,
when the U.S. want something, we just fall in line.'

Mark: 'You know we were used.'

Vanessa: 'I fully understand your indignation. We've been informed
by the U.S. that now they've got him they won't be letting him go. But,
they are happy for you to maintain links with him at Denver. All
expenses paid if you visit him, and Richard Ericson can go as well.'

Mark: 'I'll let Richard know.'

Vanessa: 'The U.S. are particularly pleased at getting Zhou's son
because of his knowledge of the way Beijing currently operates. Neither
of them will be travelling far beyond Denver as the risk of them being
snatched back is too great.'

Mark: 'Would it be safe if Richard and me travelled to Denver?'

Vanessa: 'I expect so. The U.S. authorities will be keeping close shadowing of Zhou, and his visitors. Zhou may be e-mailing you shortly.' Pause. 'There is another matter. We have a building in Cornwall that requires a geological assessment to enable an extension. Do you think you can handle that?'

Mark: 'Couldn't you do the assessment?' He was being a little indifferent, conscious that he was being sucked in further.

Vanessa: 'I've studied it but I'm required to get a second opinion. It will be a three day visit to a top secret establishment, and you will need to sign the Official Secrets Act. No written report required, just a verbal assessment. You'll get a large tax free payment.'

Mark: 'I'll need to think about it. I've got a lot in my diary at the moment.'

Vanessa: 'I appreciate you're finding all this rather difficult, but it will be useful for your career. You'll get an e-mail from Stephen.Heath37@zxz59.com with the date and place. Dominic Wright and myself will meet you.'

Mark got out of the car and went in for breakfast. He felt he was being controlled. He didn't enjoy his breakfast.

Graham knocked on the door of the B&B; the landlady opened it: 'Hello, I've come to meet Mark Scott, please can you tell him I'll wait by his truck.'

Mark was coming down the stairs with his overnight rucksack and his day sack: 'Hi Graham, another dry day, we're doing well for November in Cornwall.' He was trying to brighten himself up.

Friday was the day they had selected for the cliff area near St Agnes. Luckily there was hardly any wind which was an advantage for an exposed area.

They started in the Porthtowan valley. Graham had identified the mines and spoil tips he thought were the most likely to produce minerals.

Many of the sites were on access land, so difficulties with farmers were not a problem. Friday became colder as the North West breeze increased through the day. They could get the truck to most sites along narrow minor roads. The major geological feature of St Agnes Head area is the satellite granite pluton. The numerous mines were related to metamorphic zones around the pluton and other igneous intrusions subsequent to the formation of the granite. Like so much of the North Cornwall coast the rock at the cliffline is Devonian sandstones, shales and slates. Not all the slate is particularly hard, its creation from mudstone is a result of variable amounts of metamorphism.

The whole area of the St Agnes coastline has a similar industrial archaeology to that of St Just to Pendeen where they had been surveying two weeks earlier. The main difference is that Penwith is all Granite whereas St Agnes is mostly Devonian sedimentary. The exposed Granite only accounts for a few square kilometres on the surface but the igneous rock pluton underlies all of it at depth.

They worked their way North and East. Quite a bit of coastal footpath walking. Mark was cheering up. He was getting interesting signals from PIRSy. Quite a few rare earths identified and many samples bagged. By the time they had completed their day's work, near Perranporth, Mark had 38 samples.

It was nearly 17:00 and getting grey. Mark drove Graham back to Porthtowan to collect his bike. Mark said: 'Thanks for all your work planning out sites this week, I appreciate it. I'll send you a summary of the sample results next week. And thank Jean again for a superb meal last night.'

Mark drove home. He wasn't happy. The three days fieldwork had been a great success, but he was concerned that the security services were still imposing on him. Vanessa Wyndham was a pleasant woman but she was taking him for granted. How should he respond?

*Michael J. Fennessy*

# 21

Mark got back home at 21:00. Emma was elated. She'd had a good week at school and nobody was dumping jobs on her. She had interviewed her maternity leave replacement and was happy that the woman would follow her curriculum. Added to that, the visit to see the health visitor this evening had given her an "excellent". She brought Mark his late dinner but could see he was less enthusiastic than usual.

Mark unloaded the latest request from the security services. Emma was worried when Mark said he felt he was being sucked in. What exactly did they want from him. Mark said a geological assessment on some building. Emma responded: 'You could say you'll do it but on your terms, but you don't wish to be part of their system.'

Mark: 'That's roughly how I see it, but they want me sign the Official Secrets Act.'

'Well, just say you'll do the consultancy on a professional basis, but not sign any piece of paper. If they don't like that, then they don't trust you. They've got the problem, not you. There'll be another Act of Parliament soon anyway. If the Attorney General considered you had done something they considered a breach of national security they'd charge you anyway.'

Mark was quite tired, he'd had a successful fieldwork tour but just wanted to get to bed and then have a relaxing weekend. Saturday he did his usual domestic tasks, Sunday they went up to Stroud to have lunch with Mark's Mum and Dad. In the afternoon they had a walk in the

Autumn sunshine. Mark's Mum, Jennifer, remarked how well Emma was looking. Emma was getting heavier but coping well. Only just over 9 weeks to go. She found having a gentle walk each day helpful, even strolling the school grounds at lunchtime for half and hour.

Mark had a quiet chat with his Dad, Roger, about the new consultancy "request". Roger agreed with Emma's suggestion: 'Take the consultancy on your terms. They want something from you for some reason. Remember that the civil service can be rather incestuous. Try and maintain your own person. They know you're not a loud mouth, that's probably why they think you're useful to their secret world.'

Mark drove home a little happier.

Monday at Avon, Mark had two e-mails, that he was expecting. One from Professor Zhou and one from the mystery Stephen Heath, Vanessa Wyndham's spoof e-mail address.

> Mark,
> Geology consultancy, Cornwall, Monday 2nd to Wednesday 4th December.
> You're booked in at the large hotel on the headland, Newquay, for Monday night and Tuesday night. Dinner Monday and Tuesday, Breakfast Tuesday and Wednesday, packed lunch Tuesday. Fully paid.
> We'll collect you from the hotel foyer at 09:30 on Tuesday 3rd.
> V and D

Mark thought he would leave the e-mail for today and reply to it on Tuesday. They would know he had opened it.

As for Zhou's e-mail, it was a softly worded e-mail to him and Richard inviting them to engage in collaboration on the processing of rare earths. A lot more detail as well, but it was clear that this was a carefully worded offer. Probably prepared with the assistance of the group responsible for setting him up in Denver. They needed collaborators for Zhou as it was certain that the U.S. would not be allowing him out of their sight for fear of having him abducted, or worse.

There was a scheduled supervision with Richard and Kevin Tranter on Wednesday so Mark decided to leave any form of reply until after that meeting.

Mark spent all of the rest of Monday on his samples from Carnmenellis. He followed his usual protocol: Clean and dry samples, scan with PIRSy, crush the sample and put part of it through the Bench XRF, another part would be put through the mass spectrometer. With his 38 samples he would only do the third examination with samples that showed some interest from the Bench XRF. All that would take most of the week, and he wasn't sure yet how busy the chemistry department's mass spectrometer was going to be.

The supervision meeting on Wednesday was partly on the Zhou invitation. Richard had received the same e-mail, he would need to think about it. There was a discussion amongst the three of them on how Mark was going to shape his thesis, together with the hint that he might need to consider when he was going to start writing it up. Mark acknowledged the hint.

Of the 38 Carnmenellis samples Mark put 14 through the mass spectrometer. Some of those because of signals for multiple rare earths but also a couple which were high in Tin. He was thinking of providing information for Graham. He sent him an e-mail with the results.

Thursday he sent his reply to V and D:

V and D,

I'll undertake the geological consultancy in December as
detailed in your e-mail. It will be on a professional basis,
and I'll have conditions.
Mark

At 15:00 on Friday Mark felt he'd had enough of the office. There
had been no reply back from Vanessa Wyndham, so he assumed the
Newquay consultancy was going ahead.

Back home he tried to put on a smiley face for Emma. She'd had
another good week and was keen to do some shopping for baby items on
Saturday afternoon. In the morning Mark did the supermarket run with a
long detailed list. The afternoon list was baby buggy, papoose, two car
seats unless they could find one with two sets of seat fittings. Also,
assorted changing accessories, two sets, one for home, one for her Mum
and Dad' home. That lot cost just shy of £800. Mark could feel his life
was beginning to change, but Emma was happy and that cheered him up.

Sunday was solid drizzle. Neither of them wanted to go anywhere.
Emma was prepared for this, she started on the Christmas Card list,
although she wouldn't post them until December. Mark did some
domestic cleaning.

Monday at Avon Mark looked at Ordnance Survey and geology
maps of the St Austell pluton. That was the next fieldwork campaign for
him and Graham. The huge area of China Clay workings meant the
landscape was different to the other granite areas. China Clay is the result
of the breakdown of the Feldspar crystal in the granite. It is generally
assumed that the breakdown of the feldspar arises from hot gases rising
up after the granite has solidified. Because granite is a matrix of Quartz,
Feldspar and Mica crystals, chemically altering one crystal means the
whole granite changes from being solid to being a loose white gravelly
porridge. The Quartz crystals are unaffected as they are chemically

resistant to most gases and liquids. To remove Quartz and Mica crystals from the raw mix the quarry workers wash the clay away with giant hosepipes. Clay particles settle slowly. Adjusting the time when the milky white water is directed into various pools allows different particle sizes of the Kaolin clay to settle out. Pharmaceuticals, paper manufacture, and many other manufacturing processes require specific sizes of clay particle.

Aware that days were shortening and the weather was becoming less usable, Mark wondered whether it was practical to do another visit. There was an area around St Blazey with several mines printed on the Victorian map. He looked up the geological memoir on the internet. After much consideration, including Emma's forthcoming confinement, he decided to leave the St Austell area until the Spring. He phoned Graham and had a long chat. Graham was of a similar view. He said that with all the Penwith and Carnmenellis data they had plenty to work on. They could have a get together in a few weeks time to work through the text for the Penwith mines article.

Mark didn't like working on Sundays, although Emma was happy to have a day at home. Perhaps it was useful for her to adjust to imminent motherhood.

On Monday Mark decided to tidy up his fieldwork spreadsheet. It was getting unwieldy. He could have a summary spreadsheet, but then have the full data in separate files: Exmoor, Overseas (Austria and China), Penwith, Carnmenellis, and whatever else arose. He bumped into Richard on Wednesday to explain his decision. It was met with a gentle smile: 'Good idea, I wondered if you'd get around to that. Organising datasets is a key part of effective research. On the Denver matter, I've decided I'll decline Zhou's offer of collaboration, but you may wish to take advantage.'

Mark wasn't expecting a discussion on Denver: 'I think I'd rather pause at the moment. Emma's only got nine weeks to go, so it would be useful to stay local through the winter, and I think I'll work on your hint about the thesis.'

Richard responded: 'Yes, that's a wise decision. There are several other considerations as well. Zhou won't be up and running with a new lab for several months, although I guess he'll have plenty of offers of funding, from government and multi-nationals. The other thing you need to reflect upon is whether you wish to stay with academic geology, or move into processing technology.'

Mark realised he needed to give that more thought. Richard made some valid points, and Mark was getting the feeling that he was being gently steered away from processing technologies. Zhou had been generous of spirit when he first invited him to China, but the Fudong situation had changed radically. He may have been dragged to an academic institution in Denver but economic geology in the U.S. is dominated by the big multi-nationals. Mark decided to send Zhou a courteous reply along the lines of "thank you, but I'm busy for the next few months". That was true, anyway.

When Mark totted up his various fieldworks and visits through the summer he realised he had been out of the office for nearly fifty percent of his time. If he was going to complete the PhD successfully he needed to focus on further reading, publications and assembling his thesis. Whatever he decided to do with the rest of his career a sound PhD was essential. That would also tessellate with supporting Emma and the baby.

The weekend arrived, Emma was still pre-empting the Christmas season. Shopping was the focus.

The following week Mark decided to read up on the Newquay area. He wasn't sure what Vanessa Wyndham was trying to throw at him, so he needed to assess cliff erosion, ground stability, groundwater saturation, anything that might affect a building. He had no idea what sort of building he was being asked to survey.

That week Mark did some more work organising his data. He had a day at home on Wednesday. That meant he could cook for Emma on at least one day. Thursday and Friday he checked his field equipment. Because of the vague details of the consultancy he decided to take all his fieldwork equipment: PIRSy, laser range finder, geiger counter, torch, chisels, hammer, sample bags. The first four needed charging. He would be down in Cornwall for three days, but he assumed he may need to analyse materials, or photographs, back at Avon. He wasn't expecting to give a professional opinion on the day.

# 22

That weekend Mark was still apprehensive. He thought the best solution was to focus on Emma. She was getting heavier, still happy, almost ebullient at times. It was clear that pregnancy was not going to limit her celebration of Christmas. The shops in Taunton were getting busier, she was keen to do some gift shopping, but to outlets with original ideas. Sunday was a visit to a local out of town craft centre. In between shopping outings Mark gave the cars a rough wash. Autumnal road grime had made them both grubby.

Mark set off for Newquay shortly after Emma left for school. He would be there by about 11:00. The weather was dry and he thought it would be useful to get the feel of the landscape. He'd studied the geological description of the area on geological Sheet 346. That covered the coast from Watergate Bay down to near Porthtowan. He wasn't sure but he had a feeling that because the government had controlled land near the coast dating back to the Second World War it was a possibility that the "building extension" might be on one of those sites. The other idea he couldn't get out of his head was that it might be a coastal property on a problem coastline prone to cliff falls or storm damage. Whatever it was, enhancing his familiarity with the area might be an advantage. Much of the geology was Devonian sandstones, shales, mudstones, and low quality slate due to variable amounts of metamorphism. Igneous intrusions up through the Cornubian batholith were widespread. Some were now exposed on the surface but others were still covered by

Devonian rocks. Those small isolated plutons were partly known from recent gravimetric surveys.

Mark had four or five hours of daylight to roam the coastal area, a bit like the day with Graham when they were inspecting mines and spoil tips. The roaming was on the narrow lanes and some walking along footpaths. Every building bigger than a small cottage was an object of interest. This was a weird consultancy, no detail of where he was going to be tomorrow!

He arrived at the hotel as the light was fading. He unpacked his overnight bag, phoned Emma, watched the evening news, then went down for dinner. Early December meant there were few holiday makers. The guests were predominantly business suits.

Tuesday morning after breakfast he went down to the foyer with his fieldwork rucksack full of equipment plus hat, gloves, waterproof jacket and trousers, and the hotel packed lunch. Everything for an outdoor consultancy in December. He had a piece of software on his phone that recorded the GPS co-ordinates of a journey or walk. He switched that on. He could still take photographs or video without causing the background software to stall.

A black Range Rover with blacked out rear windows rolled up outside at 09:30. Vanessa Wyndham got out: 'Morning Mark, is the hotel comfortable?'

'Yes, thank you.'

'You remember Dominic Wright, he'll drive, we'll put you in the back.'

At the edge of the town, Dominic Wright pulled into a lay-by. Vanessa Wyndham turned around and said: 'Where we're going today is top secret. You have to put this blindfold on. I'll explain more later'

'I imagined the day might be like this.'

The car set off again, main road at first, then roads seemed to have more bends. For the last few kilometres the surface was noticeably more bumpy, and the vehicle speed had reduced. This was a bit like a party game. Eventually, the vehicle stopped. Mark could hear a large metallic sliding door. They set off again, but seemed to be running on electric now. A minute later, Vanessa Wyndham turned around and said that Mark could remove the blindfold. They were in a tunnel. The car headlights were on and Mark could see that the raw rock on the sides was Devonian shale. The ceiling was quite high. A lorry could pass along, but probably not a double decker bus.

Mark could see the odometer. The last two digits were 3.7 when he removed the blindfold. The ceiling had steel beams. When the odometer read 4.1 the rock type changed to a complex pattern, then it changed to granite. No steel beams any more. There were a couple of branches in the tunnel, which went upwards, but the Range Rover started to go down a slope.

Eventually, they arrived in a large darkened area. The odometer read 4.9. A total of 1.2 miles through the tunnel. Dominic Wright got out. After about ten seconds a series of lights were activated. They were in a huge chamber, flat floor, square sides and a ceiling that Mark couldn't see fully from inside the car. Vanessa Wyndham got out and opened Mark's door: 'We're here, apologies for the blind journey.'

Mark got out. The domed ceiling was high. On the floor was a sort of hydraulic digger and a large covered trailer.

Vanessa Wyndham started: 'Well Mark, this is the "building". Eventually, it will become the replacement government headquarters in the event of war. There are similar ones around Britain. Which one gets used is only assessed at the time of need.'

Mark: 'How come we're inside granite?'

Vanessa: 'It's one of the granite plutons in the area that hasn't been exposed. The rock at the surface is Devonian shale. We have an older chamber further down the coast but because it's completely carved out of the Devonian and metamorphic rock there are a number of problems. It's over sixty years old. This new one will be entirely self sufficient. Nuclear power for electricity, desalination for fresh water, filtered atmosphere to remove radioactive particles.'

Mark: 'It's a big space.'

Vanessa: 'Yes, it's got to contain 140 people. Technical staff, military and security staff, medical staff, and the prime minister with his or her spouse and children. He or she will be nominally in charge but tightly guided by government staff. There will be no other political personnel.'

Mark: 'How will you feed 140 people?

Dominic Wright answered: Five years dehydrated food will be stored on the first floor.'

Mark: 'What will be on the ground floor?'

Vanessa: 'Two nuclear reactors, British built and much improved technology to the Exmoor ones you uncovered earlier in the year. Two desalination plants, one geothermal power unit, and an air conditioning unit. Everything you'd expect.' Pause. 'The reason we need your assessment is for the structural integrity of this hollowed out granite.'

The Q and A continued. This was an unusual consultancy. With no prior information Mark had a huge number of questions. He was aware that Vanessa and Dominic were probably most concerned about the ceiling. Mark opened his rucksack and got out his various pieces of equipment. He started with the laser range finder. The dimensions of the huge chamber were 52 metres by 52 metres and the height to the centre of the ceiling dome was 58 metres. Looking up at the ceiling with his torch

Mark noticed that the ceiling wasn't a dome, it was actually a steep pyramidal shape.

Mark looking at Vanessa: 'Do you know the angle of the internal pyramidal faces?'

'60 degrees.'

'And the height of the floor we're standing on above current Mean Sea Level?'

'8 metres.'

'And the depth of ground cover at the peak of the ceiling?'

'At least 30 metres.'

'Thanks.' Mark was jotting all this down in his fieldwork notebook.

After a pause Vanessa asked: 'Would 30 metres cover withstand a direct nuclear ground burst?'

'How long is a piece of string? I don't wish to be facetious, but that's impractical to calculate, too many variables, many unknown. If it was a perfect direct hit of a ground burst then this chamber would be destroyed.'

There was a lingering silence. Mark set off to walk the perimeter of the chamber, tapping the walls with his hammer. On the East wall there was a discoloured patch near the base of the wall. His hammer tapping caused a small amount of loose material to fall to the ground. Mark put that in a sample bag. On the North Wall there were many holes about 30 cm in diameter. Poking the range finder in gave mixed readings. There was also a small sump below floor level with another hole leading from it.

Mark got the geiger counter out and switched it on. There was one click for gamma every twenty seconds although it wasn't consistent. When he switched to the alpha sensor and held it close to the floor near one of the holes, there was a significant reading. He switched it back to gamma and left it on.

He walked the West wall and then back to the car at the South Wall.

'What are the holes on the North wall for?'

Dominic Wright replied instantly: 'How do you know that's the North wall?'

'The flux gate compass in the laser range finder.'

Vanessa could sense Dominic's irritation. She responded quickly: 'Those are all the services. They mostly connect to the sea, not in perfect straight lines. They are for reactor cooling, in and out; sea water intake for desalination plant, sewage out, radon sump outlet, air inlet and outlet, spare holes in case of blockages.'

'Have you had a nuclear reactor in here already?'

Vanessa: 'Yes, all the cutting tools to carve out the chamber have been powered by nuclear electric. That unit has been removed and we now use battery power from that trailer.'

Mark thought for a moment: 'A lot of careful design has gone into this facility. Are there some concerns over its suitability?'

Vanessa: 'There are a few. You've noticed one on the East wall, the kaolinisation.'

Mark: 'That's not severe. It's only two metres across. Kaolinisation is common in this area. I'll check out the sample with chemistry when I get back. The pyramidal ceiling seems unaffected, and you've only got slight running water on the West wall. It is December so the ground is quite saturated. I'm sure you've got much more water ingress in your existing facility. Structurally this chamber should be usable, unless you get a direct hit. When do you start building here?'

Vanessa: 'Quite soon. We've had another scientist in here recently. She was concerned that we're too near sea level.'

Mark: 'Eight metres gives you quite a bit of freeboard. Spring High Water will be about three and a half metres above current Mean Sea Level. That means you've got over four metres spare before sea level rise affects you. That could be well over a hundred years and even that's debatable. This facility will have passed its sell-by date in less than a hundred years.'

Vanessa: 'Unfortunately, she's threatening to go public.'

Mark: 'What's her name?'

Vanessa: 'I can't disclose that. In the same way that I couldn't disclose yours. She was a prominent member of the IPCC (Intergovernmental Panel on Climate Change), so she thinks she'll have a supportive audience.'

Mark: 'Well, you know that IPCC predictions of sea level rise have been over stated, and shown to be so, for decades. Sea level rise is still measured in millimetres at the moment and the debate on how much rising is predicted has been rumbling on for over forty years.'

Vanessa: 'That's the problem we're trying to address.'

Mark: 'Why don't you get an experienced physicist that's working on ice melt in Greenland and Antarctica. Physicists are the ones doing the measurements of ice, and they're not as noisy as some members of the IPCC. Remember that some people use exaggeration to bolster their claims for more funds to study their ideas. You need to take some quiet advice. In your line of work you should be able to detect the exaggerators.'

Dominic Wright: 'But we can't ignore her.'

Vanessa Wyndham: 'I'll see what I can do.'

Mark: 'The floor of this chamber isn't perfectly level. When your builders come in they'll need a level base. That could add 30 or 40 centimetres of reinforced concrete at least, but that will also provide a better sump arrangement all around the chamber for the radon to drain. How are you going to build in here?'

Dominic Wright: 'It's all preformed. It already exists as hundreds of numbered interlocking concrete "bricks", a bit like giant children's play "bricks". Each weigh about a tonne, or a little more. They'll arrive by lorry from Yorkshire at night. The driver will be swapped on the A30 for one of ours, the Yorkshire driver takes the previous day's lorry back. Each lorry carries about fourteen "bricks".'

Mark: 'So, that'll take months.

Dominic: 'About 9 months for the structure. Then about another 5 months to install all the services and electronics.'

Mark: 'Who's done the work in here?'

Vanessa: 'The chamber has been carved out by two ex-military workers over the last eight years. By keeping the lorry movements low we avoided attracting attention.'

Mark: 'Where has the waste granite gone?'

Dominic: 'Into a redundant china clay pit.'

Mark: 'I'll analyse the rock samples I've taken and get back to you, but I can't see you've got much of a structural problem.'

Vanessa: 'Thank you Mark. We'll go now. I'll have to blindfold you again before we get to the road.'

They left for the slow drive out through the tunnel. Mark put his blindfold on and waited until they got into Newquay. At the hotel, Mark got out and said good-bye.

He went up to his room and wondered if he could drive home that evening. He looked at his GPS log. The out and back routes were identical. There had been no driving round in circles. The location where the GPS signal failed was clear. It was on a minor road between St Agnes and Perranporth. Mark thought he would have an early breakfast tomorrow morning and have a look. He hadn't been asked to sign any document.

He phoned Emma conscious that GCHQ might be monitoring his call. He conducted a warm conversation with a carefully worded explanation of how the consultancy day had gone. He was careful to create the impression that he was a reliable and discreet adviser to Britain's secret services. They should know that already from the way he handled the rogue nuclear reactors on Exmoor.

After breakfast on Wednesday Mark loaded his bags into the truck. He switched his phone off and put it inside the two biscuit tins he'd left in the truck from the days of surveillance during the Miners Court difficulty. He headed down towards Perranporth. He didn't take the minor road indicated by the GPS log but went up on a ridge road which ran nearly parallel. Last night, from the map on his phone, he could see where the Range Rover had turned into a building with a large metal door. He parked the truck in a field gateway and climbed to the top of a hedge which provided him with a view down into the valley. He could see an industrial building backed into the steep slope of the valley side. Mark got the binoculars out of his rucksack. The sign above the sliding doors read "INSIGNIA MEMORIALS". A link to the long history of military involvement in the area. All military units were rather proud of their insignia. The building was plain, but quite grubby. The forecourt was rough hardcore. The sliding doors were open and granite headstone blanks could be seen on the left, with bench cutting machinery behind. Most of the right side of the building was unoccupied, probably for lorries to drive in and out. The December morning light, even though it was sunny, wasn't reaching down into the valley. That meant Mark couldn't discern the tunnel entrance at the rear of the inside of the building.

The stonemason business was obviously the "front" to the secret chamber excavation, and its associated tunnels. Mark decided he had enough visual information and wasn't going to venture down into the valley. It was likely that the locality was covered with hidden cameras. It seemed that people with military connections were part of the "front".

Mark didn't wish to demonstrate further interest in the area. He decided to go back into Newquay. He found a funeral directors shop in the town. He went in and enquired how he could find a memorial inscription company to make a headstone for his late aunt. There was no one else in the shop and the young lady was quite helpful. She said that there were several in West Cornwall. Most used granite or slate. The inscriptions were cut with a computer aided machine these days. Mark asked the best ones for a local granite headstone. She said there was one in the town and another near Perranporth which only used local granite. They were called Insignia Memorials. Mark asked if they were a long established business. Yes, was the reply, they went back as far as the war years. Originally they were based near Nancekuke, but they moved to near Perranporth about twelve years ago. They had links to the air force bases which were active in the area. The young lady gave him one of the stonemasons' business cards. Mark said: 'Thank you, you've been most helpful.'

Mark had a clearer picture of what he'd been asked to look at yesterday. The whole set up must have been a long time in the planning. The use of ex-military personnel seemed to pervade the security services.

After removing his phone from the two biscuit tins, Mark drove home. Emma had left a note in the kitchen:

> If you get home before me, this is what we're having for dinner xxx

That evening Mark outlined his three day consultancy to Emma. It was a large new building and they wanted to know the integrity of the ground upon which is was being built. Emma was coping well at school and still not getting jobs dumped upon her. Unusual for the end of Autumn Term in a secondary school.

As for Mark's three days working for the government. His mind wouldn't let him drop the odd consultancy. Vanessa Wyndham hadn't lied to Mark since he'd known her, but she was a solid government operator. Mark couldn't count her as a friend and he would always need to be cautious in his dealings with her. He felt he had the measure of Vanessa but was unsure how to assess Dominic Wright. He recalled the comment in the granite chamber about wall direction when Wright was slightly irritated. He didn't think Wright had the sort of scientific ability that Vanessa possessed. He wasn't sure of his background. He was about forty, well spoken. Could he be an ex-military officer?

The following day at Avon Mark showed the loose kaolinised granite to Dr Felicity Murchison the department's granite specialist. She said the Feldspar crystals had been only partly degraded and the sample was still gritty, rather than powdery. Not sufficient to affect foundations. That was roughly what Mark was expecting, but now he had a second opinion.

He'd also picked up several small pieces of granite from the floor of the chamber. One piece had visual signs of Cassiterite. When he put it through the Bench XRF it indicated Tourmaline rather than Cassiterite. Other elements were shown to be Silicon, with some Boron, Aluminium, and Magnesium.

From his photos of the four walls there was little evidence of hydrothermal veining. At least he had sufficient information to assure Vanessa that there were no structural problems. That would mean he had discharged his professional responsibilities. Would that be the end of his use by the security services?

Mark had plenty of work to do through the winter. It would probably be March next year before he and Graham Stanley would resume fieldwork. Getting the Penwith article finalised and submitted should be the priority. Then he could decide if there was any merit in publishing something for the Carnmenellis data. His personal life would be focused on Emma and preparing for her due date on 14th January.

Christmas was now less than three weeks away, so Mark anticipated there would be a shopping expedition that weekend.

The following Monday at Avon Mark had a number of e-mails that needed attention. There was also a Christmas card from Hannah at Miners Court, She now had a partner. Mark was pleased for her. He thought that would be useful for Emma to know; she might be less suspicious about Hannah's possible intentions towards Mark.

The e-mail that was most interesting was from Professor Zhou. He'd been set up at Denver with a new department dealing with mineral processing together with the funding to establish a similar building to what he had in Fudong. He was intent on replicating the various equipment. The building would be completed in May of next year, then he had a budget of 23 million dollars to equip it. That would be an eye watering amount for geology departments in Britain!

Zhou wanted to attract some of his technicians and PhD students from Fudong but that wasn't possible after his highly undiplomatic extraction. He was asking Mark and Richard if they could advise on suitable people that might be interested in working at Denver.

The e-mail from Richard was an agenda for a supervision meeting before Christmas.

Several e-mail flyers for conferences next year. One caught Mark's eye. It was a conference on rare earth *in situ* processing, based at Stockholm in July next year.

In the run up to Christmas Mark spent four days a week at Avon. He had a couple of sessions with Kevin Tranter to help him understand some of the chemistry queries he'd come across recently. The supervision meeting went well. Mark's plan to spend the next few months reading, and some work on chapters for his thesis, concurred with the suggestions of both of them. Richard took on the task of responding to Zhou. He would circulate some of his British contacts in economic geology with an outline of the invitation to work in Denver.

After the supervision meeting Richard phoned Mark and asked him to come over to his office. Apparently, Vanessa Wyndham had been to see Gordon and himself the previous Friday. It was strong advice on how to pursue their careers after the China event. No further trips to China for either of them. Academic relationships with Zhou could be continued but any travel to meet with him in Denver had to be notified in advance to a specific e-mail address at GCHQ. Richard said that secret services were aware that the Avon group had been messed about. Gordon had expressed the view with a much stronger verb. Vanessa had said there was no financial compensation for waste of professional time and damage to academic reputation. It was just one of those things. If the U.S. suggested a course of events, Britain tended to fall in line. She had confirmed the earlier opinion that Zhou would never be let out of the United States. Even his movement around the country would be closely shadowed. All that was for his own safety.

The Americans were obviously pleased to get him and imagined they would get ten years of valuable knowledge out of him. Zhou, or his new overseers, had already put up a page on a public web site of eight approximate locations in Africa and South America where there were known deposits of Monazite, both mineral veins and sedimentary sands. These were sites where Chinese survey teams had detected rare earth minerals, but were yet to approach the local governments to exploit the metals.

China had so much metal in store already and had scores of places around the planet which were being held in reserve. The disclosure of these vague locations was a piece of bait to attract U.S., European and Australian multi-nationals to contact Zhou. The deposits were real but the

GPS co-ordinates were coarse, only to a resolution of 8 km. All this was probably being co-ordinated by U.S. authorities. The Chinese would be unhappy, hence the need for travel caution for Avon staff who had been involved in the inappropriate extraction.

One of the office teams at GCHQ would be monitoring the consequences of the Zhou defection. The U.S. wanted to break the domination of rare metals by China. Britain and several European countries were notionally in agreement.

Richard went on to explain that Mark would still be monitored, for safety reasons, but would be "left alone" for a couple of years to complete his PhD. Vanessa Wyndham was likely to visit Mark in February to explain the importance of the strategy.

Mark went home decidedly uneasy. He felt there was an increasing level of control being exercised. He had been most grateful to be evacuated from Ecuador, and patched up, but it seemed that the "price" was rather high in terms of his own freedom. He decided not to relate his feelings to Emma. Not just because of her imminent launch into motherhood, but because he was unsure if he was being oversensitive.

# 23

Preparations for Christmas were now in full flow. Kathleen and Henry, Emma's parents, had invited Jennifer and Roger, Mark's parents, down for Christmas Day. Emma was more than happy with that. It would certainly mean that she had less tasks to do.

The Christmas season was leisurely with much small talk. It was certainly in the style of 50 and 60 year-olds. All four prospective grandparents were patiently awaiting 14th January.

There were a few outings to friends of their own age. Peter Robinson, Mark's school friend, and his girl friend Clare came down before New Year. Their news was interesting; an announcement of their engagement and the wedding scheduled for May 2021, eighteen months away. Afterwards, Emma remarked: 'Well I did throw my bouquet towards her, and she caught it.'

Emma tried to have a gentle walk around the village each day, when the weather wasn't too off-putting. The baby turned on Christmas eve. She was confident that things were progressing well.

Mark was settling into a routine of data analysis and map analysis through the morning, hoping to establish patterns. Afternoons were chapter writing, rather draft chapter writing.

Emma, now on maternity leave, was getting heavier. It was 7th January 2020 when an informal visit from the health visitor, just keeping an eye on things, turned up. Emma was on the standard list, hospital maternity ward, vaginal birth. During the brief conversation Emma revealed that her mother lived nearby and her husband was working from home over the final week. That generated a satisfactory response from from the health visitor.

14th January arrived, no indication of an imminent birth. They went to bed that evening; Emma wondering if her date was wrong. At 02.00 waters broke and contractions started. Mark got Emma up and into the truck. There was more room in there than in the Mini. Test drives had shown that he could drive to the hospital in fourteen minutes. Probably less in the middle of the night. The journey was going well, all the traffic lights were turning green. Another contraction in the truck. Mark had phoned the maternity ward and a porter was at the door with a wheel chair if needed.

There was a bed available and Emma was taken straight to a delivery room. It all happened rather quickly. At 06:20 on Wednesday 15th January 2020, baby Katherine Jennifer was born. Weight 3572 grams, or 7 lbs 14 oz for the grandmothers. All well, Emma glowing and happy, but exhausted. Mark was overwhelmed, he was now a Dad. He'd held Emma's hand throughout the labour. After all the usual procedures the midwife got Emma into bed and advised her to sleep for a while. The suggestion to Mark was go home, catch up on sleep. Visitors could come in during the afternoon.

Mark welcomed that suggestion. Emma was happy. Mark phoned both sets of parents with the news and suggested a visit at 16:00 might be best.

All medical checks on Emma and baby Katherine satisfactorily completed; no reason to keep them in hospital. Emma was discharged that evening. Mark drove them home, particularly carefully. Big Kathleen, Emma's Mum, stayed the night at their bungalow.

Emma revealed to Mark that she wanted the baby to be called Katy within the family. Not only was it a simple short form for a child to understand, but it would lessen the confusion when her Mum and the baby were in the same place.

Thursday and Emma was up and about in the kitchen. Feeding was going well and baby Katy was content. Mark was performing general dog's body roles: cleaning, cooking, shopping. Emma was alive with energy. That evening she was phoning her colleagues at school with her news.

Friday, the health visitor called and carried out her usual checks. She stayed for 30 minutes and watched Emma breast feeding. All good, she would drop in again in a few weeks.

Saturday was a dry, cold day, but no wind. The three of them went for a walk into the village. Katy was in a baby carrier on Emma's front and wrapped in Emma's coat. They were out for forty minutes and there wasn't a squeak from Katy, she slept all the way. Emma had given her a big feed before they set out.

Sunday evening Emma suggested to Mark that he could go up to Avon if he wanted. She would be perfectly happy at home and her Mum would come over if any help was needed. Mark went in mid-morning on Monday and stayed until 15:00. Margaret Rouse, and her girls in the departmental office, wanted all the details. Mark had already phoned Richard Ericson with the news. They'd visited Richard and his family just after Christmas. Many congratulations in the staff lounge at lunchtime. Mark had one or two things he needed to look up in the Map Room and the Library. Apart from that he hadn't done a great deal. He headed home to find Emma preparing dinner. She was full of energy. Katy was feeding and sleeping well. Kathleen had done some shopping and they'd all been for a walk. The big event was gently drifting back to family normality. Emma was taking it all in her stride.

Mark's work was progressing but he wasn't finding a significant difference in rare earth mineral proportions found in Cornwall to those found on Exmoor. There was the one small cluster of higher concentrations of rare earths in Penwith, but generally the amounts were quite low. Mining and processing small quantities would be costly and impractical. On site processing would have some economic advantages but the ground up waste rock would create problems for the landscape.

It was now the end of January. Mark had a chat with Richard Ericson whose view was that for the PhD research work it was still an important finding. If he was on a Chalco prospecting mission it would be a pack up and go home situation. No profitability, but for a piece of research it was perfectly valid.

Mark should put on his academic hat rather than a business hat. What he could investigate was at what level of rare earth occurrence, alongside traditional metals, was it realistic to entertain mining. That brought them onto the suitability of attending the on-site processing conference in July at Stockholm. Richard recommended that Mark should go.

On the following Monday Mark sent in his application for Stockholm. He submitted a provisional title "At what stage does in-situ processing become viable for low percentages of rare earth minerals?".

He had a couple of months to prepare that paper, which, if accepted, would go into the conference proceedings. Richard Ericson reminded Mark to also try and get at least one article, as first author, into a peer reviewed journal. The conference paper would provide some useful focus as Mark worked through his data. Whereas six months ago he was concerned that he didn't have much data, he now had plenty and from two distinct geologies. There were also the contrasting Austrian and Chinese data sets.

Mark was in regular contact with Graham Stanley about when they should attack the St Austell area and Bodmin Moor. They both wanted drier ground more than anything. Cold and wind on the day was less of a hindrance.

That weekend Emma wanted a day out, or a shortish day out, with Katy. Mark had fitted straps in both vehicles to hold the baby cot. For the first few months Emma had chosen a rear facing lie down type. The weather for Saturday looked reasonable so they drove to Minehead. Emma sat in the back seat of the truck where she could maintain eye contact with Katy when she was awake. Katy gurgling at her Mum. Emma was doing well with feeding and Katy was gaining weight to the satisfaction of the mother and baby clinic at the surgery. Weekdays, when Mark was at Avon, Kathleen drove over to be with Emma, and help out as needed.

On Monday there was another e-mail from Graham Stanley at Redruth Institute. How about two fieldwork days on Thursday and Friday this week. The weather was looking reasonable, and the ground was drying. Mark phoned Emma. She was quite happy, her Mum would come over to support her. Mark booked a guest house at Carlyon Bay.

Mark was in his office alone. Brian Porter was back in Wales. There was a knock on the door. It was Vanessa Wyndham. She said it was a general visit. No requests. She reiterated most of what Richard Ericson had told him before Christmas. She wouldn't be imposing on his good nature for the next two years. She was grateful for his help with the "chamber". It was Dominic Wright's project because of the liaison with military types. As Mark may have noticed, Dominic was a man of words and eloquence, not numbers. He was a little out of his depth on many technical matters.

She had looked into the ice melt problem and found a long established scientist working on Antarctic ice volumes. He showed her his current data on projected ice melt. There would be problems for many coastal cities, including London, but the amount of sea level rise over the next hundred years would not exceed a couple of metres, and that was his most extreme prediction. There could also be various feedback mechanisms which would reduce ice melt. One reason that some loud commentators had been getting carried away with exaggerated predictions was that they muddled sea ice melt with glacier ice melt. Melting sea ice does not change sea level, because it is frozen sea water.

As for the IPCC member that Dominic Wright had recruited, Vanessa went to see her and asked if she had any documentary evidence for her exaggerated assertions. That produced a fudged reply. It seems she was relating some of the wilder debates she had encountered on the Panel. She'd actually left the Panel in 2015.

The composition of the Intergovernmental Panel on Climate Change (IPCC) had included many perspectives and political appointments since it was formed in 1988.

Vanessa was obviously grateful that Mark had pointed her in a useful direction. She said Mark would get a Treasury cheque for his professional consultancy.

Mark commented: 'So you're not dropping me from your list, you're giving me a sort of sabbatical.'

Vanessa: 'Something like that. We always need people who we can trust.'

Mark: 'Well, thanks for letting me know.'

Vanessa: 'Congratulations, by the way, on the birth of your daughter.'

Mark: 'Thank you. You seem to know everything about our lives now.'

Vanessa: 'If GCHQ chooses to keep an eye on someone, everything that goes through their computer or phone is easily intercepted. You've got our American cousins to thank for those intrusive technologies. Most of the public are worryingly naïve about digital communications. If you want to keep a computer secure don't connect it to the internet and keep it in a lead lined cellar.'

Mark made no further comment, he just sighed. Vanessa Wyndham left with one of her slight smiles.

The update made Mark feel a little uncomfortable. Perhaps he would be left alone for a couple of years but it seemed that secret services didn't want to drop him. It would be his all pervading shadow. In some ways he was grateful for the alarm devices that he and Emma had been given but there was no guarantee that they would work, or resolve a problem. There were always too many unknowns in the secret world.

Mark discussed the situation with Emma when he got home that afternoon. Her perspective was not to worry about it, just get on with the PhD and re-assess the situation when he was finished. If the state wanted him to do other tasks he could always decline.

The next day he got his equipment ready for fieldwork with Graham on Thursday. Home life was different but Emma had everything under control. She was attending the mother and baby group and had made a friend; Sally Butler and her baby Jonathan, born the day after Katy. Had Emma stayed another night at the hospital she would have met her. Sally's husband, Simon, worked near the Yeovilton airbase in a special army section. It was a bit hush hush. Baby Jonathan was Sally's first child, so Emma felt she had common points for discussion.

Katy was sleeping through the night and both Emma and Mark were getting undisturbed sleep. Would it last? The family day was still early mornings and early to bed in the evening.

Mark worked at home on Wednesday and set off at 06:30 on Thursday to meet Graham near St Blazey. The collection of disused mines were on farmland or in woodland. They got challenged by a farmer. It was hard going. Quite a few adits and it wasn't clear what were spoil tips. The spoil at the mines around Penwith and on the St Agnes coast were the easiest to inspect. Graham had done quite a lot of research on old mine records held in the archives at the Redruth Institute. His view was that Penwith and St Agnes were the areas he wanted to pursue for Tin exploitation. Although Cornwall was considered a Tin mining area, many mines produced more Copper ore than Tin ore. Graham's interest was only the revival of Tin mining. Part of his current strategy was to exclude the Copper rich mines. Regenerating Copper production would not be as profitable as Tin. There were many more Copper mines around the world. Tin was highly regarded in the booming microelectronics industry. Because of the health problems with Lead based solder in the 20th century, the move to new solders had become necessary. Modern solders used in electronics were about 99% Tin.

Mark and Graham had a long discussion in a local pub at lunchtime. They had both benefitted from a grand tour of Cornish mining areas but their research interests were diverging.

Graham mentioned that the main topic of conversation at Jean's hospital was the new viral infection creeping around the world. Staff were wary but much more concerned at the muddle of information coming to them through official channels.

Thursday hadn't been a brilliant day for finding minerals. The weather forecast for Friday was much drier. They agreed to meet up at Minions village on the south eastern side of Bodmin Moor.

Because much of the area was on open moorland, access to spoil tips around Minions was easier. Both Copper and Tin were mined in the area for many decades. More Copper than Tin at many of the mines. Mark collected several bags of mineral samples and was finding that PIRSy was useful on the spoil tips. It was helped by a drying easterly breeze.

The total number of Cornwall samples Mark had taken now exceeded 120. He had plenty to work on. Most significant areas had been sampled. Historic estimates of the number of mines in Cornwall was in excess of a thousand. He drove back to East Quantock quite content.

On Saturday Mark did his usual domestic routines. Emma was only using her car for short journeys now so winter grime was much less. Mud splashes in the country lanes were evident so Mark still gave it a thorough wash.

Facial expressions from Katy were becoming quite common now when Mark read to her. On Sunday they all went for a walk, Katy snuggling into Emma and sleeping.

On Monday at Avon Mark had a reply from Stockholm. The title for the paper that he submitted had been accepted. He was required to send in the abstract by 24h April.

His main task for the week was analysing the St Blazey and Minions samples. He had almost full access to the Bench XRF but booking slots for the mass spectrometer over in chemistry were sparse. Many third year undergraduates needing analyses for their dissertations before Easter. The St Blazey area samples were not showing significant signals for metals using the Bench XRF. The spoil tips around Minions were showing evidence of Copper, Tin and a few rare earths. With a limited number of slots available on the mass spectrometer Mark reduced the samples he would take to analyse.

All the spreadsheet entering could be done at home. That would give him opportunities to see Katy during daytime and help Emma as well.

Grandma Kathleen asked them over for Sunday lunch. The weather was awful so it wasn't going to be a walk day. Kathleen raised the question of a date for Katy's christening. The lady vicar had asked her that morning. Emma said they would look at their diaries and select a date. It would probably be a Sunday afternoon.

On Monday Mark received a further iteration of the Penwith article back from Graham Stanley. He could work on that during the week as he was still waiting to get on the mass spectrometer.

Katy was becoming an active baby. She responded to stories and when someone interacted with her. She was feeding well with hardly any indigestion or gripe. Emma was producing plenty of milk and was mulling over the idea of going back to work after Easter. She could fill a couple of bottles each morning which would mean that her Mum, Kathleen, could feed her through the day. Emma would be away from home from just after eight in the morning until about half past four. She'd discussed the idea with her Mum and both thought it could work. The start of Summer Term was two months away and Kathleen suggested she held off announcing her decision for a few more weeks.

Mark and Graham were reaching consensus with the West Penwith article. Mark had also run it past Richard Ericson a couple of times. It was agreed that authors would be Graham Stanley, Mark Scott, John Shackleton, Richard Ericson, in that order. Mark was happy with that as Tin occurrence was the central theme, rare earths were secondary. Also, Graham would do the submission to a journal.

The following Monday Mark had a few samples he wanted to re-run through the Bench XRF. That took him the morning and confirmed an idea he was working on. At lunch he went to the staff lounge. The major talking point amongst the researchers was the developing infection risk. One of last Autumn's PhD intake had been on a ski-ing trip to Italy and was now in hospital in Turin with a severe chest infection. Her messages to one of her fellow students was that it was much worse than flu, although she was now off the ventilator.

With Cornwall field surveys having reached a partial completion, Mark was now clear to work on his paper for the Stockholm conference. He had to stick to the science fundamentals. If he adopted a conservation theme he wouldn't receive any serious recognition. His focus had to be on analysing ways of precision mining. That would involve reducing the gross excavation of rock. Precision mining wasn't the standard of many multi-national companies who would go in with big machinery and rip out potential ores. Throw it into a fleet of heavy lorries and send it off for processing.

Although Chalco left the assigning of mining contracts to the nations that commissioned their prospecting services, enquiries frequently came back from the mining companies who had purchased the licence. It was clear from those enquiries that the companies were run by money focused administrators. They wanted to invest the minimum on equipment and labour in order to achieve the highest profits. There was little understanding of the geology and how the ores were positioned in the ground. They just relied on heavy equipment and their technicians to get the ore out of the ground. At the point where the mine's reserves were showing a slight downturn the company would pull out and look for a new project. Even where a nation had issued a carefully worded licence contract, the departure of the company rarely complied with the spirit of the tidy up clauses. Third world countries were left with a mess and few legal opportunities to enforce the contract.

The problem for Mark was that he was trying to assert that better mining technologies were economically advantageous. He had to demonstrate that precision mining techniques were beneficial to the mining accountants as well as being ecologically sound. If he was trying to sell this to an aluminium or copper mining company it wouldn't work. There were still large resources of those metals all around the world. For rare earth minerals he might be able to advance a convincing argument.

Mark realised he needed to present some data on this sort of reasoning. He spent Tuesday in the Library and on the internet. He had found several papers on mining efficiency which he thought were close to his theories, but he remembered a slightly condemnatory phrase from Bernard Hosegood: "big mineral companies are now headed by faceless accountants who know little about geology or mining". Mark had to present a theme to his paper that kept solidly to the efficiency benefits of precision mining.

With COVID cases increasing in the world's media there was a risk that the Stockholm conference might not take place. Mark wasn't too concerned about that as he could submit his paper to a journal. At the present time the response of the British Government to rising infections was to deflect the idea of a pandemic. In some ways Mark could ride through the situation as he had his field data and could hunker down with his writing. He didn't need to meet many people face to face, and he could always use the video call option on his mobile phone.

At home, Emma already had infection control instructions from the surgery on how the mother and baby sessions would operate. Katy was progressing well and Emma was happy.

Mark worked from home for several weeks. He was absorbed in his work. The endless banter on the news about COVID was becoming more serious. It was clear that Members of Parliament and the usual pundits were not acquainted with science. A great deal of talking but it was clear that politicians were out of touch. Lockdowns had been declared in many countries and a statement from the World Heath Organisation on 11th March was that COVID was now a Global Pandemic. Air transport was being affected.

On Monday 23rd March a Lockdown was finally declared in the UK. That was due to start on Thursday 26th March at midday. Schools to close, people to stay at home unless their work was essential, and only short excursions out of home for food shopping and exercise. Hospitals were experiencing problems of insufficient bed space and not enough ventilators. Several thousand new cases of COVID and over a hundred confirmed deaths each day. The nation was approaching crisis. Communication by telephone and video calls were the main methods of human interaction.

There was no end in sight to the end of Lockdown. Case numbers of COVID, and deaths, were rising through Easter. Emma had phoned some of her colleagues from school. The Summer Term was going to proceed with sending work home for children by e-mail. The internet was already filling up with animated applications to assist youngsters with their studies. Teachers were working from home on their computers.

Richard had phoned Mark to say that he would have to work from home. There was a system where staff and researchers could book a slot to come into the Department, on their own, to collect materials. No contact with any other staff.

Mark had a couple of e-mails from Stockholm. The conference would probably not take place, unless they could arrange some sort of remote participation. He should still send in his abstract.

Zoom calls on people's computers or mobile phones were becoming widely adopted.

# 24

There was considerable public debate over what constituted a domestic residence and who could meet whom. Emma strongly asserted that Grandma Kathleen, her mother, was essential to the raising of Katy.

Case numbers of COVID were rising. By mid-April there were over 100,000, and hospitals were struggling. The shortage of ventilators was a worry, many older people were not surviving. Hospital staff were succumbing to the illness and deaths were occurring even among younger nurses and doctors. Although many of the population were working from home, hospital, transport and essential shop staff were badly affected. Many older people in those areas were resigning. Emma had decided to have all the family's groceries delivered but felt terrible for the people who were doing the deliveries. Emma's father, Henry, felt he needed to visit the shops to see what he was buying, particularly the fresh foods. By early May there had been 30,000 deaths.

The range of public grumbles was wide. From non-essential shops that were prevented from opening to medical staff who were highly critical of government, particularly over the lack of protective clothing. University students who had been sent home were vociferous over the retention of their student fees, and the poor quality of remote tuition.

There were "keep you going" financial handouts from Government but a great many families were in financial difficulty.

Towards the end of June case numbers in Britain had exceeeded 300,000. Almost everybody was aware of people who had the virus, and had heard of close neighbours who had died.

Unfortunately, on Thursday 25th June Grandad Henry, Emma's Dad, was taken ill. Kathleen had been living with Emma and Mark since Easter. Henry was admitted to hospital and put on a ventilator. The hospital wasn't able to accept any visitors. Kathleen was heartbroken. On Tuesday 30th June Henry died. Kathleen received a phone call from the hospital; she was devastated. She couldn't forgive herself for not being with him. Emma said she was inconsolable. What made it worse were the rigid funeral arrangements. Only close relatives allowed.

Mark looked after Katy while Emma and her mother went to the crematorium. They were joined by Brian, who had driven across from London, not knowing if he would be stopped on the motorway for being out of his home area. Was it an essential journey? He thought so. Emma and Kathleen sat together, many metres from the celebrant. Brian sat at the back. He wasn't going to get near his sister or mother. It was the most unnatural send off they could imagine. Brian kept his distance although exchanged a few words with his mother. This was difficult for Kathleen when all she wanted to do was hug her son. This was a time when the virus was particularly virulent. The three of them found the day incredibly difficult. Brian set off to drive home visibly upset. None of them had a chance for any words with Henry before his passing.

Back home Mark did his best to welcome and empathise with Emma and Kathleen. He made them a cup of tea. Katy had become rather grisly, but was calmed when her mother picked her up. Up until then the four of them had been isolated. They were just living a domestic life without any public interaction. Even on their short village walks they exchanged greetings with other villagers from opposite sides of the road. The day of Henry's funeral had cemented the seriousness of the COVID pandemic.

His demise had been so rapid. Kathleen was never going to forgive herself. She couldn't see it, but she had been an enormous support to Emma, and an important influence on Katy. Since April, when she became a "live in" Granny, she had phoned Henry twice a day, sometimes for nearly an hour, or until the phone battery gave up, but she felt terrible for not being with him.

The following weeks were strained. The family needed a holiday, but that wasn't possible unless they had a large camper-van. In the warmer summer days Mark insisted on a trip to the beach. Other families were adopting a similar patten of escapism, so selecting a beach with limited numbers was the key to sustaining a low risk outing.

As for Mark's work he was making good progress. Several chapters of his thesis were drafted and checked with Richard Ericson.

The Stockholm conference had been changed to a Zoom meeting. Not many delegates took part but he had some constructive comments when he delivered his paper. The organisers were still intent on a conference publication so Mark spent a week tidying up his paper, checking with Richard and submitting it.

He'd interspersed his reading and writing with a number of minor jobs around the bungalow. Also regular grass cutting and weeding. The garden was much larger than the miniscule front garden at their rented house.

Mark had several telephone conversations with Bernard Hosegood, Chairman, and Andrew Norris, CEO, at Chalco. The company had kept some work going. Most of their prospecting sites were a long way from habitation. The main problem for the Company was getting teams to and from sites. Countries across the world had differing health protocols for COVID. Australasia had been problematic to get in and get out. Work in Scandinavia had been encouraged. Some charter aircraft were available and some nations offered military assistance. The countries with low population densities, and government willingness to get Chalco teams into position, resulted in successful completion of their explorations. One team had been stuck in Australia for months, awaiting clearance to fly home.

Bernard asked Mark if he could do a Zoom seminar. Possibly a repeat of his Stockholm paper. Mark agreed. It was now late Summer and not much chance for safe use of air traffic, and not many services flying anyway. Chalco had sufficient financial reserves to be able to keep all its staff on the payroll for a year or so, even without government support. Various medical experts were on the media discussing the likely progress of the Pandemic. Some of the population were adapting their work life but others, particularly those with customer facing roles, were experiencing high risk lives.

Mark felt he was fortunate to be able to structure his own route through the PhD. Emma was in discussion with her school about returning, whether it was as an e-mail teacher or a classroom teacher. The facility of having her Mother at home was a huge benefit. It was also probably therapeutic for Kathleen after the loss of Henry.

# 25

The summer passed everyone by. Wealthy families had managed to take holidays abroad, and there were efforts by many to take holidays in Britain with self contained accommodation. Camper-van hire was popular. There was a lull in the number of new cases in July but Autumn brought another wave of infections. More and more families were sinking into financial problems. The winter months were difficult and Christmas arrangements were limited. The Pandemic was going to exceed a year. Some commentators were predicting it was going to last much longer than a year. Comparisons were made with the Spanish Flu outbreak of 1918-1920. Later research had shown the prefix Spanish to be a misnomer. It was considered that the Pandemic started in Kansas, U.S.A.

Mark made steady progress with his thesis write up. He was in regular e-mail and phone contact with Richard Ericson. Richard gently guided Mark away from the mineral processing route. His main point being that processing was a technology and he encouraged Mark to retain a scientific approach to his work. His abundant skills for finding minerals in the natural environment was his strongest attribute. If he moved his focus to enhancing mineral processing techniques he would be in the same world as industrial efficiency, subject to Taylorism and the steady march of management strategies.

Katy was an alert child. She enjoyed the days out in the summer, visiting the seaside and other scenic venues. The one thing that was lacking in her upbringing was mixing with children of her own age. For several weeks, through February and early March, Emma and Katy had met up with Sally Butler and her son Jonathan. That had dwindled although the two women were in regular contact via e-mail and messages. They had planned a day on the beach in July where they were going to site themselves clear of other children. That was postponed when Sally's husband, Simon, contracted COVID.

It was now early Autumn 2020 and prospects for the winter were not good. Infections were rising again. Mark realised he was now two years into his PhD programme. Opportunities for conferences and meeting up with other geologists working on rare earth minerals were limited. In his own mind he felt that he needed to revisit some of his earlier field sites and validate initial findings. Field visits were easy. He could do those alone, but safe access to the mass spectrometer at Avon was problematic. It wasn't impossible but health safeguards limited the time available.

Discussions with Richard Ericson and Kevin Tranter were quite encouraging for Mark. He was in a much better situation than many PhD students, particularly those that had started their programmes in Autumn 2019. They had intended to run fieldwork campaigns through the Summer of 2020, but that had proved difficult for many of them. Those needing overseas travel and accommodation were advised to adopt different projects.

By October of 2020 Mark had three journal publications, in print or accepted. Richard had asserted that Mark's methodology was sound and he should concentrate on finalising his thesis. It would have been satisfying to pursue some of the resulting observations but practicalities of the Pandemic meant that would have been difficult and unwise. Throughout the previous year Mark had established productive correspondence with several co-workers. He was also exchanging e-mails with Maria Weber. She had completed her contract with BMW and now had a geology lectureship in Vienna. Her specialism was still in rare earths, particularly the radioactive elements.

It seemed she was trying to rekindle Mark's interest. Mark was happy to sustain academic correspondence but in no way was he interested in any other interaction.

COVID hindered scientific meet ups so e-mails and video calls were becoming the communication standard. Mark was concerned that Maria was pursuing nuclear aspects of rare earth metals. Maria's interest in Promethium, a particularly rare element in the Lanthanide series, was worrying. Its availability was entirely dependent on the nuclear industry. It was difficult to find Promethium in the natural environment. It was known that scientists who worked with radioactive elements were prone to cancers, and it seemed that many workers became somewhat casual about the risks. Does familiarity breed contempt?

Correspondence with Maria was a digression. Mark had to sharpen his focus to his own work. Richard had made a comment recently, that had lodged in Mark's consciousness: "A doctoral thesis should be about new knowledge." It was certainly a maxim within the hard sciences and the viva process. Supervisors were responsible for ensuring that a candidate was living up to the maxim.

Mark wondered if the focus of his thesis was sharp enough. Should he drop the claim for on-site processing of mineral ores. It may have long term economic and ecological benefits but it was not his concern. He needed to ruthlessly analyse his large data set and present his findings. He had already shown that small quantities of rare earth elements were found in close contact with more common elements like Copper, Iron and Tin. Keeping to this central theme might be the best way to conclude his thesis. He needed to demonstrate that he was dedicated to exhausting the data rather that diverging into, possibly valid, but separate ideas.

He remembered his uncle Dr Simon Jennings uttering that same phrase during his undergraduate days, "make sure you exhaust your data". He knew that Richard Ericson and Bernard Hosegood were firmly backing and encouraging his enthusiasm but he now needed to show solid focus to his work. Leave the loose ends for another day and stick rigidly to producing a conclusive thesis.

Perhaps a phone call to Uncle Simon might be a valuable. It would also be a courtesy to someone who had supported his academic career for so long. Mark hadn't seen his Uncle since the meeting at Weston over two years ago. A face to face meet-up wasn't possible during the ongoing pandemic but a video call was easily arranged. He sent an e-mail to suggest such a call.

Mark was trying to firmly root himself in data analysis at home, and writing and rewriting chapters for his thesis. He forced himself into only visiting sample sites to validate earlier findings. He valued visits to the mass spectrometer at Avon. Emma realised the change in Mark's work routine. She knew he was most happy when he was out in the field, but the necessity to complete his thesis was now his sole priority. The opportunities to interact with young Katy at home were a bonus. Both Emma and Grandma Kathleen assisted in this by stressing how valuable Mark was in Katy's development. Fortunately, the family situation was congenial in the small two bedroom bungalow.

It was a long winter. Christmas 2020 was different. There was no link up with Mark's parents. Just phone calls. It was only the four of them in the bungalow. Little different to the rest of the Autumn and early Winter. Emma tried to build up her Mum Kathleen. She realised that life without Henry left a big void. Katy was a delightful focus for Kathleen. She read to her, sang to her, tried to do artwork on the floor. Katy was crawling and realising that she could move around the bungalow.

Kathleen was doing the shepherding for most of the time that Katy was awake.

Emma's brother Brian came down to his parents bungalow on Boxing Day. He stayed for ten days. He made several visits to see Emma, Mark, and his Mum. He picked the dry days when they could all meet in the garden. Brian had a key task to perform. Henry's boat had been craned out at Watchet harbour at the end of the Summer. He knew that there was no interest within family to keep it and use it so he was working on a plan to sell it.

As for the family bungalow, Brian did some cleaning and garden tidying, but its future occupation was held in abeyance. He could see that his Mum was happy in her role as Katy's live-in nanny. He realised that he may need to put it on the market eventually, but now was not an appropriate time to raise the matter. He had several discussions with Emma about the possibilities, but neither of them were ready to raise the matter with their Mum.

Mark agreed with Emma and Brian's plan. He knew how valuable Kathleen was in Katy's upbringing. Letting things progress gently was the only practical option during this difficult time for everyone. Keeping the home free of COVID was crucial.

Into January 2021 and Mark's write up of his thesis. Having accumulated a considerable data set he realised he was in a much better position than many other geology research students. For the purposes of writing up and completing his PhD he had completely dropped the digressions into on-site processing. It actually helped him to focus on a sharper title objective. Responses on each chapter coming back from Richard Ericson, his principal supervisor, were positive.

Mark was also fortunate in seeing the article with Graham Stanley in print.

The chapters on data analysis in Mark's thesis were a bit of a challenge. He found a lot of help on line for graphical representation and statistical analysis. He was also in quite regular contact with his uncle Simon Jennings. Mark made a few repeat visits to sites on Exmoor and Cornwall to check data. That was during March and April 2021.

Richard Ericson made a tentative date for a viva in September. He had two external examiners lined up but hadn't disclosed their names to Mark. Whether it would be examination by video call, or a traditional face to face day, would need to be decided later in the Summer, taking into account health security advice and the current policy of Avon University. That meant a submission date of mid-Summer. Mark was happy with that.

If everything went to plan then he would have completed inside three years. Mark realised that Richard would have discussed this with Bernard Hosegood. Normally he could have resumed work with Chalco in the Autumn, and get the promised salary increase. He knew that prospecting work had been affected by COVID. Chalco still had a team stuck in Australia. Richard had discussed all this with Mark and said that he could be used in the department for six months working on video teaching materials for undergraduates.

The year advanced slowly. Britain was a two lifestyle society. Those whose occupations were face to face and those who could "work from home". The latter had far less occurrences of COVID. Mark was in this group.

As the year of 2021 progressed the vaccination programme was beginning to have an effect on infection rates. In the Autumn of 2020 Mark hadn't been asked to spend a week at the Chalco offices in Guernsey. With a lessening of COVID infections more work places were trying to get their staff back into normal attendance at work sites.

Government health officials were beginning to feel that the disease was moderating. More and more people were surviving infections.

Mark submitted his thesis at the end of July. Richard sent off copies to the examiners. Mark was still waiting to hear who the examiners would be, but there was silence on that matter!

Emma had finished the Summer term at her school, fortunately without catching COVID. She came up with the idea of hiring a camper van. A ten day visit to Pembrokeshire was planned. Katy was now eighteen months old, a mobile toddler and talkative. Kathleen wished them well but said she would like a quiet time at home. She was tiring by early evenings and thought a rest would do her good.

The holiday had mixed weather but proved successful. Both Mark and Emma enjoyed their first real holiday since the birth of Katy. Paddling in the sea was a delightful experience for Katy. They managed to find small campsites and kept themselves away from crowds. Mark found his true vocation as a child carrier slave. Katy was gaining weight! They did a walk most days and Mark got to explore a few slate quarries on the coastal footpaths.

Back home a formal letter from Avon was waiting in their pile of post. The date of Mark's viva was set for Friday 17th September 2021. The external examiners would be Professor Dougal McNeish from Scotland and Professor Lars Ahlqvist from Sweden. The venue was to be in the admin building at Avon, health precautions permitting, otherwise by video.

With that news Mark immediately sent e-mails with the news to his Uncle Simon at Aberystwyth and Bernard Hosegood in Guernsey.

Katy was happy and smiling to be back with her Grandma. Kathleen had benefited from a quiet ten days.

Emma knew that Mark would be intensely researching the two external examiners. That would occupy him for a couple of days at least, but he had nearly five weeks to wait for his viva. Perhaps this was a good time to suggest some domestic improvement activities. The garden furniture in the back garden, that Brian had brought over from the family home, had proved a great success for afternoon tea parties. It had enabled outdoor social get-togethers in a difficult year. Emma gently suggested to Mark that an area of paving on the edge of the rear lawn would be a distinct advantage, particularly as a dry base for the garden furniture. As it would replace some of the lawn there would be a small benefit in reducing the area of lawn that needed cutting. Emma knew that lawn mowing was not high on Mark's list of preferred gardening!

The three of them discussed the possible project later that evening, after Katy had settled. Mark could sense that there was a hint of collusion between Emma and Kathleen. Now that Katy was mobile it would be lovely for her to have an outdoor space to play in winter when the grass would be damp. The project was growing! Gentle expressions of interest and ideas developed into a patio occupying a third of the rear lawn. The women had succeeded! Mark had warmed to the idea, and was happy to tackle the project. He was keen on the idea of a play area for Katy, possibly a swing and a paddling pool. Kathleen finalised the ideas by saying she would pay for the paving stone and other materials. She also would like to see Cotswold stone slabs rather than concrete ones.

Emma was quietly pleased with the whole idea. It would keep Mark busy for several weeks. Just what he needed prior to his viva.

The following day Mark had replies from his e-mails. Generous résumés from Uncle Simon and Bernard on the two examiners. Both replies stressed the purpose of the viva. Not just an assessment of the quality of Mark's work but an opportunity to discuss ideas within a party of academic equals.

Mark's Uncle Simon phoned that evening. He reiterated the contents of his e-mail and encouraged Mark to relax, take some time off, and then just read through his thesis a few days before the viva so he was ready to respond to questioning.

The patio project was a useful diversion. Mark measured the site. Checked it with Emma and made a list of the materials he would need. Fortunately the back garden was nearly flat.

Katy was fascinated watching her Daddy working on the patio. She wanted to help. Equipped in sun hat, swimming costume and tiny wellies she took delight in wielding the hosepipe. Making big puddles where Mark was working was not a great help, but he was happy to tolerate his earnest helper. The whole project took three weeks, but that was interspersed with visits to the beach. The patio inauguration was timed to coincide with a visit from Brian. That included the grand opening of Katy's swing and paddling pool. Katy loved anything that included water.

There was a bit of a lull in the COVID pandemic but the resulting lack of caution from the less well informed was sufficient to maintain the spread of the virus. At the end of August Emma wasn't sure what the Autumn Term at school would bring. She prepared for pupils working at home as well as traditional classroom lessons. Kathleen could be back to full time child minding.

The big day arrived for Mark. He set off with a huge hug from Emma, and a hug from Katy. Richard Ericson had already briefed Mark on the protocols and format of the day. The COVID precautions involved wide seating positions. Everyone present had taken a home COVID test. All were negative.

The examiners had received their copies of the thesis five weeks earlier. They turned up with multiple pieces of paper sticking out the top of the volume. At Richard's suggestion Mark had edited the thesis to 160 pages. Massive tomes were not encouraged. Never mind the quality, feel the width, was not a wise strategy. Textual waffling didn't fit well with scientific arguments.

The viva started at 10:00. Mark was congratulated on his work by both external examiners early in the procedure. What followed was a detailed discussion of his findings. Mark was also encouraged to develop his ideas surrounding on-site processing of minerals because of the general conclusion that rare earth minerals were often found in small quantities. At 13:10 Professor Lars Ahlqvist, whose English was perfect, looked towards Professor McNeish and said: 'Gentlemen, I think we can say that Mark Scott has made a more than acceptable completion of his research degree, in difficult times. The thoroughness of his field techniques, fortunately undertaken mostly before lockdown limitations, is a great credit to him. It has been an honour and a pleasure for both of us to develop various themes with him today. We recommend a pass of distinction quality.'

Mark breathed a sigh of relief. There were several small corrections and advisories, and a few typos. These were set out on a sheet of A4. The meeting broke up with Richard saying to Mark: 'That was first class, I'll phone you about 19:00 this evening. Go home and relax, and give my best wishes to Emma.'

Mark drove home and gave Emma, and Katy, big hugs: 'Thank you for supporting me, darling.'

Phone calls, with his result, to his parents in Stroud, his Uncle Simon at Aberystwyth, and Bernard Hosegood in Guernsey. Mark was on an unusual high. Three years of intensity, not to mention a variety of unexpected hiccups. Richard phoned at 19:00 as arranged: 'I expect you're relieved.'

'Yes, it's sinking in slowly, Emma's pleased, and relieved.'

Richard summarised the comments of McNeish and Ahlqvist: 'They were impressed with your work, just from your thesis. The opportunity to meet you at the viva and discuss many aspects was a welcome interlude in their careers. The question of whether or not you had achieved an adequate standard didn't even arise. It was a refreshing experience for them both, and I must add my own congratulations. It's been a pleasure for me, and a useful addition to my career, over the last few years.'

'Thanks Richard, you have been a great help throughout. I can't thank you enough.'

'We'll catch up sometime next week, but it looks like Chalco are happy to let you stay with Avon until the end of the year. Give yourself a week or so to do the corrections and typos and get your final thesis printed and deposited with the Library. You'll need eight fully bound copies. That includes one for you and one for your Uncle Simon. After that we'd like you to work on some teaching materials for the department. Some of that is to cover possible lockdowns again this winter.'

# 26

A lot had happened in Mark and Emma's life over the last three years. Near death experience, twice. Marriage. Change of home. Birth of Katy. Pandemic upheavals. Loss of Emma's Dad. Mark realised how fortunate he was to have completed almost all his fieldwork and data gathering before the lockdowns.

Mark drove up to Avon on Monday 20th September to do the edits to his thesis. Not many people around. Students scheduled to return in the following week. COVID arrangements still not completely finalised and younger people still not fully vaccinated. Most adults had been vaccinated earlier in the year.

At home on Tuesday the postman arrived. A letter from Guernsey, addressed to "Dr Mark Scott".

Mark opened it. It was, as expected, from Andrew Norris, Mark's boss at Chalco. It started with hearty congratulations. Then details of contractual aspects for the next few months.

Mark's return to Chalco employment would start on 1st October, only nine days away. There was a significant pay rise, and a change of job title to "Senior Geologist". Because of Pandemic arrangements at Guernsey, many staff were still working from home, Mark could stay at Avon on an academic secondment basis. Mark's next field deployment was unlikely to be able to start until late Spring of 2022.

They key paragraph was:

We are currently in discussions with the Danish government for a prospecting assessment of rare earth minerals in South West Greenland. Chalco would like you to undertake and lead the project. It may be late April or May 2022 before we can establish a base, and it is likely to be a fourteen week deployment on Greenland followed by two three day weeks at Guernsey.

There were several other details, but Mark would be working from Avon for a few days a week until Christmas. There would also be a few visits to Guernsey as well. The Greenland project was a prestigious opportunity for a recently qualified PhD still in his twenties.

Emma read the Chalco letter: 'That could be quite a challenging exploration. They're obviously backing your experience and judgement. Anyway, tomorrow is your 29th Birthday, so we're having a special tea party on the new patio. Katy helped me make you a cake at the weekend, and your Mum and Dad are coming down to see you as well.'

Wednesday Mark went up to Avon for the morning. He'd nearly finished the minor edits to his thesis. He bumped into Richard in the staff lounge at coffee time: 'It looks like South West Greenland next summer.'

Richard responded: 'That sounds exciting, perhaps you can come back in the Autumn next year and do a research seminar for us.'

'I'll let you know. It's not fully confirmed yet.'

Mark got back home by mid afternoon. His Mum and Dad arrived. Then Emma got back from school. Jennifer, Mark's Mum, said: 'I've brought you a different sort of Birthday present this year. As you know, I've been working on the family history for several years. With all the lockdowns we've had I thought it was a good opportunity to put it all together in a photo book. This is an account of your ancestors and your family up to, and including, Katy. Happy Birthday Mark, we're very proud of you.'

'Thanks, Mum that's incredibly kind, I'll treasure it.'

'Your Dad helped a lot too.'

At the appropriate moment, Katy and Emma disappeared to the kitchen. Katy re-appeared pushing the tea trolley with Mark's Birthday cake, candles lit: 'Happy Birthday Daddy!'

It was a grand occasion. Mark was quite emotional. He knew how much the PhD had levered him away from family activities. He hadn't met up with his parents for five months. It was a pleasant evening in the garden, quite a useful location in times of infection risk. His Mum and Dad didn't leave until the light was fading.

The following morning he went up to Avon and had a long chat with Richard. Bernard Hosegood had made an informal arrangement with Gordon MacPherson for Mark to stay on at Avon to research Greenland in exchange for some undergraduate teaching materials. No one knew how the forthcoming winter would be for COVID infections.

The other matter that Richard revealed was that two staff would be leaving the department at the end of December; financial cutbacks. Gordon MacPherson was hoping that two of the older members of staff might take up the offer of early retirement.

Mark felt he was in a more assured career situation, for a couple of years at least. He had been asked to attend at Guernsey in October to flesh out the emerging Greenland project. Well spaced, face to face meetings with Andrew Norris and Bernard Hosegood, and also with the remote sensing team. When Andrew Norris had firmed up the contract with the Danish government there would be video calls with their civil servants and minerals department. Depending on the course of the Pandemic through the winter there would probably be a meeting in

Copenhagen next March. Details were still being negotiated. The Greenland project was almost certain to go ahead in some form.

When Mark worked under David Gresham he was involved in the preparation of four projects so he knew how the Guernsey based preliminaries operated.

Had there not been a Pandemic, Mark would be working in Guernsey from 1st October, with flights back to Bristol each weekend.

After the high of his PhD completion, Mark needed to tidy up some other aspects of his life. Chalco had told him to hang on to the truck and the company credit card through the winter. Next year the truck would need to be sold. Emma's Mini needed an upgrade. A slightly larger functional vehicle for transporting Katy and Emma's Mum on shopping trips was the objective. They decided they would get a four door hatch back of some sort.

The next few days at home without thesis commitments was quite a change for Mark. Emma was working back at school but wondering if another lockdown might close schools during the winter. Kathleen was *de facto* Nanna to Katy, an arrangement that was working well.

On Friday 1st October Mark made a point of going up to Avon. He'd arranged to meet Richard Ericson to get details of the department's expectations for the next three months. He spent the afternoon in the Map Room and the Library to beef up his knowledge of Greenland, particularly the geology of South West Greenland. Quite a lot of journal articles, although many rather dated. Not many maps. Mark realised that the more up to date material was on the internet.

The work for Avon would involve developing teaching materials for first year undergraduates. The topics would be the full spectrum of economic geology. Much of that was in his head but he would need to check out current facts and figures. The other aspect was back up for

Richard Ericson when students came knocking on doors for answers to queries.

Mark went home that evening, thinking that he needed to make his weekends, while he was home based, totally focussed on the family. This Sunday was taking Katy to a local petting farm where she could hold the animals. Kathleen, since coming to live with them, was quite insistent that their days out with Katy should be just the three of them. She actually treasured the time of being at home on her own; she would get a rest!

The following week Mark received details from Andrew Norris about a three day visit to Guernsey on Monday 18th October. The e-mail was copied to Richard Ericson.

That weekend would be just home and family. Katy was now 21 months old. She was taking in everything on the weekend days out and insisted she wanted to walk, holding Mummy and Daddy's hands. She would exhaust herself and fall asleep in the child seat on their way home. Mark found the family weekends relaxing. He would would miss them when he was away on explorations. The Greenland one was going to be longer in duration than any he had undertaken so far.

Monday, Emma drove Mark to Bristol Airport before driving to her school. Mark landed in Guernsey at 11:30 and got the minibus to the hotel, where he was scheduled to have lunch. He walked to Chalco for the first meeting at 14:00. A warm welcome from Rosemary de la Mare at reception. Andrew Norris came out of the boardroom and greeted Mark: 'Today we're having a briefing from the remote sensing team, tomorrow will be organisational and logistical matters.'

Mark knew the remote sensing group quite well from previous exploration briefings. The briefing ran for over two hours. A thirty minute history and geography of Greenland, then a detailed physical geography of Danesfjord. That included the rock structure of the possible rare earth mineral intrusions, and the proposed base camp area. This was all new to Mark. He was aware of growing interest in South West Greenland; a coastal strip clear of the Greenland Ice Sheet. It comprised many fjords and was only sparsely vegetated. Nearly all of Greenland not covered by permanent ice sheet is classified as a tundra biome. Permafrost at Danesfjord is not as prevalent as many parts of the coastal margins because of proximity to the Labrador Sea. The winters are still quite severe so geological work is confined to the shortish summer.

The name Danesfjord was a project name for the area under investigation. It was to be used for all the Chalco involvement. Explanation for the decision would become clear at the Tuesday meeting. Mark was given a large folder with all the geotechnical information. Andrew Norris wound up the briefing and thanked the remote sensing group for their detailed work.

The group left, leaving Mark and Andrew Norris in the boardroom. Andrew said: 'Mark, I'll leave you to peruse the folder this evening. Tomorrow will be the main meeting in which all the organisational aspects will be outlined. I'd like to extend my personal congratulations on completion of your PhD. I understand it was a sound piece of work. Well done. We'll meet here again tomorrow at 09:00'

Andrew left. Mark had sixty three pages of maps, charts, graphs, and text to study. He was now back in the real world of work. Expectations of him might be higher now that he had been appointed Senior Geologist. After ten minutes thumbing through the folder he decided to walk back to the hotel, have a swim, then dinner, then study the impressive document. On his way out, a quick chat with Rosemary who wanted to know all about Emma and baby Katy. After the chatter Rosemary finished with: 'Good luck with your technical briefing document; Chalco's got high hopes for you now. You'll know more in the morning.'

After dinner Mark went up to his room to study the document. It was detailed, nothing that Mark didn't understand, but an illuminating geological insight to the ancient rocks of South West Greenland.

# 27

Next morning at breakfast Mark noticed two people, a man and a woman, both in their fifties, seated at a table close by. They were looking across at him occasionally. He wasn't able to hear their discussion, but he had the impression they weren't speaking English.

It was a dry, cloudy morning so Mark walked across to Chalco after breakfast. He was four minutes early, Rosemary greeted him and said he could walk straight in to the board room. Several people already seated. Andrew Norris and Bernard Hosegood standing at one end talking quietly. Name cards around the table. Mark sat down at his place and turned his name card around. It said Dr Mark Scott, Senior Geologist, Chalco. The card on his right hand side had the name Naomi Dawson, British Government.

At 9 o'clock, on the dot, Andrew Norris sat down and opened the meeting: 'Ladies and Gentlemen, welcome to Chalco, and to the first full meeting of the Danesfjord Project. This meeting is confidential, other members of the Chalco staff are not privy to our discussions and decisions. I'd like to start by asking all of you to give a brief résumé of your role in this Project. I'm Dr Andrew Norris, CEO of Chalco. Can we proceed clockwise around the table.'

'Professor Bernard Hosegood, Chairman of Chalco, semi-retired academic geologist, mostly in Canada.'

Andrew Norris: 'The empty chair is for Dr David Gresham who will be with us this afternoon. He's my deputy and deals with organisational matters here in Guernsey, and communications with our various field teams. He's been a Senior Geologist with the company for many years.'

'Naomi Dawson, Mineral resources security for the British Government.'

That was a change, no longer Vanessa Wyndham.

Mark wasn't sure how he should describe himself. He thought he should keep it brief: 'Mark Scott, Senior Geologist at Chalco with specific interests in Rare Earth mineral detection.'

'Professor Anton Rasmussen, Economic Geology Consultant to the Danish Government.'

'Astrid Larsen, I'm the equivalent of what is termed a civil servant in Great Britain. My responsibility is Greenland and Faroes Liaison for the Danish Government, as well as the European Union.'

Andrew Norris: 'Thank you everyone. The genesis for this, the Danesfjord Project, comes from the wish of the Danish Government to establish a European expertise in searching for, and the exploitation of, Rare Earth elements. I'd like to invite Astrid Larsen to expand on the Project's aims.'

Astrid Larsen: 'Thank you Dr Norris. First, I wish to present a short history of the Danish-Greenland relationship. Greenland and the Faroe Islands are sovereign territories of Denmark. We have legal and ethical responsibilities to Greenland. The territory of Greenland achieved Home Rule in 1979, although Denmark retains control of security, foreign affairs and military issues. Further self rule was ceded to Greenland following a referendum in 2008. My Government is fronting a European funded campaign to bring Rare Earth minerals to European based companies for processing into metals required by scientific and industrial sectors . . . '

Astrid Larsen was keen to present the Danish perspective in great detail. Her English was perfect. She held the topic for over forty minutes.

It was informative, but it wasn't really moving into the geological aspects. The marker that she had tried to establish was that she was intent on holding final control on how the exploration would proceed.

At 09:55 the refreshment trolley arrived.

Andrew Norris interrupted: 'Thank you Ms Larsen. We'll break for ten minutes.'

Coffee and Danish pastries; the latter were not normally on the trolley; usually it was digestive biscuits. Bernard Hosegood went across to talk with Professor Rasmussen. Andrew Norris used his diplomatic skills to engage with Ms Larsen. She seemed to think she was going to have the floor for most of the morning.

Naomi Dawson had quiet words with Mark. She explained the reversion of her name to Naomi Dawson was because of her previous visits to Chalco in 2018 and 2019: 'It will become clear as the day proceeds that this Project is sensitive as well as being somewhat confidential. There will be portions of the British political classes uneasy with our involvement in European projects. Brexit is already being seen as a bad move in some parts of Whitehall. The civil service quietly take a longer view on matters of economic importance. I don't see my role in this one as keeping you from attacks on your life, more a case of veering domestic political campaigns away from Chalco. You already know we value your Company's activities. Congratulations, by the way, on the award of your PhD.'

Mark: 'Thank you. I intend to make minimal remarks this week, I need to listen more than talk.'

Naomi: 'That's probably a wise strategy.'

Andrew Norris went back to his seat, the others followed: 'Ladies and gentlemen, we'll have another break at 11:15, then break at 12:30 for lunch. A minibus will take us across to the hotel, or you can walk, if you prefer. I'd like to continue proceedings by asking Professor Rasmussen to develop the geology, ecological and social implications of the Project. Professor Rasmussen.'

'Thank you Dr Norris. You'll all be aware of the presence of many metals in the exceptionally old rocks of South West Greenland. There has been some planning in the way that the Naalakkersuisut (Greenlandic Government) resources department have granted licences to mine for metallic ores, but it has become increasingly important that licence allocation must be tightened for economic, ecological and social reasons. Mining multi-nationals have become larger in recent years and subject to intense political and economic pressures. Countries with the greatest persuasive power are the U.S. and China. The reason for this Project is to protect Danish sovereign territory from exploitation and enable the European Union to gain influence in world metal markets.'

At that point Rasmussen paused for questions. Most of the questions surrounded ecological and pollution control. After about ten minutes Rasmussen continued: 'Thank you for those questions. I'm pleased to see you're all keen to see a clean operation of the Danesfjord Project. In contrast to many metal extraction mines, Rare Earths present considerable problems of what is commonly known as spoil. Approximations indicate that for every tonne of metal, or its metal oxide, there can be as much as a thousand tonnes of waste material. If we intend to bring Rare Earth metals to Europe we need to leave the waste material *in situ*. Crushing and other methods of separating the valued mineral from the waste mean that the waste is usually fine particles. Keeping that from water courses and the coastline is essential if we are not to pollute the environment. As you know, Greenland's economy is based on fishing. If the Project results in any damage to the marine environment it will be an "own goal". The nations principal industry will be harmed and probably unable to fully recover.'

Mark interrupted: 'Professor, there are examples of mineral mines being packed with their own waste material. Costs are variable but it does mean that waste material is not transported around the world, or left in the environment to pollute.'

Rasmussen: 'I'm aware of those examples. What we need for Danesfjord is an efficient, low pollution industrial unit close to whatever mines are cut into the rock. You'll be aware that Danesfjord is formed of ancient crystalline rock. When you study local maps of the area you'll notice that the area defined has a Greenlandic name. For political reasons we'll continue to refer to it as Danesfjord.'

Professor Bernard Hosegood interrupted: 'Professor we've seen over ten years of metal mining further down the coast from Danesfjord. Is there any Chinese involvement with those operations?'

Rasmussen: 'Yes, there is. Financially small, but they are there, although the operations are managed by the usual Western multi-nationals.'

Hosegood: 'Is the Danish government happy with the existing operations?

Rasmussen. 'Not entirely, the Naalakkersuisut appear less keen to question these multi-national operations. The money they receive is useful to their economy. What we cannot know for sure is the extent of any personal inducements. The intention of the EU and the Danish Government is to have an exemplar operation. The indigenous communities are sparse in South West Greenland. If we can win them over by focusing on ecological and social issues we may win the economic and ethical arguments.'

Andrew Norris posed a question: 'How long will the EU fund this Project?'

'We have thirty-four million Euro over three years, with the largest slice in the first year to cover setting up a field base.'

Andrew Norris: 'Will the funding continue after three years?'

Rasmussen: 'Yes, in one of two ways. If your Company's prospecting concludes nothing worth developing there will be a clean up and restoration grant of several million. However, if the prospecting results indicate substantial reserves then a processing unit will be funded, with a claw back agreement based upon the sales of metals into Europe.'

Andrew Norris: 'Even if we find substantial reserves there is always the reality that they will be finite. What will be the view of the EU if the extent of mining is less than ten years?'

Rasmussen: 'I don't think I can answer that one at the moment.'

Astrid Larsen: 'Denmark will continue to support Greenland in any way we can. Hopefully, we will have established a mining industry concept within the local community. Long term we hope to diversify the Greenlandic economy. Currently, ninety per cent of national income comes from fishing. By example, we aim to demonstrate that diversification will have long term advantages for the territory. As for finite resources, we know that is a risk, but with the vast amount of still untapped minerals in South West Greenland we believe that mining has a promising future.'

The meeting continued with the mix of politics. Andrew Norris was hoping to get down to the mechanics of how the Chalco team was going to get established on the ground next Spring.

The bureaucratic aspects were still being raised and sustained by Astrid Larsen after the second coffee break. Naomi Dawson and Professor Rasmussen were both trying to gently subdue her repetition of points already discussed. Across at the hotel for lunch Andrew Norris sat adjacent to Astrid Larsen. Bernard Hosegood continued his discussions with Professor Rasmussen; the two were clearly of a similar mind.

Naomi Dawson sat with Mark assuring him that practicalities would be addressed that afternoon.

After lunch Andrew Norris made sure that Astrid Larsen was put in the minibus. He announced that he would walk back to Chalco. Bernard Hosegood, even though his knee was hindering his walking, joined him. Andrew sent a short text to Rosemary.

> We're walking back. Astrid Larsen is in the minibus. Can
> you engage her in any general chatter for twenty minutes.

Andrew decided to put David Gresham in the chair for the afternoon session. Andrew would listen in from his office. He hoped that Ms Larsen could be cooled from the politics and that David Gresham would stick solidly to setting up the field base.

Back in the board room with David Gresham in the chair. He'd been briefed. He opened the session: 'Welcome back everyone. I'm Dr David Gresham, deputy CEO, responsible for field logistics. I'll continue from where I left off from my meeting with the Danish Navy in September. An auxiliary naval vessel will helicopter in four timber buildings, each weighing about 9 tonnes. They will be kitchen, male accommodation, female accommodation, and a laboratory. Each building will be fully equipped. The heavy lift helicopter will then transport the mining equipment and site vehicle. Marines will ensure that the four timber buildings are firmly positioned on the chosen site.'

Gresham then put up a slide of the site area; an aerial photo with overlain contours. The site was on a low level col between two 200 metre knolls. Both knolls were rounded, heavily glaciated bedrock, free of soil and vegetation. The col was wide and near level with some grass on a thin soil covering. It was 20 metres above fjord sea level. The Marines would also be tasked with laying an alkathene water pipe to the buildings from a substantial stream two kilometres away. A hundred and eighty square metres of solar panel would be set up, linked to a six tonne battery block.

All that sounded impressive but in reality it would only supply sufficient energy for modest cooking in the kitchen and a protected supply to the laboratory. It wouldn't supply much heating, although probably enough for hot showers each day.

Gresham took questions.

Mark Scott: 'How do we get to the field base.'

Gresham, looking directly at Professor Rasmussen: 'Professor, can you explain the transport provisions?'

Professor Rasmussen: 'Yes, Dr Gresham. The Marines will take the auxiliary vessel up into the fjord, close to the field base. This will be about two weeks prior to installing the Chalco party. The heavy lift helicopter with take the four timber buildings ashore and settle them on prepared bases. The services to the buildings will be connected. When complete the vessel will return to the quay near Narsarsuaq Airport. The Chalco team will fly into the airport, either direct or via Nuuk Airport. The Chalco team will be taken by sea on the auxiliary vessel to the field base at Danesfjord. That's a voyage of about 200 kilometres. The vessel will organise an airlift of you and your equipment. The vessel will remain on standby for several days to ensure the field base is functioning safely. For the remaining part of the summer you'll have two pilots, an engineer and a four seater helicopter to do any local movements. They will have a supply of JetA1 fuel for the helicopter and petrol for the rubber boat. Denmark will be providing a competent chef for the duration of the exploration. The kitchen building will have well stocked freezers.'

Gresham interrupted: 'Can you explain the purpose of the boat?'

Rasmussen: 'Local use only in the fjord. Limited range because the two engines are thirsty. It will enable sediment sampling from the bed of the fjord.'

Gresham: 'Thank you Professor. I'll turn to communications now. Chalco will be sending two satellite phones, for emergency use and to enable data transmission back to Guernsey. The small helicopter will be able to communicate with Narsarsuaq Airport. That might necessitate taking to the air as the Airport is over 100 km away.'

Mark Scott was beginning to appreciate the scale of this operation. Much of the EU budget would be going on transport and the establishment of a field base. Andrew Norris had already explained that Chalco staff would comprise Mark, an assistant geologist, still to be determined, a mining engineer, and a laboratory based mineral chemist. The lab would have a Bench XRF, a crusher, microscopes, fridges, all requiring a stable electric supply.

Several questions arose that were debated. Rasmussen was making notes. He had accepted the role of ensuring that the team had first class support for this landmark project. He needed to show both the EU and the Greenland Government that this project had benefits for the local population as well as getting valuable metals into Europe.

Astrid Larsen judged her moment. She pointed out that Greenland was a sovereign territory of Denmark. Although Greenland had control over its own resources since 2009, Denmark was responsible for defence and foreign affairs. As such it was intent on ensuring that Greenlandic Government officials didn't make commercial arrangements with nations that the European Union judged unsuitable. She didn't mention China but it was probably at the root of her concerns.

David Gresham wound up the session by 16:00, as planned. Mark had kept to his plan. He'd made copious notes and asked a few questions for clarification purposes, but avoided getting entangled in the political tension between Rasmussen and Larsen. Mark didn't feel the tension was necessary. They both had the same objectives, but Larsen was hoping to be the person in charge. She was probably a successful negotiator and politician but her knowledge base was related to political issues. Rasmussen, on the other hand was the pragmatic operator. He was fully conversant with the geological imperatives and the practicalities of completing complex tasks in remote and environmentally challenging locations.

Mark knew that the summer temperatures at the field base were going to be cool. The summer season was short. It was likely that a start date was going to be in May rather than April, and they would have to finish before the end of August.

The meeting broke up and the Danish pair left for the airport. Naomi Dawson, quietly said to Mark: 'You're strategy was the right one. You can see that this prospecting expedition is going to have many eyes watching you. I expect you might be receiving several visitors while you're over there. Diplomacy, diplomacy, diplomacy. My role is to support Chalco, and you. Best of luck.'

David Gresham said to Mark: 'That was a necessary meeting. The Danes wanted to meet the key operators in "their" Project. Tomorrow at 09:00 we'll have a Chalco meeting; just you, me, Andrew and Bernard. We'll finish in good time for your flight back to Bristol.'

Mark left and walked back to the hotel. He would go through the remote sensing folder again, and the copious notes he'd made during the day.

The wind was getting up and dark clouds looming. Mark decided to forego his swim. He had an early dinner, phoned Emma, then settled down to his reading.

# 28

Wednesday, Mark walked across to Chalco. The overnight rain had stopped and there was a cool North Westerly breeze.

At the meeting Andrew Norris started in a much more relaxed style: 'Thank you all for your participation at yesterday's meeting. It was a necessary performance to satisfy the Danes, and the EU, that we're on the ball. We could all sense the tension between Rasmussen and Larsen. One of my golfing acquaintances told me that EU projects can be heavily dominated by meetings. We have to remember that we operate in a different business arrangement with this Project. We have definitely been appointed to do the first year's prospect. We also get a substantial fee, even if we find nothing. What we cannot predict is whether we get appointed to do years two and three. Chalco will not lose on the 2022 summer, but we will be being watched to see if we're a sound outfit to undertake the following years. No pressure then!'

Bernard Hosegood. 'We're also getting a lot of high quality equipment and transport provision for which we don't have to account.'

Andrew Norris: 'Yes, this is a different contractual situation to our standard pattern. We're being paid up front.'

David Gresham: 'The other thing that we need to remember is that we've never operated in such a remote location. There are no roads or tracks between settlements, everything moves by sea or air. If we break anything we can't replace it for many days and a great deal of flying. We have to ensure that we pack spares. Fourteen weeks at the field base is also much longer than we normally programme for a prospect.'

Andrew Norris: 'The auxiliary naval vessel will berth for one day at St Peter Port *en route* to Greenland. The container it will load must have everything we need, except for the rucksacks our party travel with. So extra clothing will need to go in the container.'

David Gresham: 'We haven't been given the travel dates yet, but we should plan to have our equipment, plus extra personal luggage, ready for the container by the end of March.'

Mark was making notes throughout the meeting. He was already designing a critical path diagram. There were five months to get everything right. It wasn't quite the same as planning for a Moon landing, but errors could still prove embarrassing. Mark asked: 'When will you know the staff list?'

David Gresham answered Mark: 'That'll take place through January 2022. You'll be on the selection panel. I'll be inviting the candidates, but you'll have the final say.'

Mark hadn't needed to select staff before. It was going to be a new experience, like much of the Project.

Andrew Norris joined the discussion again: 'With the Danish Navy providing a chef we don't need to consider vittels. I expect the freezers will be packed full of herrring!'

Much discussion continued through the morning. The emphasis was on planning for a long stay in a remote location.

Bernard Hosegood, who had considerable experience of fieldwork in the tundra of Northern Canada, stated that he wanted a reserve battery unit held at Narsarsuaq Airport. The whole field base would be heavily dependant on a reliable supply of electric. He then changed the subject to security: 'We understand that the two pilots are also doubling as our lethal force security. Polar bear curiosity can't be ruled out, although it is less likely in South West Greenland than further North. The field base total crew will number eight. Measures must be set up to ensure that flare guns and pistols or rifles are available at all times. There will be many days when a prospecting party will be out, sometimes many kilometres from the field base, while chef, navy engineer and mineral chemist will be in the field base buildings.'

David Gresham: 'Yes, that's been alluded to already, but I'll get something more rigid instigated at my next meeting with the Danish Navy.'

Andrew Norris butted in. 'Security, is paramount for this Project. Mark, this bit is highly confidential to you only. Other members of the field base team don't need to be told. There will be visits, from the three of us, and almost certainly from European Union and Greenland Government personnel. David will be monitoring all these visits to give you, and only you, fair warning.'

Mark: 'Thanks, I'll bear that in mind.'

David Gresham: 'We know that Igneous Metal Ores, a multi-national, have had a presence, about 80 kilometres to the South East of Danesfjord, for several years. They'll be watching what Chalco are doing. How they'll go about their surveillance operations we cannot be sure, but we need to be prepared. Remember that China has a part investment in that company. Vigilance, and making immediate use of the satellite phones will be essential.'

Andrew Norris brought the meeting to a close: 'Thank you everyone for the last few days. We've all got plenty to work to do, and Mark, we'll bring you over for a progress meeting in December, then several, about every fortnight, after Christmas.'

Mark had an hour before he needed to be at the Airport. He had a long chat with David Gresham who was now fully based on Guernsey, with his family. David was looking much stronger after the near fatal event in Ecuador. He was walking smoothly and without a stick.

Back home Mark had a lot to unload with Emma. He kept to the physical aspects of how they were going to operate, but kept away from the micro and macro politics of the Project. Emma's only negative comment was that it would be nearly September next year before Katy would be able to play on the beach with Daddy. She realised that this was a significant career step up for Mark and she was fully behind him.

Mark spent Thursday at home sketching out his new set of responsibilities. He started with his list of what Chalco would need to pack; doubling up on key essentials. The new role was not just "Senior" Geologist, he also had the task of managing three other Chalco staff, as well as the Danish naval attachments. They would all be English speakers and would be told that Mark was their "Director of Operations". That was new to Mark. He couldn't get it out of his head. What if the chef produced food that the Chalco staff found unappetising. He hoped that over the next few months these irrational fears would be subdued.

Pete, Mark's school friend and Best Man had recently taken over the workings of his agricultural consultancy. He had eleven staff under him, none of which he had appointed. Mark knew that this had given Pete some headaches. At least the selection process starting in January would give Mark the opportunity to vet the three candidates for the Danesfjord Project.

Anyway, a meet up with Pete might be a useful starting point to resolve his apprehensions. He'd also seen a documentary where the conclusion was that fear only exists because of a lack of information!

Friday, Mark went up to Avon. He checked out the library to see if there were any useful articles on South West Greenland. The only ones of possible interest was a paper on flora and fauna, published in 2015, and a mineralogical article on the gemstone finds near Nuuk, the capital of

Greenland. The latter was published in 2019. As for printed maps there were few large scale maps of Greenland. Some rather old small scale of the whole island. He tracked down Christine Trevelyan, his enormously helpful retained custodian of the Department Map Library. She said his best starting point was the Danish Government's mapping agency. Their geology wing were involved in a development to put a lot of interactive maps on line.

Mark felt he should also put some hours into developing the teaching materials for Richard Ericson. The COVID Pandemic wasn't over and the possibility of further lockdowns were a recurring problem for universities. He had six or seven weeks to his next Chalco meeting over in Guernsey so he needed to make sure he was making full use of the Avon facilities. That would formally end at Christmas.

At home Mark thought he should invest more time with Katy. She was now 22 months old. She loved stories. A quiet discussion with Emma agreed that Mark should read the bedtime stories every other evening when he was home. That would leave Grandma Kathleen and Emma to do the other evenings.

Talking of Grandma, Emma said that it was her Mum's birthday on Monday so could they take her out to lunch on Sunday? She'd be 62.

The weekend was dry and sunny. Mark went with Emma to do the supermarket run on Saturday morning. Then to the garden centre for a potted plant for her Mum. In the afternoon Mark had an energetic session winterising the garden. The Birthday lunch was a great success. Katy was on her best behaviour sitting in the high chair provided at the olde worlde pub. It was a change for them all. Kathleen had insisted that weekend days out should be just the three of them, so it was a new experience for Katy to have her Grandma at her side. It may have been why she was so well behaved.

Kathleen raised the question of her bungalow. It had been mothballed by Brian since Henry's death. Kathleen was concerned that Katy was reaching the age when she should have her own bedroom. There were three bedrooms at Kathleen and Henry's old bungalow. Katy could have her own room. Emma gently engaged with her mother saying that it was a nice idea but that it would change the unwritten arrangement that Brian, her brother, should eventually take over the property. Mark said nothing. This was a delicate area holding a discussion without Brian. After the exchange of ideas, possibilities and the money aspects, Emma thanked her Mum and said we all need to think about it. The weather outside was pleasant so they had a short walk after the lunch.

That evening in bed Emma asked Mark what he thought of the bungalow swap. He raised the matter of financial adjustment for Brian, and what Emma thought of the schooling provision if they moved. Emma summed up by saying they needed to sleep on it for a few weeks and consider how to approach Brian.

As well as his preparations for Greenland, there were now several domestic decisions looming. Andrew Norris had asked him to dispose of the truck in the New Year. That meant they would only have the Mini. A larger family car was now on the horizon. Family matters needed attention. When he was not on explorations Mark realised that the five weekday daytimes were career time, but evenings and weekends were for the family.

It was now November 2021. Mark had set up his critical path on his laptop. A key date was the end of March, everything had to go in the shipping container. No ifs or buts. Mark's lists of items were headed personal, computing and communication, prospecting equipment, lab equipment. This wasn't so different from previous Chalco prospecting trips. Because replacements were many days away for lost or broken items, it was essential that some critical items were doubled up. Mark recalled that a couple of his earlier explorations had made use of local hardware stores for basic items. Those had been within a couple of hours from their prospecting base. That luxury wouldn't exist in Greenland.

One thing that wasn't resolved at the October Guernsey meetings was the gap in armed security. If the two pilots were on a trip back to the airport at Narsarsuaq they could be absent for several hours. More if the weather turned against them. Chef and engineer would also need to be armed.

Mark thought he should devote most of November to digesting the available geology information. Maps, and documents from the Danish Geology Institute, gave the dominant bedrock as Syenite. A coarse grained alkali igneous rock. Exact chemistry can be variable. To a casual observer much Syenite has the appearance of granite, although the principal crystal is feldspar. Syenites are typically low in quartz crystal composition. There are often pegmatites within the syenite. These are noticeable from the large crystals, in excess of several centimetres.

As for soils and subsoils on the Syenite, the steeper slopes would be devoid. Although their base site was described as thin soil, it was likely to be fragile. Whoever was selected to be mining engineer would need to be prepared for hard rock. That meant, rock drills with many spare bits. Also the crusher in the lab would need a supply of spares. It would be essential to take a second crusher. If the exploration was to be 14 weeks, that would mean about 12 weeks of actual fieldwork, nearly double the typical Chalco trips with which Mark was familiar.

Mark would try to do two days a week up to the end of November on teaching materials for Richard, and three days on Greenland research. He needed to have a clear plan of how he thought the exploration would proceed by the time he was called over to Guernsey in December. He was heartened by Bernard Hosegood's demand for a second battery block to be kept at Narsarsuaq. That needed to be kept on the quay because its weight meant it would need to be transported to the site by ship. The Danish Navy Auxiliary vessel and its heavy lift helicopter would be needed to move it.

The remote sensing team's sixty three page folder had many aerial images of the terrain. Mark felt the need for a drone was probably a valid addition to the prospecting equipment list. It would save time when investigations needed to tackle a new area. Two drones should be taken so there was spare. Hopefully, the assistant geologist might be persuaded to bone up on their use. A great many popular drones were manufactured in China. Some use a mobile phone as a screen. In such a remote environment, with no internet, that type of system wouldn't be reliable. Also, Chalco would not wish third parties to have knowledge of the sites the field team would be surveying. Perhaps someone on the Guernsey staff could investigate suitable drones. Perhaps the ones used by wildlife photographers in the Amazon, New Guinea and Antarctica might be appropriate. Programme makers wouldn't want drones that could be monitored by plagiaristic film companies. Drones could be a more effective viewing device than the helicopter when close up detail was required.

Equipment planning was somewhat hypothetical and almost frustrating because "on the ground" knowledge of the proposed site was absent. It was already too late in the season to ask for a quick site visit. In some ways Mark was pleased to have the teaching materials task as focusing solely upon equipment planning for the next six weeks was likely to become intense when all possible scenarios were considered.

Previous explorations were never more than a day away from some sort of hardware store or general store. The Guernsey office could provide replacement equipment within about 48 hours. International couriers were expensive but the Company policy was to use them, irrespective of cost. This was because exploration downtime was more expensive. The remote base site at Greenland would entail longer delivery times, and that would involve use of the Danish helicopter crew. They were a safety back up at the site and not having them close by was a risk for all personnel. Thorough preparation, and taking appropriate spares, was paramount for the smooth running of the Project.

At home Katy was making rapid progress. She saw as much of Daddy as she saw of Mummy. That would be modified next year, and was clearly on the mind of Emma. Mark would be away for nearly four months.

Probably because of his recollections of Ecuador, Mark was focusing on security aspects. The Chalco team and the Danish Navy attachments would be on site for fourteen weeks. There was currently no provision for security through the winter. Whether to cut trial mines, usually horizontal adits, could be an important question. He needed to discuss this with Bernard and Andrew Norris. It was pertinent to the selection of the mining engineer. Could all the investigations be done from just drilling. That would mean they could leave the site with few indications of were they had been working. Conversely, if an adit was cut then it was clear to any malign visitor where the mineral focus had been concentrated. So much money was now being invested by the big multi-nationals. Some were using any methods to undermine competitors and capitalise upon their discoveries.

It was the third week of November and COVID was causing travel problems again. Mark decided he needed to check his planning with Guernsey. He sent an e-mail on Thursday 18th November to Andrew Norris requesting a half day meeting with him, Bernard, equipment staff and the remote sensing team.

An e-mail reply from Andrew Norris came back Friday:

Good idea. I'll get Rosemary to bring you over next Wednesday, returning Thursday, if she can get you flights. Details to follow.

The following Monday an e-mail from Rosemary with flight details arrived. A slight difference; flying from Exeter, arriving about 11:00. Short meeting with Andrew and Bernard before lunch, then separate meetings with equipment quartermaster and remote sensing team after lunch. Emphasis on extreme hygiene and infection control.

On Tuesday a package arrived by courier. A box of a new type of face mask. It was labelled as being ordered by Chalco. Working from home Mark hadn't realised that some companies were investing in infection minimisation. He spent Tuesday afternoon on preparing a couple of slides detailing his thoughts from his equipment planning exercise.

He drove down to Exeter Airport on Wednesday morning, not forgetting his supply of high quality face masks. At Guernsey Airport a car with all windows open was there to meet him.

The meeting with Andrew and Bernard and David was valuable. All three were supportive of Mark's security and safety concerns. Bernard Hosegood stressed the continuing need to keep the politics and security aspects of this unusual exploration away from staff. The two afternoon meetings would be just one staff member plus Mark and David Gresham.

The meeting with the equipment quartermaster, Reg Boston, was useful. He would be happy to research drone specifications, and seemed to have already considered the spares aspects of key equipment. The budget indications he had been given were generous. Definitely no problem with two Bench XRF spectrometers, and two crushers. In the case of the latter, a package of spares had already been ordered. Firearms were being ordered, with necessary documentation. The quartermaster had been advised that this was in anticipation of the small risk of polar bears. The firearms would be issued by the Danish Navy on arrival at the base camp.

The meeting with the lead of remote sensing was much less specific, but she agreed that a greater degree of environmental background information needed to be supplied. The aspect that Mark stressed was climatic data. She responded that with so few permanent weather stations in Greenland the data package she would try to provide would be largely generated through interpolation.

Mark had one night at the local hotel then back to Exeter the following morning. He would be returning in about two weeks time to go through the field staff selection procedure.

# 29

Mark's time at Avon was nearing an end. Richard was pleased with the teaching materials, and suggested that Mark should now focus all his time on Greenland preparations. Richard repeated his request; would Mark be able to come back to deliver a research seminar in the Autumn of 2022. Mark assured him that would happen.

At home hints of Christmas were becoming more frequent. Emma and Kathleen were doing a lot of knitting. Emma wasn't keen on doing much shop shopping. COVID infections were rising again. Although the three of them had been given jabs, Katy hadn't. With much regret Emma had used the internet to obtain deliveries of wool for their current cottage industry. It was likely she would be ordering more presents that way.

Mark had been perusing the internet for books on staff selection. He felt he needed to get his head around the topic before going back to Guernsey. He also had a couple of calls to Pete, Best Man at his wedding and friend since school years.

He was more confident in his equipment listing since the recent meeting at Head Office. David Gresham had complimented him on his thorough planning and said that even if an item isn't used it will come back and go into the quartermaster's store. The shipping container they were being provided with was a 20 foot type, weighing a little over two tonnes empty. The heavy lift helicopter could transport up to ten tonnes. Mark's back of the envelope calculations showed that his equipment list came out at three and a half tonnes. That was allowing each team member to pack 150 kilogrammes of personal luggage. It would almost certainly be less than that and each person would travel with a rucksack containing their close personal items. The heaviest individual items in the container would be drilling equipment; nearly half a tonne including spares.

Because the Danish Navy were supplying the huts, catering equipment, bunks and mattresses, there were less things to take than on some previous explorations that Mark had undertaken. In fact the comfort level of this trip was going to be quite high. That was key to the objectives of the fourteen week exploration. It was a long time in a remote field location.

A letter had been received from the Danish Navy. The two accommodation huts would each have eight cabins with bunks, showers, lavatories, washbasins. Also one large stainless steel sink for cleaning boots. There would be two washing machines, two tumble driers, supplies of washing chemicals, and 200 toilet rolls. No towels. The kitchen and refectory hut would have full cooking facilities including fridges and freezers, plus a large table, chairs and two satellite video players. The laboratory hut would have standard benches with sinks, two fridges, one freezer and a satellite video player. Chalco would need to pack the geological equipment needed for their work in the shipping container.

The one item not mentioned in the letter was heating. It would be cool. As far as Mark could determine daytime temperatures could be five to ten degrees on cloudy days, but risk of night frosts. Perhaps that assessment might be clarified if the remote sensing team could provide better climate data. In any event, this was going to be a cool exploration. The equipment list needed an addition. High insulation factor sleeping bags for all sixteen bunks. That would mean any overnight visitors could be accommodated. If visitors came for a day visit there was always the risk that poor weather might prevent them returning to Narsarsuaq Airport.

Mark wasn't too concerned about the lack heating. Appropriate clothing would cope with that. It would be an easier working and living environment than a hot desert.

The other aspect mentioned in the letter was food. With the installation of the kitchen hut, the freezer would be stocked with a seven week supply of frozen food, and chilled fruit and veg. The auxiliary ship would return after seven weeks to restock the kitchen. That was encouraging because there was an opportunity half way through the visit for Chalco to replace, or provide, technical equipment. Anything that was beyond the carrying capacity of the small helicopter could be sent on the ship. That could be be crucial for extra drilling equipment.

Things were looking far more optimistic for Mark. Key items were being ordered and there were still four months before the shipping container deadline. He was content that equipment was meeting his critical path targets. His next challenge would be the staff selection.

Mark received an e-mail from David Gresham with the dates of the December meeting to define the staff selection criteria. It was only ten days away. He was booked in for Monday 13$^{th}$ to Thursday 16$^{th.}$ That would mean three nights at the hotel, full board. Early flight Monday; afternoon flight Thursday. Departing from and returning to Exeter Airport.

Emma had Christmas fully planned. Relying mostly on deliveries, it was going to be a low key affair. Brian would be coming down to Somerset for Christmas Day and Boxing Day, camping in his Mum's home. Emma hoped that Mark could go over a few days before and switch on the heating. Brian had made several visits through the year, so the property hadn't become too run down.

If the weather was calm and not too cold they would have Christmas Dinner outside and Brian could come over. Brian and Emma communicated frequently on their phones but for Kathleen the face to face meetings with her son were emotionally important.

Mark thought the best use of his time for the next ten days was to get stuck into personnel management textbooks. He would be leading three Chalco staff, and liaising with the four Danish Navy people. He would soon be involved in appointing his Chalco assistants, but the Danish Navy contingent would be "as provided". Diplomatic and negotiating skills would be needed with them.

Emma had their second cautious Christmas celebrations well in hand. The focus would be around Katy, two years old in January.

Monday 13th December came quicker than anticipated. After a turbulent flight, most of Monday was spent with David Gresham. He outlined the roles of the assistant geologist, the laboratory analyst and the mining engineer. It was all fairly familiar to Mark except that assistant field geologist and laboratory analyst were now two roles. In his expeditions, over three years ago now, Mark had been doing both roles himself. David Gresham explained that now the focus was on Rare Earth metals, rather than just Copper, the lab work was much more time consuming. Copper mineral ores could often be identified by a trained eye, plus a few simple physical tests. Rare Earth minerals needed considerably more detailed assessments.

The pair worked together during the afternoon to define roles and responsibilities. The mining engineer normally did operations, like drilling, or directing the cutting of an adit, and some of the surveying. Because of the advances in GPS technologies, and the use of photographic drones, accurate recording of locations of every drilling and sample site could be done digitally. The remote sensing team back on Guernsey would assemble all the digital data and assist with the survey report. The Chalco plan was to make the assistant geologist responsible for drone deployment, as well as its maintenance and recharging.

David Gresham invited Mark over to his house that evening. It was good to hear how he and his wife Jill were now firmly established as Guernsey residents. Their children were all working in London and the home counties. One was in law, another teaching English and a third was in health administration. They were all scheduled to return to Guernsey for Christmas. David mentioned, humorously, that none of them wanted to follow him into geology – too many risks!

Tuesday was a session with Andrew Norris; going through the applications for the three roles in Greenland. Andrew had advertised two of them within the Company and whittled the applicants down to two for each role. No decisions today, just an outlining of the qualities and skills of each person. The laboratory chemist had been advertised outside of Chalco. Interviews for the appointments would be held in January. Mark noticed that both lab analyst applications were female. Andrew pointed out that many women geologists follow a lab based career after graduating. Across the industry it was recognised that women were often tidier and more efficient in laboratory settings.

After lunch there was a meeting with Bernard Hosegood. This covered all aspects of the planning, particularly relations with the Danish Navy. Bernard congratulated Mark on his safety and security concerns. The Danish Navy supported the idea of additional guns for the civilian members of the expedition. They would provide the training and safety protocols. There would also be Very Pistols, for use as flare guns, to warn off any intruding polar bears. Chalco had ordered two satellite phones, one for field work and one kept in the lab. Mark raised the matter of electric power supply. If it failed for any reason they would be severely hampered in their work. No ability to recharge field instruments or lab equipment. No cooking facilities. They would be in a remote location and restoration of an electricity failure would take many days. Bernard responded that he had agreement with the Danes for a spare battery to be kept at Narsarsuaq Airport. That was Bernard's original request but it was unclear how the spare battery would be transported to the Huts base if there was no ship and heavy lift helicopter in the vicinity. Many days could elapse before electricity would be restored.

The last matter that Bernard raised was medical emergencies. Mark had already doubled up on first aid kits. Apparently, the Danes were ahead of the curve on this aspect. The helicopter would have two pilots. That had been declared a few months earlier. The career summaries of the Danish Navy personnel had reached Bernard last week. The pilots were both fully qualified Captains. One male, one female. The female was also a qualified doctor, speciality emergency medicine.

Wednesday was a day with the quartermaster: Reg Boston. He'd received nearly all the equipment Mark had requested. He was particularly interested in the two drones. He'd been practising with one of them locally. Certainly user friendly. If the user stops flying it, the machine just hangs stationary in the air. He took Mark outside to demonstrate its performance. Mark was quite impressed with the handling and image quality. In survey mode the machine printed the exact Latitude and Longitude on every image and video. That came from the built-in GPS unit which was also used by the machine to return to its take off location when a dedicated button was pressed. Mark discussed the need for the quartermaster to thoroughly train the assistant geologist, when appointed in January.

The exploration plan was to record every drilling site with a drone image, and the associated GPS data. Prior to leaving for the winter the drill holes would be plugged with the original core top, and the site brushed clean. Because the Chalco team would be leaving before the end of August there would be several weeks before the onset of winter that a competitor organisation could inspect the whole area.

Bernard stressed that Chalco's intention was to continue the Danish/EU contract into the following summer. Maintaining security through the intervening winter was a priority if they didn't wish for rogue operators to move in on the fieldwork area. Denmark had special services teams on Greenland all through the winter. Unfortunately, the size of Greenland meant that they couldn't watch everywhere all the time. There would be security cameras installed for the winter, with a programme to maintain battery power. The Danes considered August/September to be the high risk time. Chalco would be leaving about mid August as this was the wettest time of the year. Not conducive to productive surveying.

It was becoming clear to Mark that Bernard was in close contact with the Denmark authorities. He saw his background influence role as pivotal to the success of the Project.

Thursday's meeting was with Andrew Norris, Bernard Hosegood and David Gresham. The latter was to be the prime contact with the expedition on a day to day basis. His home telephone number, as well as the number of Chalco Head Office, had been labelled on each phone. Because of time zone difference, the expedition work day would correspond with British afternoon and evening. If things were going well there was no need to have a voice call each day.

Andrew Norris asked Mark quite pointedly if he was confident in his preparations. Mark replied with a firm yes: 'I realise this is a big development for Chalco, as it is for me. The Danes and EU will be demanding clients who are sinking a lot of money into the Project.'

Andrew summed up the session and said that Mark would be brought over, probably mid January, for the staff selection interviews. The successful candidates would be decided immediately after the interviews, so that Mark was fully aware of his team leading up to the final preparations.

With that Mark left Chalco for the Airport. The flight back to Exeter was inconsequential and sunny with exceptional views.

The staff application forms were being retained by Andrew Norris. Mark had made his own notes. He realised that all six candidates were competent and suitable. He felt he would defer any decisions himself until January. He needed to see and hear the candidates in order to assess if he could form a working relationship. Andrew Norris had clearly indicated to Mark that the final choice of personnel would be Mark's.

Back home Emma had almost completed her Christmas preparations. Katy had a sense that something was afoot. She told her Daddy that Father Christmas was going to visit soon and he would be bringing presents. Christmas was now a reality, and only eight more sleeps to go. It appeared that Kathleen had been priming Katy! Emma thought she would just follow the traditional arrangements and stories. She was almost as excited as Katy!

Mark had two key tasks to fulfil before Christmas. He needed to go through his notes on the candidates for the Danesfjord team. Andrew Norris wanted the appointments to be made on the day of the interviews. Mark's second task was to clear his desk at Avon University and foster his relationships with the people he had worked with over the past three years. Maintaining professional relationships was key in any career, but with the world of geology being relatively small, it was likely that many paths would cross again.

Emma's main concern through Christmas was to keep the family free of COVID. This had been a problem for Katy's development. She waved to other toddlers when she was out on walks but couldn't understand why she couldn't play with them. On children's television programmes she could see lots of children playing together.

Two days before Christmas Mark went over to Kathleen's bungalow to switch on the heating for Brian's visit. On his return Emma greeted him with a wide smile: 'Is Mum's bungalow ok.?'

'Yes, it seems ok. The gas boiler started up and I checked all the radiators before I left.'

Emma, with a widening smile: 'That's good, I hope it's going to be cosy.'

'Why are you smiling?'

'Oh, no reason, I just want him to be comfortable in rural Somerset.'

Mark sensed something was strange. Emma was almost in a mischievous mood. He thought he would change the subject: 'When can I assemble Katy's dolls house?'

'You could do it now before dinner. Katy's out on a walk with Mum. You've probably got half an hour.'

The elated Emma wasn't giving anything away, but there was an air of an imminent announcement. Mark knew he would have to wait. Had she won the lottery? Was she pregnant?

Kathleen and Katy returned. Mark put the doll's house back in the large box. Katy was running around excitedly: 'Mummy, we saw a squirrel.'

Emma, still with her glowing smile, gave Katy a big hug: 'That's lovely, darling. You could go and draw a picture of it with its big fluffy tail. Dinner will be in twenty minutes.'

Mark laid the table. The atmosphere was pensive. Even Kathleen had noticed the strange atmosphere.

They all sat down to eat. Emma seemed to be enjoying the tension. Whatever the announcement was going to be she was dragging it out, watching the frustration in Mark's eyes.

Classroom teachers have many tactics for ensuring everyone's attention. Emma really was milking this one. Kathleen realised that something was different. Emma cleared away the plates and brought over the bowls of strawberries and yoghurt. The teacher was firmly in charge. They just sat there saying nothing until everyone had finished.

Realising that she had full attention Emma said: 'I have an interesting announcement to make.'

The pause seemed endless: 'As you know Brian is coming down on Boxing Day.' Long silent pause. 'He's bringing Susan, a personal friend.'

Mark: 'Well, that's a surprise, how long has he known her?'

Kathleen: 'Over a year. They went to Madeira for a week, in September.'

Emma, in exclamation, and the wind taken out of her sails: 'You knew Mum. Why didn't you tell us?'

Katy, still licking her spoon, looking at everyone around the table as this unusual story unfolded.

Kathleen: 'I like to keep my children's confidences until the appropriate moment.'

Emma, in astonishment: 'Well, can you spill the details now?'

The atmosphere returned to more normal dinner table conversation as small details were slowly trickled out in stages by Kathleen. At least the prospect of a dull COVID Christmas had been usurped by the imminent arrival of Emma's bachelor brother and his personal friend, Susan.

Christmas Day arrived. Presents, turkey, singing and dancing from Katy, the Queen's Christmas Message, a Christmas cake made by Kathleen, but the big event was to be Boxing Day lunch.

Brian and Susan had been to Susan's parents for Christmas Day.

It was a benign, slightly sunny Boxing Day so all was set for lunch in the garden. Emma was insistent that Brain and Susan kept their distance. She didn't want to risk anyone catching COVID. Particularly in the case of her Mum. There were still a lot of cases around, and hospitals were not able to save many older people. Despite having received several vaccinations Emma was still concerned about safeguarding her Mum.

Mark had borrowed two long trestle tables from the village hall which assisted the idea of keeping Brian and Susan well away from Kathleen. The weather was calm, glimpses of sun, and not too cold. Katy wore her new highly coloured woolly hat throughout lunch. It had been knitted by Grandma.

Lunch was a convivial event, gently questioning Brian and Susan about their relationship. Kathleen interposing general questions to reduce the pressure on Susan.

Susan was a year older than Brian, and worked in a museum in London as a senior conservationist. After college she had worked for four years on field archaeology projects in East Anglia. She'd worked at the museum for seven years and was now their principal ceramic specialist. She had two brothers, younger than her. The family was based in Saffron Walden which was where she and Brian had spent Christmas Day. Susan was enchanted with Katy, although Katy couldn't understand why everyone was spaced out around the two tables.

Brian thanked Mark for starting the heating at his childhood home. He and Susan had arrived at ten o'clock the previous night after a misty drive across from Essex.

It was an odd family lunch but at least Brian and Susan were staying until New Year's Day. Despite the forced distance rule imposed by Emma, it was a great pleasure for Kathleen to see her son, the first time since Henry's funeral.

No one enquired about marriage plans, nor was any indication given by Brian, although Susan was wearing an engagement ring. Kathleen probably knew more about the relationship than she was letting on, but was content to let the couple retain control of any announcements. They seemed happy together.

Brian and Susan had brought a supply of COVID tests with them. After five days had elapsed they both did a test; negative. They'd had several days of walking around Somerset footpaths and hadn't met with anyone else or been into any shops. Emma finally agreed to take Kathleen over to her old bungalow to spend an afternoon with her son and his fiancée. New Year's Eve Brian and Susan came over to Emma and Mark's. It was a more relaxed family get together. It was also an opportunity for Katy to show Susan her dolls and toys and books. Susan read a story to Katy which was a great success.

The parting surprise was a quiet announcement from Brian that they were intending to marry sometime in the Summer. Kathleen obviously knew already, but it was now public. For the normally exuberant Brian it was a gentle matter of fact statement. Susan gave a relaxed smile. The next day they would be returning to their London flat.

# 30

The Christmas holiday had been warmed by the news of a family wedding. Emma was pleased for Brian. Katy would soon have an Aunty as well as an Uncle.

After New Year's Day Mark changed his focus back to work. There were no e-mails on his computer, but he guessed that he would be over in Guernsey within the next two weeks. He spent some time reworking his ideas on health and safety matters. The information that the female Danish Navy pilot was also a qualified doctor gave him more confidence that the fourteen week exploration would proceed without difficulty. He decided to order additional COVID test kits through the quartermaster. They would be isolated as a team at Danesfjord, but if they had visitors then they needed methods for sustaining a COVID free site. The most likely initial threat came from the time of their flights and their transfer to Danesfjord on the Danish Navy vessel. It was not clear who would be visiting them while they were working. Mark knew that any Chalco visitors would be thorough with infection control, but others, some possibly unannounced, were a potential problem.

On the 4th January 2022 Mark had an e-mail from Andrew Norris. The interviews would take place in Guernsey during the week 17th to 21st January, details to follow, but he would need to fly out Sunday afternoon, returning Friday afternoon. Rosemary would send him the tickets.

Mark spent the two weeks after New Year with his head in personnel management books. Some texts were rather forthright in tone and content. Perhaps written by military types or factory managers. The team that Mark would be leading would need a more collegiate approach, hoping that their long term career interests would keep them focused on a common purpose.

The post Christmas winter gloom was also a good time to go through all his equipment lists and fieldwork plans to make them intelligible. Once the team members had been appointed he would need to produce a Project plan and joining instructions booklet that would be post mailed to each member of the team. More sensitively he needed to produce an information booklet for the Danish Navy personnel: the two pilots, the engineer and the chef. He would need them on side to liaise with the captain of the auxiliary Navy ship to ensure that their transfer and support operations would be unimpeded, and with no breakages.

Saturday 15th January, Katy's second Birthday, came quicker than expected. Emma wanted a day out with Katy and the weather was calm. For nearly all of Katy's life Daddy had been around nearly every morning and evening. He would be away for six days now and then several more weeks prior to the fourteen week exploration. Keeping the parental connection with Katy was going to be a key part of Mark's life.

Mark was already packed for Guernsey. Emma would drive him to Exeter Airport on Sunday afternoon. There wasn't much difference in the drive time to Exeter or Bristol airports, it was more a case of the most suitable flight times. The usual hotel on Guernsey was almost empty when Mark arrived. Standard room again. He had dinner and then an early night.

On Monday he hadn't been given a time to arrive at Chalco but he intended to be there by 09:00. Greeted by Rosemary who said: 'Meeting with Andrew and David at 10:00, but Reg Boston, the quartermaster, would like to see you about a few things first.'

All the other equipment that Mark had ordered had arrived. Reg Boston strongly recommended: 'I know your assistant geologist will be responsible for flying, maintaining and recharging the drones but I think it essential that you fully understand the basics of their operation. You never know when you might need to step in. I gather you'll be free after lunch today, so I'll see you about 14:00 in my workshop.'

Ten o'clock Mark knocked on the door of the boardroom. Andrew and David called him in. The schedule for the week was explained to him. Tuesday morning would be interviews for the assistant geologist role. Both candidates were already on the Chalco payroll and had done explorations for Copper minerals. Wednesday morning would be the candidates for the mineral chemist role, based largely in the laboratory Hut. Both candidates were young women, not currently employed by Chalco. Andrew made it clear to Mark that questions related to their personal relationships and pregnancy were to be avoided during interviews. A clause in the contract for the successful candidate would state that immediate return to Guernsey would be necessary in the event of pregnancy. This was because of remote location and lack of suitable medical facilities. Mark asked if that was necessitated by employment law. Andrew replied: 'Yes, we have three women on field operations now and all have the same contract wording.'

Thursday morning would be the two candidates for the mining engineer role. Both currently employed by Chalco. Because the use of drilling equipment was similar for Copper and Rare Earth sampling, existing Chalco staff should be suitable.

For each of the three roles both candidates would be interviewed by Mark, Bernard and David or Andrew. Bernard would chair the panel, but Mark and David would ask most of the questions. Bernard would only intervene if questioning became bogged down, or a fair atmosphere was being infringed. Questioning should alternate between Mark and David.

David gave Mark a card with eight standard questions on it. It was more an *aide memoire* to start things off and put the candidate at ease. Additional questions could be added as appropriate. After initial introductions and welcome were completed Bernard would ask David to ask the first question so that Mark could feel the tone of the process.

It was a familiar procedure for David, who had probably interviewed many candidates over the years.

There was a session with David evaluating the six candidate application forms again, to refresh his memory. Mark had no preferences for the moment. He wanted to meet and listen to the candidates before making up his mind.

After lunch Mark went over to Reg Boston's workshop for a hands on session with the drone. It was a robust quadcopter design, European manufacture. It had a diameter of about 45 centimetres when unfolded. It was larger than the many hobby machines on the popular market. The control panel with hooded video screen had a neck strap. Reg took Mark out into the adjacent field for a practice. He placed a take off and landing board on the ground. Mark was now in control. The drone took to the air. Reg suggested he let go the forward, turning and up/down controls. There was a slight breeze but the drone just hung in the air. It hardly moved. Reg said: 'It will stay there until the battery runs low, then land itself on the board and switch itself off. You're unlikely to cause it to crash. Today, just fly it around to get the feel of the controls.'

The more he practised, the more his confidence increased. He said to Reg: 'This is going to be particularly useful. My assistant geologist will be responsible for its use. I understand you'll be training, whoever we appoint, in all the handling and maintenance.'

Reg Boston: 'Yes, the boss has allocated two full days for that task.'

Mark: 'That's great. The Latitude and Longitude data etched into each photo it takes will be a key part of our surveying record.'

That was day one complete. Mark walked back to the hotel for dinner then another early night. He wanted to be thoroughly refreshed for the Tuesday interviews. He had a long chat on the phone with Emma that evening. She told him to relax, it would all go quite naturally.

Tuesday morning Mark made sure he was at the offices by 09:00. First candidate was scheduled for ten. David would meet and greet the two candidates who had been asked to arrive at 09:45. Mark would be in the boardroom with Bernard.

The first candidate, Harry Wilson, came in with David and shown to the seat. Bernard conducted the preamble then handed over to David to begin the questioning. Mark asked questions mostly related to the Greenland environment. The second candidate, Simon Cawston, was shown in by Rosemary at 10:30. The interview followed the same pattern.

At the end of the second interview, Bernard said: 'We'll give ourselves a maximum of twenty minutes. Mark can you present your assessment.'

Mark started: 'Both candidates were equal on paper. Harry Wilson has been with Chalco for two years and seemed to show an eagerness to experience a new area of geology. Simon Cawston, three years with the company and had done more explorations. Sadly, he sees his employment with Chalco as just a job. He lacked enthusiasm. I'd feel more content with Harry Wilson.'

Bernard: 'David, would you like to add anything?'

David: 'I think Mark has a point, Harry Wilson was more enthusiastic. Academically, they are similar, but Simon Cawston has been a little pushy with his last two explorations. He was keen to wind up before the team had fully completed their task. That could be a problem on a fourteen week deployment. The longest he's done up to now has been six weeks.'

Bernard: 'I think we're agreed then. I also concur. David ask Harry Wilson to come back in.'

Harry Wilson returned and was formally appointed for the role. He, David and Mark retired to the side room while Bernard called in the unsuccessful candidate: 'Simon, we'd like to thank you for applying for this position but we've appointed Harry Wilson. This won't affect your career with Chalco, and I'd like to thank you for taking the trouble to apply.'

In the side room. David and Mark outlined the key features of the Danesfjord project. He would need to return to Guernsey in February for training with the drone, as well as other aspects of the preparation. Mark explained that there would be a booklet for all the team members mailed to him in early February which would expand on details and include suggested lists of all items he would need to take.

Handshakes, and departures. David congratulated Mark on his questioning during both interviews.

Mark strolled back to the hotel. He was quite pleased with the result of the interviews. He felt he could work with Harry Wilson. That was important as he would be spending more time with the assistant geologist than the rest of the team.

Wednesday would be different. How to select the laboratory based mineral chemist? Rosemary would be part of the interview panel, because of the women candidates. Mark arrived at 09:00 as planned. Rosemary welcomed him and said there will be a brief meeting in Andrew's office. As CEO Andrew Norris recognised that some aspects of the Danesfjord Project would reflect on him. The concept of a dedicated laboratory chemist in the field was new for Chalco. Most exploration teams were field based, some teams even living in tents. With an infrastructure of four large huts, well staffed, and an admirably equipped laboratory with electric power, Chalco was well set up to produce high quality analysis on site. The bench XRF instruments, although not as discriminating as mass spectrometers, offered significantly better determination of metals than hand held spectrometers.

Andrew Norris remembered the days when mineral samples were taken back to the original Chalco headquarters in Bath. Depending on their importance, or need for better quantification, some samples were parcelled off to university chemistry departments. Because the company were only interested in finding Copper ores, visual identification of the various Copper minerals meant that spectrometric analysis of the ores was less of a priority. Rare Earth minerals are much less easy to differentiate visually, so use of electronic methods was much more appropriate. Modern technologies were speeding up analysis, but Andrew knew that it was important to have competent analytical chemists overseeing the important work of mineral assessment. As the only trained mineral chemist on the current Chalco staff, he was best placed to sit in on the interviews today. Andrew explained to Mark that he would replace David for today's interviews.

Both women candidates were recently qualified chemists, with first class honours, who had specialised in mineral preparation for spectrometer analysis. Rosemary would join the panel for gender balance and the aim of reducing any implied intimidation for the candidates. Each interview would last forty minutes and Andrew would make a strong recommendation for the successful candidate. Mark was quite pleased with the arrangement as his own training within the chemistry department while at Avon had been partial. It was just enough to enable him to process samples for his PhD, but he couldn't claim to have experienced the full rigour of a chemistry education.

The first interview started at ten. Bernard was still in the chair. The candidate was Esme Blackall, 22, a Cambridge graduate. Quite petite, spectacled, immaculately dressed. Bernard briefly welcomed her and passed over to Rosemary for the first question. That was to put her at ease. Mark followed, but used his questions on outdoor environments rather than anything on chemistry. He knew that Andrew would pursue those. The chemistry questions were mostly focused on mineral preparation standards. Esme responded well, with succinct answers. Andrew seemed content with her laboratory ability.

The second interview followed. Bethany Davies, 23, with a strong mid-Wales accent had graduated over a year ago from Durham. She'd been on a hiking trip through South America. She wasn't as precise as Esme Blackall in her answers but she was confident and assertive. She wasn't phased by any of Andrew's questions and clearly demonstrated that she was a first class honours chemist. She'd worked out that Mark was the exploration leader and was maintaining eye contact with him even when responding to Andrew's questions.

An interesting discussion amongst Bernard, Andrew, Mark and Rosemary followed after the interviews. It was clear to Mark that Andrew was firm in his opinion to appoint Esme Blackall. Rosemary commented that Bethany Davies was more adventurous and outgoing, whereas on first impressions Esme presented as a shrinking violet, although she recognised her as an intelligent, well organised and competent young woman. Mark didn't offer a view. He was pleased that Andrew was taking the initiative. Listening to the two candidates responding to Andrew's questions Mark was aware that his chemistry understanding was still quite weak. For fourteen weeks Mark would be relying on the appointed candidate to provide hard data on the quality of the exploration samples. He followed Andrew's recommendation.

Wednesday had been an odd day for Mark. How well was he equipped to appoint a staff member in a technical area for which he was not fully familiar? He recognised that in any future interviews he needed to listen carefully to the other members of the panel.

Thursday was the appointment of a mining engineer. A fieldwork skill with which Mark had plenty of first hand knowledge. Over the years he'd worked with three different engineers, although none of them were up for these interviews. The panel was the same as Tuesday; Bernard, David and himself. Often an adit is cut for Copper explorations, but in Danesfjord the current version of the contract involved only taking drill cores.

At 10:00 the first candidate, Humphrey Hutchings, 41 years of age, was confident, firmly spoken and had thoroughly researched the Greenland environment. Mark was uneasy about him, particularly the confrontational nature of his answers to technical questions. How would he manage him.

The second candidate, Leighton Jones, 24, and had only worked for Chalco for just under a year. He was keen and gave succinct and clear answers to questions. He expressed a willingness to learn. Mark was certain which candidate would fit in with his evolving team.

After the interviews, Bernard commenced discussion, by asking Mark for his decision. Unequivocally, Mark responded Leighton Jones. David Gresham nodded. Bernard responded: 'I'm inclined to agree with you. Humphrey Hutchings has worked well for many years with Sidney Pollock, one of our Senior Geologists, but that may be due to Sidney being 12 years older than him. I feel he might be unpredictable if he is being directed by someone many years younger than him.'

David Gresham remarked that was a fair analysis. He also suggested that we should give it another few minutes before calling Leighton Jones back in to offer him the role.

This was a different aspect to the work of Chalco for Mark. It was useful for him to have been supported in the selection process. Later that afternoon, Rosemary had remarked that during interviews we place candidates in different hotels to the one near the Airport. She also explained that Andrew and her would be holding mini seminars for new entrants to Chalco. That includes explanation of the company objectives and expectations for staff. When Mark meets Esme Blackall again in the February team building week she will have been inducted into the Chalco company ethos.

Mark went home satisfied that he had the basis of a sound team to carry out the fourteen week exploration. His role, in addition to finding Rare Earth minerals, was to reinforce the team, keeping everyone focused, regularly praised and happy.

Mark flew back to Exeter Airport to be met by Emma and Katy. He had a lot to unpack about the whole process, but he told Emma that he was pleased with the team they had appointed.

It was comforting to see Katy at the airport. It made Mark realise that she was moving into being a little girl with a personality of her own. Being away for a full week was a big gap for Katy. Mark was determined to give her a lot of attention that weekend. He found his job fulfilling and challenging but he knew that his most important role in life was to be a successful husband and father. He wouldn't be doing any work for Danesford until Monday.

There were three weeks at home, to work on the briefings for the team, before he flew back to Guernsey for the first of the team meetings. Those three weeks were to have a clear pattern of activity with Katy. Always one story each day, hopefully a walk if the weather was clement. Emma had abandoned ideas of playgroup while the COVID Pandemic was rising again. Adults had been vaccinated but not children. Emma hoped that the summer months would see an easing of the Pandemic, similar to last year.

Mark had promised his team members "the booklet". That would occupy him for a few days. His team had to be ready and well briefed before the departure in April. There was the mid February meeting and probably two in March and April. Mark knew he had to get the preparation period right. Once they were in Greenland there was little opportunity for accessing standard modern facilities.

# 31

Kathleen announced one morning at breakfast that Brian had been offered a position at Bath. Something to do with supporting the Naval equipment inventory. Brian, classic civil servant, was never detailed about what he did. Information was always a little vague. He'd asked Kathleen, his Mum, if he and Susan could move into his childhood home, Kathleen didn't know what to do, because she was thinking that Emma, Mark, Katy and her might move back to her home. Her reasoning was simple; Katy was growing fast and really needed her own room. Kathleen and Henry's family home had three bedrooms, whereas Mark and Emma's only had two. Mark didn't really want to join the discussion, he hoped that Emma could diplomatically handle her Mum and Brian. He was aware that if Kathleen continued to live with them then a larger home would be essential. It was clear to everyone, including Mark, that Kathleen's relationship with Katy was incredibly valuable.

If there was a Brian-Susan wedding in the summer, Mark could still be in Greenland. He thought the best he could do was make sure Emma had his most up-to-date schedule. It was likely that the wedding would be at Saffron Walden, Susan's family home. That would mean a return journey of over 350 kilometres for Emma, shepherding her mother and Katy. It was a venture for which she would benefit from Mark's presence.

Mark decided to leave the situation with Emma for the time being. He focused his efforts on writing the exploration booklet he had promised his team. Equipment lists, travel details, even though exact dates where not yet available, but mostly an explanation of the four hut base camp in a remote section of Greenland. He wanted to produce the text by Wednesday, then send the draft by encrypted e-mail to David Gresham for approval. Hopefully, he could post mail a physical booklet to the three appointees on Thursday. He had the Chalco encryption software for communicating with David, but he felt it safer to post mail a paper version of the booklet to the three team members. Naomi Dawson had warned him that any unencrypted e-mails were likely to be monitored by nefarious organisations.

David Gresham must have given it his instant attention on Wednesday as it was returned the same morning with a few minor edits. David had also emblazoned the word CONFIDENTIAL on the front cover.

The next task was to plan his February visit to Guernsey. He would have the Tuesday and Wednesday to build his team. Harry Wilson would spend two days with Reg Boston learning how to use and care for the drone. He did a couple of slide presentations on his computer covering climate at Danesfjord, physical environment, responsibilities of each member of the team, details of the Danish Navy support personnel. Hopefully that would enhance the equipment lists by alerting the team to the need for taking everything they would need, plus spares. There was also the Rare Earth metals lecture. This was a new area for all three of his team. Rare Earth minerals required a greater knowledge base than Copper. There was also the factor of radioactivity. Thorium was often present with Monazite. They would not be processing any radioactive minerals on site, but would place suspect samples in a double lead lined box for transport back on the Auxiliary Navy ship.

During his lead up to Greenland Mark was conscious of the need to take Katy up to see his parents in Stroud. He was aware that his mother wasn't her normal self, although she hadn't disclosed if there was a reason.

In early February a brief e-mail from David Gresham. The team building week would be Monday 14th to Friday 18th February 2022. Monday would be Rosemary's induction procedures. She would also deal with passports, visas and general bureaucracy. Tuesday and Wednesday would be Mark's briefings. Thursday and Friday Reg Boston's drone training days for Harry Wilson. Mark would need to be with Harry on part of Thursday to see how the drone training was going. Explaining the necessity of using the drone for GPS co-ordinate recording on each site photograph was key to the record keeping.

The day he took Katy up to see his parents was mixed. Katy knew she was on display and was eager to act for her audience. She had a faint recollection of her paternal grandparents but mostly reliant on Mark's briefing while in the car. Both parents, Roger and Jennifer, had been testing for COVID for the past three days. They were delighted to see Katy. For a two year old she was unusually socially aware. The afternoon went well. It was only in the last five minutes that Jennifer told Mark that she had been diagnosed with multiple myeloma and was having treatment for the cancer. She ushered Mark and Katy out the door, obviously not wishing to dwell on a discussion.

Back home Mark looked it up. No cure, although patients can live for several years. Later that evening, after his wife had gone to bed, Roger Scott, Mark's dad, phoned him. He explained the details of Jennifer's diagnosis. She probably had only four years left.

It made Mark feel how important family was, he would need to create as many occasions as possible for his Mum to see Katy.

The Friday before his trip to Guernsey for the team building week Mark had an e-mail from David Gresham:

Team building week postponed for one week. The offices are closed because of a COVID outbreak, including Andrew, Rosemary and Reg. We're all home based. More later.

Mark realised that was squeezing the Danesfjord schedule. He tried to look at the positives. He would use the week to focus on the family.

The following Friday another message from David:

Team building week is on for next week. Andrew and Rosemary, and most of the rest of the staff are now clear of COVID. Reg Boston still positive but he should be clear by next Thursday and Friday. We've revised your airline tickets for next week. You'll receive updated e-tickets. See you next week.

Mark packed his bag and checked through his presentation slides. Friday afternoon David sent an encrypted e-mail to Mark. The Danish Auxillary Naval vessel would dock at St Peter Port for 12 hours on Tuesday 29th March. Everything except the team's air travel rucksacks had to be loaded into the shipping container on that day. Mark made up another couple of slides for his team building days. Tuesday 29th March was the first hard date for the exploration.

Each member of the team would have two aluminium flight boxes, total volume per person would be 360 litres. All extra clothes, footwear, personal items, had to go in.

Mark's flight for the team building week was Monday afternoon 21st February. He didn't need to go to the offices that day so he checked in to the usual hotel. At dinner, the three others turned up, they'd been at Rosemary's Company induction. They were all in the same hotel for the week. That was useful for the team to blend. The following morning Mark started his series of lectures, or seminars. The slide presentation that prompted the most questions was the Rare Earth minerals introduction. This was all new to the three of them. Even Esme Blackall hadn't worked with Rare Earths. Discussions ranged between the economics of why Rare Earth metals were being pursued, to how they were going to live for fourteen weeks. It appeared to Mark that all three were enthusiastic about the novel exploration. Esme Blackall, a young women with no experience of the Chalco prospecting culture, was eager to get to Greenland. Mark was satisfied that the two days, and two dinners at the hotel, with his new team, were successful. He couldn't detect any signs of irritation and all three were accepting of the specific roles within the group.

On Thursday morning Mark introduced Harry Wilson to Reg Boston for the drone training. Harry was completely new to drones but he was picking up the theory quickly. Reg Boston, a product of the British Army, was a "hands on" instructor. There was only one way to do anything, his way, the right way. It was similar to the way that raw recruits were inducted into cleaning their rifles Fortunately, Harry was aware of Reg's teaching style and just went along with it. Mark gently asked Reg if he could make two photocopies of the instruction manual. One for Harry and one for himself.

The bit that Mark needed to see was how to ensure that the video monitoring display was visible on the screen. There was a dedicated switch to display, or not display, the GPS data. Whatever was on the screen automatically got included in the photo when the "capture" button was pressed. As far as Mark was concerned the most important aspect of the drone was producing photos of each site, particularly where they were drilling, so that the survey was accurately recorded. If Harry was able to build up his flying skills that was a bonus.

Mark was content with his morning out in the field. Reg would send him a copy of the instruction manual. Thursday afternoon for Harry was to be cleaning, maintenance and effective charging of the drone. That would be in Reg's workshop. Friday morning would be flying skills.

Mark left them for the airport and the flight home. He was pleased that the week had gone smoothly. The two dinners together had been convivial and Mark had detected an air of excitement within the team.

Back home Emma could sense that Mark was encouraged by the team building week. Katy bounded up to him with: 'Daddy, Daddy, come and see my toys.'

Life for Mark was slowly changing. He was well qualified but the most significant aspect of his life was the way that responsibilities were mounting. He had a young family with a live in grandmother, his own mother with a terminal illness, a major European project, and responsible for three young scientists soon to be launched into a remote location.

He now had a week off, but Andrew wanted him back in Guernsey on Monday 7th March. Professor Rasmussen would be visiting that week with the Senior Captain of the helicopter.

How to make the most of his week off with Katy was a welcome distraction. He had been mentally focused on the emerging Danesfjord Project for five months. It now appeared a reality, just waiting for the summer season. Mark wanted to widen Katy's experience. Emma was still uneasy about sending her to playschool, although COVID numbers were dropping. Could Mark find short days out that were inspiring and attuned to the needs of an active two year old?

In bed that weekend Emma suggested taking her to a petting farm which had a range of animals and was highly regarded for their safety and hygiene. It was part owned by a local vet. Taking Katy out for the day or even half a day was a respite for Kathleen. As Katy was growing into an active toddler Kathleen was finding her quite tiring. Even though she was an experienced teacher, energy levels were declining. Emma was working back at school now so Kathleen was on duty for the best part of the day.

The day at the petting farm was a great success. Rabbits, young lambs, baby calves and a Shetland pony. The lady running the farm that day wasn't sure about placing Katy on the pony but Mark was keen to see his daughter have the experience. Katy watched all the procedure of saddling up with interest. Fitted with a junior helmet, Mark lifted her on and walked the pony out into the small paddock. The farm lady was leading on the other side so there was little chance of Katy falling off. The smile on Katy's face was amazing. Mark took a photo, she didn't want to stop. The farm lady was surprised that such a young child could manage five laps of the paddock. When Mummy arrived back from school Katy was eager to tell her all about the pony.

Mark concluded that whatever he dreamed up for the rest of the week it would not beat the pony day. Through the rest of the week he took Katy swimming, to a flower farm where they were harvesting daffodils, to an aquarium, and to see the steam train at Minehead. Nothing captured her interest as much as the Shetland pony. She did take pride in picking some daffodils which she presented to Mummy and Grandma.

For Mark it was a relaxing week. Monday morning 7th March Mark caught the flight from Bristol Airport to Guernsey. The meeting with Rasmussen and the senior helicopter pilot Captain Oscar Hansen was informative. The four Huts were complete and temporarily on a quay at a military base near Copenhagen. There was an invite to Mark and David Gresham to fly over and inspect them. The invite would last until 18th March, after which the Huts would be loaded onto the deck of the vessel and secured under tarpaulins. David Gresham thanked Captain Hansen and promised he would get back to him.

Because of continuing COVID infections Rasmussen outlined procedures for checking every visitor to Danesfjord and also when the Chalco team embarked the vessel. The voyage from Narsarsuaq Quay to Danesfjord would take about 16 hours. There were enough cabins for each person to have one each. If anyone tested positive for COVID at the Quay prior to embarkation they would be placed in one of the isolation cabins and have their meals delivered.

This emphasis on health security was acknowledged and welcomed by David and Mark. David told the Captain that the Chalco four had received three vaccinations so far and scheduled for a fourth one in early April.

After the meeting, Rasmussen and Hansen returned to the Airport for flights back to Copenhagen. David Gresham explained to Mark that he couldn't really spare the time to go and inspect the Huts as he was dealing with a staffing difficulty in New Zealand. Three days away would not be helpful at this time. He suggested taking Reg Boston, the quartermaster. It will be good public relations if the Danish invite was accepted. It would also be beneficial for the final days of equipment provision. There would be several days before the vessel arrives at St Peter Port in case any additional items needed to go in the container.

Mark went see Reg Boston to check if he was available and then ask Rosemary to find some flights. Mark stayed overnight at the usual hotel and flew home the following morning. Kathleen and Katy greeted him when he arrived home.

The following day an e-mail from Rosemary arrived late afternoon. The Copenhagen flight from Bristol was booked for Monday afternoon 14th March. Reg Boston would fly to Bristol and join Mark for the flight to Copenhagen. They'd be met by a Danish Navy vehicle and taken to the naval base. Two nights accommodation at the base with a guided tour of the four exploration Huts by Rasmussen and Hansen. Fly back Wednesday.

Mark's schedule was becoming compressed. Less time with young Katy. When Emma arrived home he explained the additional excursion: 'I'll bring you back some Danish pastries and herrings.'

Emma's response was: 'Herrings yes, pastries no.'

At least Mark still had three days in the current week with Katy while Mummy was at school. The weather was brightening and days were getting longer. Katy wanted to go back to the petting farm to see the Shetland pony. Mark wasn't sure if that was the best plan. He tried to find new venues each day.

On Saturday Emma, Mark and Katy went across to Minehead to see Emma's Aunt Mary and Uncle George. It was nearly four years since Emma's last visit. A lot had happened since then. Mary and George hadn't seen young Katy.

At Emma's suggestion they had done COVID tests; all clear. That was useful as it was a rainy day and they were all indoors. It was an opportunity for Mary to see if Katy had any interest in music. She had taught hundreds of young children over the years and was skilled at setting a suitable ambience. The piano was in the spare room. Katy was intrigued. Mary sat her on a couple of cushions to bring her up to the level of the keys. Emma stayed in the sitting room with George and Mark. Katy randomly pressed the keys and gradually, with Mary's help, started to touch the keys gently and with a degree of order. After about 20 minutes Mary suggested that Katy should go and fetch Mummy. The piano session ended on a positive high, which is what Mary had hoped. She said: 'When children find even small episodes of success, they come back eager for more.'

Mark was engaged with George's accounts of his Exmoor bird watching. He knew it would give Mary undisturbed time with Katy.

George did ask a few questions of how Mark's work was progressing. Mark was careful not to reveal the Danesfjord Project in detail. He described his next exploration as being in a remote part of Scandinavia. George realised that Mark wasn't able to give a precise location. Although Emma knew of Mark's real destination they had agreed that in conversation it would be prudent to refer to a remote part of Scandinavia. In an historical context Greenland could be described as part Scandinavia!

The visit was another educational experience for Katy. Mary remarked that Katy was a quick learner and eager to sample new challenges. Mark agreed, and acknowledged that it was partly due to the amount of contact she had with Emma's Mum, Kathleen, Mary's sister.

Monday, Mark set off for Bristol Airport. He met up with Reg Boston. At Copenhagen Airport they were met by two men in naval uniform. Fast tracked through the usual security and customs, along a narrow corridor and straight to a waiting car. At the naval base they were shown to an accommodation block and given a visitor pass to wear at all times. A printed schedule said dinner in Block F at 19:00 with Captain Oscar Hansen.

It was a cool evening when they walked across to Block F. Greeted by Captain Hansen, Mark introduced Reg Boston to him.

Hansen explained the next day's schedule in detail. His English was flawless.

After breakfast on Tuesday, Captain Hansen and Professor Rasmussen escorted them to the auxiliary quay. There was no ship but four Baltic pine Huts, and several containers on the quay. Rasmussen said: 'We'll examine the four Huts first. We'll give you some copies of the detailed inventories, but feel free to take photographs.'

The kitchen Hut was well equipped. Fridges, freezers, dish washer and a washing machine. A long table that would seat about fourteen people. There were two large video screens on the wall.

The female accommodation Hut was different to what Mark was expecting. Several compact rooms, or cabins. Four for single women, two for married couples. Also washing machines and a large stainless steel sink for general cleaning, particularly boots. All the cabins had their own lavatory, wash basin and shower cubicle, together with bed, several cupboards and a chest of drawers.

Mark asked Rasmussen: 'Is there a reason for the two married couples cabins?'

'Captain Hansen can answer that one.'

Hansen: 'One cabin is for myself and my wife, Captain Doctor Frida Karlsen. The other is spare. We have planned extra accommodation capacity to cope with any visitors who may not be able to return to Narsarsuaq due to poor weather.'

Mark and Reg looked rather surprised.

Hansen: 'I should explain. The Danish military is a little different to that of the UK. My wife and I have worked for several years on special operations in The Faroes and Greenland. Normally she is the active medic and I do the flying. Purely from a safety and versatility standpoint it is important to have more than one pilot, particularly in remote regions. I am also a qualified nurse. Our military planners considered we were a suitable combination for this unique European experiment.'

The party moved onto the male accommodation Hut. Again, all laid out as cabins. Quite compact but with the same high quality specification as the female Hut. Mark was shown his cabin. A little larger and with a desk. There were a total of eight cabins. Three males from Chalco and three males from the Danish Navy, although Captain Hansen would be sleeping with his wife. That left three spare male cabins available for visitors.

The last Hut was the Laboratory, the base for Esme Blackall. It had an impressive bench set up. Cleaning areas with sample crushers. Although it was a hut it would do justice to the labs and workshops in any university or research unit. Electric power points throughout, all with UK sockets. Reg Boston was taking numerous photos with his phone. As quartermaster it was his area, and it was beneficial for him to see the layout. There was a small cupboard for the Bench Xray Fluorescence Spectrometer which was lead lined. All the lighting was LED.

Mark and Reg were told by Rasmussen that when the Huts were in position they would be linked by telephones and back up radios. Rasmussen stressed the need to make the exploration base as polar bear proof as possible. The risk was small, but it couldn't be ignored. The plumbing would take the installation crew the most work. That involved water supply connection and a complex waste disposal system which would be downslope towards the fjord but only releasing clean water.

Mark realised that this was Rasmussen's personal project. He was an experienced geologist who had worked on many exploration sites. He knew that, for a team to operate for fourteen weeks, domestic and research support was essential if everyone was going to produce their best work.

Captain Hansen asked if they would like to return to any of the other huts to photograph facilities. Reg responded: 'Yes, that would be worthwhile.'

Reg Boston knew exactly what he wanted to photograph. Within five minutes he returned to the group. Captain Hansen told them that lunch was just about ready and escorted them to Block F.

After lunch a meeting with the three other Danish Navy staff had been laid on. Mark wasn't expecting this. He quietly went through the key features of the Danesfjord Project in his mind. Objectives, safety, domestic arrangements. He needed to convince his Navy team members of the chain of command: 'I will be scheduling the daily programmes of prospecting work. Captain Hansen will assist me if we have any security or serious safety issues.'

Mark knew that he had to leave the Danish Navy people with a clear message that he was the competent exploration leader. He spoke individually to all four, asking them if they had any questions. They were all fluent in English. At least they all seemed keen to take part. He told Peter Schmidt, the chef, that he was the most important person in the team. He responded, with a chuckle, that the fridges and freezers would be stocked with both British and Danish popular foods. He asked if any of the British team were vegan or vegetarian. Mark admitted that he hadn't considered that aspect, but he remarked that his wife was gently moving him in that direction. Mark confirmed that he would check with everyone and send a message back.

Anders Heiberg, was next. His main role would be servicing the helicopter but he'd also worked with Rasmussen on the design and specification of the Huts. He would be the first line of action if anything in the Huts needed maintenance or repair. He was being sent with two engineers toolkits; one for the helicopter, one for the Huts and domestic equipment. There would be a small container installed which would contain spares.

Mark had several questions for Captain Doctor Frida Karlsen. All related to the level of medical treatment that would be possible on site. That was met with a confident reply: 'Everything. You may have noticed a large cupboard in one of the bedroom cabins that had a range of equipment and drugs and plasma. The plasma was stored in a small freezer.'

Mark admitted he hadn't noticed the cupboard, but thanked her for her convincing assurance.

Captain Hansen asked Anders Heiberg, as armourer, to explain the use of heavy pistols that would need to be always available when anyone was more than 5 metres from the huts. Although the risk was small, everyone should always be alert. Heiberg also explained the waste disposal skip which would be just downslope of the huts. It was a Norwegian design which had polar bear proof hatches.

Navy catering staff brought over a tray of teas and coffees. Having covered the key formal information, conversation moved to more general questions and answers.

Mark and Reg Boston had one more night in the accommodation block then a flight back to Bristol on Wednesday morning.

# 32

Mark was pleased he'd visited Denmark, not just to inspect the purpose built Huts but also meeting the Navy crew with whom he would be depending upon for a great deal of support. It would leave him and his Chalco team to focus solely on the search for Rare Earth minerals.

Having Reg Boston along was more valuable than he realised at first. David Gresham's suggestion was practical. Reg would be the on-call person for equipment queries. If there were any breakages or malfunctions then it would be Reg's job to place a solution on the next plane to Iceland and onto Narsarsuaq Airport. As an ex-military technical specialist he knew how crucial it was to ensure that his subjects were kept properly equipped. No excuses, no bureaucratic delays. Just achieve a remedy. He had *carte blanche* to sanction orders 24 hours a day if necessary. The EU budget had plenty of spare funds for replacement gear.

The visit for Reg was illuminating. The Danesfjord Project was now much more real to him. With the printed copies of Hut inventories provided by the Danes, together with his own photographs, he felt a key member of the Danesfjord team.

There were now 12 days remaining before everything had to go in the container at St Peter Port. The auxiliary naval vessel would only be alongside for ten hours. Chalco would be hiring a removal van to be parked outside the offices. Everything that went in would be transferred to the container by the crew of the naval vessel.

Mark had told the three Chalco members of the team to bring over their spare clothing and personal items, and even specific bedding if they wished. They each had a weight limit of 150 kg, and their gear had to fit inside two 180 litre flight containers. They had a three day window before the 29th March to bring their stuff to Guernsey.

Captain Hansen had told Mark that the ship's crew would need two weeks to establish the accommodation and services at Danesfjord. The provisional fly out date had been set at Monday 25th April. Rosemary would book the flights for them.

Mark had just over three weeks with Emma and Katy before his departure. He wanted to make the most of it as he was aware of the long summer gap before he saw them again. It was an expensive choice but Emma suggested booking a large house near St Ives for a week over the Easter weekend. Mark wanted to be back home a few days before the fly out day. They were in the process of booking when Mark has a message from Rosemary.

> Exploration site still covered in snow. Danish Navy need
> an additional week for the set up. Fly out date now
> Tuesday 3rd May.

Mark was quite pleased. Emma could book a holiday for a week later. His exploration schedule would still be in a reasonable weather and daylight window. He knew that Professor Rasmussen wanted a clear fourteen weeks on site. That would now mean early May to mid August, allowing about three days at both ends for travel and set up and close down.

With three eager team members now just waiting to get to Greenland, Mark was conscious of maintaining communication with them. He sent out a general update to all three, also copied to David

Gresham and Reg Boston. He described many of the new things he'd found out about the Huts, and also stressed the importance of getting their personal stuff over to Guernsey before the 29th March. His idea of responsibility for his team was in some ways similar to the way he was keeping Emma, Katy and Kathleen up to date. Just as he had relied upon David Gresham for honest information in his early days as assistant geologist he knew he had to adopt a professional stance of being totally straight with his staff. They were all keen and he needed to respect their energy and enthusiasm. If he could demonstrate that he had their best personal and career interests at heart then they would do their best to make the Project work. This was an important step in Mark's career and the business integrity of Chalco.

Mark had several e-mail replies with genuine questions which he endeavoured to reply to on the same day. He told them he would be on holiday with his family in the last full week before the revised fly out date, but insisted they could still e-mail him with any questions.

The week near St Ives with the family had good weather. Even one sunny day on the beach making sand castles. Not a full day but a few hours until a breeze set in. The week went well in their self catering abode. Mark realised that Kathleen was weakening a little. Katy was even helping her on occasions, picking up things she'd dropped on the floor. Katy could sense that Mummy was Mummy and that Kathleen was an older person. Kathleen's great benefit for Katy was her story telling ability. Katy would select the book and the story within the book. Kathleen could assimilate the story within seconds and deliver it in her convincing style.

Mark had seen considerable progress in Katy's development in the months since Christmas. He was a little resentful to be away for nearly four months. He knew that Emma was the principal influence on Katy's education, quite a common occurrence where the mother in a family was a teacher. Perhaps the child development lectures, within her teacher training, were the advantage. How could all that be successfully imparted to the general population of young mothers?

After the St Ives holiday Mark lifted himself out of family mode and went through his extensive checklist of personal items for Greenland. By Monday afternoon everything was in his rucksack. Early Tuesday 3rd May he gave Emma and Katy big hugs before he climbed into the taxi to Bristol Airport for the first flight to Reykjavik.

At the Airport all four met up as arranged. They were on their way. Reykjavik, then Nuuk and the last flight down to Narsarsuaq. Only an hour to wait between each sector. They were met by the two Captains and a military truck to take them to the quay. COVID tests and fortunately everyone was negative. As they boarded the ship Mark introduced everyone. Up to then, Mark was the only one to know the whole Danesfjord team of eight. The snow and ice of the Greenland Ice Cap was visible behind the Airport. There were also small icebergs in the fjord. The ship's Captain explained the voyage. Departure in fifteen minutes, then dinner in the Officers Mess. They each had a separate cabin, clean and comfortable although no attempt to panel over the hard steel structure of the ship.

The voyage was smooth, mostly through fjords and between islands. They arrived in Danesfjord at 14:00 the next day. That's when the off-loading started. The Chalco members of the team, with their rucksacks, were taken ashore to a tiny gravel and sand beach in a big Zodiac by the construction team leader.

While the large Zodiac took the Chalco team ashore, another smaller Zodiac was launched with the Navy engineer, Anders Heiberg. He beached the boat into a special cradle with a winch that allowed him to pull the boat up well clear of the fjord.

The small helicopter on the rear deck of the ship started its engines and flew the short distance to the top of the col where it was almost level. Captain Hansen and Captain Doctor Frida Karlsen, and the chef Peter Schmidt climbed out and joined the party down at the Huts, about 100 metres away.

They all met by the four Huts and were given an instructional tour by the construction team leader, who was carrying a pistol in his holster.

The Huts had all been positioned perfectly level, abutting each other. Connecting doors would allow the team to move between the Huts without needing to go outside. The whole site was sloping at about one degree towards the fjord. The Huts were raised up on blocks. The waste pipes ran downslope for about 50 metres to the waste treatment cylinders. A huge array of solar panels had been constructed behind the Huts. The Chalco container, collected at Guernsey, was next to the large battery and solar panels.

The ground was short grass on a thin soil. Patches of bare rock showed through. The site was just downslope of the wide col between two unvegetated hillocks. The outside doors and main windows of the huts faced South West. On arrival, the Sun, low in the sky, was illuminating the Huts. In the distance, about 30 km away, the edge of the ice sheet was catching the sunlight. It was a cool day even though there wasn't a cloud in the sky.

The construction team leader said the last of the winter snow had only completely melted a few days ago. They'd seen one polar bear swimming in the fjord two weeks earlier while they were installing the solar panels. He wished them all well and told them the ship would return in seven weeks to restock the freezers and bring in fresh food. He said his goodbyes and returned to the ship in the big Zodiac.

# 33

They were now on their own. Captain Hansen said: 'We'll all go into the Kitchen hut and sit down while Peter makes us some warm drinks.'

They sat down at the long table. Peter Schmidt had obviously practised this welcoming event. Within five minutes two teapots were planted on the table, one marked decaf. Then two coffee pots, again one marked decaf. Then the UHT milk, they would grow to love that, according to Peter. Lastly a huge plate of Danish pastries. 'Tonight', Peter announced: 'We'll be eating dinner at 20:00. For the rest of the expedition it will be served at 19:00. Breakfast will be at 07:00. Lunch, if you're on site, will be 13:00.'

Captain Hansen said: 'Thank you Peter, over to you Mark.'

Mark: 'Welcome to our home for the next fourteen weeks. When we've finished our drinks we'll go over to the container and carry our personal gear to our cabins. We'll do the Chalco fieldwork gear tomorrow. So, the rest of the afternoon you can focus on getting yourselves sorted and settled in your cabins before dinner in here at 20:00.'

Doctor Frida was on polar bear watch while her husband carried their stuff into the Hut. Esme Blackall had a quick peek into her Laboratory Hut, then back to establish herself in her cabin.

Because they were now in the West Greenland Time Zone, UTC.+ 2, their first day had been two hours longer. After dinner it was time for bed.

All the showers and other plumbing worked. Everyone assembled in the Kitchen Hut at 07:00 on the next day. Peter, the Navy chef, determined to show he was up to his task, laid on a full cooked breakfast. He would soon learn that many of the team were opting for the alternative continental style. He made a note of individuals preferences for tea and coffee. This was a new venture for him, only eight people to feed, including himself. He was more used to feeding up to a hundred hungry matelots on a ship.

Mark had decided to produce a hand written schedule each day which went up on the magnetic board. That was mainly to cover time critical events, particularly later in the day. During breakfast he made a point of announcing the priorities of the day. This was day one and he wanted to establish clear communication patterns for the following 97 days. He would be working with his team and did not wish to be a faceless administrator secreted away in an office.

The first task after breakfast was unloading the Lab equipment from the container. All hands, except Peter, helped with careful carrying. Esme Blackall was mostly in the Lab Hut unpacking and checking her equipment. The outdoor fieldwork gear, particularly the drilling equipment, would be stored each night in the container. The expensive electronic field equipment would be parked in the Lab on the wide bench next to the door. Much of it would need charging every night.

After lunch everyone, including Peter, were taken on a familiarisation tour of the site. First a two kilometre walk to the freshwater spring on the other side of the North hillock. Not a navigation problem, Anders Heiberg led them along the blue alkathene pipe which had been laid on the surface of the ground. Slight frosts were still possible, even though it was May, but permanent hard freezing of the water supply was not anticipated. Anyway, burying the pipe in the rocky ground was impractical. If the team were to return next year, a replacement pipe would be installed as winter would almost certainly cause it to fracture. At the bubbling spring, the strum box in the small pool, was inspected. Anders explained that if the water supply appeared to be blocked or slowed down then clearing away any material should be all that was needed. If that were to occur then at least two people, equipped with a pistol and Very pistol, had to be sent to inspect and clear the strum box. Only a strong animal could lift the strum box and pipe out of the pool. Greenland musk ox were unlikely to appear on the site because of it being on an island. As for polar bears they were always a risk.

On return from the spring Captain Hansen showed them over the helicopter and explained the headsets, lifejackets and four strap seat belts. Only the pilots and Anders Heiberg were to do any refuelling using the hand operated pumps on the top of the large drums of Jet A1, the fuel for the helicopter.

Behind the Huts, Anders explained the solar panels and large battery. Cabling was on the surface of the ground, again burying not practical. If a polar bear was to raid the site there was a small risk that cables could be compromised. The battery monitor display screen on the kitchen wall would indicate if the electric supply was not functioning correctly.

The last familiarisation topic was waste disposal. Only toilet paper to be flushed down the lavatories. Bins in each cabin were to be used for anything else. The last thing was the skip for bin waste and kitchen waste. The skip had a substantial top. The only way to dispose of waste was to open hatches that had ingenious handles; polar bear proof. Anders explained how the handles on the hatches worked. It was essential that any marauding bear didn't get a whiff of food waste. The hatches had to be properly sealed every time. An unforgivable error if the hatches were left ajar. A bear was not to be given the slightest indication that the base could be worth a repeat visit.

The whole team now knew where everything was located, and the purpose. They'd been outside for three hours. The temperature was about 6°C, but a breeze was increasing, and dark clouds were building in the West. Peter said: 'Hot drinks and cake in the kitchen in ten minutes, then dinner at 19:00.'

Everyone assembled the Kitchen Hut. Mark took the opportunity to outline the programme of work: 'Tomorrow we'll start prospecting. All of us will be addressed by our first names from now on. Military rank will still be observed by the four Navy personnel, particularly in relation to matters where Captain Oscar Hansen has to take command because of hazards. Also, when the auxiliary vessel returns. Esme will be based most of the time in the Lab Hut. Harry, Leighton and myself will be out in the field. Tomorrow, we will start on the hillock behind the Huts. When we've finished our drinks we'll assist Esme in the Lab with any help she needs to set up all her equipment. Sundays we'll endeavour to keep as a rest day, and we can each do a phone call on the satellite phone.'

Thursday, Mark, Harry and Leighton set off up the hillock to do a visual assessment, then start sample collection. Away from the col, the thin soil and grass gradually petered out. The hillock was smooth igneous rock. It was like a large *Roche Moutonnée*. There were clear signs of crystalline mineral intrusions running across the bedrock surface, which was similar in appearance to granite. The Geological Survey of Denmark and Greenland latest maps gave it as Syenite, in other places as Granodiorite or Diorite. Visually it was similar to the stone facings that most people would recognise on the fronts of public buildings and banks. The bedrock formation must have been smoothed by the Greenland Ice

Cap when it covered the whole landmass. How long ago that occurred was not accurately known. It was evident that the edge of the ice cap was receding each year, and it was now about 30 km away in this part of Greenland.

The first task was to put the drone up and take a photo of the whole hillock, an area about 500 metres wide. Harry was ready. He'd mentally rehearsed what he had to do. He took the drone up to about 200 metres and checked with Mark if that was a suitable view. Many of the wider intrusions were visible on the screen. A lot of the intrusions were a metre wide some nearly two metres. The team had plenty to work on.

Then the start of sample collection. Leighton, didn't need his drilling equipment. He used the hammer and chisel to release samples and bag them. Harry flew the drone up to about four metres and took a photo of the sampling site. The drone key pad had a numbering facility. This sample was "1". The other data printed automatically on the image were GPS data and the day's date, 2022-05-05 (yyyy.mm.dd). If they could do this routine at every sample site the surveying record would be consistent and thorough.

The main mineral containing Rare Earth elements was Monazite, a milky grey crystalline intrusion, not that dissimilar to milky coloured quartz. Some Monazite was brownish or reddish or greenish. Flat surfaces of the crystalline mineral had a waxy feel.

Thorium could occur within the Monazite and is determined from Alpha and Beta particle emissions. Chalco's agreement with the EU was not to analyse in the field but take Thorium samples back in the double lead lined trunk for analysis in a specialist nuclear laboratory. Thus field checks on prospective samples would include a radiation sensor, a portable infrared spectrometer, and a photograph. The team were fortunate in sampling from an advantageous environment: bare rock completely free of soil. On this first site they were fortunate, although Mark realised that some sites may be covered in thin soils or gravel.

The job for Esme back in the Lab Hut would be to reduce each sample to dust in a crusher and analyse its elemental content with the Bench XRF (X-Ray Fluorescence) spectrometer.

The main radiation emission from Thorium is Alpha particles. These are identical to a Helium-4 nucleus. Because of the short path length, about 2 millimetres, many radiation sensors are ineffective. To detect Alpha particles the Geiger-Muller tube used in most radiation detectors needs to be engineered so that it can be placed close to the mineral of interest. Mark had made a point of ordering several of these specialist detectors so that the Lab, and the field team, were always able to check for all types radiation. This was particularly important for Esme. Using a crusher to reduce samples to dust ran the risk of some fine particles being entrained in the air which she was breathing in the Hut. In the case of Alpha particles that was a considerable health risk which had to be avoided.

Mark felt he couldn't be totally reliant on just the drone photo to record each sample. He used his field notebook to make a note of the sample number, date, time, intrusion width and a remark on the characteristics of the minerals in the intrusion. In some ways this area, completely clear of any soil covering, was one of the easiest environments he'd ever worked on. He'd equipped Leighton with a box of surveyors' nails. The ones often seen on pavements and roads in urban areas following a survey by council staff, engineers or architects. Getting Leighton to hammer one into the rock was intended to enable a sample site to be marked for a return visit. Unfortunately, hammering into crystalline rock is not always easy. The nails are like masonry nails and their hardness is comparable to the rock material. Leighton managed to chisel out a hole to insert the nail and fix its position with some silicone sealant. A small aluminium strip attached to the nail had the sample site number embossed.

The intrusions were easy to identify and through the day the team managed to take from, and record, 27 sample sites. Four of them had an amount of Thorium, identified by the spectrometer as well as the Geiger Counter These samples were still bagged and recorded but they were destined for the lead lined box. As long as Leighton didn't breathe in any dust and washed his hands before handling food the radiation risk was nil.

Back at the Huts Mark, Harry and Leighton took the samples into the Laboratory to explain to Esme. She'd had a busy day readying herself for the first samples. The four Thorium containing samples had been placed in the lead lined box which was kept in the container. Esme said she didn't mind processing the Thorium samples but Mark insisted that they needed to go to a specialist lab where sample crushing and analysis could be undertaken in a specialist fume cupboard type of environment.

That evening at dinner Mark explained that the day's sampling had been successful because of a particularly favourable environment. Some other sites might not be so accommodating. He wanted to include the Navy personnel so they could get the feel of the purpose of the exploration.

Friday Mark took his team up on the South hillock, which was also bare rock. A similar survey procedure, first a drone photo of the whole hillock, then collecting samples from 33 intrusion sites. There wasn't much difference to the previous day. Only two samples had Thorium. Nine samples were taken from intrusions that were three metres wide. Mark's general experience of volcanic intrusion gave the impression that the intrusions so far had been near vertical. He was happy to continue these preliminary surveys with hammer and chisel surface samples. If there was any indication that intrusions were not vertical then bringing in the drilling gear to collect sub surface material would be necessary. At the moment that wasn't part of the plan.

Back at the Lab Esme had processed the previous days samples. Nine rare earth elements identified in total and they were represented in most samples. Mark asked her if she'd had enough time to do the 23 samples from yesterday. She replied enthusiastically that it was ok, not wishing to admit that she couldn't cope. She gently stressed that the crushing process was the most time consuming because she needed to change rollers to get the fine particles. Mark could sense her meaning. He asked if 15-20 samples in a day might be a more suitable collecting target. She responded that could be an easier work load, and it would also enable more thorough crushing so that the sample particle size was all down to dust level.

Saturday, Mark had arranged with the Captains to take the helicopter across the fjord to the other side of the island. With no heavy drilling equipment the helicopter could take all three of the field team. The weather was grey, not much breeze. Captain Hansen wanted to download an aero weather forecast. He took the helicopter up to 3000 feet and got a signal from Narsarsuaq Airport. Today the weather was settled, but Sunday and Monday would see a deepening Low Pressure. At this altitude Mark took several photos. The vegetation pattern was similar all across the island, bare rock on the hillocks and struggling grassland on the lower slopes. They landed, as intended, near a hillock close to the fjord. They could see the Huts at their base about three kilometres away.

Their plan of action for the day was similar to the previous two: Leighton chiselling out samples from the intrusion sites that Mark selected. The intrusions were of similar colour and texture, but their width was much narrower. Some were only 20 centimetres wide. No sign of any radiation. Mark limited sampling to fifteen locations. He wanted to signify to Esme that he was listening to her concerns. He knew she was a perfectionist and he was happy to accept that enabling her to do her best work would result in higher quality analyses.

It had been a useful day. The aerial photo of the whole island would be used to plan a sampling campaign. After three days of sampling Mark had evidence that Rare Earths were definitely present. If the weather was obliging he could accumulate well over a thousand samples during their exploration. More important than the number of samples would be the areal distribution. Plotting all the results on a map would show the key sites for mining, although it could be be quarrying. Esme's work would provide information on the likely concentrations of minerals in different areas. Although the first target area was the island on which they were based, they would use the helicopter to do checks on the adjacent mainland and smaller islands.

Mark was quite insistent that Sunday was to be a rest day. Peter had prepared the day's meals and put them in the freezer or fridge. It was to be a day for washing machines and general cleaning. A rota for family phone calls was set up. Everyone had ten minutes on the satellite phone located in the Lab. Mark put in a call to David Gresham as arranged. He would be flying over for a two day visit within the next few weeks. Reg Boston would accompany him so Mark needed to let them know about any equipment needs.

Lunch and dinner that day was more relaxed. Conversations were much more personal than during the working week. The consensus was that the well designed Huts and facilities were particularly valued by the whole party. It was an easy living space, compared to low grade huts or tents.

Harry, assistant geologist, offered to set up a spreadsheet of the sample data. He'd practised this several times as a student, specialising in spatial mapping of the data.

As well as the voice call to David Gresham, Mark used his ten minutes of personal calls to talk to Emma and Katy. All was fine at home and Katy was developing fast.

There were a couple of spare laptop computers and Esme offered to link one to the Lab satellite phone. Mark thought that was an excellent idea, live pictures. It would mean that the weekly ten minute calls to loved ones were more intimate.

During the following week six further areas were prospected across the island. Harry was getting used to the drone procedure of grabbing a photo and precise Latitude and Longitude of each sampling location. Samples were chiselled out by Leighton from the bare crystalline rock. Mark had never known such a straightforward collecting environment. His plan was to do several weeks with a similar strategy, focusing on bare hilltops. With that in the bag he would expand the search area but also attack the more lowland areas where soil and vegetation would require gardening tools to get down to the bedrock.

Weather was reasonably conducive to the sampling programme with only one heavy rain day in their third week. The team used this down day to review the accumulated data. Harry's printed out distribution maps were a great help. They didn't have a single sample site which hadn't recorded any Rare Earth minerals. Sampling sites had been visually selected by Mark but every single one had shown at least six Rare Earth elements in the Bench XRF analyses. Pinpoint sampling alone couldn't numerically assess the concentration of elements at each site, but Mark felt confident that the area was rich in Rare Earth minerals. Compared to his experience of working on Exmoor, Danesfjord was a significantly better prospect for realistic mining.

Esme's XRF analyses showed that Neodymium was the most abundant element. That would would please the industrialists with interests in manufacturing high efficiency electric motors for vehicles, and wind turbines. The next most abundant element was Samarium, valued for X-ray lasers, and magnets that can withstand high temperatures. Other elements were Terbium, used in solid state electronics; Cerium, a glass additive; Praseodymium, used in optics. All the above were found in nearly all samples. Terbium might be of interest to the EU accountants as it commanded a high price on the metals market.

Unlike China which had accumulated huge stocks of metals, and were able to control World markets, Europe had minimal stocks.

An e-mail came in on Thursday, David Gresham and Reg Boston would be arriving at Narsarsuaq Airport on the afternoon of Tuesday 24th May, with a return a flight on Thursday afternoon at 14:00. That meant the helicopter would be needed to collect and return them. Mark decided to do samples sites on the North of the island during Monday and use Tuesday for trial drilling near the base on a piece of ground near the fjord. They could use the quadbike to carry the drilling equipment. The selected sampling site had grass and a thin soil, although the soil was underlain by gravel. This would be a trial. Up to now they'd enjoyed easy site selections simply because the exposed bedrock clearly showed where the Monazite intrusions occurred.

Friday and Saturday they did sampling on the hillock tops but came back early Saturday afternoon as a storm was developing. Sunday was grim with sleety snow and strong winds. The planned volley ball match, Navy versus Chalco, had to be postponed.

Monday they went to the North of the island and collected 15 samples on a bare hill top.

Tuesday Oscar and Frida set off early in the helicopter for Narsarsuaq. They wanted to have the rotor blade angles checked and adjusted if necessary. Then they filled the fuel tanks to the maximum. This meant that the day's flying would have used hardly any fuel from their base stores. David Gresham and Reg Boston arrived on time. Reg had some equipment spares requested by Esme. They weighed 65 kg so Oscar had to do some quick calculations. Personal luggage wasn't all that heavy, David was of normal stature, but Reg was a large man, about 120 kg. With full fuel tanks the total payload was only 15 kg below recommended maximum. Oscar and Frida considered their strategy. It was a cold day so flying low down the first fjord would be the best plan. The flight went without incident. They landed back at base about an hour before dinner. All the Chalco team plus Anders the engineer, were waiting. They carried the spares down to the Huts while Mark greeted David and brought him up to date on sampling results. Reg explained to Esme the contents of the spares package. He had doubled the request for crusher rollers, commenting that skimping on those would inhibit her aim to prepare samples for the bench spectrometer. There were also two extra laptop computers.

Mark's lowland sampling exercise near the Huts had been hard going. They had to dig a long trench through wet gravel and soil until they encountered a Monazite intrusion. The vein was nearly a metre wide so Mark asked Leighton to chisel out two samples. Both exhibited a lot of radioactivity. Mark used paper towels to dry the pieces. Not ideal conditions to use the infra red spectrometer but a couple of scans revealed that the crystals contained Thorium and Thulium. Minor signals for a few other rare earths but the samples seemed to be quite different to the many hilltop ones taken so far. Those samples were bagged and placed in the lead lined box back outside the Lab Hut. It had been the dirtiest field day the three of them had experienced so far.

Dinner was a chatty affair as team members recounted their experiences of the first three weeks. David was pleased that the team were impressed with the Huts. All the planning and preparation had paid off, of course with the up front EU money. David took time to talk with

Peter. He knew from his many years field experience that competent catering was an essential element for maintenance of happy and healthy geologists! It was more than evident from the meal that the team were content with their feeding.

Reg had long chats with Esme, Harry and Leighton. He realised that if equipment wasn't up to scratch some of the frustration would be focused on him. Reg had only been with Chalco for four years after 24 years in the military. This was the most innovative field project with which he'd been involved. He liked the job and was determined to make sure he was an effective member of the Company.

Bringing in 65 kg of kit to Narsarsuaq was actually cheaper than if the package had been sent with one of the international couriers. Reg and David also knew that it had reached the correct destination and at the designed time, with no breakages. They'd both had a long day of travelling and were happy to be shown to their cabins.

On Wednesday, Mark had arranged to take David and Reg out to the North of the island. That required two helicopter transfers, but they were only six minutes each. Mark wanted to show David the routine they had developed for sampling on the bare hilltops.

Mark: 'It's the first time I've had such clean bare rock for sampling. As you can see the Monazite intrusions are clearly visible. We should be able to obtain over a thousand samples on this prospect. We can do the actual sampling and drone recording in less than ten minutes for each site. Because of the clean rock we haven't used the core drilling gear at all yet. We're limiting to 15 samples a day as Esme can just about manage that number. Most of her time is taken up with the crushers. Working down through the rollers to get a fine powdery sample is essential for the Bench XRF spectrometer.'

David: 'How about using the backup crusher so Esme can prepare two samples at the same time?'

Mark: 'That may not work as might be expected. The crushers need attention all the time so that the rollers can be changed at the appropriate time.'

David: 'I could suggest you need two lab scientists, but you already have a large data set. As for sampling strategy, your best option is to increase the areal coverage, rather than collect a high density of samples in a small area.'

David was actually challenging Mark to evaluate his methodologies. He was more than satisfied with the quality of the first three weeks data. Chalco had never benefitted from such an advantageous support infrastructure. Mark knew that from his own experience. They had use of a helicopter for placing geologists wherever they chose, and amazing technologies for recording their work. So far, the data was showing consistency. Just doubling or trebling the number of samples in a small area wouldn't add any more scientific value. They needed to examine just how far these intrusions of rare earth extended. That was what the eventual mining organisations would value. Scientific niceties were one thing but in the end money was at the root of this whole campaign. Mining organisations and governments measured success in billions, not the esoterics of academic geologists.

David was clearly overwhelmed at the economic potential of the site and the whole area. Ease of working was a tremendous asset. He sent Reg back in the helicopter with Harry and Leighton. He and Mark would return on the second flight with the gear.

David's purpose was to acquaint Mark with the almost certain success that Danesfjord was revealing. But, even though the initial data transfers had been fully encrypted it had become clear from week one that cyber hacking was being attempted. The geeks were now full time on defeating interferences with their systems. David was briefing Mark on what the Danesfjord team needed to do to resist hacks and any other form of information gathering. The strategy needed to be one of disinformation, obfuscation, confusing whoever was trying to capture the team's progress.

The satellite phones were part of the problem. The location from which they were transmitting was easily available to even low level hackers. Weekly phone calls to loved ones had to be curtailed. Outgoing messages had to be routed through Mark who would need to edit out any comments about work. He would then put them through a piece of encryption software to an e-mail address set up for the group.

David had brought two new satellite phones and would take back the originals. Only emergency voice calls to be made. Mark could make urgent calls to David through a new number.

Mark felt that for staff morale these changes were akin to practices for prisoners, he was sure that David wouldn't be introducing them without good reason. Because Chalco was involved with an EU project Andrew Norris had decided not to involve GCHQ with the hacking problem. He wasn't sure how anti-EU culture was operating in the some parts of the security services. Another complication was a request from Naomi Dawson to visit Danesfjord. David was fending that off for the moment, but would deal with it sensitively on his return to Guernsey.

The helicopter returned. Mark and David climbed in and flew back to the base. As they walked downslope to the Huts, David said he will meet all four Chalco members in the Lab after breakfast tomorrow: 'I want them to know that I've made the decision to limit outgoing communications. I don't want them thinking that you're the one who's turned into a dictator.'

Reg Boston was engaged in a friendly discussion with Anders Heiberg. Their careers as military "fixers of problems" gave them a common bond. Anders revealed that the four of them, the Navy personnel, had been threatened with court marshals and imprisonment if they leaked any information about the Danesfjord Project.

The auxiliary support vessel that had delivered the team was dealing with more than one discreet operation in Greenland. It was also keeping a number of military groups further North supplied with food supplies and equipment. They were there to watch over any attempts by foreign groups to establish surveillance bases on the shores North of Nuuk, the capital of Greenland.

Denmark's responsibility for defence was continually being tested by potential threats. The recent loud assertion by the U.S.A. to buy Greenland had sharpened the Danish military approach to security. The bigger worry was surreptitious financial persuasion of the Greenland government, and population, to accept a U.S. acquisition. The largely urbanised Inuit population of the capital city were not wealthy, and exhibited considerable social problems. Completely unlike the social atmospheres of other Nordic cultures.

Dinnertime everyone headed to the kitchen. Peter had conjured up a splendid culinary spectacle for the last night of the Chalco visitors.

David sat next to Oscar Hansen, the pilot and senior officer of the Naval party.

Reg Boston made a point of sitting next to Esme. He realised she was rather a shrinking violet, unlike his own daughter who had all the brazen assertiveness of military life. Reg said he had doubled up on the crusher spares and spare computers. If she needed any further gear she should put in a request via Mark. There was no problem with the project budget, and in any case, equipment not used would travel back in the container and go into stock. Reg had seen Esme's Lab, she was meticulous. Not the sort of try-it and chuck-it attitude of some military deployments that Reg had experienced. He encouraged Esme to speak up more strongly for anything she needed to do her work.

David's discussion was more restrained. Oscar was careful not to provide any detail, but admitted that there was concern in Copenhagen that Greeenland was under threat. He was a key part of a discrete military grouping that was the eyes and ears of the Danish government. Security and caution were their watchwords and he was pleased that David was tightening communications for the Chalco staff.

Breakfast the next morning was brief for David and Reg. Peter surprised them with large foil wrapped sandwiches "for the journey". Mark gathered the other three in the Lab for the communications clamp down. David didn't pull any punches. He wanted to leave them with the impression that he was the grumpy old man, but he also explained that Chalco was being hounded by cyber hackers. He wished them well and then headed up the slope to the helicopter. Mark detected that there wasn't too much disgruntlement amongst the other three. They were on a bonus payment for the fourteen week tour of duty, to be followed by an eight week leave. To them it was just a part of the job. Some of their friends were in jobs where phones were removed at work, and they had to sign horrific non disclosure agreements which contained career wrecking conditions and threats of legal action.

Oscar and Frida had worked out how much fuel they needed to fly to Nasarsuaq where they would refuel. The Chalco return luggage was much less; personal rucksacks and a box with the two decommissioned satellite phones.

At the base it was a clear sunny day. Without the helicopter they could only work locally. Mark wanted to get core samples from the crystalline bedrock up on the North hillock. The drilling equipment was brand new and Leighton needed a trial drilling to familiarise himself. The samples which they took at the surface, one metre, and two metre depths were a sort of control samples. The Prospect Report would need to have analysis of the principal bedrock. Visually it was quite similar to fine grained granite. It was professionally important to understand the native rock. Any future quarrying needed to know its hardness and composition. Tools can wear out rapidly cutting into most types of crystalline rock.

Going back on the planes David and Reg discussed the efficacy of the Huts base. Reg pointed out the slender staffing. No back up for Peter the cook. He also felt that for such a highly prestigious project Esme was irreplaceable by the other three. At least the helicopter had two pilots, but one of them was also the sole medic. For such a remote location the team of eight had little in reserve. David acknowledged the slenderness of the Project. So far sampling was progressing well and he was hopeful that it would continue successfully.

In some ways David felt that the Project would succeed. It was one of the best funded explorations ever undertaken by Chalco, but it was also in a unique environment. He fully realised that the location was totally reliant on a ship that had other responsibilities in one of the most challenging environments of the world. Reg had used his military experience in making his assessment. Unlike military units where life was sometimes regarded as disposable, Chalco had legal obligations to its staff for safety and stress.

Although David didn't admit it he had found Reg's direct comments useful.

# 34

Friday Mark decided to start the revised sampling targets. Wide area coverage, rather than multiple sampling within a small area. That meant daily use of the helicopter. He still had a few parts of their base island to sample, then Saturday would be a start on the mainland and some of the smaller islands.

Saturday was a glorious sunny day, low humidity and exceptional visibility. They flew across to the mainland and Mark asked Harry to put the drone up to 5,000 feet, 10,000 feet and 20,000 feet to take vertical images of the wider area. How far did the crystalline rock with the intrusions extend? Also, were all the hill tops free of soil and vegetation? The small scale geology maps produced by the Danish Geology Institute showed the area as being of similar igneous, but there was no indication of how many analysed samples had been taken to arrive at that conclusion.

Using the drone at high altitudes had exhausted the battery so the reserve one was attached for images of the nine individual sample sites they had taken that day. Mark kept the helicopter on stand-by so they could increase the sampling interval to about 2 kilometres. They were still sampling from bare rock so the collection time was still the same. It had been a superb day, even slightly warm when the breeze wasn't present.

Back at base Mark asked Harry to put the three high altitude images onto a memory stick for him. He studied them carefully in his cabin after dinner. It appeared that the same geological structures existed over a wide area. Hilltops clear of soil and vegetation. There were well over 20 kilometres by about 12 to 14 kilometres of potential sampling sites.

Sunday was another bright day. Conditions were ideal for the volleyball match. Mark remembered one exploration he went on for three weeks where they worked every day; mainly because the weather window was short. He was aware that everyone seemed to value the "day off". He had an interesting chat with Frida before the picnic lunch. She felt that yesterday, when they were on stand-by out in the field with the helicopter, made her and her husband feel they were involved with the Project. Often they were considered taxi drivers, shifting people from A to B, but to see how the prospecting was operating out in the field added a new dimension to their duties. The landscape was dictating where they went and what they did. That was quite different to a military career where it's all about following orders that cascade down from, sometimes, faceless superiors.

So far Mark had learnt that Peter was enjoying his deployment as chef to a geology team. Now it seemed that Oscar and Frida were valuing their involvement with the Project. Perhaps he should try and engage with Anders Heiberg to hear his comments on the Danesfjord exploration. He would try and find a suitable opportunity for a relaxed conversation. One thing he knew already was that Anders was a skilled volleyball player.

Into the fifth week and it looked like the weather was becoming more settled and a little warmer. Mark was quite hopeful that he should be able to continue with the wide area sampling. Although the helicopter was being used much more, Oscar said it wasn't making a significant dent in their supplies of jet fuel. Each change of sampling site was only one or two minutes in the air. At the end of each day there were only about 30 km of air miles logged.

As for results, Esme was performing her analyses methodically. She was pleased with her new rollers for the crusher. The rare earth elements list was largely unchanged and it seemed that quantities were consistent. About five percent of all samples had small amounts of Thulium and Thorium. They were all bagged and placed in the lead lined box. None of the Chalco team had any training or experience in handling high risk compounds. So they would follow the procedures laid down in the EU contract to hand over the Alpha emitter samples to an EU regulated laboratory.

Unfortunately, the weather broke down by the weekend such that the party came back early on Saturday. Worse still, the Sunday volleyball match had to be cancelled!

On Monday morning the rain had stopped but it was cool. Just before they set off for further sampling, the satellite phone rang. It was Bernard Hosegood. Naomi Dawson had advised him that she would be arriving at Narsarsuaq Airport, from Nuuk Airport at 10:15 on Wednesday for a brief visit. She would need to be back at Narsarsuaq Airport at 17:45. Mark thought this was part of the general plan. He assumed that this visit was part of the British Government's continued support for Chalco. Bernard rang off without any further conversation. That probably meant not much sampling would be done on Wednesday.

Mark got Oscar and Frida to fly them out to the mainland again to continue the hilltop sampling. He was conscious of limiting collections to 15 but as a number of samples were quite radioactive he decided to collect from a further six sites. Site intervals varied between two and three kilometres so the areal coverage was growing fast. The radioactive samples were clustered at the most Northerly extent of the area. In some ways that would be of interest to future quarrying companies. It turned out to be quite a sunny but cool day with a drying wind from the North West. The extra six sites lengthened their day and it was 18:40 before they landed back at the Huts base. Mark was exhausted. After dinner he gave a brief description of the day to Esme: 'The fifteen samples for processing are all clear of radiation, and I've put the six Thorium samples in the lead lined box.'

Mark spent the evening on his own in his cabin. He needed to update his own fieldwork log book. Keeping accurate records on such a long exploration programme was essential. He had also been impressed by Esme's laboratory log book. Much data was on the computers but keeping paper records still had a value. There was an e-mail alert on the new satellite phone.

> Thanks Mark for giving Reg and myself a comprehensive introduction to the Danesfjord base and operations. We got back late last Thursday after a couple of delays and weather re-routing. Since then I've been brought up to speed by the geeks. They are convinced that serious hacking is continuing which is affecting all our teams, not just Danesfjord. I've been in touch with Professor Anton Rasmussen and he has been experiencing similar problems. The Danish Government have set up a watch team to monitor their communications; military and civilian. We're still not sure where it's coming from but the general consensus is that we limit communications, but also use obfuscation techniques to confuse the perpetrators. As for any visitors to Danesfjord, just be vague, do not give data to anyone, except myself and Bernard.

Mark was intrigued by that message. He sent a brief reply:

Thanks David. I fully understand. It was good you came last week to get a feel for the landscape we're working in. I had a brief phone call from Bernard this morning advising me of Naomi Dawson's visit on Wednesday.

A reply came back, rapidly.

Bernard has been in hospital for the last week having his knee done. He doesn't even have the new Satellite phone numbers.

Mark thought for a moment. It had been an odd brief phone call from Bernard. Not his usual style of conversation. He sent David another reply.

That makes the phone call highly suspect. I'll let you know what happens on Wednesday. We'll be particularly cautious.

The security situation was becoming peculiar. He would brief the rest of the team, including Oscar and Frida, that something odd was going on. He had followed Naomi Dawson's requests and suggestions for several years, but he knew she worked in the murky world of so called "government security". Had the phone call "from Bernard" been made by someone using speech manipulation? Speech copying software was now widely available. Were the cyber hackers now widening their armoury to include impersonation tactics?

Tuesday at breakfast Mark briefly mentioned to Oscar that another visitor needed to be collected from Narsarsuaq on Wednesday. He thought it better to leave the details until breakfast on Wednesday in case further messages were received.

They had a successful sampling day on Tuesday. No sign of any radioactivity, so Mark limited the total samples to 15. The pattern he was adopting with the helicopter was to take three samples at each helicopter landing site. Those samples were spaced about 50 metres apart along the selected intrusions. That meant five helicopter landing sites during the day, each taking about 50 minutes on the ground. They were back at base just before 16:00.

No further communications from Chalco. Mark thought he would go to dinner but not give any details generally to the team until breakfast the next day. He mentioned to Peter that there would be one extra for lunch tomorrow. He went back to his cabin to make up his handwritten log. At 21:00 a phone call from David. Mark was quite sure it was David from the usual banter. David had been to the hospital to see Bernard. He hadn't made the unusual call, so they were both agreed that the call Mark had received on Monday morning was from an impersonator. David suggested sending the helicopter across to Narsarsuaq tomorrow morning to see if Naomi Dawson was there. If she was then bring her back to base but give her minimal information because of a contractual statement from the EU to restrict all data. If she wasn't there then ask Oscar to phone you for instructions. Then you phone me.

Wednesday morning Mark briefed Oscar and Frida. They would take a satellite phone while Mark would carry the other with him all day. Mark realised that there would be no real data collection today. If Naomi Dawson did arrive they would walk her down to near the fjord where it was damp and do a trial trench "to take a sample". If she asked what we had found so far Mark would stress the EU contractual statement, but also quietly and "confidentially" admit that what they were finding were the low value elements like Cerium and Lanthanum, and in not great quantities.

So the strategy was set. It was just a matter of waiting to see if Naomi Dawson appeared.

As the helicopter set off towards Narsarsuaq Airport, Harry and Leighton went down to a soggy section of the banks of the fjord. They dug a trench 3 metres long, lifting out the thin soil and then the muddy gravel. Nearly an hour elapsed and the satellite phone rang: 'We've collected Ms Dawson, estimated flight time to base is 45 minutes, listening out.'

Mark said to Harry and Leighton: 'Looks like the day is going as advised. We'll get back to the Huts, grab a warm drink, confirm to Peter that lunch will be needed for one guest, then we'll wander up to the col and await the visitor.'

The helicopter arrived and Naomi Dawson stepped out. Mark introduced her to Harry and Leighton, and welcomed her to Danesfjord. They took her down to the female Hut and showed her to a cabin so she could freshen up. Mark was the soul of discretion and deliberately diplomatic. He didn't wish to give her any indication that they were treating her visit with a huge amount of distrust and caution.

At the trench, Mark explained: 'We've started another trench to see if we can encounter any Monazite. Harry is using the geiger counter first, then the spectrometer. Because the trench is rather damp we can't rely too much on the backscatter from the field spectrometer. Then we bag up a small sample which Esme will put through the crusher and the XRF spectrometer in the Lab tomorrow. Harry is labelling the bag with the date and sample number. Then he'll put the drone up to about ten metres and take a vertical image. If you look at the control screen you'll see that the Latitude and Latitude is captured and recorded on the image. That's the basis of our location recording, and we also have a handwritten logbook as a back up, and to make a textual description of the site.'

Naomi: 'So when will you know the accurate analysis of the sample?'

Mark: 'Tomorrow.' Pause. 'Leighton will do one more sample at the other end of the trench then we'll go back to the Kitchen Hut for some lunch.'

Naomi imagined that she would be shown the Laboratory Hut after lunch. She'd been using her camera phone extensively during the demonstration. Why was she so intent of photographing everything?

Mark hoped that his planned fieldwork act might be working. He knew that Naomi had done economic geology for her PhD. That probably meant she had done little fieldwork herself, and certainly not with a field spectrometer. In all other respects he was totally welcoming to the woman who had extricated him and David Gresham from the Ecuador tragedy in 2018. If she maintained her position within British security services he might need her support on a future project which wasn't connected to an EU confidentiality contract. Mark couldn't forget the unusual phone call that had set up Naomi's visit.

Back at the Kitchen Hut Mark introduced Naomi to Peter the chef and Anders the maintenance specialist. He gave the two sample bags to Esme and asked her to clean and dry the morning's samples. He'd briefed her earlier in the day about the Cerium and Lanthanum pieces of Monazite that he'd used for demonstration purposes while at Avon.

Peter announced: 'If you'd all like to take a seat I'll serve lunch.'

Peter had prepared one of his Danish specialities: mop herring salad and warm bread. The kitchen was already effused with the unmistakeable bakery smell.

Naomi joined in the general banter over lunch hoping to elicit information on the Danesfjord field base. She'd been using her camera phone continually while down at the trench.

As lunch and coffee was coming to conclusion, Mark asked Esme to fetch the Monazite samples, that she had dried.

When she returned and sat down at the large Kitchen table, Mark took the field infra red spectrometer out of his rucksack. He showed Naomi the procedure of scanning, and the result coming up on the screen. Quite clearly it listed two elements: Cerium and Lanthanum, but in small quantities. He then went on to explain the campaign they had followed to date: 'The results have been consistent to date, mostly Cerium, much less Lanthanum. We've sampled quite densely around this island, but also across on the mainland, up to 20 km from here.'

Naomi: 'That's interesting. Can you show me the Laboratory?'

Mark: 'We'd love to, but the Danish government have provided that, indeed all four Huts, and have stipulated that access to the Lab wasn't to be made available to anyone not included in the EU contract. Peter was loading the dishwasher, but the other three Danes around the table, Oscar, Frida and Anders, were stern faced. They were solidly supporting Mark's constructed story.

Naomi showed the first signs of not believing Mark. She responded: 'That's a pity, I may as well get back to the Airport.'

At that Oscar and Frida rose from their seats. Oscar: 'We'll prepare the helicopter. We'll be ready to depart in about ten minutes'

Mark had achieved his aim, but at what cost. Naomi Dawson had been a beneficial "aunt" to him over the past four years of his career, even though she had expected a range of *quid pro quos*. If she feels she had been snubbed what were the consequences for him and Chalco?

The helicopter with Naomi departed, Mark thanked everyone for their support but now he had to revert to the central programme.

Unfortunately, without the helicopter that afternoon they were confined to the immediate area. Harry could see that Mark was feeling a little disturbed. He asked: 'Shall we return to the banks of the fjord and backfill this morning's trench?'

Mark thought for a moment: 'Thanks Harry, but I think we'll leave it open, we don't know if we might need it again.'

Anders came across to Mark and pointed out that there was a small bare topped hillock down on the other side of the fjord. It was at the South end of the island, and it was an area that they hadn't sampled a few weeks ago. Anders said: 'I can take you down the fjord in the Zodiac. You'll only have about 600 metres to walk up to the hillock.'

Mark thought for a moment. It was a sunny afternoon, no wind and the weather seemed settled. They wouldn't need shovels, just the drone, the Geiger Counter and the spectrometer. Mark thanked Anders and within ten minutes the three Chalco team joined him down on the small gravel beach. They climbed into the Zodiac and set off down the fjord. It was about four kilometres to where Anders found a small beach to land.

Anders stayed with the Zodiac while the team walked up to the summit of the hillock. It was only about 40 meters above sea level, the lowest hillock they had found, but it was just about bare rock. There were a few plants seemingly rooted into the bare rock but it was still easy to visualise the lines of Monazite intrusion. It was the densest pattern of intrusions they had seen, and some were more than a metre wide. Mark wanted to take the now standard three samples. It was 15:30 and Mark said: 'We need to work quickly.'

He selected the first site. Leighton checked for radiation, none, then used the infra red spectrometer. A positive reading for many elements. Leighton chiselled out some samples and bagged them. Harry took the drone image at about four metres. Mark asked him to go up to 100 metres and take the whole hillock. Within six minutes they were walking to the next intrusion. They completed another two sites and headed back down the slope to the Zodiac. There was still no wind, the fjord was flat calm. The 12 hp engines didn't give them much speed but they got back to the base beach in seventeen minutes and they were all bone dry. A rare sight occurred as they neared their beach, a single orca was heading seaward in the opposite direction. It paused and raised its head to reveal the characteristic black and white markings. Leighton captured it on his mobile phone.

They helped Anders winch the Zodiac up clear of the water. The tidal range wasn't more than about 40 centimetres but the winching system was a precautionary measure in the event of a severe storm.

Back at the Huts Leighton handed over the three bagged samples to Esme. Harry added: 'We got positive signals for all three.'

Esme responded: 'I'll process them first thing tomorrow. I've given the crusher a thorough clean this afternoon. It'll dry overnight.

The helicopter hadn't returned. It had been away for nearly five hours. Anders said that Oscar was planning to refuel at the Airport but that shouldn't have taken long.

The helicopter landed up on the col at just after 18:30. Oscar took Mark to one side: 'Can Frida and me see you in your cabin?'

Mark said to the others: 'You grab a warm drink and I'll see you at dinner shortly.'

Oscar, Frida and Mark headed for Mark's cabin. Oscar started: 'Your colleague, Ms Dawson, was sullen all the way back to Narsarsuaq, no communication whatsoever, and she couldn't have had a better day to view the Greenland scenery. She went across to the terminal building. We had to wait for the local tanker lorry to finish collecting jet fuel from the ship down at the quay. That's why we were delayed. Frida went across to terminal for a comfort break. While there she saw Ms Dawson talking with several men and another woman.'

Frida: 'They departed and walked across to a Lear Jet with Canadian markings. I went up to the control tower and talked my way in past the security guard. I had to present my special ops military pass. The plane had filed a flight plan to St John's Newfoundland where it was based. The plane had been chartered by an Adam Tilby. I asked if they could find out who paid the charter. That took a while, then a reply came back from St John's. It was paid for with a company credit card in the name of Oronazite Minerals.'

Oscar: 'I was wondering why she was away so long. I'd finally got the helicopter fuelled and was waiting to leave.'

Mark: 'Thanks both of you. That's all new to us. I'll phone Chalco after dinner.'

There was lots to talk about over dinner. Mark didn't want to reveal all the oddities of Naomi's visit so the conversation was mostly about the interesting hillock they had surveyed that afternoon. Leighton was showing everyone the photo he had taken of the Orca. Mark announced that if the weather was stable again tomorrow they would resume wide area sampling.

After dinner Mark quietly left for his cabin. He decided to send an encrypted e-mail to David:

> We're working through the sampling steadily, still no appreciable finds. Naomi Dawson arrived today. We showed her a sampling site down near the fjord. I explained that we couldn't show her into the Lab because of the EU contract, so she went back early. When the pilots returned they said she was met by a group of men and one woman who all climbed into a Lear Jet with Canadian tail markings. The flight plan was for St John's Newfoundland. The charter aircraft was booked by an

Adam Tilby and paid for with a Oronazite Minerals business credit card. We think Naomi Dawson found the visit useful although she was disappointed at not looking into the Lab. We're not really sure of the reason for her visit. Peter provided an excellent lunch and everyone was most welcoming.

Twenty minutes later a reply came back:

Thanks for your communication. I'm glad you were able to show her around. I'll get back to you.

Mark assumed that David would look into the details. Perhaps getting some information on Tilby and Oronazite. One thing that complicated the Naomi Dawson personage was that it was difficult to determine exactly what and who she was. The secret world of any government was always clouded in the dark world of lies and misinformation.

Thursday the weather was still favourable so the resumption of wide area sampling was back on.

A successful day. Not just the fifteen samples from five landing sites. The weather and visibility was exceptional so Harry did vertical images at multiple altitudes. He got the drone up to over twenty thousand feet which produced an image that covered from the Danesfjord base to nearly at far as the ice sheet. With the Danish geological maps and their own images they now had a comprehensive record of the area they were surveying.

Friday was similar. Another fifteen samples. When they got back they were met by Esme, Peter and Anders up at the landing pad. Esme was trembling. She waited for Mark to disembark and then broke into tears: 'We've been raided.'

'When?' replied Mark.

Esme: 'This morning, three men in a purple helicopter. I saw them coming down to the Huts. I locked myself into the Lab but they broke down the door. They took lots of photographs and asked where you were.'

Anders interrupted: 'I'd taken Peter with me to go round to the water intake to check the strum box. We had the satellite phone with us. Esme was busy in the Lab so we left her there.'

Mark: 'Did they take anything?'

Esme: 'A computer.'

Mark, alarmed: 'With all your data?'

Esme: 'No, I'd put that one and my desk log book in the fridge. I'd put one of the spare computers on the bench. That's the one they took, but it didn't have anything on it. My back up memory sticks are always hidden.'

Noticing that something was unusual Frida got out of the helicopter and came over to comfort Esme. Peter and Anders had heard the intruder helicopter and were on their way back. Frida urged everyone to go down to the Huts.

Back in the Kitchen, Peter got some warm drinks ready. They all sat round the table. Mark had brought his expedition log in with him, the one he made up each evening. He carefully tried to record as much detail as possible, mostly from Esme. Anders had remembered the registration markings as the rogue helicopter flew over him. It was a Danish civil registration. Oscar said he would get it checked out. Esme remarked that they were almost laughing when I said you weren't here. The man doing the talking had an Australian or New Zealand accent. The other two didn't really talk, they just chuckled and laughed. They were quite intent on photographing all the Lab equipment. The photographer was the second man. The third man, probably the pilot, appeared to be Far East Asian.

Mark asked Esme why she thought he was the pilot. She said he went back up the slope to the helicopter while the other two went round the back of the Huts, presumably to look at the solar array.

There were many questions from the team, particularly surrounding general security. Oscar said he was going to put in a request for two special services soldiers. There were many up North on coast watching duties: 'We should be able to transfer a couple of them down here for the next eight weeks. If its approved they'll be willing volunteers who would value Peter's cooking over ration boxes.'

Mark reminded the team that the auxiliary vessel is scheduled to arrive next Friday to restock our food supplies.

Mark had a private word with Oscar: 'If Anders and Peter go to check to water source again, they must take Esme with them.' Oscar concurred.

Peter had started preparing the evening meal. He announced to everyone: 'Dinner will be ready by 19:00 as normal.'

The group chat and debrief broke up and most went back to their cabins to tidy up. Mark caught Esme's eye: 'If there is any need to check the water source again, you must go with Anders and Peter. You're not to remain at the base on your own.'

Mark was beginning to realise that the security of the whole base, and all the personnel, was not satisfactory.

After dinner that evening, he typed up an e-mail to David Gresham. He sent it fully encrypted via the satellite phone. He hoped that it wouldn't be intercepted by any rogue operators. The new satellite phone numbers were probably already known to the cyber hackers, and it probably wouldn't take them many days to decode the "so called" sophisticated encryption software.

Within half an hour a reply came back from David. The decrypted text was as follows:

> Thanks for update. We are concerned that things might be becoming awkward at your end. Myself, Rasmussen and Reg will be flying to Nuuk next Thursday to join the auxiliary vessel while its taking on food. We're getting assistance from the Jersey government for cyber problems. They have a new department with specialists. It's independent of GCHQ. They're trying to track down the real name of Naomi and perhaps we can find out why she now has a seemingly unexplained different agenda. I've spoken with Bernard; he's furious and is also using his connections to unravel the problem. Will keep you informed.

Mark sent an acknowledgement and asked for a third satellite phone, specifically for Esme. He settled down to sleep hoping that tomorrow he might be able to do another 15 samples on the wide area programme.

# 35

At 00:20 Mark awoke. It was early on Saturday 11th June. There was buzzing in the Hut. Wires were burning out and his mobile phone was inoperable. Mark wondered if they were being attacked. Then a knock on his cabin door. It was Harry, then Anders, then Leighton. What was happening?

Mark peered out of his tiny window; deliberately made small to hinder inquisitive polar bears. It was dark outside; a heavy cloud layer. Oscar knocked on the connecting door. Anders let him in. Oscar asked if there had been any buzzing in their Hut. It was self evident when another buzzing started. Oscar asserted: 'I suspect we're experiencing Electro Magnetic Pulses, usually abbreviated to EMP.'

Mark was aware that devices capable of delivering such effects had been built in physics research labs for years. There were plentiful rumours that military had been assessing such devices for warfare purposes. EMP generated electronically did not harm people, in contrast to nuclear explosions which produce much more powerful pulses, in addition to the radiation.

Oscar continued: 'A great deal of electrical power is needed for such weapons. It was likely that the source is a vessel down in the fjord.'

None of the lights were working in the male accommodation Hut. Two lights were working in the female Hut. Anders and Peter went through to the Kitchen Hut. Several lights working there. Peter switched on a kettle. That was working. Oscar assumed command: 'I think were under some form of attack. No one go outside.'

Esme had put on most of her clothes and came through to the male Hut: 'Will someone come through to the Lab Hut with me?'

Anders already had a gun in his hand. Frida had dressed and came through with the pilots' gun. She gave the gun to her husband. Oscar. Anders and Esme unlocked the connecting door to the Lab. No lights were working. Esme opened the fridge and the light came on. Her computer and lab logbook were still in there from yesterday's malevolent visit. She left the fridge door open to provide some illumination. She checked some other electrical items. Not much was working. Anders looked out of the small window that faced the fjord. He asked Esme to close the fridge door to reduce the light. He could just about see a dark shape moving down the fjord. Oscar looked as well. He said it looked like a ship about the size of a minesweeper or a coastal patrol vessel.

Mark said: 'Can we all assemble at the Kitchen table. Oscar, you lead the debrief. I'll write notes in my logbook.'

Oscar: 'I'm convinced we've been subjected to an EMP. We'll know more at first light. For the remainder of the night we have to assume that there are malicious operators outside. If the ship has departed then that accounts for the current absence of buzzing in the wiring.'

Frida went back to her cabin and brought through an aluminium flight case. She asked her husband if she should open it yet. He said we can probably take that risk now that the ship has departed. She opened it and took out the pilots' satellite phone and Oscar's mobile phone. Oscar checked the phone; it was working. He then switched on the satellite phone; it also appeared to be working. He phoned the Danish Military Base at Nuuk. The night operator picked up immediately. Oscar announced his military details and the Danesfjord codes. The rest of the call was mostly in Danish and gobbledegook, it was all military speak.

Oscar finished the call. He spoke to everyone clustered around the table: 'Helicopter team will arrive at first light. Keep guns by your side, but the best thing we can do is all get some sleep.'

It was now nearly 01:00. They kept the Kitchen lights on but went back to their dark cabins.

The Huts base was at about 61° North, and it was nearly midsummer's day. That meant sunrise shortly after 04:00. Oscar set his phone alarm to 03:40. Because his phone had been in the flight case it was probably the only phone still functioning. Aluminium flight cases behave like Faraday Cages. Electrical equipment inside is protected from electromagnetic fields.

Mark had been writing assiduously while everyone was around the Kitchen table. This was another problem that could wreck the Danesfjord Project. He turned in but didn't sleep well.

Oscar's alarm went off. He leapt out of bed and started listening for helicopter rotors. Frida got up also and was fully dressed. Outside at 04:00 wasn't likely to be all that warm. Oscar went to get Anders. All the guns were checked, safety catches off. They went into the Kitchen Hut where there were still some lights. They could hear a large helicopter approaching. Oscar said: 'We'll stay near the door, but inside, until we're sure it's one of ours. Anders, you watch through that window. I expect they'll circle first, then check out the site, then land near our helicopter.'

Anders could see the Danish military helicopter land. About eight soldiers climbed out, then they checked the whole site, including the solar panels and battery. They found no physical damage or any unwanted characters hiding in the area.

Oscar recognised the group leader. It was Major Lars Nielsen, currently acting senior officer of the coastal protection group. Oscar had been on several courses with him. Oscar decided to go out to meet him.

Hello Oscar, are there any casualties?

'No, only our nerves and patience. We think we've been subjected to an EMP. It happened shortly after midnight. Buzzing and so forth. Most of our lighting is inoperable, and many other electrical items don't work. We got a faint glimpse of a small ship moving down the fjord once the buzzing stopped. Nothing else has happened since the ship left.'

'My men haven't found anyone lurking on the site. Probably the best thing we can do now is make a complete inventory of electrical items.'

'I agree. My chef, Peter, is already in the Kitchen. He's trying to cook up some breakfast. Our Laboratory Hut has suffered the worst of the attack, but because the Kitchen is the farthest Hut from the fjord we've still got some appliances working. While you and your men are eating I'm going to check out our helicopter.'

Before he left, Oscar introduced Lars Nielsen to Mark. The military group stripped off their battle gear and settled around the Kitchen table to eat. There wasn't quite so much finesse in Peter's catering skills. He had nearly twenty mouths to feed so everything was done industrially. Fortunately, there were ample stocks of protein remaining in the fridges and freezers. One freezer wasn't working so that one was emptied first.

The two pilots of the big troop helicopter chatted to Oscar and Frida as they checked over their small helicopter. Oscar said the avionics seemed unaffected. He and Frida would do a quick search for the rogue ship. It was now over two hours since the ship departed so it could already be in international waters.

Lars and Mark had discussions. Lars had been on a specific EMP course as part of his duties with the Danish military. He filled Mark in on the effects of a ship borne device. The range of the pulses was directly related to the power of the device. That power would have to have been taken off the ship's engines or batteries. The fact that there was more electrical and electronic damage in the Lab Hut than the Kitchen Hut showed that the range of the ship's device was at the limits of its destructive effect. Mark said that the Lab equipment was badly affected. He would need to get Chalco to send over replacements.

Lars asked if there was any equipment in the shipping container. Mark said there were some spares. Lars suggested they have a look. He was hopeful that the steel container provided a full Faraday Cage effect.

Mark went to find Esme. Lars rounded up his special services team. They unlocked the container and the troops carried in some items. Anders had already replaced many of the light bulbs in the Lab and most were working, except one corner where the lighting cable had burnt out. They found that three power points were working. That included the one powering the fridge. The crusher was found to be working, but not the Bench XRF spectrometer. The troops carried in the spare and that worked. By and large the Lab damage wasn't as bad as they had first thought.

Outside the troops were checking the solar panels and battery. Some slight burn out of connecting cables but the monitoring display panel in the Kitchen Hut was still showing a moderately healthy battery capacity and only eight of the 140 panels had failed.

The small helicopter returned. Oscar and Frida walked down to report back to Lars and Mark. They had found an old, probably 1960s, minesweeper anchored in a bay about 15 nautical miles down the coast. The vessel had no markings whatsoever. Lars rounded up his men and said they would assess if a boarding party could be contemplated. Within five minutes they were airborne.

Since breakfast Anders had made a preliminary inventory of all the Danish equipment and services. That was mainly cabling, one freezer, possibly eight solar panels. The electric shower heaters were all working, but two washing machines needed replacing. He'd also checked the outboard motors on the small Zodiac at their beach. They were in bad shape and needed replacing along with the battery and the navigation unit. He was hopeful that next Friday's visit of the auxiliary vessel could bring the essential replacements.

Similarly, Esme had tested all her equipment and computers. She had a list of what she needed. The spare XRF spectrometer in the shipping container that the troops had carried in for her was now in service. She intended to request another one, as a new spare. If Reg Boston could source the various items before the Chalco group left for Nuuk then they could arrive next Friday. It was tight, but their best prospect for keeping the whole Project on track.

Mark and Harry had totted up their requirements. A new drone, field spectrometer and Geiger Counter. Above all, replacement mobile phones. It seemed that devices with fine wiring, or extensive silicon chips, were the most badly affected. Fortunately, Harry had left the spare drone in the shipping container, and it was unaffected.

The whole team currently had only one satellite phone that worked. The one that Oscar had put in his aluminium flight case. Mark took that into his cabin to send a message to David. Another significant piece of luck was that Mark's desk in his cabin was a utilitarian steel variety. Not the most attractive piece of furniture for the leader of the expedition but the fact that it had acted as a Faraday Cage for his computer in the top drawer meant that he could still use it.

Mark was more than thankful that his cabin computer was functioning. Although he methodically made up his handwritten log each evening, there were several files on the computer including copies of Harry's ongoing spreadsheet cum mapping exercise. Additionally, Mark had daily backups to a memory stick.

The long e-mail to David started with a description of the second disrupting event in 24 hours. Then a long list of items that they needed replacing. The first part of the list were the items that were absolutely essential for arrival next Friday on the auxiliary ship. Those items would mean that the sampling strategy could be fully back in action for the second seven weeks of the Project. Another part of the list were items that would replace the spares in the container. Mark realised that the cost could exceed £100,000 but that was not his worry. The Project must not be allowed to fail. For some reason it was becoming clear that there were organisations that wanted them to fail. If that was for political reasons, or business interests, he was not in a position to unravel. An outstanding question was who was behind the disruption. His role was to keep things running. He was pretty sure that the whole Danesfjord team was behind him.

Having encrypted the message he sent it to David. He couldn't do much more until he got a reply from Guernsey. Perhaps it was time to send a message to Emma. He didn't want to give the impression that things were dire, so he focused on a theme of the ship returning next Friday to restock the base for the next seven weeks. He needed quite a bit of replacement equipment because they'd been working so hard, but the team were fully supportive of the enterprise so all was looking quite promising for the second half. Mark hoped his theme was upbeat enough.

# 36

At about 11:00 the big helicopter returned. Lars came down to the Huts. He called a meeting in the Kitchen of himself, Oscar, Frida and Mark. He prefaced the meeting with: 'This is now a military matter of the Danish Government in pursuit of its constitutional role: the defence of Greenland. We flew over the location where the minesweeper was anchored. Another vessel was tied up alongside; a small coaster. She had a Canadian flag, and a name – *Baffin Angel.* I decided not to lower my troops until I can get authority from my superiors. I want to get to the bottom of this matter, but without causing an international incident. The other thing of note is that there were men on the deck of the minesweeper who were dismantling large sheets of plywood to reveal a fishing trawler underneath the "minesweeper" The EMP device is now clearly visible on the front deck. We've got photographs. It's not large but it fits the structure of a magnetron with lots of coils. Another reason we had to return without intervening is that we were low on fuel. If I get authority to intercept I need jet fuel from your store. I appreciate we cannot leave you, or us, with insufficient fuel to get to Narsarsuaq. I can requisition your supplies but I feel I have a duty to seek your agreement.'

Mark replied: 'With the incidents we've experienced in the last 24 hours we can't be sure there aren't more attacks on our operations. How much fuel will we have left if you refill?'

Lars: 'Not much, my helicopter drinks three times more than what your four seater uses.'

Mark: 'Where is your nearest ship?

Lars: 'It still way up North, in the Disko Bay area. If it started to steam South now it would be nearly thirty hours before it gets here. Do I have you agreement to refuel my helicopter from your base reserves?'

It was so much a question, more a statement of intent.

Mark thought for a moment. His professional duty was to ensure that he could get his team back safely to Narsarsuaq.

Mark voiced his decision: 'Yes, provided we can get one flight out to the Airport.'

Lars said thank you. He went up to his helicopter and put through a call to Copenhagen.

An hour later Lars returned: 'We're going, but I have to take the small helicopter in support.'

Mark felt he was losing control. He and his Chalco team were now on an uninhabited tundra island without a helicopter, and with a Zodiac whose engines didn't work. This was now a military operation and he was almost powerless. He stated calmly to Oscar: 'Leave us with the satellite phone, you've got your military radios.'

Oscar realised that Mark was trying to defend his position, and placed the phone on the Kitchen table without any comment.

Within ten minutes both helicopters were in the air. Unbeknown to Mark, Anders had been ordered to refuel both helicopters while Lars waited for authority from Copenhagen. Peter had been briefed to prepare two big bags of sandwiches and a supply of water.

Mark felt the risk of isolation. If both helicopters were shot from the sky by who ever was on the coaster *Baffin Angel* then he would have little more than the one satellite phone.

# 37

Mark rounded up Esme, Harry and Leighton, and gathered them around the Kitchen table. He explained the situation. There was little he could do to get further samples. The priority for all of them was a general tidy up, but also be prepared for evacuation, or Heaven forbid, further attacks. He was rather downbeat, not his normal self.

Peter had gone with Anders and the pilots in the small helicopter. The Kitchen was now theirs. Esme put the kettle on. They all rustled through the well organised food supplies. No bread left, but plenty of rice, and a fridge full of salad stuff and cheese.

Two e-mail replies had come through. Mark went over to his cabin to transfer them to his computer. The reply from David was upbeat. He and Reg would be working flat out to get the equipment to Nuuk for next Thursday. The reply from Emma was much warmer and homely. She sensed Mark was up against it. Lots of accounts of Katy's progress.

Mark went back to the Kitchen where the team had cooked some rice and knocked together a lunch. Mark was most grateful. He suggested to the team that he would send messages for them this afternoon. He felt buoyed up by his three assistants. He was just hoping that the two helicopters would return without any harm, to machines or personnel.

Mark thought he would have a look at the Zodiac down at the fjord he asked Leighton to accompany him, and of course, with a gun and a Very pistol. Esme asked if she could come too. At first sight the engine looked ok, but when they looked closely they could see that the wiring to the battery was fried. The boat, high and dry on its berthing frame, was in the firing line of the EMP attack. Probably less than a hundred metres from the damaging electronic device. Mark thought that the boat with its two tiny paddles gave them few transport options. He was not raising his confidence. Esme said brightly: 'Can I show you some gadgets I brought with me. My boyfriend is studying for an MSc at Southampton University. He asked me to plant some cameras at the edge of the fjord. Peter helped me install them when we arrived. There's one camera over there.'

The three of them walked about forty metres to the North. Unfortunately the whole camera in its plastic case had been fried.

Esme explained: 'He asked me to plant them so they covered visiting whales in the middle of the fjord. So this one looked South East and the one further down the fjord looks about North. Can we walk along to that second one?'

Mark perked up a little. This was a novel digression from his worries about the Project. They walked seaward down the bank of the fjord for about three hundred metres. Past the bluff trench they had dug for Naomi Dawson's visit. The second camera didn't appear to be fried. Esme lifted a small cover which had a tiny screen and various buttons and LED indicator lights. The screen lit up to show a clear infra red image of the last thing to trigger the video capture. There was the minesweeper on its way back down the fjord. It was a high resolution camera. Esme changed the SD card so she could recover the stored videos and images onto a computer.

Mark: 'That's a bonus. At least we've got some evidence. I hope your boyfriend isn't too disappointed to have images of ships rather than whales.'

They started walking back to the Huts. As well as the guns, Mark had brought their one remaining satellite phone with them. It began to ring. Mark answered it. A strong Danish accent announced that she was calling from Military Command HQ at Nuuk. There was a problem; one helicopter has ditched in the sea. A major rescue attempt had been activated. There was no further news at the moment. The phone rang off.

Mark was feeling that things were going from bad to worse. Where would the Chalco team be placed on the priority list of the Danish military?

Esme brought her computer into the Kitchen to show the others the images and videos captured by the camera trap. There had been several orcas swimming up to the head of the fjord over the past few weeks. They were all single male whales recognised by their high dorsal fin. The Zodiac had been videoed over a week ago when the boys went down the fjord on a sampling trip. The last items were the minesweeper, or what they had assumed to be a minesweeper. It came up the fjord in the dark. The camera trap defaulted to the infra red lens. The ship turned to face the Huts. Some crew folded up a large sheet behind the magnetron. It stayed in that position for about fifteen minutes. That was about the time of the buzzing pulses experienced in the Huts. It turned and slowly steamed seaward. All the timings were printed on the videos. When there was no further movement in the fjord the camera switched itself off.

The videos were clear evidence of their midnight nightmare but they were still in a powerless situation. They just hoped the remaining helicopter would return soon.

Amid the afternoon gloom and pensive state Leighton surprised them. He was now in chef mode. He'd found Peter's notebook of the food stocks and was cooking up an evening meal. Not just for the four of them, but for the Navy guys and the helicopter troops. He was being deliberately optimistic. The only comment he made was that there was enough frozen food to last the four of them for about four months.

The smell in the Kitchen was charging their appetites. Mark wanted to phone David again but thought it was pointless until he knew the outcome of the helicopter mission.

Leighton announced: 'Dinner will be served at 19:00 as usual.' That raised spirits a little.

At 18:40 the sound of a helicopter was heard. Mark, Harry and Esme went outside. It was the big troop helicopter. Mark was sure it was the one he'd seen earlier because he remembered the markings. That meant their small helicopter must have been the one that ditched. The troops climbed out, assisting two others wrapped in space blankets. Then a stretcher was lifted out, accompanied by a third person in a space blanket. The 150 metre walk to the Huts seemed to take forever. Eventually Lars approached Mark: 'We have one casualty I'm afraid. Peter has hypothermia.'

Frida, still wrapped in a space blanket was tending to him. Lars ordered his troops to sit down at the table. Oscar and Anders went for a hot shower and a change of clothes. Frida had the stretcher placed near the cooking range, propped up on four chairs, to take advantage of the warmth. Peter was still unconscious. Frida asked Esme to fetch any duvets she could find. Harry thrust a cup of milky tea into Frida's hand. He could see she was shivering. Leighton carried three large pots of hot food to the table and started feeding the troops. Oscar and Anders came back from their showers heavily dressed in dry clothes. Oscar went over to Frida and told her to get a shower and dry clothes. He watched over Peter who was just about conscious and warming up.

The temperature on the Kitchen wall thermometer was now 22°C. Eight troops plus Lars and two pilots, together with the Danesfjord eight had all contributed to warming the Kitchen Hut. Anders was studying the solar panel display on the wall. The electric was nearly all coming from the battery. The cooking range was still on full, the battery reserve was dropping fast. It would be flat in an hour and a half. Most had been fed, but there was still the treatment of Peter. Frida came back fully dressed in dry clothes. She wanted Oscar and Anders to take Peter into a hot shower and remove all his wet clothes.

Lars took Mark to one side. The afternoon's incident with the ditched helicopter was unsuccessful and the loss of the machine was a disaster for the military. He'd have to take it further up the line for resolution.

Mark asked how the helicopter had ditched. Lars was hesitant: 'I can't really comment at the moment. We did everything by the book, but we were attacked by some electronic devices. Myself and Oscar will need to go back to Nuuk and file our reports and be debriefed.'

Mark pointed out: 'Without a helicopter we can't complete our work.'

'I realise that. I'll have to get authority but I propose we take your group to Narsarsuaq. There's enough fuel in the helicopter to get there with a light load. Then I'll refuel. Then I'll return for my troops.'

Mark asked: 'What's happening about the *Baffin Angel* coaster?'

Lars responded: 'We have one of our frigates leaving the East coast of Greenland now. They'll try and intercept. The Canadian government are in agreement. They're tracking the coaster by satellite and relaying that to our frigate. The coaster can steam at 14 knots, our frigate can exceed 30 knots. Copenhagen is sending two F35s to Nuuk. They'll overfly the coaster as the frigate moves in. Fortunately the whole matter is being accepted by Canada as a criminal activity, not political.'

Mark directly to Lars: 'Do you know what's going to happen to my team of four: Me, Harry, Leighton and Esme.'

Lars: 'I'm going to make a call to our Command Centre at Nuuk as soon as Dr Frida has assessed Peter's state. I guess it will be a full evacuation for you, while we set up a guard team here and wait for the auxiliary ship to arrive with replacements and a repair team. Don't quote me on that yet. In the military we just follow orders from our superiors.'

Frida came over to speak with Lars: 'Peter is out of immediate danger and his body temperature is nearly back to normal. He'll need some tests in hospital to see if there are any secondary issues. I hope we can get him to Nuuk first thing in the morning.'

It was gone 20:30 and getting dark. Lars agreed with Dr Frida: 'I'll prioritise that but I'll have to send our helicopter to Narsarsuaq early tomorrow to refuel. I'll phone HQ now.'

Lars went outside with the phone. He was on the phone for a good fifteen minutes. He returned and spoke with Frida and Oscar first. All Danish military personnel will go to Nuuk tomorrow, except four troops who will guard the base until another unit arrives in the afternoon. That new unit will be fully self contained and comprise twelve personnel.

Lars then spoke with Mark: 'Yes, evacuate for at least ten days. Tomorrow there will be an 07:00 flight to Narsarsuaq for the Chalco four. All personal gear must be removed from the Huts and placed in the Chalco container, so that a team can revamp the entire Hut complex when the ship arrives next week. Apparently, your colleague Anton Rasmussen was at the Command Centre and insisted on the evacuation.'

Mark gathered the other three: 'This evening we have to put all Chalco equipment from the Lab into the container. Early in the morning all our personal gear comes out of the cabins and also goes into the container. We're going home for about ten days. It's imperative that every piece of data, in books, on computers, on memory sticks goes in our rucksacks for the flight out. We also need to take our broken phones back. We leave at 07:00. No trace of our work must be left in the Huts. We can't exclude further attacks on this base from persons trying to obtain our data.'

There was some relief that they were leaving as without repairs and replacements they knew they couldn't continue the Project. They got to work immediately on clearing out the Lab. The only things to remain were the Danish fixtures and fittings. They also lifted the lead lined box with the radioactive samples into the container. There were no indications on the sample bags of what was inside, just day number and sample number. The key data was in the log book, Esme's computer, and the SD card from the drone. As far as the drone handbook indicated no other location or image data was left in the machine. Mark was trying to cover all bases. If another attack raided the container he wasn't worried if instruments were taken because they could be replaced. It was critical for the EU Project to keep a tight hold on all data. Chalco was a knowledge based company. It would lose its credibility if others had access to its raw data.

It was 22:30 when the team had cleared the Lab. Leighton had his bedside alarm clock; totally clockwork and unaffected by the EMP. He set it to 04:30, when he would wake the other three. He also offered to get in the Kitchen and knock up some breakfast. Anders had pointed out earlier that evening out that the battery was low. Probably only a few kettle boils remaining.

The troops billeted themselves down on the Kitchen floor. Their breakfast might need to wait for daylight to reach the solar panels. With their mid-morning departure they didn't need to set any alarms.

Peter was tucked up in his bed covered with two duvets. Frida was content he should be alright.

# 38

Sunday morning went smoothly. Leighton had tea, coffee and luke warm porridge ready for the Chalco four and the pilots of the Merlin helicopter who would take them to Narsarsuaq. Lars wanted Oscar to travel with them to ensure no hiccups with the refuelling.

Lars admitted that the aircraft was low on fuel. Hovering to rescue the four from the small helicopter that ditched had depleted reserves.

The payload to the Airport was light and it was hoped that the flight would make it. A second ditching was not even being contemplated. It was a cool morning, no rain and no wind so the environmental conditions were favourable. The plan was to fly direct but mostly near sea level and along fjords. The Chalco team had only their personal rucksacks, albeit stuffed full of notebooks, computers, phones, memory sticks and SD cards.

Oscar was in the jump seat between the two pilots. He was watching the fuel gauges. The Chalco four weren't aware of the delicate flight strategy. Visibility was good. An announcement by one of the pilots over the intercom said: 'Airport in sight, 4 miles.'

That was nautical miles. Within a minute, a lot of odd noises from the engines. Then the sound of one engine winding down. The aircraft was now on only two of its three engines. Its speed dropped but the pilots held the altitude. No other announcements. They reached the edge of airfield and more spluttering. The pilots put the helicopter down as the spluttering continued. It was a rather heavy landing but at least they were on the ground. Two fire engines were approaching. Oscar came back into the main cabin: 'That was tight'

With the engines silent the sound of one of the pilots communicating with the control tower could be heard. It was all in English; aviation clichés and acronyms. The control tower was treating it as a major incident. The pilot was insisting: 'Not an incident. Military, we're on a special mission. We're scheduled to depart in twenty minutes. Send minibus and a jet fuel tanker.'

The Chalco evacuees disembarked. Mark turned to Oscar: 'Thank you for getting us out. Hopefully we'll see you again soon.'

A minibus arrived. The four climbed in with their heavy rucksacks . At the airport terminal two officials met them: 'This is irregular. We'll need statements from you.'

Then Professor Anton Rasmussen arrived and interposed. He waived some documents under the officials' noses: 'High priority, I have to get these people back to Nuuk.'

Rasmussen walked straight through security and outside towards a waiting transport aircraft with the familiar red markings. The five of them ascended the steps, to be welcomed by a steward in military uniform. They were shown to seats and asked if they'd had breakfast. Leighton quickly responded: 'No we haven't.' He was conscious of the minimal offering he had rustled up with almost nil electricity nearly two hours previous.

The seat belt sign was on. The steward went to his seat and strapped in. Within a minute they were racing down the runway. Mark looked out the window. He saw a tanker with fuel lines connected to the helicopter. He could make out Oscar waving to them as they climbed rapidly and banked steeply. They were heading North. The plane continued to climb, then levelled out. Another steward arrived with a trolley and served them breakfast. Harry was impressed: 'This is much better than you get on a flight to Majorca.'

For Mark, this was reminiscent of his evacuation from Ecuador. At least he wasn't injured this time, and no missiles were chasing them. He just hoped that the Danesfjord Project could be recovered.

After they had consumed their second breakfast, Anton Rasmussen called to Mark and invited him to come over and sit for a chat. There was certain to be some sort of military debriefing, and Rasmussen hoped that it wouldn't go into detail over what geology had been found. He suggested to Mark that he used the phrase – we've collected some interesting samples but can't really assess them properly until we've analysed them in our lab. Could Mark pass that on to the other three. Mark nodded. Rasmussen warned Mark that there would be quite a high level inquiry because of the loss of the helicopter.

The plane landed at Nuuk airport. They disembarked and were shown to two military vehicles. They didn't go near the terminal but out through a gate and along to a military base about a kilometre away. The vehicles were waved straight in.

At a separate building they were ushered into a large hall with many paintings. They sat down and waited. An officer, in full parade dress came over and asked, in perfect English, for Miss Esme Blackall. Anton Rasmussen got up and quietly told the officer, in Danish, that he would be her advocate during the meeting. Mark didn't know what was said. The three of them walked off down a corridor.

Mark turned to Harry and Leighton and said we're under a military authority, if we get questioned, keep to bare facts but imply ignorance of why we were being attacked over the past few days. Obfuscate on questions related to our findings. Say we won't know until we've analysed our samples back in Guernsey.

In a small office the officer started questioning Esme. He was beating about the bush a little but two things were clear. He was uncomfortable at having one of Denmark's leading academics sitting in, but he was also aware that he shouldn't be interviewing a civilian woman on her own.

Esme's recollections afterwards was that he was attempting to discover the organisation behind the strange disruptions. The officer had to explain to his superiors why a helicopter had been lost. In Copenhagen this would be a serious matter. Esme explained several times that she was alone at the Lab Hut when three uninvited men raided the Lab and took many photos. They didn't acquire any data, although that was probably why they'd been sent. Esme inferred that they weren't particularly knowledgeable in geology or science in general. The man with Far East features didn't seem to be a part of the raiding group. He'd just been sent as an add-on. As for the EMP attack Esme pointed out that electronic warfare was not part of her scientific repertoire.

Esme had to go through her explanations several times, then suddenly the officer said he needed the computer with the infra red photos of the attacking minesweeper. Esme said that was not possible, or legal. Anton Rasmussen didn't need to say anything. Esme was holding her own: 'What I can do to assist your enquiries is give your military people copies of the infra-red photos. If you'd like to go and find a new, unused, memory stick I'll copy them for you.'

Rasmussen, in Danish, gently asserted: 'That seems to be a satisfactory solution to your problem, officer.'

The officer got up from his seat behind the desk and walked out.

Rasmussen explained quietly that the problem with military personnel is that they're not skilled in discussions with ordinary people. They're locked into a system in which their only leverage is rank. Their understanding of science and its practices is weak.

Five minutes later, the officer returned with a memory stick still in its plastic wrapping.

Without any further words, Esme took out one of her computers, she had three in her rucksack. She found the camera trap videos of the minesweeper, showed them to the officer, then copied them to the memory stick. As she handed over the memory stick she calmly added: 'If you use these videos in any report, please acknowledge the copyright of Southampton University.'

At that, Anton Rasmussen got up from his seat, Esme likewise. They both gently smiled and left.

Rasmussen, in his long academic career, hadn't encountered a young scientist quite so confident, and competent, in defending her position.

Back in the Hall, Rasmussen indicated to the other three that they were leaving. At the entrance hall they were met by a startled corporal. Rasmussen ordered formally, in Danish: 'Will you arrange for transport to take us to Hotel Glacier, please.'

Two minutes later they were shown down the steps and into an armoured car. In ten minutes they were deposited at the hotel, probably the most expensive in the small city. Rasmussen led them in and to the reception desk: 'Lunch for five please. Charge it to my account.'

Over lunch Rasmussen admitted to the Chalco four that the military were fully aware that they had to support the Danesfjord Project. However, they were unfamiliar with looking after geological survey teams. Rasmussen knew his power base was that Danesfjord was a high priority EU project. Nothing was to hinder its success. He explained: 'The last few days have been a hiccup for the Project but it won't curtail the work. I'm staying here in Nuuk to ensure that everything is put in place, so that when you return you'll be able to continue where you left off. I've already been in contact with David Gresham and Bernard

Hosegood. Together we're endeavouring to get to the bottom of the Naomi Dawson visit and her possible connection to the other incidents. As for all of you, I've booked you on flights to Reykyavik early tomorrow. Then a flight to Bristol and another to Guernsey. David Gresham will meet you there. He'll give you replacement phones. He needs you for two days to debrief and make back up copies of your data. He and the expanded geeks team will also brief you on methods for keeping data secure for the second stage of your work. It's vital that your data is for your eyes and Chalco only. Not even me, or Astrid Larsen, should have access to it until Chalco formally presents its findings. Anyway, you should be able to fly back to England on Thursday and have a week at home, David will contact you when we know the reconditioned base is ready. Any questions?'

Mark: 'I think you've covered most things. Thank you for shepherding us out of these problems. On Saturday we thought we were stuck on the island with no support, hardly any electric, and no helicopter.'

It was mid afternoon. Rasmussen booked them into the hotel for one night and suggested they could have a ramble around the unusual capital city.

# 39

After breakfast next morning, Rasmussen ordered them a minibus and sent them off to the airport. The flights interlaced perfectly with only one hour change-overs at Reykyavik and Bristol. At Guernsey David Gresham met them as promised. It was 16:00. The two geeks were with him. Within half an hour all four of the field team had a brand new phone and most of their messages and photos restored. David dropped them off at the local hotel.

That evening Mark phoned Emma. She and the other families of the evacuees had been informed by Rosemary de la Mare that the team was coming back to Guernsey for a mid-Project break and they would be coming home for a week's holiday.

Mark kept to that politically correct story. All he wanted from this phone call was a family chat, particularly with Katy. She was so excited: 'Can we go to the beach?'

It was a welcome interlude following a chaotic week when Mark wasn't even sure they were going to get out safely.

The following morning the four of them turned up at Chalco offices to be welcomed by Rosemary: 'We've been worried about you. They're all in the board room.'

David Gresham, Andrew Norris, and Bernard Hosegood were waiting. Bernard had crutches, following his recent knee operation.

Bernard: 'It's good to see you all. We still haven't sorted out what's been going on but we'll update you when we're certain. Two days here so we can secure your data so far, then you should be able to have a week, or a bit longer, as a holiday. You deserve it. David will debrief you today and get your views on how the Project has progressed. Tomorrow we'll put you in the picture, as we see it, of the political, or business, interests trying to intercept our Project.'

Tea and coffee were wheeled in. A relaxed chat followed between all seven of them. Bernard was intent on creating the feeling amongst his geologists that they were highly valued and that their physical and mental welfare were a high priority. It gave the younger members of the team an opportunity to relate their experiences and concerns.

Following refreshments Bernard and Andrew left the board room. David explained how he wanted the data archived at Guernsey. 'As little of your first seven weeks data should go back to Danesfjord on your computers. We can't be sure it will be safe from interception and copying by rogue operators. In order for you to carry out your work you obviously need to know where you have sampled up until now. It's clear that the chemical analysis has shown consistent promise of high mineral content for the elements which we've been been asked to investigate. I'd like the full chemical data to remain here, but the Latitude and Longitude data, encrypted, should remain on Harry's computer, with a back up copy on Esmes's and Mark's. That will mean your coverage mapping is fully available. The wide area survey will benefit from expanding, possibly from another two weeks sampling. Then it may be worth increasing sampling density in areas which merit further sampling. I'm suggesting that we avoid further sampling in areas with radioactive content. We intend to submit our report to the EU in November. We anticipate that we'll get a continuation contract for next summer. If that's the case then the EU will indicate if the Thorium and Thulium elements are of further interest. That would require a higher level of Lab safety, and an additional building with full radiation cupboard facilities. We would also require an additional chemist experienced in radioactive material handling. Even if there is no interest in the Alpha emitters, we will definitely be recruiting an assistant to support Esme.'

Mark was pleased that David was acting on the weak position that Esme had been in when the spurious visitors raided her Lab.

All the computers were on the table. One of the geeks, Joss, came in with memory sticks to clean up the field computers. He also had some software to install that would resist any attempt to capture data via the possibility of a rogue WiFi unit installed under the Lab Hut.

The spreadsheet with Lat and Long data that Harry had developed was studied. Harry explained the rationale, and how it linked to his mapping programme that he'd created from the wide area drone image. This was a valuable tool for the planning of further sampling.

The team knew that they were finding consistent and valuable chemical data. Joss suggested that they develop a coding system for the elements and their value. It was clear future attacks would use intercept methods more than a direct robbery of machines. So developing their own methods of recording scientific data would be an additional safeguard.

It was a busy morning with all four of them contributing ideas to the data security strategy. They walked back to the hotel for lunch. The afternoon was equally focused on data protection. They had to learn alternative names for the fifteen Lanthanides, the Rare Earth elements, plus Thorium. That list would reside in the geeks office on a sheet of card. No copies on any computer. They decided to use names of wildlife and birds:

squirrel, fox, robin, swift, bear, lion, eagle, heron, rabbit, horse, puffin, thrush, leopard, deer, cuckoo, parrot.

None of these wildlife names had any cryptic connection with the Rare Earth elements. Their mapping to a particular element just had to be memorised.

Quite a bit of humour coloured their brainstorming session, but they all realised that the strategy was pivotal to ensuring Project security and integrity. The internet could not be considered secure.

They walked back to the hotel for a welcome swim in the pool. Then dinner and more phone calls to loved ones.

The second day at the Chalco offices was a tidy up of the method to record spectrometer value to any identified element. It was decided to use an algorithm. That meant the spreadsheet could be translated easily when back in Guernsey.

At a mid morning coffee break, David introduced Sandra Boston to Esme. It wasn't so much an interview for a career position but an opportunity to see if the two would get along. Sandra was keen to have a work experience prior to taking up an MSc course in Maths at Exeter in October. She'd just completed a Maths degree at Bath. Esme twigged that she was Reg Boston's daughter from a conversation back in May. They certainly didn't grate and David could sense from the body language between the two that it might be worthwhile to send Sandra over to Danesfjord when the team returned in about ten days.

For the next session there would be a slight delay as Bernard wasn't due to arrive until 11:30. His wife would drive him over. David sent the team out in the garden for half an hour. He took Esme to one side and asked if she thought that Sandra could be useful as a lab assistant for the next six weeks. Esme didn't look surprised as she thought there must be a reason to introduce the two of them. Esme, conscious of the delicate situation she had encountered with the uninvited visitors, was happy to agree to the suggestion.

David checked with Mark about the arrangement; he thought it would be useful. Mark could see that it would solve several problems for Esme; security, intellectual support, and assistance with time delays arising from the crusher routines.

The two women were both quiet listeners and competent in several areas. What no one else knew that morning was that Sandra had a number of skills in the martial arts area. Undoubtedly a product of Reg's persuasive military parentage. It wasn't a set of skills that Sandra was eager to advertise now that she was a grown woman, but it did provide her with a degree of confidence in many situations.

Bernard arrived with a broad smile: 'Morning everyone, sorry to keep you waiting.'

It would have been pleasant to hold the next session in the garden but the information was highly sensitive. Mark, Harry, Leighton and Esme were shepherded back to the board room by David and Bernard. As they sat down they were joined by Andrew Norris and the Company geek Joss.

Bernard: 'While you were wondering if you would ever be rescued from Greenland we've been trying to unravel who is behind the disruptive activities. One of my contacts, now retired, appointed Naomi Dawson about fifteen years ago. She was one of the sharpest operatives he had known.'

Bernard, with assistance of Joss, full name Jeremy Moss, went on to describe a sequence of incidents that may have led up to the recent problems. Naomi Dawson had, as is not uncommon in her line of work, used aliases for most of her special services career. As well as the alias Vanessa Wyndham there were four other names that she had used. Her birth name was Carol Anne Saunders, and her married name is Carol Anne Tilby.

Bernard: 'If we now turn to her husband, Adam Tilby, we can start to see who might be behind some of the strange occurrences that have caused the Danesfjord Project to be disrupted. We've had the marriage certificate checked. Carol Anne Saunders married Adam Benjamin Tilby in London in 2009. Even before they were married Adam Tilby was working for an American company, Oronazite Minerals LLC, based in Oregon. Tilby had been a sort of agent, based in London, for the company. He used to engage graduates for the prospecting arm but now spends most of his time wheeler dealing on the metals market. Any questions?'

Mark: 'How big is Oronazite?'

'Huge. Probably several hundred billions invested all around the world. I remember it in the 90s when it was quite active in prospecting. It was doing small surveys in Northern Canada. Now it's more like a private equity group, headed by lawyers and MBAs. It gets an easy ride with the US tax authorities because it tries to control who holds stocks of all noble and rare metals. It appears to be trying to balance the massive stocks of Rare Earth metals that China has accumulated. It's the control freak of the Western metal market. It operates quietly. It doesn't need to advertise. If you're a factory that needs specific metals to make stuff you soon get pointed in the direction of an Oronazite agent. It has unobtrusive offices in Los Angeles, New York, Toronto, London, Tel Aviv, Dubai, Zurich, Melbourne, and probably some others that we haven't tracked down yet. Oronazite is a concatenation of Oregon Monazite. Their agents live in a world of spreadsheets these days, they've gone beyond hammer and chisel geology.'

Mark: 'So you think Naomi Dawson, or Vanessa Wyndham, real name Carol Anne Tilby, is being used by her husband.'

Bernard: 'We can't rule that out.'

Joss: 'We also believe that Oronazite has a traditional timber dwelling in Nuuk, capital city of Greenland, that they're using as an intelligence base. Presumably keeping an eye on prospecting in Greenland.'

Esme asked: 'Are we safe going back to Danesfjord?'

Bernard: 'We think so. Companies as big as Oronazite don't need to use force. They can just bribe and persuade in order to get their way, or silence anyone that threatens them. Obviously they are using disruption tactics against Chalco. They have so much money, that hiring Lear jets or coasters, or fishing trawlers is just petty cash.'

Joss: 'One thing they don't like is bad publicity. Like all control freaks they like to operate quietly in the shadows. They're like the investment funds that operate in New York and other banking centres.'

Mark, Harry, Leighton and Esme were somewhat amazed by what they were hearing, but it was providing a rational explanation for what they'd experienced over the past week.

Esme raised a question: 'So you think that all we've experienced is American, rather than Chinese.?'

Bernard: 'Almost certainly. The far eastern gentleman who accompanied the raid on your Lab, was probably added to confuse us. We know there are Australian prospecting groups working legitimately in Southern Greenland. They have some Chinese investment.'

Bernard went on to describe what would be happening shortly at Danesfjord. This was being intensely co-ordinated by Professor Rasmussen, with the backing of the EU. He'd bypassed Astrid Larsen and was now working with the top bureaucrats. The ones determined to resist activities of right wing American politics and their multinational patrons. 'A permanent self contained military base is being set up adjacent to the four Chalco Huts. It will have a detachment of six troops, their own helicopter with two pilots, a chef, and an engineer, plus a large fuel store. They will be there as your security, and back up transport. Captain Oscar Hansen will have full command of their daily activities. When you finish in August they will be responsible for maintaining the site through the winter, keeping all snoopers and disruptors at bay. We aim to return next Spring and the accommodation and equipment should be as good as when we leave it.'

Joss took over at this point. He explained that Chalco should be able to resist raids on its computers. Although the Company was using bog standard laptops, with commercial operating systems, Bonzo had been working on software that prevented rogue operators from switching on any of the computers remotely. 'We get some help on this from GCHQ. Almost everyone who purchases a mobile phone or laptop lets their files be uploaded to a cloud these days. In fact, it's difficult for many people to resist it. Because Danesfjord doesn't have any WiFi facilities, access to the cloud shouldn't be possible. However, if a rogue operator were to install a WiFi unit under the Huts, with a link it to the new breed of satellites, Chalco computers and mobile phones could be compromised. The cost of the satellite uplink for WiFi could be a couple of thousand dollars a month, but the knowledge benefits to Oronazite would be considerable. Coverage from these satellites is roughly up to the 60° parallel. That means the satellites can reach Danesfjord.'

Bonzo, Pierre Aubert, was Joss's co-worker. He was the coding wizard, fluent in six different programming languages. He was not interested in world politics or business strategies, he just loved solving problems numerically. Joss and Bonzo now had two young coders, straight out of local schools. They were Ivor Griffiths and Mary Richardson. Both from a similar mould as Bonzo. Mary was an exceptional mathematician who had turned down an offer from Cambridge in favour of working near home.

Joss was the unappointed "manager" of the geek team. He was the one that Andrew Norris, or anyone else, went to with tasks. Joss was insistent that they were a collaborative group. Bonzo and him were paid the same salary. Joss was a social reactionary. His father Isaac Moss had sent him to Oxford to study economics but he rapidly changed to Mathematics, then to computer science. Joss's father was rather controlling. Isaac brought his family to Guernsey when Joss was a teenager. This was following a large inheritance from his own father's banking fortune. Isaac bought one of the largest mansions on the island but his marriage broke down. Joss's mother separated and Joss decided to live with her. Chalco and computing had provided Joss with independence and a life.

Another benefit to Chalco occurred back in 2018 when GCHQ geeks were sent over to Chalco to improve data security following the Ecuador report file copying. Joss didn't tell Andrew Norris at the time but one of the GCHQ geeks had been a fellow student on the computer science course at Oxford. That relationship had flourished, unofficially, over the last few years and helped Chalco with data security across its world wide operations.

Joss had explained his GCHQ connection to Andrew Norris about a year ago after Andrew had asked him in one day for a chat. Isaac Moss had called to see Andrew about a possible buy out. Andrew had humoured him, not wishing to alienate one of Guernsey's money men. He explained courteously that Chalco was a specialist scientific consultancy operating in a rapidly changing commercial environment. The board of directors required people with a sound knowledge of geology and Isaac Moss's undoubted banking skills were different to what Chalco needed.

Nothing further had come from Isaac's visit, but the sharing of the details had led to a mutual respect between Andrew and Joss.

According to Joss, his father had gone back to buying up cafés, shops and hotels all over the island and some on Jersey.

The morning session finished late. David sent the Danesfjord four back to the hotel for lunch.

The afternoon session back at the offices was about arrangements for resuming the Project. Bernard sat in but it was David who delivered the plan: 'The earliest you'll need to fly back to Guernsey is Thursday 23$^{rd}$ June. Rosemary will contact you with your flight details when we get confirmation from Denmark. It may be a few days later but you can safely plan a vacation up to and including the 22$^{nd}$. You'll be flying to Nuuk or Narsarsuaq on a military transport plane. There'll be the five of you, including Sandra, plus all the replacement gear for the Lab, and the reconfigured computers from the geeks. Reg and Joss will accompany you to Danesfjord to check out some security aspects. Professor Rasmussen will also meet up with you. Any questions?'

There were none. David summarised: 'We'll leave it like that then for now. Have a well earned break and await the call from Rosemary.'

They all went back to the hotel for another swim. Nearly mid summer and it was a warm day. After breakfast on Thursday they caught flights back home.

# 40

Mark got a taxi from Bristol Airport. At home he was met at the door by an excited Katy. She'd grown!

Kathleen was looking tired, but she was ecstatic to see Mark. Mark said he had a week's break while some of the equipment was being updated. He wasn't going to worry Kathleen with the real reason for his week off. Katy was jumping up and down with excitement: 'Daddy, Daddy, take me to see the goats.'

Kathleen smiled, and said it was only a little way along the lane: 'We have to visit every day.'

Katy was already putting her wellies on. Mark just dumped his rucksack, Katy couldn't wait. Kathleen said she would have some lunch ready for when they got back, and gave Mark a bag of carrots. To be able to take Daddy to see the goats was a treat for Katy and made her feel grown up. They set off, hand in hand, with Katy showing Daddy the way.

At the field gate Katy was jumping up and down and waving. Six nanny goats and one billy goat came trotting across. Katy grabbed the bag of carrots and started showing Daddy how to feed them. This tiny adventure made Mark realise what he was missing. A child growing up when every day was a new adventure, and he was missing much of it. The week off had to be totally involved with his family. There was nothing else to do; no reading, no writing, no communications. He needed to take full advantage of the unplanned week at home.

Katy knew that only one carrot per goat was allowed, or else they get tummy ache. They walked back to the bungalow. Lunch was waiting. Kathleen said it will be bananas tomorrow and parsnips on Saturday. The owner of the goats had carefully explained to Kathleen of the need to vary the treats for an animal whose diet was predominantly grass. After lunch Katy brought a book so Daddy could read to her. She listened intently, even joining in the story.

Kathleen suggested a walk in the woods. Katy could pick some flowers for Mummy. That was a great success.

Later that afternoon, Emma's car drove up the concrete drive. She'd skipped her usual visit to the shops knowing Mark was arriving home. Katy and Kathleen waved from the front window. Mark went out to meet her and gave her a big hug. It was an unexpected break. Emma had been priming herself for a family reunion in August.

Emma knew her Mother had slowed down these last few months. Probably due in part to a highly energetic two year old. She mentioned that she was trying to persuade her to see the doctor.

Anyway, Emma had stocked up with plenty of food yesterday for a grand home-coming feast. She made a cup of tea for everyone, including Katy who was now having slightly tea flavoured warm milk. Hers was made with a decaf tea bag. Emma ordered her Mum out of the kitchen to sit down and rest. Dinner was under way.

Emma had a young kitchen assistant now and the current activity was shelling peas. For the last three weeks Emma had bought a few grams of peapods from a local farm shop. This proved a useful activity for a toddler determined to help Mummy. It was also a time consuming activity as every pea had to taken out of the pod individually. Mark was fascinated by Katy's thoroughness to do everything right.

Having Daddy home was exciting. She was following all the conversations over dinner, so much so that her eating was much slower than usual. Questions regarding the progress of the Danesfjord Project were answered positively. Mark was trying to construct a modified account. He stated that prospecting progress was moderately promising, whereas he knew that the quantity of Rare Earth metals was actually quite remarkable. On accommodation he was particularly praiseworthy, describing the individual cabins, warm showers and washing machines. He awarded great credit to Peter, their cook, who was going out of his way to match everyone's appetites and dietary preferences. The reason for the week back home was a total lie. He didn't wish to disclose the difficulties, as they were not yet fully understood. He did explain that they needed an additional chemist and improved equipment to be able to process the complex minerals.

This was Katy's family and she made sure she was fully involved. She had grown in confidence and ability in the seven weeks since Daddy was at home. Over the past few weeks Emma had used the weekends to team up with Sally and her little boy, Jonathan. They were only meeting outside in the fresh air but events were advantageous for both toddlers. Sally's husband, Simon, had experienced poor health since he'd contracted COVID and his convalescence had been slow.

After dinner, Katy was getting tired but it was Daddy who had to give her a bath and read her a bedtime story. Towards the end of the story she fell asleep. It had been a surprisingly different day to recently.

Bedtime for everyone was early. Kathleen was sleeping longer and often didn't have the energy to read to Katy.

In bed Emma explained her fertility mapping. She'd abandoned the pill when Mark left for Greenland, thinking she'd have over three months when she could study the natural cycles of her body. Mark could sense there was more to come.

They were both immensely happy to be in bed together again. It was only a few days earlier that the opportunity had presented itself. Emma was particularly loving. She said quietly that she would be ovulating on Monday and explained in detail how she had been working it out. Then she asked calmly: 'Would you like another baby?' The emphasis was on "you".

It was a direct question, but it carried a clear signal that she wanted another. Mark would love another child and had been weighing up the realities since Emma had made some slightly pointed comments over dinner. The rather analytical remarks earlier about mapping her fertility cycle was another hint. Mark knew she had followed a highly logical route through Katy's first two years, balancing her teaching job, her Mother's loss of Henry, Mark's PhD demands and the whole COVID problem. Mark's equally analytical assessment concurred. Emma was still under 30, two and a half years since Katy's birth, and was in blooming health. In fact when she arrived home she looked amazing. As for himself, he knew he was on good form, had been active for the last six weeks, and had been eating well, thanks to Peter's catering skills.

On the practical side, two salaries, a mortgage that was manageable. Only the new car had introduced a minor financial hiccup. Above all, if Emma was eager then he was sure it was a good idea. Actually, they were well on their way. Emma hadn't been so passionate since last Christmas. Mark just had to reciprocate. No further rationalising was needed. They slept well. For Mark it was a joy to be back in the marital bed.

Friday was a pleasant summer's day, sun and cotton wool clouds, not too hot. After Emma had zoomed off to school Mark thought he would take Katy on a long country walk. He realised that Katy would insist on walking as they set off, but he took the pushchair with the big wheels in case they went across the fields or through the woods. Katy wanted to be the school teacher, mimicking her Mummy, showing Daddy all the flowers in the hedges. She certainly knew the names of many plants. Kathleen had been tutoring her well over the past few weeks.

Weather permitting they had been on short morning walks nearly every day for over a month.

Katy had walked for nearly an hour when Mark thought she might like to sit in the pushchair. Within a few minutes she had nodded off. He turned around and headed home. Kathleen was in the garden with her weeding fork. He parked the pushchair in the shade and sat down with Kathleen. There was already a jug of orange squash on the patio table. Kathleen was quite keen to talk to Mark. She admitted she was finding a full school day of child minding quite demanding. Mark praised her efforts over the past few years and gradually brought the conversation around to visiting the doctor's surgery. Kathleen had already had the suggestion from Emma, but she seemed worried about something. Katy woke up so Mark helped her out of the pushchair and gave her a drink. Katy joined the conversation around the table and said she wanted a rabbit. Where had she got that from? At least it wasn't goats!

That night in bed Emma explained her strategy for conceiving. She wanted Mark to rest that night and then resume love making Saturday evening. If this was what she wanted Mark was more than happy to oblige.

Saturday was the beach day. The weather looked ideal. It was nearly mid-summer's day. Emma packed up some lunch, Kathleen said she would have a day in the garden. They drove to a beach near Minehead. Katy got to work with her bucket and spade, and, with help, built herself a sand castle with a pond in the middle. A number of trips to the water's edge to fill the bucket resulted in puzzlement: 'The water's gone?'

Initially, Mark thought that was a question that merited a detailed explanation but though better of it. Instead, running to the water's edge to refill the bucket, then running back, was a much more appropriate activity for a child.

Saturday night Mark was on husbandry duties again. Emma was totally receptive. She'd obviously given this a great deal of thought and had imagined that it would all happen in August. To bring it forward to June presented an opportunity of which to take full advantage. They were both very happy. It was a different experience to their usual spontaneous intimacy. It was akin to animal husbandry on a farm. Mark thought it rather humorous.

Sunday they set off for Stroud to see Mark's Mum and Dad. They hadn't seen Katy since Easter so it was a special day. Katy had picked some flowers from Nana's garden. It had become known as Nana's garden because of all the care that Kathleen had put in.

Jennifer and Roger were waiting in the garden. They both looked well. Jennifer had been receiving treatment for the multiple myeloma, but was now in a sort of rest interval.

They were delighted to see Katy. Emma described how she had developed through the summer. The weather was glorious and Jennifer had lunch ready to eat in the back garden. Katy loved picnics. Sitting on a high chair at the table she said: 'I had a picnic on the beach yesterday.'

It was a relaxing visit. Emma spent some time with Jennifer in the kitchen, catching up on Jennifer's treatment. Katy was playing in the garden, while Mark outlined to Roger the recent events in Greenland. Mark didn't feel it appropriate to share his experiences with Emma, particularly as her mind appeared to be totally focused on conceiving. Emma was not a worrier but he preferred to keep the idea of Danesfjord as a safe expedition. He always knew he could confide in his Dad, Roger, and trusted his advice.

Although, Roger now had the details of last week, Mark was careful to explain that the incidents were still not fully joined up. He hoped that, when the team returned next week, Rasmussen would have a clearer picture. They'd had the experience of working with the Danish military but that didn't mean they would be told everything. Denmark retained the security of the Greenland territory, which was why military units were keeping watch on the coastal margins.

Since the political claim, in 2019 by the United States, that they wanted to buy Greenland, the political sensitivities between Denmark and Greenland were entering new ground.

Roger's advice to Mark was to stick to Chalco's aims and objectives for the Project. Leave the organisational arrangement between the EU, the Danish Government and its military, to Rasmussen.

The visit had fulfilled it primary objective: Grandparents seeing Katy. Emma drove them home. She was aware that Jennifer was finding life difficult. The diagnosis of only a few years remaining was hard for her to accept.

Back home, Kathleen had taken advantage of the continued dry weather to tend her flower borders. Watering was now a priority. She loved her "new" garden and it was giving her a feeling of ownership. As for the garden at her own house, it was now being minded by a local gardener, a competent woman but it was mostly tidying. Kathleen didn't really enjoy visiting her bungalow any more. The negative feelings from Henry's death were upsetting. Mark and Emma discussed how they were going to get her to the doctor's surgery. The plan was for Mark to phone for an emergency appointment at 16:00 on one day next week, then Emma would take her along after she returned from school.

Emma told Mark that he was on husbandry duties for the next three nights; her ovulation peak. It was a bit of a novelty but Mark could see that this was something that Emma was treating seriously!

Mark focused his energies on Katy during the following week. He probably wouldn't get a call from Chalco for several days. It was a useful diversion to be able to spend time with his rapidly developing daughter. It would be another six or seven week gap before he saw her again.

The phone call to the surgery was moderately successful. He was able to get Kathleen an appointment for Wednesday at 16:20. Fortunately it was with the doctor she had known for several years. That didn't necessarily mean that the doctor knew her well, but it was likely that Kathleen would feel more confident in discussing how she was feeling. That evening Emma said that for the last few minutes of her Mum's consultation she had been called in by the doctor. The outcome was that several blood and urine tests were requested, and taken that afternoon. The doctor was fairly confident that there was nothing too serious.

Thursday morning Mark still wanted to take Katy out for a walk, but was conscious that a call from Chalco was imminent. He got back from the walk; Katy was asleep in the pushchair; his phone rang. It was Rosemary; just a short call to say that fly out day would now be Tuesday 28th June; more details soon. Also, David would be phoning him later today.

Showery after lunch so Mark occupied Katy with stories and then playing with toys. The little plastic characters in her toy farm all had names so Daddy listened attentively as Katy explained the various reorganisations of her farmyard.

The phone rang, David's mobile number. After the usual exchanges he announced that the four of them needed to be at Chalco for 09:30 on Tuesday. Rosemary couldn't get early flights for three of them so they'd fly to Guernsey Monday afternoon and overnight at the hotel. David would drive over for a short briefing session about 20:00. Then there would be a team briefing at Chalco offices on Tuesday. Sandra, Reg and Joss would be joining them then. All Chalco staff must remain detached from the military personnel. The Danes were there to service Chalco's needs, but Chalco staff must avoid engaging in any discussion with the military security detail relating to their engagement on the high seas with the coaster. There was a difficulty because the arrest of the ship was being challenged by the US and Canada. Mark would get more details on Monday evening.

Mark had three more family days. Emma returned and Mark gave her the news and a big hug. Kathleen had entertained Katy while Mark was on the phone. Mark said he would cook dinner. That left all the ladies of the household to sit in the garden. The Sun was out again and everything had dried out.

In bed that night Emma said that Kathleen had found the week with Mark home quite a relief for her. The second topic was her friend Sally Butler. Could they meet up on the beach on Sunday for an hour? Sally's husband Simon was recovering his strength slowly from the Long Covid problem and would like to meet Mark. The third topic was a close cuddle: 'Shall we have another go, just to be sure?'

Saturday morning was a big shopping expedition, including five pregnancy testing kits. Katy stayed at home with Kathleen. In the afternoon Mark and Emma took Katy to the petting farm. That triggered the plea for a rabbit again. The usual parental defences were explained: you have to feed it every day, and clean the hutch out. That probably didn't register.

Sunday, last full day with the family for Mark, but Kathleen said she would like a day in the garden. It was the beach day near Minehead to meet up with Sally, Simon and their young son Jonathan. It was a glorious day. The women played in the sand with the children. Mark and Simon had a long conversation. Simon was getting stronger but progress had been slow. He was signed off by the Army as long term sick, but was hauled in every three months for an interview and medical tests. His biggest fear was that he might be removed from the military list. That had happened to several ratings. He was hoping that his rank of Lieutenant Colonel would keep him in. The sort of work he'd been doing for three years was closer to covert security and diplomacy than soldiering. He was mostly liaising with comparable ranks in NATO on similar tasks. He knew he wouldn't get over an assault course but his mental faculties were sharp. He just hoped that his skill set of strategies and negotiation was valued.

Mark mentioned his reason for having a week home from Greenland. He was careful not to detail the real reasons for the break in their Project as he didn't want details leaking back to Emma via Sally. Simon had worked with the Danish Army several times, once on their coastal defence patrols. Danish personnel were at a disadvantage in Greenland because of the problem of enforced contraception of the Inuit population by the Danish Government, back in the 1960s and 1970s. It was this authoritarian action which had led, in two stages, 1979 and 2009, to a sort of self rule from Denmark. The constitutional arrangement still left Denmark in control of, and responsible for, security and defence.

Katy and Jonathan played well together on the beach and Emma and Sally were obviously close soulmates.

It was an interesting afternoon for Mark. It was clear from Simon's military career that he had been a high functioning action-man soldier who had been hit hard by COVID. It had floored him physically for well over a year. He was keen to get back to his earlier activities and career but the body was holding him back. Mark hadn't realised the impact the virus had made on younger people. He had just accepted the death of Henry, Emma's Dad, as being the fate that affected older members of the population.

Sunday on the beach was Mark's last day with his family. A family that might be growing.

Monday morning he gave Emma a huge hug as she set off for school. He then took Katy for a short walk and a quick story before his taxi was due to arrive. He gave Katy a tight cuddle and a kiss: 'Daddy's going to work today but he'll see you soon.'

At Guernsey he booked into the hotel. Esme and Leighton had already arrived. They'd both enjoyed their mid-Project break.

After dinner David Gresham arrived for the discrete briefing with Mark: 'The EU are putting quite a bit of pressure on Rasmussen over in Greenland. He is trying to balance the tasks of the Danish Military and the EU pressure. Relations with the Greenland Government were not always easy. They wished for complete control of their country but were well aware that Denmark's military muscle was something they still needed. It was imperative that Chalco staff stayed clear of any controversy. Rasmussen and I have been careful not to discuss politics in our telephone conversations, because it's becoming so difficult to know if we're being listened to. We haven't discussed who might be behind the disruption of two weeks ago but he is going to brief you in person, when you arrive in Greenland. You'll route via Reykyavik to refuel, then on to Nuuk to offload some cargo and pick up Rasmussen. Then you'll fly down to Narsarsuaq. A Merlin helicopter will take you all to Danesfjord. Oscar Hansen will be your only point of contact while you're there. The soldiers now have their own accommodation huts, and that's also where the Merlin crew will live. Rasmussen and Hansen will update you on the developments with the coaster problem. It's imperative that you don't discuss that with the rest of your team.'

The sole focus for Mark and his team would be the prospecting. He could have full confidence in Hansen and his task of getting Chalco to selected sites. The Merlin helicopter and crew were there to provide the shuttle to Narsarsuaq as well as their role in coastal surveillance. Only Hansen would command their services.

The team assembled at Chalco offices early the following morning. No longer four but five with Sandra Boston, Esme's lab assistant. Also Reg Boston and Joss who had loaded all the new gear onto the plane the previous afternoon. Final briefing from David then minibus to the airport.

They were ushered through a separate security lane then out to the waiting Danish military transport plane with four propellers. Functional seating down both sides of the large cargo space was secured by wrap around netting type seat belts. This wasn't going to be the height of comfort. A couple of large metal pallets in the middle of the plane were on rails. People and cargo had entered the plane through double doors at the rear.

At 09:30 they took off, steep ascent, the plane was probably lightly loaded compared to other deployments. After three hours the first officer brought out lunch, military rations, but quite filling. Mark wondered if they were going to be issued with parachutes next.

Nearly four hours to Reykjavik. Thirty minutes on the ground, then up again. They flew low over the Greenland ice cap and landed at Nuuk. The larger of the metal pallets was off-loaded, and Professor Rasmussen boarded. Polite conversation with everyone. It wasn't easy to hold long conversations when the plane was in the air. The final sector down to Narsarsuaq was again at low altitude. Ideal for scenery viewing but windows weren't available to everyone and straining the body around to look out wasn't comfortable for long. Fifty minutes later they landed. A useful leg stretch then they climbed into the Merlin helicopter. Reg Boston sorted the items off the pallet that were needed at Danesfjord. In the spacious helicopter there were now eight of them plus about half a tonne of cargo, mostly electronic items for the Lab.

Twenty minutes later they landed at Danesfjord. It was nearly dusk but they could see the many changes at the Huts base.

The military accommodation huts were a little higher up the slope than the Chalco base. Adjacent to the Chalco shipping container, just downslope of the Lab hut, was a second container. This was where the new cargo would be stored. The soldiers were instructed to carry the boxes down to the new container.

In their Kitchen Hut a welcome evening meal was being served by Peter. He was even more chatty than usual. He told them of his week in hospital after the exposure incident, from when the helicopter had ditched. After dinner, Esme showed Sandra to one of the empty cabins in the female Hut.

Mark, Oscar Hansen and Rasmussen met in the Lab for the briefing by Oscar. The Danish Government had increased military resources in Greenland following the incident with the minesweeper, camouflaged as a trawler. That had led to the finding of the coaster followed by the downing of the small helicopter. A Danish frigate had intercepted the coaster *Baffin Angel* in international waters as it was sailing towards Newfoundland. It had a crew of nine Chinese, but commanded by three white Americans. The political implications of this were still rattling around Washington and Ottawa. What had been discovered on the coaster were two devices. One was a multiple laser beam instrument; the other a rocket launcher for bulky projectiles.

The auxiliary naval vessel that had brought the replacement items last Friday had then been diverted to the site of the helicopter downing. They recovered the helicopter and found stainless steel wire and carbon fibre netting entangled around the tail rotor. That had resulted in a jamming of the gearbox which caused the turbines to shut down. Captain Oscar Hansen disclosed this with much enthusiasm, because it provided a defence for his potential court martial. Losing any aircraft without a rational defence is a major error within a military organisation.

All this was politically volatile. The frigate had arrested the three Americans and replaced them with three naval officers to take command of the coaster and return it to Newfoundland, where it had been chartered. All this information was for the ears of Rasmussen and Mark only. What was happening now the coaster had docked in Newfoundland was

317

unknown. So far the respective authorities of the U.S. and Canada were keeping the whole affair under wraps.

Oscar Hansen continued his explanation: 'As far as is known up to today is that the three Americans are one Canadian citizen and two U.S. citizens. The Canadian is the skipper of the chartered coaster and may be an innocent party to the helicopter downing. As for the nine Chinese crew. They may have been taken along to provide confusion as to the nationality of the whole incident. For the time being the person who is being quizzed in Newfoundland is the commander of our frigate. He's not keen to release any information yet. That's all I know at the moment.'

Mark thanked Oscar for the briefing: 'All I will be doing is continuing with our prospecting programme. The only connection that Chalco has with this affair was the odd visit of one of Britain's security services personnel, namely Naomi Dawson.'

It had been a long day. The briefing broke up and they all turned in. The next morning Peter had breakfast ready for everyone, making a point of asking Sandra, Reg, Joss and Rasmussen what were their preferences for tea or coffee.

Mark hoped to get back to sampling, but he needed to liaise with Reg and Joss over security matters of the whole base first, particularly the Lab. He also checked in with Esme, but she was already inducting Sandra into the procedures for processing samples.

Rasmussen was in deep conversation with Oscar Hansen. That appeared to be highly confidential. Rasmussen knew that the military were there to wholeheartedly support the Danesfjord Project but he probably was not privy to the machinations and protocols of the Danish military. That was Rasmussen's problem, not Mark's.

Mark thought he should have personal conversations with Peter and Anders. Both had been casualties in the helicopter downing and it was a near fatal experience for Peter. He had been the last to be winched up out of the cold water by the Merlin. Mark listened closely to Peter's account. All four of them in the small helicopter had been completely disoriented by the multiple laser attack. It must have been low powered because none of them had suffered permanent sight loss. The purpose must have been to disguise the firing of the netting and wire towards the tail rotor. Mark didn't admit that to Peter as he didn't know if Oscar had disclosed the findings of the helicopter recovery. Mark praised him for his good humoured catering abilities. He felt part of his role as expedition leader was to maintain appropriate relations with their military assistants.

Since the return to Guernsey of the Chalco team for a break, the military had rewired much of the Huts' electric supply and replaced the failed solar panels. Because the soldiers' accommodation was taking electric from the solar array another hundred solar panels had been added. Reg checked over the Lab equipment with Esme and swapped some items for the spares in the containers.

# 41

Joss spent his morning checking the entire base for hidden WiFi units. It would be quite easy to install one under the Huts, particularly under the Lab hut, where the floor was about 50 to 60 centimetres above the ground. With a link to a satellite it could easily be switched on, and take over, any computers left unattended. The malign purpose, to upload any data on the device.

Joss had a detector that could find erroneous electronic gadgets. He found nothing but his next step was to provide Esme with several devices that she could use to monitor for rogue gadgets every morning before she switched on any electronics.

Mark sat down in the Kitchen with Harry and Leighton to plan a sampling campaign. He wanted to do two things over the next few weeks. First, extend the wide area further inland with samples taken about two kilometres apart. Second, the area about 10 km to the East had shown the highest values so far. That area needed an increase in sampling density to see if the high values were consistent.

Reg and Joss came into the Kitchen and sat down for refreshments. Joss was content that there were no rogue electronics anywhere in or under the four Huts complex. He'd briefed Esme on how to use the detector devices he had left for her. Most of the morning she was giving Sandra an introduction to all the equipment in her Lab. She had six samples still to process. They were left over from the day when they were evacuated nearly two weeks ago. After lunch Esme used one of the samples to give Sandra training in the use of the crusher. It seemed that she had the same attention to detail, and laboratory cleanliness, as herself. As a maths graduate Sandra hadn't had any lab experience since school, but she was highly methodical and a quick learner.

While back in England Esme had spent a week with her boyfriend in Southampton. He'd acquired a replacement camera trap for the one that had been fried by the electro magnetic pulse. Esme wanted to install the new one on the bank of the fjord. She went to find Anders and asked him to accompany her and Sandra down to the fjord. This was also an education for Sandra into the Danesfjord rule of always being accompanied, and with a gun and a Very pistol. The polar bear risk couldn't be ignored. Bears can easily outrun humans.

Mark felt that things were almost back to normal. Harry had checked the spare drone and it was working perfectly. The next few weeks probably wouldn't need any drilling gear so Leighton just needed his hammer and chisel. Oscar and Frida were all set for the following day. The replacement small helicopter was the same model but with a slightly higher performance rating. Because the large Merlin helicopter was now stationed at Danesfjord there was a huge fuel dump up on the col. There were 34 drums of 208 litres and also an electric powered pump. Sounds a lot but the Merlin drank a lot of fuel in its three engines.

Dinner that evening was for twelve although three would go back to Narsarsuaq the next day. Rasmussen's presence through the day had obviously had an effect on all military personnel. They had sharpened up. It appeared that Rasmussen was considered the central person in this whole Project. For him to put in an appearance just underlined how important the Project was to Denmark.

Thursday after breakfast were generous good-byes to Rasmussen, Reg and Joss as they left in the Merlin helicopter for Narsarsuaq. Mark, Harry and Leighton climbed into the small helicopter and headed off East to the new locations. They'd lost about two weeks but now were back on task. Mark kept the day's samples to fifteen again. He wanted to get some feedback from Esme before he increased the daily total. The day went well and they touched down at Danesfjord at 16:30.

Friday was similar. Still fifteen samples. At dinner Mark asked Esme how the processing was going. She said that Sandra's assistance was making a huge difference. She could easily take 24 samples a day now. Sandra seemed happy and the pair appeared to be working well together.

Saturday was a little hindered by a heavy rain shower at midday, but they still managed to return with 24 samples. Mark could see that the landscape in which they were working was changing. They'd probably reached the Eastern edge of the rock type with the intrusions that were providing the favourable samples.

On Sunday Mark insisted on an enforced rest day. The weather was fine; perfect for another volleyball match.

Monday the three prospectors set off for what Mark thought could be their final day in that area. They managed to get six useful samples but then the bedrock changed, and although there were still prominent intrusions, unfortunately they were nearly all radioactive. Mark called it a day at 21 samples, but most would go in the lead lined box. He was adamant that the Lab was not appropriately equipped to handle Thorium and Thulium.

For the next ten days Mark switched the focus to increasing the density of samples in the areas that had already shown valuable data.

They were becoming quite efficient. Sites were selected using Harry's map of the whole wide area; about 30 km by 12 km. Oscar and Frida would get them to suitable landing sites and then Mark's team would endeavour to sample at 500 metre intervals in the area with already proven quality data. They were getting fewer showers through early July which made their task easier. Esme and Sandra were happily getting through over 20 samples every day, and the central area of the mainland was free of radioactive minerals. It was the area that Mark was sure the mining or quarrying operation would concentrate its efforts.

Stocks of Jet A1 fuel for the helicopters were being conserved. The small helicopter was using less than 100 litres a day. The Merlin was taking the soldiers out every other day and was refuelling at Narsarsuaq Airport at the end of each patrol. This meant it was only using the Danesfjord stocks to top up.

By Saturday 16th July, at the end of the ten days high density sampling, Mark had a meeting with the Chalco five. The data was clearly showing high levels of Monazite minerals in the centre of their wide area. Mark had noticed that there were also more intrusion veins in the central area. The centre of that area was about 12 km from the Danesfjord base. If, or when, a mining organisation started to extract the minerals they would need a different base and access to a navigable fjord. That wasn't a decision that Mark would be making. As far as he was concerned the data they had collected proved this area to be a significant extraction prospect. From what they had observed there could be several thousand tonnes of mineral in the surface veins. With a deep large scale operation that could exceed a million tonnes. The value would be in the region of several billion Euro. Mark didn't share his notional integration with the others.

In some ways Mark felt they had achieved their principal objective, but from Monday there was the ancillary task of raising sediments from the depths of the fjord. Because this was likely to be fine sediment it would mean the Lab tasks would be about removing most of the salt, and any organics, then drying. Putting the fjord bed samples through the crusher would only be needed if samples were gritty. Mark decided to use the following Monday as a training day.

On Sunday evening when Mark connected the communication computer to the satellite phone, he printed off the family messages for Esme, Sandra, Harry and Leighton. Then he studied the one from David Gresham.

> Considerably better security since the mid-Project refurbishment and installation of more military. . . . . . . . .

Mark guessed that this introductory sentence was to provide misinformation to any hackers or disruptors. The use of code words for people and places was David's idea following the coding of Rare Earth Element names. Mark would need his diary to decode the main content in David's message.

It was abundantly clear that intercepts to phone calls and messages was now standard practice in the digital world. All hacking was possible if disruptive governments or rogue operators placed a focus on a person or organisation. Encryption could be broken with the processing power of modern computers. Why banks and large companies were continuing to state that their systems were secure across the internet was laughable. The best anyone could do with their messages was have a unique pre-arranged system between themselves and another person. The internet was inherently open access. It's original specification by the Department of Defense in the U.S. was not security, but to continually reroute until a message had reached its destination. This was because the U.S. was anticipating a nuclear attack and wanted a communication web of telephone lines that would still remain workable if some lines were destroyed.

Mark took out his diary and checked the code words in David's e-mail. Squirrel Mouse Hare Tiger Elephant Reindeer Marmot Panther Fox Reindeer. He deduced that to be Squirrel Mouse Hare meeting Tiger at

Elephant on Reindeer Marmot, Panther on Fox Reindeer. Which translated as David Gresham, Bernard Hosegood and Naomi Dawson meeting Anton Rasmussen at Nuuk on 19th. Then Danesfjord on 21st.

Mark replied with the agreed acknowledgement words. That meant he had Monday, Tuesday for training, Wednesday for prospecting. He needed to keep Thursday 21st for the visit.

Sampling the fjord sediments would require the Zodiac boat and Anders to helm it, and bring the guns. There was a large reel of polypropylene rope and the Shipek Grab in the container. The grab device would be lowered open. On hitting the bed of the fjord it would automatically close and grab whatever was on the surface of the fjord bed. It was a coarse device, but for initial sampling it would mean they could haul up surface sedimentary material. A mucky job, wet mud, several kilogrammes, although only a few grams were needed.

In the practice session adjacent Danesfjord beach Leighton spooned out a small quantity into a poly bag. Harry passed him a label written with an indelible pen and it was all placed in a second poly bag. Methodical care was needed for mud and soil samples because of the water content. Harry said that there was a spare rectangular storage box in the first container. He went up to collect it. The Grab would be placed in it when it was lifted into the boat. It was ideal and would help to keep the floor of the boat fairly free of mud.

The next stage was to take the sample to Esme and Sandra in the Lab. Esme was ahead on this. She emptied the mud into a small tray. Put the tray into a small oven. Set the temperature to 550°C. That was to dry it and turn any organics into ash. It needed at least an hour in the oven. So they went to the Kitchen for a cuppa. Esme suggested that washing to remove salt wasn't necessary as when it was analysed in the Bench XRF spectrometer the Sodium and Chlorine from the sea water, and the Carbon from ashing would show up in the output data. The objective was to determine the presence of any metals. The Sodium, Chlorine and Carbon would be ignored and excluded from the mass analysis.

Esme's comments over tea were that the oven could dry eight tray samples at a time so many samples could be processed in a day. Sandra listened to all this intently, aware that it was likely to be her job. The use of the crusher would only be needed if the sample was gritty in texture.

Mark attempted to explain why the fjord samples were worth analysing: 'While the ice sheet was still covering this part of Greenland there was a slow glacial movement towards the West. That had an erosive effect which is why we see all these hillocks polished smooth. Over time the material that was eroded, as stone, grit and fine particles, eventually became deposited in the fjord. What we're unsure of is the structure of the fjord bed sediments. Are there gritty layers, sand layers and mud layers? Because we don't know the erosional history we cannot answer that question. Perhaps we may need to use some of our coring equipment to try and recover a profile of about one metre of the bed layers. We'll take a few samples, analyse them, and then decide if a coring approach would be of any value.'

Anders asked if two people could come back down to the boat and assist him with cleaning. Any residues of mud, stones and sand in the boat were not helpful to the self draining flap valves at the back of the boat. Anders was determined to keep his boat as clean as possible!

Mark noticed that they were getting short on polythene sample bags. He suggested that the outer bag from each sample be saved in the Lab, cleaned, if necessary, and returned to stock. That should mean they had sufficient for the remainder of the expedition.

Over the next two days, prior to the high powered visit, they would endeavour to bring back samples from their local fjord. They had about six kilometres of sheltered fjord before it opened out into the Labrador Sea. Two of the 208 litre fuel drums were petrol for the outboard motors.

Anders Heiberg estimated that would give them about two weeks of fjord sampling.

Taking samples with the Grab wasn't difficult, but it was rather messy. The other thing the team noticed was the water temperature, about 5°C. After the first day Leighton asked Peter if he had any spare washing up gloves. To his surprise, a large box was taken out of a cupboard by Peter, who said: 'Take what you need.'

Over two days they had samples from the centre line of the fjord, at 100 metre intervals. Harry was cautious with the drone. He wanted the GPS location on the photo, although the photo wasn't as useful as the land based ones. They'd collected 21 samples so had covered just over 2 kilometres down the fjord. On return Mark spoke with Esme. She'd processed the Tuesday samples and had found small signals of several Rare Earth elements, but they accounted for much less than one percent of the fine sediment. Mark had anticipated that result simply because glacial erosion had abraded the whole surface of the bedrock, most of it being Syenite. Esme's results were quite consistent. It was not Mark's task to assess the value of continuing the sediment survey, he was there to just measure it. In some ways the sediment might have a value because bringing a dredger up the fjord and scooping up the sediment was relatively cheap considering the quantity that could be dredged in a few hours.

The two days had been the coldest of their work so far. At least the rubber gloves had made Leighton's Grab handling tasks a little more tolerable.

Mark felt it had been useful to have started the fjord sediment survey before the arrival of the Chalco bosses visit on Thursday. One thing he was still puzzled about was why were they bringing Naomi Dawson with them?

It was a welcome comfort to get back to the Huts. Leighton had a warm shower. His hands had been cold all day. If he had to do more sampling he was going to wear his silk gloves under the rubber gloves. His girlfriend had packed them for him. He hadn't thought them necessary at the time, but was now realising her wisdom.

At dinner that evening Mark asked Leighton if there was any chance of using the core drilling gear to sample below the surface of the fjord bed. Could he work on some method of dropping it in vertically, using its weight to penetrate the sediment, then lifting it out so that it was raised to the surface in the horizontal position. No motor involved, just gravity. If they could work on that tomorrow it could be useful.

After dinner, Oscar Hansen said that the visitors should arrive about 10:30 in the morning. The pilot of the Merlin helicopter had been commanded to be at Narsarsuaq Airport for 10:00 to collect four persons and transport them to Danesfjord.

Mark went to his cabin and made up his expedition log. They'd learnt a lot about using the Shipek Grab to obtain bed surface samples from the fjord. As for tomorrow, he felt he was in a good position to report to Chalco and Rasmussen. The land based sampling had shown up consistent and high value data.

What he couldn't work out was how to respond to Naomi Dawson. He pondered the possible scenarios, but concluded he would just have to follow the lead from the bosses of the Project.

Breakfast next morning was a cheery carefree start to the day for Harry, Leighton. Esme and Sandra. They knew that they would be playing second fiddle to Mark. Esme and Sandra would probably be asked to demonstrate their Lab processing tasks to the visitors. Harry and Leighton could play with ropes and pieces of drilling tube in the shipping container. Mark was less relaxed. He wasn't nervous although he realised that this was a big, planned visit. He couldn't rationalise why Naomi Dawson was in the group. That played on his mind.

It was just a waiting game now. Before Harry went off to the container to help Leighton, Mark asked him to be ready to show the distribution map of their mineral finds. Harry said it was all ready.

Two minutes before 10:30 the Merlin helicopter landed. Four people got out and walked down towards the Huts. As advised in the cryptic e-mail to Mark Scott they were Professor Anton Rasmussen, Professor Bernard Hosegood, Dr David Gresham and Naomi Dawson. Mark couldn't detect any body language oddities. All four were walking side by side and chatting. Mark welcomed them to Danesfjord; formal handshakes all round. Mark took them into the Kitchen Hut for warm drinks. Naomi Dawson softly apologised to Mark on the way in: 'I'm so sorry for my visit on the 8th of June. I know it was strange. Professor Rasmussen will explain what's been going on.'

Captain Oscar Hansen and Captain Dr Frida joined them at Rasmussen's request. Peter placed teas and coffees on the table and said: 'I'll leave you to your meeting now but I'll be returning at 12:00 to prepare lunch.'

After the pleasantries Rasmussen started his explanation: 'The Danish Government and its military have been trying to unravel the various incidents that have beset Danesfjord. The coaster was stopped by one of our frigates in International Waters. The skipper, who went with the charter of the coaster, was quite pleased to have been intercepted. The Chinese crew, all hired hands scooped up from the restaurants of San Francisco, were interrogated. They had been flown to Labrador on behalf of Oronazite by some staffing agency. The two others, white Caucasians as they wished to be called, were interviewed separately on the frigate. They initially denied any criminal activity, but when they were shown the video evidence taken by the large helicopter, they ceased all answers to

329

questions. The skipper confirmed that Ethan Becker aimed the laser device at the small helicopter, and Adam Tilby fired the netting onto the tail rotor. It was the latter that brought the helicopter down because the engines stalled. Following the inquiries the frigate has taken Becker and Tilby to Copenhagen to hand them over to the Ministry of Justice.'

Naomi Dawson continued: 'As you've worked out by now, my name is Tilby. I married Adam Tilby in 2009 when I was 28. For several years we lived in Guildford and we had two children, Daniel and Natalie, who are now 10 and 8. The marriage broke down and we drifted apart. In 2016 Adam moved to Oregon. He's been working for Oronazite for 19 years, first as their London agent, and now at the Headquarters in Oregon. I've been asking him for a Get, a religious divorce, for several years. It's been difficult, but recently he said he would agree to it if I brought the children over to Oregon to see him. My mother came with us, but Adam said he was keeping the children with him to be looked after by his mother. That wasn't all. I was kidnapped by two of his henchmen, with a sack over my head, and taken to an airport and flown to Newfoundland. If I didn't co-operate with his plan I would never see the children again. You know the rest. I realised where we were headed when I could sense that the Sun was rising in the starboard window as we left Newfoundland heading North.'

Captain Dr Frida Karlsen asked: 'Have you reported this to the Oregon authorities?'

Mrs Tilby, alias Naomi Dawson, replied: 'Not yet. I've reported all this to my superiors in the security services in London. They're going to advise me how to deal with the illegal detainment of the children. It's a waiting game at the moment. My mother is in a hotel near the children.'

Mark: 'Is this going to become a trade off between the Danish and Oregon authorities?

Rasmussen: 'It's a delicate issue. All sides are avoiding an international incident reaching the tabloid newspapers, worse still the internet gossipers. Tilby and Becker have been charged with criminal activities against Danish military personnel, so legally it's almost certain that Denmark is in a strong position. Dealing with any American authorities is often much more to do with money than moral or legal arguments.'

Mrs Tilby interjected: 'I've come over today at the request of Professor Hosegood. I need to apologise to all of you for the disruption. I realise it's not my fault, but I am responsible for the circumstances that have resulted in the chaos.'

Bernard Hosegood: 'The child abduction problem for Mrs Tilby is tragic, but cannot be resolved by the Company. The Chalco position, and that of the EU and Denmark, is to complete our contracted survey without further interference. Mrs Tilby has supported Chalco since the evacuation of staff from Ecuador in 2018. We are most grateful to her for her attention to detail. As she pursues the recovery of her children we can't be sure what interrogation, legal or otherwise, she may be subjected. It's almost certain she will need to be present in the U.S. at some time. She is fully aware that Chalco can't disclose any details to her about the progress of our work.'

Rasmusen took over the conversation again. He outlined the historical position with Greenland, and American attempts to have influence over it. The desire for the U.S. to purchase goes back decades. In 1946 the U.S. government offered to buy Greenland from Denmark for $100 million. That was after World War Two and the anticipated rise of Soviet power. The U.S. had three airbases in Greenland during World War Two. Those still exist. They played a major part during the Cold War of the 1950s and 1960s when surveillance of the polar regions was considered necessary.

Further pronouncements from the U.S. to buy Greenland in the 21st Century have continued. The interest now is two fold: defence bases, but also the untapped minerals in the ground. The latter, of course, is also the motivation for the EU in funding the Danesfjord Project.

Rasmussen explained: 'I can't speak politically for Denmark, or Greenland, only the EU project with which you're all involved. How the politicians will handle the several incidents of Mr Tilby and his Oronazite colleagues remains to be seen. As for the junior members of the Chalco team the content of this meeting will not be disclosed. We'll adjourn this meeting and go to join them.'

At that point Captain Dr Frida and Mrs Tilby remained seated at the Kitchen table; the others went off to the Lab.

Harry and Leighton came in from the shipping container. Harry demonstrated the mapping of the mineral data on his computer: 'As you can see from this map we've surveyed an area 30 km by about 12 km. The Danesfjord base is here but the highest density of Rare Earth mineral is in the centre here and occupies an area about 5 km by 3 km. So our base is currently about 9 km from the edge of the high density area.'

David Gresham asked: 'Are there still economically valuable minerals at the margins of the surveyed area?'

Mark Scott responded: 'Every sampling point had been logged, the content analysed and the bagged samples have been archived if further analysis is required. The margins of the area have significant mineral content but also include Alpha emitters, almost certainly Thorium and Thulium. Those radioactive samples are bagged and stored in the lead lined box. They're available for analysis in a nuclear lab.'

All sampling locations have been located by GPS from the drone, and also photographed. Centimetre precision of location have been recorded and photographed. Up until now 746 samples have been crushed and analysed in the Bench XRF, and 68 samples have been bagged and stored in the lead lined box.

As for exploitation, Mark declined to give firm answers: 'The high density area is likely to prove exceptionally interesting for quarrying or mining. The density of the mineral intrusion veins is also greatest in the central area. We've only sampled the surface, and it could be the thickness of the veins is wider at depth. It will be for the mining companies to decide how to extract and process the mineral ores.'

David Gresham asked: 'What are the physical advantages and disadvantages of getting the metals out of the ground?'

Mark: 'The primary advantage for whoever takes on the extraction is that the whole area is polished smooth igneous rock. Some of the cols between the hillocks have patchy grass on thin soil but apart from that the cleanly exposed rock, and the mineral veins are easily visible. As for access, that could be expensive simply because of the remoteness of the environment. It will have to be a ship based operation. Whether the minerals are recovered by mining or quarrying is for the extracting company to decide. Disadvantages include how the quarry waste will be handled. Environmental policies may be pivotal to some of those decisions. The coarse and fine processing of the ore, on site or shipped away, will be another question for debate,'

Rasmussen: 'Thank you Mark. What do you think the last two weeks of your contract should focus upon?'

Mark: 'We're currently sampling the mud at the bed of the fjord. It has shown slight signals for Rare Earth minerals, but because the sediment is almost certainly a product of glacial scouring over the last few thousand years it is predominantly ground up bedrock. So far we've taken 21 samples at 100 metre intervals, the data is consistent.'

David Gresham: 'It might be worth switching back to land based sampling, but using the drilling gear to get cores down to several metres.'

Mark: 'We can give that a try. I presume you mean drilling in the high density central area.'

David Gresham: 'Yes. It will enhance the data set. Some accountant might be a bit put off if you only have surface samples. Remember that the big mining corporations are run by accountants, not geologists. The major success you have already is certainly the wide area survey with hundreds of samples. That to a geologist is convincing. It is highly unlikely that mineral content beneath the surface will be less. It's much more likely to be higher as some of the veins could be wider the deeper you drill.'

Mark: 'That's logical.'

Bernard Hosegood: 'Yes. I agree, and you should devote one day for each core. That might get you down 4 or 5 metres. You should have enough drill bits. You might get 12 or 14 samples. Then you'll have a robust, three dimensional, data set.'

Rasmussen: ' I fully agree with that. It'll make my task with the EU much easier. Remember they'll be advised by accountants who will be trying to integrate the data to work out the value.'

Mark: 'Will the extracting company be European?

Rasmussen: 'Definitely. We need to show our politicians that we don't need the Americans, the Chinese or the Australians.'

It was time for lunch.

In the Kitchen Hut Peter had excelled, again. The Frida and Naomi, woman to woman, conversation had boosted Naomi. She was obviously a strong competent woman but with such a complex family situation she was finding it difficult. How the security services would support her was unlikely to reach many ears, but there was little more that Chalco could do.

They all enjoyed the lunch and it was time for the return to Narsarsuaq. Rasmussen pressed a small envelope into Mark's hand: 'For your eyes only, don't quote it, our enquiries aren't complete yet.'

Mark quietly acknowledged and said: 'Thanks for keeping an eye on us.'

Mark made a point of wishing Naomi, Mrs Tilby, all the best with recovering her children. Sharing her problem must have been difficult for someone with a reputation for being a competent problem solver. Mark had seen a different side to her.

The four walked back up to the col where the Merlin helicopter crew were waiting.

# 42

Mark was somewhat relieved following the high level visit. The three hour inspection and guidance must have cost the Project budget, and Danish government, over ten thousand Euro, but it was clearly important for several reasons.

That evening, after dinner, Mark opened Rasmussen's envelope. There was nothing that indicated it's source, or a date. It was a just a succession of notes.

Oronazite currently valued at 270 billion U.S. dollars.
Registered in State of Oregon as a geology and mining company.
First registered 1958
Currently a Limited Liability Company (LLC)
CEO Saul Horowitz
Only one mining project active at present in Northern California.
Geology consulting activities appear zero although still advertised.
No listing of mining projects completed.
Activity in the hedge fund area shows year on year increase.
Investment operates mostly in New York.

Activities in Argentina appear to be entirely property and company acquisition and asset stripping.

Office in Buenos Aries listed as mining consultation but that appears be a front.

Metals and mining contract trading seems to be a large source of income.

Company takes considerable amounts of money from a large range of shell companies in South America, South Africa and Israel.

Many tax fraud cases outstanding in South America and California.

Three outstanding claims for safety breaches from employees in Oregon dating back to 1980s.

No trace of Adam Tilby or Ethan Becker in current company staff lists.


The Danesfjord schedule for the next two weeks was unambiguous. Helicopter across to the high density zone with the drilling gear for the next twelve days and see how far down they can get with the drill. This would be Leighton's opportunity to shine. So far he'd been mostly involved with a hammer and chisel, and a mucky two days lifting mud out of the fjord.

Friday Mark, Harry and Leighton set off in the brand new small helicopter. It had a slightly higher power rating so it was possible to carry the drilling gear which weighed 120 kg in total.

Mark used the Lat and Long data and the sampling site photograph to make sure they could find the earlier sampling sites. The final confirmation was the surveying nail driven into the vein. By drilling a few centimetres away they could assert that they had a surface sample and a sample from 4 metres below.

The drilling gear had a petrol driven motor. Leighton got everything ready and they started. The rock was hard. It took nearly three hours to reach 4 metres depth. Leighton took the sample, checked it for radioactivity, and bagged it. The rest of the core was pushed back in. Mark realised that they didn't really need the Infra Red Spectrometer. The sample from 4 metres was definitely Monazite. The vein width at the surface was 80 cm. Fortunately, the vein must have been intruded vertically.

The weather was now milder than when they first arrived in May, and it was much more pleasant working on the hillocks than lifting wet mud from the fjord.

Esme and Sandra had been working well in the Lab over the last few weeks. They would be under utilised with only one sample a day to process. Esme created a small project for herself. She planned some changes to the Lab which would allow more samples to be crushed and analysed in a day.

Saturday Mark, Harry and Leighton drilled another sample site. Getting the drill down to 4 metres was the greatest use of their time, but there was nothing they could do to speed it up.

Sunday was a rest day. Fine and dry, so volleyball. Lars Nielsen said the soldiers would put forward a team. At the end of the afternoon, seven games had been played. The soldiers were good, but the star player of all the teams was Sandra, not just a martial arts specialist but an agile volleyball player.

Sunday evening Mark, connected the communications computer to the satellite phone. Several e-mails came in for the Chalco team, plus one from Emma. He had a quick look:

Darling Mark,

We broke up on Friday, so a six week break. Katy missing
you. Mum coping quite well, still loves gardening. Three
plums on the new plum tree. Saw Mrs Anderson the other
day, everything going well.
Looking forward to seeing you soon, love Emma xxx

Mark smiled. Plums was the code word for positive pregnancy tests,
three of them. Mrs Anderson was Dr Anderson, her GP. That marked a
new era in their family life. Nineteen days before he flew out from
Narsarsuaq Airport, then probably a week at Guernsey. It would be
nearly six weeks before he saw Emma again. He hoped she wasn't having
any sickness problems. He sent a reply:

Darling Emma,
Good to hear plums are growing. Hope you'll enjoy the
summer vacation. Give Katy a big hug from me.
Love Mark xxx

Absence makes the heart grow fonder. Mark could see why that was
such a well used phrase. He turned his attention to printing off the
messages for Harry, Leighton, Esme and Sandra. They all found the
limited content e-mails a little frustrating, but it was essential that nothing
was sent that had any prospecting relevance to hackers.

Mark took the messages to the Kitchen Hut where several chess
matches were being feverishly contested.

A winding down plan was needed for Danesfjord. Oscar Hansen and
Frida Karlsen, and Niels Larsen, would need to be consulted and briefed
on how Chalco was going to depart Danesfjord. There were now two
containers on site. David Gresham had suggested that one container
should be used to return expensive equipment to Guernsey. There was no

hint from Rasmussen of a further exploration at the same Huts base next year, so a complete departure from Danesfjord was necessary. The accommodation Huts should be left as they found them. The previous week Mark had given memory sticks to both Bernard Hosegood and David Gresham. That meant Chalco had the bulk of the data if anything went disastrously wrong at Danesfjord over the next two weeks.

The other thing of value was the lead lined box, almost certainly containing Thorium and Thulium ores, which would travel in the container. That would need advising to the commander of the auxiliary naval vessel, although the bagged samples were not hazardous unless someone started handling the bags in a sustained manner.

Monday was another drilling day. As was the whole week through to Saturday. They would be on their second drilling bit. The Monazite veins were wearing the cutting teeth. They had plenty of spare bits. The main problem was to find a way way to speed up the drilling. The weather was quite settled so Mark asked Oscar if they could try and do two cores in a day. Instead of getting back to base at about 16:00, it would be nearly 20:00. All agreed they could give it a try as a one off.

Thursday was the two cores trial day. An early start. The first one was finished by 14.00, then a short flight to the second site. That's when the problems started. Even with a new bit the drilling was slow. Leighton pulled the whole rig out to have a look. It was clear that at about three metres depth the drill was trying to cut through the Syenite bedrock. In other words the vertical drilling line had crept out of the sloping vein. That was always a risk. A bodge was needed. Leighton suggested taking the sample from the 2.5 metre depth, which was still Monazite. The team got back to Huts at 19:30. Mark decided not to try that again. One drilling sample a day from now on.

Friday and Saturday were more relaxed. For both days they got their samples at 4 metres depth and they didn't hit any Syenite.

On Saturday afternoon they returned to the Huts at about 16:00 to be met by Anders and Esme. Esme looked as white as a sheet: 'I think we have a problem. I did my morning scans with the gear that Josh left for us. Two of the instruments flashed up a warning. Anders got a torch and looked under the Lab hut. Wedged between two floor joists was a black box. The instruments confirmed that it was the source of the warnings.'

Anders: 'I found the spare geiger counter in the shipping container. When I switched it on it was registering a reading for Beta particle radiation. I suggested to Esme and Sandra that they should stay out of the Lab. I went to find Major Nielsen. He came down and suggested we lever the box from under the floor with some pieces of angle iron left behind when the solar panels were installed. It fell to the ground. We got some polypropylene rope and passed it around the box so we could drag it out.'

Mark: 'Where is it now?'

Anders: 'Over there, about 200 metres away.'

Mark could see a small black box in the distance. He asked: 'Where is Nielsen now?'

Anders: 'He's still out on a coastal patrol in the Merlin, but he reported it to HQ at Nuuk before he left. They're sending down some techies.'

Mark thanked Anders and Esme, but realised he couldn't do anything more until Larsen arrived back. He suggested everyone goes to the Kitchen for some drinks. It was a cold day, a bitter wind from the East, dropping down off the ice sheet. While they had been drilling Leighton had got cold handling the gear, nearly all metal.

Mark was pondering this latest disturbance. Was it a WiFi unit, or a bomb, or both? The noise of the Merlin could be heard. It landed and ten minutes later Major Niels Larsen came into the Kitchen. He didn't think it was confidential matter so announced to all present that it has to be treated it as a bomb. A bomb disposal unit was arriving from Nuuk about 20:00.

Esme showed Mark a photo she had taken while it was being wrapped in rope. The box was similar in size to a Christmas biscuit tin, just a bit bigger. Mark asked Esme if she had switched on any computers in the Lab this morning. She said no, not until after Anders had removed the box. Mark thought that was fortunate. Josh had said that the facility for WiFi to switch on the Chalco computers remotely had been disabled. However, once switched on by a user the WiFi unit could still be used to interrogate the files on a computer.

In a further conversation with Larsen, Mark asked if his soldiers could search the whole site, particularly under the other three Huts. That would be a problem for the Kitchen hut as it was higher up the slope and there was hardly any space under it.

Mark asked Esme if the camera trap down by the fjord was still working. Esme answered yes. She'd also installed the replacement for the one that was fried by the electro magnetic pulse.

Mark asked if she would take him down to check the video. Esme agreed. They grabbed Anders, and his gun, and walked to the fjord. The Northern most camera, the one that had been replaced, had video of a large white motor cruiser. That was picked up on the infra red camera at 02:40, early in the morning. There was not enough definition to identify its name. It was probably 10 metres in length. Esme scrolled back and came across a daylight video of a polar bear swimming North towards the shallow water at the head of the fjord. That was dated 2022.07.27 at 06:15, about three and a half days before. There were no other videos. Having only been in position since they returned, its memory only went back for about four weeks. That raised the question of where was the polar bear now? If it had swum seaward again, it hadn't triggered the camera trap. They decided to go and have a look at the Southern camera a few hundred metres down fjord.

The large motor cruiser had been recorded twice, once coming up and once going back down the fjord. There were two files recorded, one at 02:34 and the second file at 03:12. Again, not enough detail to read any boat name, or perhaps it had been blanked out.

Esme was keen to unravel the polar bear puzzle. The up fjord video was triggered at 06:11 and there was no second video. So, did the polar bear climb out onto land? Esme had the SD cards of the two cameras as she wanted to copy them to her computer. She asked Anders if he could accompany her back down after dinner to replace the cards. She didn't want to miss any future triggered events, particularly overnight ones.

Mark thought carefully about the video information. Perhaps David Gresham should consider equipping every Chalco field team with camera traps. In these times of dubious organisations trying to spy on prospecting activities, and even disrupting them, then video surveillance could prove to be valuable evidence.

Camera traps had become much more sophisticated over the last two decades. They had found favour with wildlife teams; their principal advantage being the motion sensors that triggered the camera to record. Having daylight and infra red cameras meant that 24 hour coverage was enabled.

Back at the Huts Esme copied the SD card files onto her computer. Anders took her back down to the fjord to replace the cards. She didn't want any gaps in potential recordings, particularly for her boyfriend who had supplied the cameras. Anders and Esme were a little late for Dinner at 19:00. As she walked in she explained that a polar bear had been recorded swimming up fjord three days ago. There was no recording of it swimming back out to sea, so there was the possibility that it may be lingering in the area.

Oscar said thank you. He would pass that warning onto to Larsen and his soldiers. He also said, quietly, to Esme, that she needed show the images of the large white motor cruiser to Major Larsen as he had been based at Nuuk for three years.

The polar bear caution was still an unknown. Everyone had been most careful using the waste skip with its tightly sealed hatches. The primary food for polar bears was seal; they feasted on their thick layers of blubber, rarely eating the meat parts like muscle. Non blubber foods were often scavenged for during times of hunger, although Polar Bear digestive systems did not respond well.

At 20:10 a second Merlin helicopter landed up at the col. A team of three soldiers came down to the Huts. They were led by a Sergeant Jorgen Brasch of the bomb disposal unit. He asked the location of the suspected bomb. Anders took him across to the small black box. Anders explained that it was registering Beta particle radiation and was thought to be a WiFi unit connected to a satellite up link. The team walked away for a few moments, then approached with several pieces of equipment. Sergeant Brasch told Anders that they would disable it on site. They drilled a small hole in the black plastic box then injected some foam. They walked away for ten minutes then returned. Brasch had heavy gloves on, and goggles. One of his team used a type of jigsaw to open the plastic box. Inside was a satellite phone, a smaller box, presumably the WiFi unit, and two plastic packs connected to a couple of wires. Brasch turned to Anders and said: 'Should be ok now. We'll tidy up, put the contents into separate special boxes and take it back to Nuuk. I'll be over to your Kitchen to give you a debrief shortly.'

The daylight was getting fainter. Anders walked back to advise Oscar Hansen and the others: 'If we all hang on in here for a while the bomb disposal team will come over and explain what they've done.'

Five minutes later a small explosion was heard. Anders and Oscar Hansen went outside. The light was failing, but they could make out three persons standing over near the bomb location. They were moving around, looking as though they were packing up. Then they started walking up to the col and their helicopter.

Ten minutes later, the three men came into the Kitchen Hut. Peter had drinks and sandwiches ready for them. Sergeant Brasch gave his explanation: 'We've dealt with your bomb, and detonated the explosive charge. It's as you advised, and it was emitting Beta particles. Inside the black plastic box was a WiFi unit and a satellite phone. One of the plastic packages is definitely radioactive. We've put that in a special container and will have it analysed back at base. A full report will be sent to Major Larsen and Captain Hansen and the Prospecting office at Nuuk with Professor Rasmussen. You did the right thing letting us know. You're at the top of our task list. We're under orders to keep this location safe. Thanks for the refreshments. We'll head back, via Narsarsuaq, to refuel. Best of luck.'

The three men left briskly, the two assistants stuffing extra sandwiches in their pockets.

It was now 22:15, Mark said that hopefully we can sleep safely now.

# 43

Sunday at breakfast it was decided that there would be no volleyball today. It was cold, windy and drizzly. Everyone agreed it was a day for relaxation, e-mail writing, cleaning, tidying, playing backgammon, chess and cards.

Monday was a sunny day. Mark got his team up and away to do another drilling. In the Lab Esme and Sandra were processing the two drilling samples from Saturday. Major Larsen knocked on the door. He'd been asked by Captain Hansen to come and have a look at the images of the large white motor cruiser. He said he recognised the craft; it was a charter vessel in Nuuk Marina. Could he have copies of the two videos. For the second time Esme put files onto a memory stick for the military. Larsen thanked her. He would endeavour to have the use of the vessel traced.

Mark was concerned that the second Saturday drilling had moved outside of the Monazite vein and entered the syenite. He examined today's selected site which was on a vein measuring 128 cm in width. That was wider than the Saturday vein but he needed to assess whether it was a vertical vein, or not. That wasn't easy because they only had a two dimensional surface view of the vein. Leighton suggested he chip away at the edges to see if he could identify any departure from the vertical. He spent about 20 minutes on that exercise. It was evident that for this particular vein it did appear to have a vertical form. Drilling commenced, three hours later they were down to 4 metres. The core was extracted.

Definitely still within the Monazite vein. That was a relief. Back to base in the helicopter.

The next five days were similar for the sampling. That took them up to Saturday 6th August. There were no further problems of the drill departing the Monazite vein. As far a Mark was concerned that was the last prospecting day. They would use Sunday to tidy up and pack, and be ready for the ship arrival on Monday 8th August.

Sunday morning he called a meeting of his Chalco team in the Lab. He explained that there was no guarantee that Chalco would be contracted to return next Spring. Even if they were, it wasn't clear within Chalco who would be returning, and also if they would return to the current Huts base. That meant everything had to be packed away in the shipping container, or personal rucksacks. Cabins to be completely cleared of personal items. Travel arrangements were return to Narsarsuaq Quay on Monday in the auxiliary naval vessel. Rosemary would be sending flight details for return to Guernsey. The unknown at the moment was the date that the naval vessel would dock at St Peter Port to offload the shipping containers. What went into personal rucksacks was up to each person. Luggage placed in the container might be delayed.

Esme stated that she and Sandra would pack up after they had processed the one sample from yesterday. That would take them about an hour. Later they would need help carrying boxes to the shipping container. Also, borrowing Anders to cover them while retrieving the camera traps down at the fjord.

By mid afternoon they were almost packed. In the Kitchen at 16:00 Peter had made them a huge cake to celebrate the end of the Project. He said he would be back on a ship in September, almost with a tear in his eye. Apart from the chilly dunking in the sea he had greatly enjoyed his time at Danesfjord. Oscar and Frida came to join the cake feast. Oscar announced that Danesfjord Huts might be relocated on the mainland, or turned to military use. The coastal protection operation could be using the base as its Southern HQ. The deep water fjord was a perfect harbour, and almost ice free through the winter.

That further confirmed to Mark's team that the summer of 2023 might be a different operation for Chalco.

Mark wished to express his thanks to the Danish Navy support team: the pilots and Peter and Anders without whom they wouldn't have been able to complete the survey. Before the light failed, Mark suggested that they should take team pictures outside the Huts. The late afternoon Sun was ideal for photography.

On Monday morning they could hear the auxiliary naval vessel dropping anchor down in the fjord. They peered out of the tiny cabin windows of their accommodation Huts for the last time. Breakfast, then the Chalco team did their final packing of personal gear. The vessel's captain came ashore in the big Zodiac and explained the schedule. Chalco team members aboard first. Then the ship's heavy lift helicopter would transfer both containers onto the deck of the ship. Estimated time of departure set for 11:00.

They arrived at Narsarsuaq at about midnight. They'd had a calm cruise through the fjords. It was mostly sunny although it was evident that the Sun was setting earlier each evening now. At the Quay they were told they could stay in their cabins overnight, with breakfast scheduled for 07:00. It was rather drizzly as they disembarked and were shuttled to the Airport in a couple of military jeeps. They had a direct flight to Reykyavik at 08:30. A two hour wait at Reykyavik then arrival at Bristol at 17:45. Rosemary couldn't get flights to Guernsey so the five of them found their way home on a variety of transport. Mark found out later that it was nearly 01:00 on Wednesday before Harry reached his parents' cottage in Norfolk. Fortunately Mark arrived home by taxi at 19:15. He declined an offer from Emma to collect him knowing that settling Katy into bed would be upset.

Katy was asleep as Emma welcomed Mark at the front door. She was looking well. No problems with morning sickness this time, so far at least. She had a cup of tea ready, made with real milk. The UHT milk diet was now over. Mark said: 'It's only a short stopover because there were no seats available on the evening plane to Guernsey. I've got to be back at the airport tomorrow afternoon for the 16:00 flight.'

'Katy and I will take you up. We need to get to bed soon as Katy wakes just after 06:00 at the moment. She'll come bouncing in to find that you're home!'

Emma made Mark some cheese on toast and salad, followed by strawberries and cream, and another cup of real tea. Mum's gone to stay with Brian and Susan for a few days. Brian's driving her home on Friday.

Mark said: 'That's a lovely dinner, darling, thank you. I'm going to have a soak in the bath now. Although we've been looked after incredibly well for the last fourteen weeks, compared to other expeditions, the absence of baths was noticeable.'

They had a particularly warm, loving cuddle then fell asleep in each other's arms.

Just after six, no alarms necessary, in came Katy clutching her teddy: 'Daddy's here!' She snuggled in between the pair of them.

The family was together again, if only for a few hours. Emma had brought Mark up to date on the pregnancy. She was enjoying the experience and waiting to see Katy's face when she was presented with a young baby brother or sister.

Kathleen had been to see her doctor following the blood tests. She was given some tablets to address low blood count and hormone levels. On a return visit three weeks later she was feeling much better and her doctor said she had nothing to worry about. That boosted her confidence. Since then she'd been much more active with Katy.

Mark took Katy for a walk in the woods after breakfast. Her language skills showed a huge development over the past seven weeks. In fact she hardly stopped talking the whole way.

After lunch, Emma drove them all up to Bristol Airport. This was a new experience for Katy. She waved Daddy off enthusiastically but then cried. Daddy had told her that he was only going to be away for seven sleeps this time.

At Guernsey, Mark checked in to the usual hotel near the Airport. The others had already arrived. Harry had only been home for seven hours so was a bit sleepy. Sandra had been met by her father and taken home. The other four had dinner together reminiscing over their experiences.

Thursday was dry so they all walked across to Chalco offices to be welcomed by Rosemary: 'David will be in the boardroom at 09:15.'

Sandra was already at the offices. David arrived and asked them all to join him: 'Welcome back everyone. Chalco extend a big thank you to you all. You've had a much longer expedition than we normally design and you've had more than your fair share of disruptions. At least you're back safely and you've managed to complete a comprehensive survey.'

David uttered a few more adulations then asked everyone for their comments on how the expedition could have been more effective.

Esme thanked David for sending Sandra over for the last seven weeks: Having a second person in the Lab gave a comforting feeling of security. It also meant that she could process samples more quickly. If there were three crushing units to each Bench XRF spectrometer that would help as well. Sample preparation was essential for high quality analysis.

Leighton followed a similar theme: 'Using the coring drill to penetrate down four metres was taking about three hours in the crystalline rock. Perhaps some consideration could be given to more suitable drilling equipment, possibly thinner cores. The Lab only used a few grams of ground up mineral for the analysis but the drill was delivering 50 mm diameter cores. Much more than needed.'

Harry was particularly complimentary about the drones. They behaved well for the purpose to which they were put. There was only one day when it was too windy to fly. That was about 24 knots and gusty. Having the location and date/time logged to such precision and printed on the image was a massive advantage. Harry said he found the whole expedition a tremendous experience.

Mark didn't need to say anything. He knew he would be in many debriefings with David and Bernard, and probably Andrew. He was pleased that the other three had shown constructive ideas in their comments.

David summed up by saying that he'd studied much of the data that he'd brought back a few weeks ago. Considering the team lost over 20 days a more than reasonable data set had been achieved. He made no comment on the data quality, as he didn't want that to leak out at this stage. Later he revealed to Mark that the data showed a huge financial value to whoever retrieved the minerals and processed them.

The whole team had been impressed with the accommodation, considering where they were. The domestic arrangements allowed them to live comfortably and keep healthy.

Refreshments arrived. David said that today they needed to see Reg Boston, or Dad in the case of Sandra, and write out a list of all the Chalco equipment in the container, then a list of all personal effects. The date of docking and offloading of the container still wasn't known.

Mark had to gather the data from Harry and Esme and ensure that nothing was left on the field and lab computers. They would do that with Josh. He would take backups.

Back to the hotel for lunch, then Mark had a meeting with David, Bernard and Andrew at 14:30.

Bernard started: 'Mark, I think you've tackled the expedition with competence and success. David tells me that the responses of your team demonstrated enthusiasm. The data that's been accumulated appears to be more than was anticipated. We imagine that the Danes and the EU will be pleased with the Chalco performance, and that's down to you. Professor Rasmussen couldn't go into detail over the phone but he's been impressed by the ability of the team to keep focused on the work through several incidents outside of our control. Those events will obviously receive a lot of forensic and causal analysis. Hopefully that won't involve too much of your time. I'll deal with that. For now we want you to write the Report, sidestepping the incidents and focus on your findings. Involve Harry and Esme as much as you can. We can send Leighton home tomorrow but we'd like you, Harry and Esme here until next Tuesday to get as much of the Report prepared as you are able. We still have the hacking problem so want to avoid any significant e mail correspondence between you three.'

Mark replied: 'It will be useful for me if you can sort out the disruptive incidents. We lost nearly three weeks due to those. Before he left last week Professor Rasmussen passed me a note of his interim inquiries into Oronozite. None of the team have seen it. I gather that he gave you copies. This photocopy is a report from the bomb disposal team led by Sergeant Jorgen Brasch on the 30th July. The military are still checking out the motor cruiser that appears to have brought the bomb.'

Nuuk Bomb Disposal Unit

Report: Danesfjord Bomb Saturday 2025.07.30
Analysis
The black plastic box (280x280x135mm) was taken apart
on site following xxxxx foam injection. Contents:
satellite phone
WiFi unit
plastic explosive xxxxx approx 20 grams
connecting wiring
polyethylene bag containing granulated metal, mostly
Strontium 89
Names of restricted chemicals have been redacted (xxxxx)
The explosive material was small. It would have disabled
the electronics and it was sufficient to spray the Strontium
granules over a wide area. The thin plastic casing would
not have posed a shrapnel problem to personnel. Although
the contents were capable of intercepting digital
communications, and receive a remote signal to detonate
the explosive, it would appear that spreading radioactive
material was a central purpose. We have been advised that
the radioactive material, which had a Half-Life of only a
few weeks, would be almost harmless after about 8
months. That would coincide with next Spring when the
winter snow melts and personnel might return to the site.
The bomb purpose appears to be mainly disruptive rather
than fatal.

Andrew Norris: 'Mark, I'd like to echo Bernard's complimentary
remarks. He'll follow up on the disruption and disruptors. Chalco needs
to keep its staff clear of anything that hinders their contractual role. The

current Report will be pivotal as to whether or not Chalco is invited to undertake further work.'

Bernard: 'I've read the note from Rasmussen. I'll put that together with some other inquiries we have underway. I'll be seeing him in Copenhagen when he gets back. We're determined to get to the bottom of all this. I'll keep you informed but, rest assured that I need to take this problem off your shoulders.'

The discussions lasted another hour. Mostly about the framing of the Report to the EU. There were also some pointed questions about the Naomi Dawson (Mrs Tilby) relationship. Mark reported that she had been rather demanding, particularly in relation to the China visit last year. He had no prior knowledge of her family connections, or her marital situation. That was all new. The only thing he was concerned about was the feeling that she was trying to suck him in to being an informer for the security services. He told her he wasn't happy about that, but felt a bit of a duty to assist her because of the help she had given with the Ecuador evacuation in 2018.

The other four had spent the afternoon with Reg. Keeping track of all the gear was essential in an expedition tidy up. As more and more technologies and gadgets were accompanying the Chalco field teams Reg's job was to ensure minimal wastage.

Mark asked Sandra if she would like to come over to the hotel this evening for dinner and a send off to Leighton who could now start his holiday.

On Friday Mark, Harry and Esme met in one of the spare offices. Mark explained the Report. It was going to EU staff and Denmark politicians. Chalco had to present their findings in such a way that the readers would think they had performed a successful exploration. Harry's map graphics would form quite a prominent part of the Report, although it would be based on Esme's spectrometer data. David didn't want any communication by e-mail because of the ongoing hacking problem, so the team had until next Tuesday to get most of the Report completed. Then it would go to David for edits. He would liaise with Rasmussen to ensure it would fulfil the objectives, Denmark's and Chalco's.

Harry asked if the Report was the basis of Chalco's chances of continuing the Greenland work next year.

Mark said quite probably. Next year was still an unknown. Rasmussen was keen to see Chalco retained, but he could only recommend. The EU committee would have the final say.

Mark wanted Harry to produce distribution maps of eleven elements they had detected across the wide area. They were the ones of highest value per kilogramme as well as having significant quantities in Esme's data. There were another seven elements in the data but with much lower occurrence. They could be extracted if needed but the cost benefit proportions would, at current world prices and demands, be uneconomic.

The prospecting advantage that the team had enjoyed would be equally useful to any quarrying activity. The removal of soil and other overburden was always a high cost during any surface exploitation. To have a site of smoothed bedrock would be a significant cost saving for quarrying.

If mining was the chosen method of extraction then the clearly identifiable pattern of mineral veins would be a great aid to planning the mining levels. The bedrock throughout the wide area was all extrusive igneous, mostly Syenite, some fine grained, some coarser grained but the major differences were chemical, running the full range from acidic to alkaline minerals. That was somewhat academic. Miners would just treat it as a hard crystalline rock which would wear out drills and cutting equipment. Quite likely explosives would be employed to open up mine tunnels and levels. Because of the shape of the landscape it was likely that adits could be used extensively in the first instance. If the economics dictated and the quality of the minerals in the veins were increasing with depth then shafts could be sunk. The team needed to hold these thoughts in mind as they were writing the Report as at some point mining companies would be casting their eyes over it. It would be they who decided if it was to be quarrying or mining.

Mark was keen to put in a paragraph supporting the repacking of processing waste back into any mine. That would concur with the idea that on site processing was an effective methodology. Ships were already in existence with processing equipment. Processing nearly always required clean water, not salt water, in separation methods. In the wide area that Chalco surveyed there were few springs from which to pipe water to a processing plant, or ship. If it wasn't sufficient then desalination of sea water could be employed.

Conservation minded personnel in the EU might welcome ideas of repacking mines or quarries with processing waste. They might include a stipulation to that effect in any contracts issued to prospective contractors.

Mark quietly imagined that next year an opportunity could exist for Chalco to establish a pilot extractive operation. He knew that David was fairly supportive of such ideas, partly because during his long career he had witnessed many quick and dirty operations in Australia and Africa where mining multinationals had gone in. The ore had been extracted, ground into fine particles, the metal ore separated out, and the residue left on site. The problem with that type of extraction was that ground up waste had other elements, some of which were toxic. Being ground up into fine particles they were easily absorbed into the environment. A further problem was fine particles getting washed into water courses and causing siltation and flooding. Mark's task was to frame these various points in a Report that would endear itself to the EU staff and politicians.

They would be the ones allocating money for next year's activity in Greenland.

Throughout the day the three of them were throwing out ideas to test their validity. It was useful for Mark but he knew that he was the one whose name would be at the top of the Report.

Saturday he put Esme in one of the spare offices to work on the presentation of the data, specifically the seven key elements. He put Harry in another office and stressed that his mapping, and symbols, were clearly advantageous to Mark while they were working across Danesfjord, but they needed simplifying for presentation to civil servants and politicians.

He would give both of them Sunday off to have a wander around the island, while he attempted to piece together the bulk of the Report.

Monday Mark had finished his Report by mid-morning. He printed it off and took it round to David Gresham. At 15:00 he got a request from David to join him in his office. The first comment was: 'I like it.'

Mark sat down while David went through, agreeably, each paragraph. David dwelt on the sections referring to repacking waste into mine levels. He seemed to think that would go down well with the EU committee. They had to negotiate with the Greenlandic government with regard to mineral licencing. Anything that assisted the idea that Denmark was looking after the natural environment was an advantage. The political tension between Denmark and Greenland had a significant history. Denmark also provided several billion Euro a year to the Greenlandic government. There was a "you need us and we need you" tension between the two and anything that Denmark could do to demonstrate its honourable status was a bonus. David said that he would meet with Rasmussen in a few weeks and they would tweak the final wording between them. Mark gave David the file source on the internal network. David told Mark he wasn't required back at Chalco until 3rd October: 'Have a good rest, you deserve it.'

Mark got the flight tickets from Rosemary then went to find Harry and Esme. They had been working with Reg to sort through the gear. Some just needed cleaning, some minor repairs, and some thrown out, to be replaced. Mark said they started their holiday tomorrow and wouldn't be needed back until 3rd October.

The three of them went back to the hotel to meet up with Sandra for a swim and their last dinner together.

# 44

Tuesday Mark caught the early flight to Bristol. Emma and Katy were there to greet him. Mark said: 'I'm on leave until 3$^{rd}$ October, that's almost seven weeks.'

Emma: 'Monday 29$^{th}$ August I've got my 12 week scan.'

Emma was looking well. She'd had a few bouts of morning sickness, but quite mild. For the last two weeks she hadn't experienced any at all.

Mummy and Daddy were talking continuously on the drive home. All of a sudden, Katy piped up: 'Can we do Daddy walks now?'

For the last four weeks of term Kathleen had taken Katy out for a morning walk along the lane to the village shop. Since the start of the school holidays Emma had joined them. Katy was obviously hoping to go on the longer woodland walks with Daddy. She liked the flowers and mottled light shining through the trees.

Kathleen had been much brighter and energetic since the doctor had prescribed her some tablets. She'd regained her playtime activity with Katy, which was fortunate as Katy was now even more active than she was in June.

Back home the first thing that Daddy did was the woodland walk. He took the pushchair, but Katy walked the whole way. That was a first. Daddy was also given a commentary on all the flowers.

Kathleen had prepared lunch. They ate outside on the patio. Lunchtime conversation was dominated by Katy, so much so that she hardly ate anything. Emma whispered in Mark's ear: 'I think our catch up chat might have to wait until later. It won't be too long, she'll tire soon. She did the same a few weeks ago when Brian and Susan came for lunch.'

Mark relished the idea of his seven week holiday. He anticipated there would be some communication coming in from Guernsey, but hopefully he wouldn't need to fly over again until October. It was likely that his next job could be in the Southern Hemisphere, or at least an area with a usable climate. His major task for now was to cement his "Daddy" relationship with Katy. He realised he was the novelty today, particularly on the woodland walk. It was interesting that Katy had an agenda. She had a new strategy. She didn't actually say that she wanted a rabbit, but during the walk there were many references to rabbits. Mark had been shown three rabbit holes, and she was first to spot two young rabbits nibbling at plants on the footpath. That prompted her strongest reference: 'Rabbits are my favourite "aminal".'

The consonants "m" and "n" are commonly switched by young children. Mark had several questions for Emma. He was aware that the toddlers of teachers are frequently more advanced in language development than most children. Emma was ultra precise in her conversations with Katy, as was Kathleen. Baby talk was avoided. This was undoubtedly advantageous to Katy's conversational progress. Mark couldn't help thinking that his daughter was particularly advanced. It was like holding a conversation with a bright teenager.

Emma hadn't suggested anything yet but Mark was conscious that a short family holiday was necessary. Perhaps the best approach would be to ask Emma what sort of holiday she would like, and where.

In bed that evening they were not short of topics of conversation. At least they could talk openly and intimately rather than having to anticipate the responses of radar ears Katy.

Emma was one step ahead of Mark. She'd already selected a cottage she'd like to rent for a week on The Lizard peninsula in Cornwall. It was close to a small sandy beach and quite sheltered. It wasn't cheap, but it was well appointed. She hadn't mentioned it to her Mum, Kathleen, yet. Emma said she would phone up first thing in the morning to enquire.

The cottage was a family owned and operated cottage, not an agency. It was free for the following week, 20th to 27th August, Saturday to Saturday, because an earlier booking had been cancelled. They decided to take it.

Emma asked her Mum if she would like to join them, but she declined. She'd had her holiday for this year when she went to stay with Brian and Susan following a quiet family wedding in June.

In any event Kathleen liked to be able to potter in the garden. Keeping weeds down in August was her challenge. She said thank you for asking and wished them well.

It was Wednesday so they only had three days to prepare. Emma wrote out a list of shopping. Mark suggested getting one of those children's wet suits that covered the torso. They left Katy with Kathleen while they zoomed off to the superstore.

Back home just before lunch to be greeted by 'I want a Daddy walk'.

The next two days were general household tidying, car cleaning, lawn cutting for Mark. As well as walks in the woods.

Saturday the three of them set off for the East side of The Lizard. The road was busy, it took them just over three hours. A long time in the car for a little one. They arrived at the cottage mid afternoon. It was exceptionally clean. A small village store was close by but the road traffic was a problem. The weather was settled and sunny for all but one day. The pattern was a local walk in the morning, then stories, then lunch, Afternoons on the beach. Katy loved playing at the waters edge. The wetsuit was a great success. One afternoon was breezy and waves were unsuitable for a small child. That meant that Daddy was building sand castles with some help from the chief architect. All was going well then Mummy called them over for drinks and nibbles. That was intentional as the tide was coming in and the sand castle extravaganza was due for imminent inundation. It was the only time that Katy cried throughout the whole holiday.

On the Friday, the last full day, Mark suggested going to Penzance and try swimming in the Jubilee Pool. It was quite crowded but Katy and Mummy enjoyed it. The slight buoyancy afforded by the wetsuit gave Katy confidence in the water. Although Mummy had a firm hold of her all the time it was clear that Katy was trying to swim. They were in the warm childrens' pool where Katy could see the other children swimming, or nearly swimming, with an assortment of arm bands and other floatation aids. Katy wasn't going to be left out. Mark was busy taking photos, trying not to get his phone wet.

The holiday was a great success. Emma was keeping well, no sign of morning sickness. Katy made a lot of progress, not just confidence in the water, but also in her language development. In the car it was like having a third adult in the conversations. Lots of questions about trees, animals in the fields, odd shaped buildings in the towns.

Back home on Saturday afternoon, Katy rushed to see Grandma Kathleen and gave her an excited account of all the holiday highlights.

Monday morning Emma and Mark set off to the hospital for the 12 week scan. Mark holding Emma's hand. All clear, normal progress. The whole visit was quite short. The 20 week scan was scheduled for Monday 24th October. Mark noted the date in his diary, but would need to see how his work commitments would fit in with that date. The sonographer said that they could phone up to arrange another date if necessary.

Back home for lunch. Emma was relaxed and confident. She asked Mark what he was thinking about extra accommodation for the new baby.

Mark pondered how he was going to phrase his response, he didn't wish to unbalance the family. 'We definitely need to have more bedrooms. At the moment everything is working. Kathleen is happy to have Katy in her room, but that would change as Katy grew older. It's not for me to comment on the suggested house swap with Brian. I get the feeling that Kathleen doesn't wish to return to her old home now that Henry's not there. That leaves putting another floor on this bungalow, or moving to another house.'

Emma replied: 'You're right about Mum, she feels comfortable here. This is a new chapter in her life. She knows about the pregnancy and I think she's looking forward to another baby. Her influence on Katy has been exceptional.'

The conversation batted to and fro for nearly half an hour. Emma couldn't face the prospect of several months of dust in the home so would prefer a move to another home, although still in the village. She'd been sizing up the various primary schools in the area and was hoping that they could live in walking distance of their local school. Could they find a suitable home nearby?

Emma had been thinking through a house move since she first knew she was pregnant again. She'd been walking the village lanes, with and without Katy. Two contenders looked promising. One on the market, but still occupied, was a five bedroomed house with a large garden. The other a four bedroomed bungalow on the edge of the village, about 300 metres from the school. That one had been occupied by a retired colonel who had died in February, but it was still not on the market.

Mark asked Emma if she'd like him to make enquiries about the bungalow. Emma was keen on that suggestion. A bungalow was much more pragmatic as Kathleen aged. Mark would like to have been able to raise a nuclear family, but he was well aware that being away for months at a time meant that Emma would be bringing up children largely on her own. Kathleen's sensitive grandmother role had been an enormous benefit for Emma and Katy. With two young children Emma would need even more support.

On Tuesday Mark told Katy they were going on a different walk today. He set off for the four bedroomed bungalow that Emma had described. It was on the other side of their village. The grass was a bit long but the almost level garden had been well tended. Probably built late 1980s. Solar panels on the roof, and there was a double garage. Being a near level site it would be an easily managed garden, and probably would be admired by Kathleen for garden pottering.

Katy piped up: 'Daddy can we go to the woods now.'

There was another wood nearby with a public footpath through it, so that's where they went next.

Back home Emma was deeply engrossed in her school work. She had a staff meeting the following day. Mark said he could see why she had warmed to the property. He could spend the next few days making enquiries as to when it might come on the market.

Emma's plan was to go back to school without any mention of her pregnancy. She could hold that position until half term. If they did attempt to make a house move before the baby was born then she intended to maintain her teaching salary. What she hadn't disclosed to Mark yet was that her Mum, Kathleen, had offered them £200,000. That was an advance on the fact that Brian would probably take on the family bungalow. Kathleen was determined to balance any family assets passing to her two children.

While Emma was starting the new term at school, she hoped that Mark could make enquiries on the possible bungalow acquisition.

Casual visits to pubs, estate agents, and the local vicar gradually built up a picture of the 92 year old colonel who had lived at the bungalow until recently. The discussion with the vicar was the most illuminating. The colonel had been a sidesman for nearly 30 years. His wife had done the church flowers until she passed away 10 years ago. They had been quiet pillars of the community for all their retirement. Rather different to the more exuberant retirees who take over the local parish council and adopt a role of "lord of the manor".

Mark thanked the vicar. It was someone who the family would be approaching for a christening next Spring. He didn't need to mention that yet. In any event, he imagined that Kathleen would engage with that task.

The hints from the vicar led Mark to an estate agent who dealt with many properties in the village. He played it cool, although he wasn't sure if his approach was being seen through. He told the agent, it was probably the owner of the business, that he was looking for a four bedroomed home within five kilometres of the village school. That resulted in details of three properties being run off from the office printer. Mark graciously accepted the details and said he would look through them with his wife. As he was leaving the agent mentioned that there could be another property of interest fairly soon. Mark responded: 'Right you are, we'll peruse these first and get back to you.'

On his way home Mark drove past the bungalow of interest. As accommodation it would suit them well. He studied the location. Several other properties along the lane. Medium sized gardens, nothing in poor condition. The only adverse feature was a small timber yard cum agricultural engineers about a hundred metres from the bungalow's front gate, but it appeared a tidily run business.

That evening Mark laid out his progress to Emma. It was a good start, but it might be a waiting game. He was hoping that the interest he had shown to the estate agent might be kept in mind. Mark suggested that they ask for a viewing on one of the three property details given to him. If they selected the one closest to the village that would send one message, another message would be to say thank you for showing us around the house but we think the stairs might be a difficulty for Grandma. The big unknown was how long would it take the solicitors to handle the colonel's will, and put the bungalow on the market. Possibly there might be a relationship between estate agent and solicitor handling the will. That might lead to a quicker appearance of the property on the market.

Mark and Emma did a viewing of the selected house. The agent who accompanied them was the daughter of the man that Mark had seen in the shop. They were most complimentary to the current owners, but, as planned, they had to admit that the steep stairs would be a problem.

That was as much as they could do at the moment. They drove home via the late colonel's bungalow. Emma was definitely developing a yearning for the property. She had a maternal vision that this would make a perfect home to raise her two children.

As September progressed Mark's intention of doing as much of the housework as possible was keeping him busy. Emma was coping with school with her usual calm enthusiasm. Mark was spending his spare time scanning the internet, trying to build up a picture of the mineral mining multi-nationals. He called in at Avon University to talk to Richard Ericson, his PhD supervisor. If Richard still wanted him to lead a research seminar, it would need to be within the next few weeks. He wasn't sure what the winter months would bring but he assumed that another seven week leave wouldn't be presenting itself for a while.

Walks after breakfast with Katy were still a major feature of Mark's weekday schedule. He even dispensed with the pushchair. All Katy's toddler support gear was now in a small rucksack.

Post was arriving mid morning, which meant that on the days where there were deliveries, Mark would open the envelopes while Kathleen was doing stories with Katy. An envelope from Guernsey arrived. He was anticipating such a communication. It was good practice for the Company to keep their staff apprised of future commitments. The same letter went to all of the Rare Earth team: Mark, Harry, Leighton and Esme.

The letter was dated 16th September and Mark received it on Tuesday 20th September. Roughly two weeks notice. The first paragraph was a guarded comment about the Danesfjord Report. It had been approved by Rasmussen and read by the EU committee responsible for the Greenland projects. They were more than satisfied and wished to offer Chalco another prospecting contract for next summer. That would be at another site licensed to Denmark, but many kilometres to the South of Danesfjord. A similar project but with greater security support.

The second paragraph referred to the team's winter work. Two four week prospects in Portugal; October and February/March. Again an EU supported contract. Hotel accommodation throughout. They would be away for about four weeks in October and early November. Two weeks leave in mid-November, then four weeks at Chalco in November/December for lab work.

The team would have an addition: a female lab assistant. Esme was being invited to Guernsey to sit in on interviews of the candidates on Monday 26th September. If that was inconvenient, then the appointment would be made by directors. That probably meant Bernard, who was aware of Esme's needs for assistance, and a harmonious work environment. Having one woman working alone in difficult environments was not good for the Company's health and safety policy.

Mark could see that Chalco communications were being cautious and not too detailed. They couldn't risk key details being intercepted. At least the four of them could map out their diaries for the next few months.

Mark thought he should to read up on Portugal's mineral resources. He could also quiz Richard Ericson when he was up at Avon, probably next week. He knew that metal mining had been a key feature of Portugal's long history. And, of course, as a colonial power in South America over several hundred years.

It was now evident that the EU was pursuing a quiet project to enhance its stocks, and control, of critical metals, particularly the Rare Earths. Mark wondered who would be extracting the Monazite crystals from Danesfjord, and would the minerals be processed, or part processed, on site.

The following day, an e-mail from Richard Ericson. Could Mark do a one hour research seminar on Wednesday 28th September at 14:00. Title of his choice, but something related to Rare Earth minerals within the wider topic of economic geology. That wouldn't be difficult. It had occupied Mark's mind for nearly five years. He had plenty of photos on his computer so would make up a presentation file.

That morning another letter arrived from Guernsey.

Dear Mark,

I'm bringing you up to date with a letter. Josh and Bonzo are still fending off hacking attacks on our e-mail systems, so were being advised to put sensitive content in snail mail. This letter is for your eyes only.

The T problem is unravelling slowly. Denmark is treating his attack on the helicopter as attempted manslaughter. Oronazite is denying everything, although the U.S. authorities are embarrassed because they admit the evidence is compelling. Oronazite has been creeping its way into Wall Street circles but they're being somewhat sidelined for the time being.

Mrs T has got her children back. T's mother was rather glad to hand them over. The children wanted to be back home.

Oronazite has been making applications for mineral licences to the Greenland Ministry of Natural Resources. Their application was stalled because they wouldn't fill in the names of the scientific team who would do the exploration.

My contacts in the U.S. and Canada advise me that Oronazite have been getting licences all around the world, but then selling them on to prospectors and mining companies. It seems their scientific geological work is now minimal, they are trying to move into the world of metals brokerage. They grab the money but get others to do the work. Their reputation has been declining in the geological world.

Anyway, Chalco's guardian angel, and your professional acquaintance, ND (Mrs T) is now rather relieved.

Rasmussen is liaising with the Danish Government with a view to getting a sort of apology to Chalco. So I'm reasonably happy that we might be in their good books, and that could have benefits for future work.

Treat all this as confidential.

Regards, Bernard

The last few weeks had been quite busy. Katy had Mark's full attention for over a third of her waking day, with Grandma and Mummy covering the remainder. The total amount of adult contact time was considerable, but Emma was conscious that Katy needed more time with toddlers of her own age. Emma was still concerned about the COVID outbreaks, particularly through the winter months. Katy's main "friend" was Jonathan, son of Sally and Simon Butler. Emma felt quite comfortable with that. She knew that Sally had a similar approach to protecting her family from the virus. A phone call that evening revealed that Sally was also pregnant again. The other surprise news was that Simon, her husband, was gradually moving out of his Long Covid problems, and he was due to restart his military career without any loss of rank or pay. Mark would be welcome to bring Katy over for a few hours next Monday [26th Sept]. Sally would entertain the toddlers, and Mark and Simon could have a catch up.

The day was a success, the children got on well playing together. Simon was looking much stronger and was looking forward to getting back to work. He was being given a new role, shadowing ministers on international meetings. At these he would be out of uniform and wearing a dark suit. His duties would be primarily protection, but also updating ministers and diplomats on security aspects. Back home he would be keeping up to date on world politics and the characters involved. He was curious about the intensity of security interest in the metals market. Economic spies were everywhere and the big mining multi-nationals were building up their private security operatives.

They had a long discussion about Greenland. Simon said the big U.S. companies were showing a great deal of interest in the goings on in Nuuk, the capital. Currently, the U.S. government was not supporting those activities, but that could change.

They all had lunch together. Katy was on her best behaviour. Jonathan always had a sleep after lunch so it was a good opportunity to leave. The playtime had exhausted both of them. Katy slept in the car all the way home. When she returned from school, Emma had a full report on playtime from her young daughter.

On Tuesday Mark did his usual woodland walk with Katy in the morning, then passed her over to Kathleen for stories. That allowed Mark to concentrate on his seminar at Avon the following day.

An e-mail from David Gresham. Ferry schedules had changed, Mark and his team now needed to fly over to Guernsey on Tuesday morning, not Monday, of next week. That meant one more day with his family.

The drive up to Avon University on Wednesday 28th September brought back memories of his three years focussed totally on producing his PhD thesis. It had been a solitary experience. Quite different to his last few months in Greenland where he had to lead a team to gather the information required. He guessed that part of his audience would comprise students and post docs whom he had known 12 months ago. He wanted to present his work in Greenland as an intellectual challenge but with mildly humorous characteristics. He wasn't going to include any international politics or the various hindrances they had experienced. He knew he had to explain the term Rare Earth minerals and the reason they were coming to the fore. Any chemist or geology student was aware of the elements, but they were probably less familiar with the huge international attention they were now receiving. He couldn't leave out the economics and politics entirely but would try to focus on the technical aspects of why competent geologists, and chemists, were needed for the work.

For centuries the principal metal minerals gleaned by mankind had been recognisable by colour, texture, density, hardness, physical appearance and scratch colour. It was also relatively easy to obtain the metal from the collected rock simply by heating. Some, like Lead would be released at low temperatures, others like Iron needed furnaces equipped with modern day equivalents of bellows to achieve higher temperatures. That forced more oxygen into the heating process.

For centuries in Cornwall Tin had been obtained in similar ways. Copper smelting required higher temperatures, but it was still easily achieved. Rare Earth elements required much more complex processing to obtain pure metal, and that required considerable understanding of geochemistry and physical techniques to remove the bedrock particles. Also, some modern industries required highly purified metals which increased processing requirements.

Mark thought how he could enliven his delivery. He would focus on the advantages of modern technologies to assist the detection of minerals in the ground; Coring drills, Geiger counters, and portable spectrometers. Some of his audience would be unfamiliar with economic geology, the world of monetising whatever was recoverable from the Earth's Crust. The scale of some operations had led to larger and larger multi-nationals who were able to invest in expensive equipment to recover the valuable minerals.

The seminar was well received by the students and postdocs. That was evident from the number of intelligent questions that Mark received, and later confirmed by Richard Ericson.

Afterwards Mark had his opportunity to quiz Richard in his office on Portugal's long history of metal extraction. He stressed the need to keep the name of the country confidential, and led on to the one aspect that Mark had omitted from his seminar. His recent experience of continual surveillance of prospecting and the rather hazardous interventions. Richard had heard of several similar incidents, and it was making it difficult for prospecting organisations to retain key personnel. The amount of financial persuasion was on the increase. Some from the Far East but most from the multi-nationals operating out of free world nations. Company registration could be anywhere. The approaches from China were often quite subtle, such as providing health centres for indigenous peoples. The large free market multi-nationals were less subtle and often much more assertive.

The conversation with Richard carried on for some time, eventually turning to respective family news. Richard also commented on the state of Avon University. Staffing cutbacks were continuing. Mark concluded with a gracious thank you to Richard for all the support he had given him during his PhD.

It was nearly 18:30 before Mark arrived home. Emma had anticipated his late arrival and cooked him a dinner. The first time in his seven week "vacation". Emma was coping well with her teaching and was happy. Mark felt a little guilty that he was soon to be away again for four or five weeks. He had set out all his thoughts on how to handle the purchase of the colonel's bungalow, should it come on the market while he was away. He was perfectly content that Emma would handle the purchase competently. After all, she had done much of the negotiating when they purchased their current home. Although Emma hadn't taken her Mum to see the colonel's bungalow they were both confident that she would welcome such a move.

# 45

That evening Mark wanted to cut the grass before it got too dark. The new electric lawn mower was fairly quiet so it wouldn't disturb Katy's bedtime. While mowing Mark received an unexpected telephone call from Simon Butler: 'I've been chewing over what we were talking about a few days ago. I have a work meeting early October. Prior to that I was wondering if we could have a meet up to flesh out some of the points that you mentioned back in June.'

Mark could sense that Simon was being deliberately vague. He guessed that there were topics that he'd rather not mention over an open telephone line.

Mark realised he ought to respond in a similar manner. He knew he was on a tight schedule prior to his departure for Guernsey. He mentioned to Simon that he only had Friday free. If that would work then how about meeting on the beach at midday. The same beach as they were on in June.

Simon: 'Yes, that will be convenient.', and he put the phone down.

Mark thought that was a similar style of communication he sometimes had with Naomi Dawson. Avoidance of specifics from both of them. Middle of the day on Friday now had been framed into an innocuous event. He was aware that the close friendship between Emma and Sally was a risk for transfer of information. He didn't want to quash that relationship in any way. It was mutually beneficial for both women, and an important opportunity for Katy and Jonathan to play together.

After some reflection Mark thought the best story for the family was that Simon had come across some military maps of Greenland that were issued to him about eight year ago. Mark was going over to collect them on Friday. Could he drive Emma to school in the morning then pick her up at the end of school.

He hoped his story didn't sound too implausible. He also had to parcel up the story for Kathleen. He could drive Emma to school, drive home, take Katy for a woodland walk, then drive across to Minehead. He already had some Greenland maps that were given to him on the auxillary ship. They were rather worn and heavily folded, but they would work. He would take them in his rucksack.

Kathleen was quite happy with the Friday plan. The woodland walk would give her an hour clear of her active granddaughter.

The false narrative was a little surreptitious but Mark felt it was necessary. Until he met up up with Simon he couldn't be sure if it was something that Simon was perfectly happy to reveal to his own wife, or something that was better left between the two of them.

Friday was a dry day. Mark explained to Katy that he would be home for her walk quite soon. He hadn't driven to Emma's school for a couple of years, the last visit had been a Christmas concert before the Pandemic.

Mark assured Emma he would be at her school to collect her at 15:30. Their new hatchback was an excellent family vehicle, but there would be times when they needed two cars.

Katy's walk went well; she walked all the way. Mark was still on schedule for the midday meet up. At Minehead parking was easy. The summer season was nearing its end.

Simon was on the beach, at the same location to within a metre, as when they were there in June. He was looking much stronger than when they met recently. The Army had pushed him over an assault course last week. He got round although not as fast as a couple of years ago.

Both of them agreed they would ramble along the beach and local promenade.

Now they were free of any listening ears Simon explained his reason for requesting the meeting. He was unambiguous. He was now in a military grouping that was involved in maintaining ties with key European forces. They were unofficial but comprised several Whitehall characters and vetted military operatives. Politically it was a risk. Formal statements by the government still implied that the U.S. was the key ally. The possibility of a change of government in the U.S. was the prompt for increasing links with European forces It wasn't known what could develop if the recent Ukraine invasion was unresolved. Keeping close military associations with principal European nations was considered essential. The grouping was considered "under the table" as there were some politicians and some senior civil servants who treated links with Europe as philosophically unsound.

Mark could see that Simon's new position was also a development central to re-establishment of his military career after his Long Covid difficulties.

Mark asked: 'If this relationship is "under the table" aren't you worried it could lead to a career demotion, or worse, if you get found out?'

Simon: 'That was an early concern but now large areas of government, elected and civil service, are acknowledging that Brexit was an ill-conceived idea.'

Simon had been promoted to Lieutenant Colonel in November 2019, a few months before the Pandemic. It was a step up from Major. Up until then he'd had a flourishing military career. His soldiering career was free of any blemishes. He was considered reliable. Hence his selection into more intellectual and diplomatic circles. The Long Covid problem had been a significant knockdown but he obviously had backers in the General Staff who were firmly behind him. As an accomplished soldier with a comprehensive school background he was in an uncharacteristic role.

Simon's reason for laying all this before Mark was that he'd had a suggestion from an ex-commanding officer that he should cultivate links with civvy street academics and professionals: 'After our chat about Greenland earlier this Summer I put in a security analysis check as to whether I could reveal my position to you. The reply that came back was "high confidence".

Mark asked: 'Are those checks done by the Army or security services?'

'Both, I guess. We put them in through official Army channels, but how it operates is just a black box to me.'

'Does the name Dominic Wright ring any bells?'

'Not to my recollections. Why do you ask?'

Mark replied: 'Oh, just someone I came across on a consultancy for the military a few years ago.'

Simon: 'You know that government people working on public facing roles often use different names.'

Mark: 'Yes, I'm familiar with that.'

Simon: 'Sally said you had an unfortunate incident in Ecuador several years ago.'

Mark: 'Yes, I was slightly hurt but we lost a mining engineer and my immediate boss was in a critical condition. That's why we were evacuated by Whitehall.'

Simon: 'That might be why you're on lists.'

Mark: 'Who do you think keeps the lists?'

Simon: 'Probably all sections of government. It's one of the most secret aspects of the nation we live in. Whitehall is rather paranoid about who can be trusted.'

The walking conversation continued. It descended further and further into deep state activities. They both avoided sitting at sea front cafe tables. Cardboard cups of tea and coffee on the move were a safer way of avoiding any eavesdroppers.

It was nearly two o'clock. Mark was aware that he needed to ensure he was on time at Emma's school. Mark asked directly: 'How do envisage making use of my Greenland experience?'

'Perhaps you could be persuaded to explain strategic changes in the world's critical metals to the grouping.'

'Surely you already have civil servants who can voice those issues.'

'Partially, but they can be a little too office based. You could relate the up to date risks.'

Mark: 'You know I'm often away for a couple of months at a time.'

Simon: 'I can work around that. The grouping meets every month at the moment. Suits, not uniforms.'

'Where do you meet?'

'Mostly, In a northern Europe city.'

Simon continued: 'You could present in English. Simultaneous translation is provided for a number of languages. You would receive an honorarium via a Channel Island Bank.'

Mark: 'Ok, I can probably put something together that would enlighten your members. Will Sally be aware of all this? I ask because we both know that she and Emma are fairly close since we've been able to re-instate the children's play dates. I don't have any secrets from Emma, but I am inclined to tone down the day to day difficulties of my work, and specific confidences. With two new pregnancies we wouldn't want to expose either of them to controversial, confidential, or high risk events. They need to feel we're just two blokes who exchange male banter.'

Simon: 'Yes, I fully appreciate that. When we have anything that requires a meet up we'll tell the women we're having a walk over The Quantocks. We need to avoid using phones for messaging. Just short phone calls. I've written out meet venues on this card.

| Code Name | Real Place Name |
|---|---|
| Taunton Museum | Green Oak Inn |
| Bridgwater Library | Kings Arms |
| Watchet Harbour | Horse and Plough |

Mark: 'Ok, I know where those three pubs are?' As of Tuesday, I'm on fieldwork for nearly four weeks. Good luck with your new role. Might see you in November.'

It was just before 14:30 when they said their good byes. Mark returned to his car. Carefully removing the Greenland maps from his rucksack and spreading them across the rear seat.

He was in good time at Emma's school. The end of lesson bell rang. Within two minutes there were numerous chatty girls crossing the car park on their way to the coaches. 'Who's that in Mrs Scott's car?'

'It's probably her husband, silly.'

Five minutes later Emma arrived. Mark got out and gave her kiss.

Emma responded: 'You get back in, I need a chauffeur.'

Back home, Kathleen and Katy were waiting at the front door.

'Daddy, I've painted you a picture.'

Mark made a fuss of his aspiring artist daughter. As well as entertaining Katy most of the day, Kathleen had prepared the family a salad dinner, for eating on the patio.

Mark expanded on his meet up with Simon. They had recounted their various experiences of Greenland. Emma was quite pleased that Mark had a male friend with whom to relate shared interests.

The day had gone as planned. Mark thought he now had another "responsibility", a shady relationship with some obscure European defence grouping.

On Tuesday, he would be off to Guernsey and switch all his geology and staff leadership skills into another project. Life was speeding up, but he was happy.

----------------------------